A Year At Meadowbrook Manor

Faith Bleasdale lives in North Devon with her eight year old son and her cat. She studied history at the University of Bristol, has enjoyed a wide variety of jobs but is now lucky enough to write full time. Having lived in Bristol, London and Singapore, she now enjoys the countryside and seaside life in Devon, happily swapping the city for wellington boots, although she dusts the heels off frequently to visit London. She has previously written six fiction books and one non-fiction.

A Year at Meadowbrook Manor

Faith Bleasdale

avon.

AVON

A division of HarperCollins*Publishers*
1 London Bridge Street,
London SE1 9GF

www.harpercollins.co.uk

A Paperback Original 2018

1

Copyright © Faith Bleasdale 2018

Faith Bleasdale asserts the moral right to
be identified as the author of this work

A catalogue record for this book is
available from the British Library

ISBN-13: 978-0-00-828727-6

Typeset in Minion by Palimpsest Book Production Ltd, Falkirk, Stirlingshire

Printed and bound by CPI Group (UK) Ltd, Croydon CR0 4YY

MIX
Paper from
responsible sources
FSC
www.fsc.org   FSC™ C007454

This book is produced from independently certified FSC™ paper
to ensure responsible forest management.

For more information visit: www.harpercollins.co.uk/green

For my mum who has spent so much of her life
rescuing animals

Chapter 1

'Wow, Meadowbrook,' Harriet Singer breathed, as she smoothed her black Prada jacket and stepped out of the car onto the driveway of Meadowbrook Manor, her childhood home. She watched the driver take her cases out of the boot and she paid him, tipping him heavily. He'd met her at Heathrow and driven her all the way to Somerset. Thankfully, he had sensed her mood and hadn't tried to make polite conversation, so she'd been able to spend the journey with her own tortured thoughts.

As he drove off, she turned her attention back to the house. Even at thirty-seven years old, the sight of it made her feel like a little girl again. The late May sun served as a spotlight for the house – an imposing Georgian manor which looked like a giant doll's house. She breathed in the sweet air as she stared at it; impressive, grand, full of memories of her childhood. She hadn't been here in years but Meadowbrook still felt like a family member. Silently, she greeted it and told it she had missed it. She was almost surprised to find just how much she had.

Her father had passed away a week ago. It was a shock to her and to her three siblings, but as she recently discovered, not so much to him. He had heart problems, and for some reason had chosen not to share this information with his children. Harriet was the oldest of the Singers living in New York, working for a big investment bank, so coming home had taken a few days to organise. Dumbfounded, she had booked a flight, delegated any outstanding work and, still unsure of how she was feeling, boarded a plane. Just in time for his funeral.

Confusion wrapped itself around her like a shawl. She had been away for so long, her life had changed, she was more city slicker nowadays, not a country girl anymore. But seeing Meadowbrook made her think of that child she used to be and she wondered, how on earth it had come to this? Why had she stayed away for so long? And why had only a death, the death of her only remaining parent, brought her back?

She shivered and pulled her jacket tighter around her. She was cold, despite the fact the weather was mild, she felt her bones chill with what she could only identify as fear.

As she prepared to greet her family again, she tried to calm herself. Her three siblings were almost like strangers to her. It had been five years since she had seen them – at her youngest sister, Pippa's wedding – and they only kept in touch by email sporadically. Her father was her only link, she Skyped him weekly from her New York apartment, and they chatted for ages. God, it hit her, that would never happen again. But the worst thing was that the Singer siblings, once so close, were now fractured; she didn't know them anymore, not like when they were children. Not only that but they didn't know her anymore either.

She shuddered again as she made her way to the imposing black front door. Meadowbrook was waiting for her, and now Harriet was going to set foot inside for the first time in five years, to quickly shower, change and then attend her father's funeral.

Harriet found herself once again standing in front of the house. They had returned from the local church where Andrew Singer's – her father's – funeral had been attended by most of the village of Parker's Hollow. It had been organised by the elder of her brothers, Gus, and Gwen, the family's housekeeper, to her father's precise wishes. Had he organised the sunny day too? she wondered with a wry smile. Although thinking about it, he probably would have wanted rain, hail, thunder; for the sky to be as upset as the mourners were.

Andrew Singer was a successful businessman, he'd built a tax consultancy from nothing and sold it for a ridiculous amount – floating it on the stock exchange and making millions. He was a man who always knew what he wanted. He had also been a single parent for most of their lives; their mother had been killed in a car accident when Harriet was only nine, so he had brought up his four children alone, with the help of Gwen, a series of nannies and, for most of the Singer siblings, boarding school. His exacting standards, his success, his ambition was something each of his children had been indoctrinated with to some extent. But he was also a loving father, refusing to marry again because he loved their mother too much, and he was always there for his children, even when they were adults, right until now when they had to bury him.

Her father had specified a big service – the church was standing room only – where his children all shared memories of him and the congregation sang his favourite hymns. It was followed by a burial where he was laid to rest next to their mother. Naturally, instructions had been left for

3

an elaborate headstone to be erected in due course. Her parents would dominate the graveyard, just as her father wanted; the lord and lady of Meadowbrook Manor. Not that he was a lord of course, but a self-made man, who had come from nothing to own one of the most beautiful houses in the Mendips. And not only that, but he was devoted to Meadowbrook and Parker's Hollow, so it was somehow extreme but fitting.

Harriet was sure that he would have enjoyed the service, although he would possibly be disappointed that no one had tried to throw themselves onto his coffin as it was lowered into the ground. Harriet smiled, which soon turned into a grimace; burying her father next to her mother had been a stark, savage reminder that the Singer siblings were now orphans. And she would miss her father dreadfully, just as soon as she was able to accept that he was gone.

Although she had been there, seen the coffin, watched it going into the ground, it still didn't feel real. Although usually logic-driven, she felt as if the surrounding air was filled with disbelief, clinging to her. Yes, her father was gone, but when would it feel so?

Watching the others in church and at the graveside, she felt she came up short. Yes she looked the part, the grieving oldest daughter, black designer dress, Louboutin heels, Armani jacket, but although she was carrying a Chanel clutch full of tissues, she had needed none of them. Others – friends, neighbours, the postman – had shed tears, she – his daughter – had not. Her eyes remained resolutely dry and she resented them for it. Thankfully her oversized sunglasses hid the fact. It was as if her heart felt everything but that didn't translate to her eyes.

She felt herself stumble slightly in her heels and

4

instinctively she reached out and grabbed the nearest arm; her brother Gus's. Surprise flickered in his eyes, before she regained her balance and they walked across the drive to the front door. She glanced behind her to see her other brother, Freddie, and her youngest sister, Pippa, just inches behind them. The front door loomed in front of her, and for a moment she felt something akin to panic.

'Right,' she turned to Gus, Freddie and Pippa, 'shall we go in?'

Harriet was the oldest; Gus – Angus – was thirty-five, Freddie was thirty-two and Pippa was the baby, about to turn thirty. Being the older sibling was a role she had taken seriously, especially after her mother died. But in adulthood, she had neglected that role; instead throwing herself into her career in London and then New York, opening up a distance between them that contained more than just miles. She told herself her siblings didn't need her as much, and vice versa, although now, being with them, she felt guilt prodding her like a hot poker.

Harriet turned the large brass handle and pushed the door open. Of course it wasn't locked, the house was expecting them. Meadowbrook had always been a house that seemed to own the family rather than vice versa. Her father's dream home, it had been the only house Harriet had lived in before she left for university. But for ten years she had been living and working in New York and they had become estranged, along with the rest of her family.

When her father bought Meadowbrook it was as a wedding present for him and their mother, Victoria. Before they stepped inside it had been renovated. Money being no object, he had poured it into the house, using interior designers, the best materials; it had always been an amazing house both inside and out. Her father had updated rooms throughout their childhood as well, and Meadowbrook was such a part of him, Harriet could barely think of the house and her father as not being together. She was unsure how she would feel staying here without him. Wrong didn't begin to cover it.

As she heard her heels echo on the chequered tiled floor, gazing as she always had as a child at the huge chandelier that commanded the impressive entrance hall, she turned and looked at her brothers and sister.

'So, we made it. Now, shall we fortify with a drink before the hordes arrive?' Harriet tried a smile but she feared it would be more like a scowl. She also hated how formal she sounded to her own ears. She was with her family yet it felt as if she was with strangers.

'Good idea,' Freddie said, breaking away and heading for their father's study. Or what *was* his study, Harriet thought, wondering if she would get used to thinking of him in the past tense anytime soon.

'Um, OK, Mark's driving some of the villagers who didn't have a car.' Pippa's eyes clouded; as the baby of the family she was probably feeling their father's loss more keenly than the others. Pippa had always worn her heart on her sleeve, not like her older sister. For Harriet, emotions were something she tried to avoid like cheap shoes. Harriet knew she should give her a hug, but she could only manage a slightly weak pat on the arm.

'Where's Fleur?' Harriet asked, having only just noticed her twelve-year-old niece's absence.

'Her mother felt it better to take her home. She felt going to the funeral was enough.' Gus's eyes strayed to his shiny black shoes. 'She was so upset . . .' His voice broke.

6

She knew she should offer some comfort, but she was at a loss where to start with each of them.

Freddie headed to their father's old-fashioned drinks trolley as soon as they entered the study. It was definitely her father's room. His personality stamped on every inch, from the huge imposing mahogany desk that had dominated the room forever – Harriet vaguely remembered when she couldn't even see over the top – to the large wooden backed chair that she used to love spinning in until she was dizzy. The art on the wall, all landscapes – her father believed paintings should be only of landscapes, people or fruit – were achingly familiar. As were the antiques that he had carefully chosen, an old floor-to-ceiling map, a ship, a globe. Strange objects that had captivated her as a child; her father rarely travelled and he hated the sea. She glanced across at Gus, who was transfixed by the wall, and she wondered if he was thinking the same. Perhaps reliving their childhood, even just in their heads, would help them find their relationship with each other again.

'Right, well, I think we should drink the very good stuff,' Freddie announced in his usual dramatic way, selecting a bottle of expensive whisky.

'I suppose I better go and see if Gwen is OK,' Harriet said. The housekeeper kept a low profile, Harriet had barely seen her after the service.

'Can you get ice as well, please, Harry?' Freddie thrust an ice bucket at her.

'I'll get the ice, Harry can chat to Gwen,' Gus said, sensibly, taking the bucket from her.

They walked across the large hallway to the kitchen at the back of the house. The aroma of food hit them as soon as they entered. People, strangers, wearing black and white uniforms whirled around the large kitchen, unwrapping food, plating it up, polishing glasses.

'Harriet.' Gwen emerged from behind the crowd. 'Are you OK, love?' The closest thing Harriet had had to a mother figure growing up, she let Gwen hug her and Harriet was surprised by the warmth of the embrace. She couldn't remember the last time she had been hugged like that.

Gwen had been the family housekeeper for years. She'd arrived at Meadowbrook as a young single mother, shortly after their own mother had been killed, and she had never left. She was part of the family; her father's companion in a way, although nothing romantic had ever happened between them. Just as her father maintained their mother was the only woman he would ever love, Gwen was the same about her son Connor's father, Thomas, who had been taken far too young by cancer.

'I was checking you were all right, actually.' Harriet even at nine had liked to think she didn't need anyone to take care of her. That was the character of her childhood, the oldest of four motherless children, she took her responsibilities seriously and along the way she had somehow forgotten to let anyone take care of her.

'And I'm on ice duty. Freddie wants to drink all Father's expensive whisky before the guests arrive,' Gus laughed dryly, as he shuffled from foot to foot. He was wearing a smart black suit but Harriet couldn't help but see him as the distraught nine-year-old who begged her not to go to boarding school. To her he would always be that boy. It had broken her heart to leave them when she was eleven, but her father insisted. Boarding school would be the making of her, he said, and wouldn't listen to her pleas to let her stay at home with her siblings. Gus had followed two years later – a different school. Her father held old-fashioned ideas about education and was unmovable on the topic.

'Here, I'll get the ice.' Connor, Gwen's son, appeared, took the ice bucket and went to fill it. Although she had spoken to Connor at the church, seeing him, properly seeing him, now gave her a jolt. She immediately felt jittery and uncomfortable in his presence. Again, they used to be so close, he was her best friend growing up, but she hadn't seen him for so long that familiarity had definitely faded. It was as if standing in front of her was a man she knew so well, but also a stranger. One that she wanted to reach out to but who made her feel unsure of herself.

'Thanks, Connor,' Gus said, taking the filled ice bucket from him.

'Connor!' Harriet breezed, collecting herself, a smile plastered to her face. 'It's been so long,' she said, hoping her voice wasn't as squeaky as she suspected.

'Harry, you look exactly the same as you did ten years ago,' he teased, wrapping his eyes around her. She disentangled herself from him as rapidly as she could without being offensive.

'You git, I've aged horribly,' she giggled. Goodness, that was the first time she had giggled in a long time. Connor had always had that effect on her. He was two years older than her, and she had adored him as a child, followed him around like a shadow. Well, the less said about that . . .

'It's really lovely to see you, Harry,' he enthused.

'So, you came back to Meadowbrook?' Harriet said. She felt shy, awkward. Like the time she first got braces and refused to smile, lest Connor see them. That hadn't turned out well of course.

9

'You are the only one of the Singers I haven't seen, and I've been back for three years, Harry.' He shook his head reproachfully. 'Living in one of the cottages, but anyway, I'll fill you in later.'

Harriet opened and closed her mouth, goldfish-like, at Gus, who shrugged, and with his newly filled ice bucket headed out. And as she turned to follow him, she felt such a gulf between her life and her *life*. How had this happened? All her siblings had been part of Meadowbrook and only she had not. How and why had she let that happen?

'Connor, Gwen, come join us,' Harriet said, recovering, determined to resume control, of herself mainly.

'Yes, it'll be nice to toast your father, just the family,' Gwen said, her voice catching as if on a rusty nail. Harriet felt her grief. It was all around her. In her siblings, in Gwen and Connor. She knew it was there, but even though she hurt inside, she was angry that she couldn't see it in herself.

'Goodness, how long does it take to get ice,' Freddie cried, grabbing the ice bucket from Gus, as they returned to the study, and organising drinks for everyone. Finally, everyone had a very large, expensive whisky in their hands.

'I propose a toast, to the old man,' Freddie said, with a grin. They all drank.

'And to his children,' Gwen added. 'He'd be very proud of you all today.'

Would he though? Harriet was pretty sure that he wouldn't be proud of her in the slightest.

Chapter 2

'Thank you for coming,' Freddie said for the millionth time as people began to leave the wake. Pippa pinched him. 'Ow. What?' he asked, glaring at her.

'It's Mark, Pippa's husband,' Mark pointed out, shaking his head.

'Oh goodness I didn't recognise you.' Freddie was slurring his words and Harriet knew he had put away enough whisky to render him almost blind. Freddie had always liked a drink, he was almost expelled from school for trying to brew his own vodka from potatoes when he was thirteen, but he excused it as part of his job as a party organiser in some of the hottest clubs.

Mark smiled, patiently. 'I was in the pew with you in the church,' he pointed out. He had his arm around Pippa, Harriet noticed with a pang of something akin to envy; he had been by her side for the whole of the wake. Although Harriet hadn't had much of a chance to talk to Mark, she was grateful for him being there for her sister. Sad that she didn't have anyone but happy Pippa did.

'Oh, I'm sure you were, dear brother-in-law,' Freddie said, pleasantly. 'But unfortunately you have one of those forgettable faces.'

Harriet gaped at Mark, who looked a little red-faced,

but then, to everyone's relief, he laughed. Harriet let herself relax, and Pippa giggled. Freddie was a terror, but so lovable. She'd almost forgotten.

Her relationship with Gus over the years was distant, and Freddie was well, Freddie. Pippa had kept in touch via email but those emails didn't tell the story of what was really going on, nor did Harriet's replies. Harriet felt as if her siblings were out of her reach in many ways. Being back at home with them, having to say goodbye to her father, it hit her how much she actually missed them. How she should have tried harder to keep them together. How much she wished her father was still here to tell her how.

Thank goodness the wake was winding down – if Harriet had to smile any more, she felt her face would split in two. Her feet were killing her, she hadn't anticipated how much standing she would have to do, but it had definitely been an event. The Singers didn't have any other family; her father had been an only child, her mother's family was pretty much an unknown quantity, but the villagers had shown up in full. It seemed as if most of Parker's Hollow had come to her father's send-off and it was clear, touchingly clear, that her father was a very popular man.

Either that or the village had heard about his wine collection.

Impulsively Harriet grabbed Pippa's hand.

'Come with me,' she said, dragging her away as Mark was being cornered by one of the village's older ladies.

Harriet ushered Pippa into the study, where she sat down and started spinning in her father's chair. She felt dizzy and a little nauseous, so it possibly wasn't her best idea. Pippa sat on the desk, cross-legged, taking up most of the available space. It was a scene from their childhood. But Pippa was no longer a child, she was a woman, a married grown-up. A stunning grown-up woman.

Harriet didn't think she was beautiful like her younger sister. Pippa looked like their late mother with her white-blonde hair, blue eyes and slender figure. Harriet took after their father more. She had dark hair, was taller than Pip and her features were even, some would say striking, but not ethereal like Pippa's.

'I miss him,' Harriet said, simply.

Pippa's eyes filled with tears, but Harriet remained dry-eyed. She wanted to cry for her father, but it was as if the tap of tears had been turned firmly off. Not that Harriet was much of a crier. She had cried a lot when she was a child, well she probably had; she assumed she did. But after her mother died, she realised that she was the oldest and that meant she had to behave as such. She had to look out for her brothers and sister and suddenly tears didn't seem to have much of a place in her life. Harriet had become so good at shutting off her feelings, she wasn't sure how to conjure them up anymore.

'Me too. I still think he's going to walk in any minute. It's funny isn't it, how long it's been since we've all been together.' Pippa sighed. 'I mean, it's been years since I've spent any proper time with you.'

'I know, it's my fault. I mean, being in New York. I didn't even come home for Christmas. I hadn't seen Dad since your wedding. I Skyped him every week, but I didn't come and visit. And now he's gone.' Harriet swung the chair violently. The guilt was strangling her.

'We didn't know he was going to die,' Pippa said quietly.

Harriet nodded. No, they had no idea that he was dying, and she knew if she had she would have rushed back to

13

see him. But what sort of daughter did that make her? One who would only fly across the ocean to say goodbye? It didn't make her feel any better about herself.

'Pip, shall we go to the summer house?' Harriet asked. She had no other ideas of how to reconnect with her siblings, but the summer house was somewhere they all spent time together when they were children. She wanted to find some of the closeness they used to have, which at the moment felt as if it was out of reach.

'Yes please,' Pippa replied, wiping tears from her cheeks.

'What do you think Dad would make of this?' Freddie asked later as the sky darkened and the four of them sat on comfy floral sofas in the summer house, their child-hood den, drinking champagne straight from the bottle.

'That we are a bunch of delinquents but at least the champagne is vintage,' Harriet laughed.

'He certainly thought I was a delinquent,' Freddie said, laughing sadly. No one argued. Freddie was tall, over six foot, with blond hair and blue eyes, like Pippa he took after their mother. He was so good-looking that often women – and sometimes men – threw themselves at him.

'But would he think we were OK?' Gus asked. 'I mean, would he, like Gwen said, be proud of us?' Gus sounded so downcast, Harriet wished she knew how to reach out to him. Gus looked more like her than the others. Dark hair, as tall as Freddie, but with features which as he got older more resembled their father. He was good-looking but his face so full of sorrow that it was hard to see how attractive he used to be.

'He loved us all, I know that,' Pippa said fiercely. 'I know he was hard on you guys, but he did love us all.' It was clear that Pippa felt guilty that she had had an easier time of it than her siblings. It was as if their father used up all his expectations on the older ones and let Pippa do pretty much what she wanted, including not going to boarding school.

'He did. I know he did. He might have been a bit unorthodox as a parent sometimes,' Harriet said, swigging from the bottle again, 'but I agree with Pip, he loved us.'

'I will miss the old bugger,' Freddie said, and she saw his eyes fill with watery tears. She wanted to reach across and hug him but she still didn't know how.

'Me too.' Gus looked forlorn.

'Let's drink to that,' Harriet said, needing to lift everyone's spirits, including her own. 'Our wonderful father, the old bugger, may he rest in peace.'

'Either that or haunt us all for eternity,' Freddie finished.

Chapter 3

Harriet felt her hangover taunting her before she was ready to wake up. Her head was pounding, her mouth dry and, as she tried to process the events of the previous day, she wanted to vomit. Bury father, be polite to strangers at his wake, attempt to bond with siblings. Cry? No, her eyes were still resolutely dry.

It had been bittersweet spending time with her brothers and sister yesterday. They had got drunk, yes, and they had also talked, or at least tried to. It was still slightly awkward between them, they were all lost in their own thoughts about their father, but it was progress of sorts. There had been no terrible row, but they had all drifted and it felt as if she was in the company of three polite strangers – or two polite strangers and Freddie. Harriet knew that she had to ensure her siblings didn't drift apart again, and she had to find a way for them all to reconnect. Keeping the family together would be her priority even when she was back in New York. After all, now that her father was gone, she was head of the family.

The summer house party had ended when Mark and Gwen arrived, asking if they wanted anything to eat. Pippa had got up, stumbled, so Mark had said he would take her back to the house for a lie-down. He practically had to carry her as they all went back up to the house where leftover food from the wake served as supper.

She woke up in her childhood bedroom, although at first it seemed alien. When each child turned twenty-one, the rooms had been redecorated one by one, starting of course with Harriet's. Her father said it would always be her room but a grown-up version, suitable for her becoming an adult. It had been transformed, a beautiful king-size bed with a fabric headboard, the bed linen matched the curtains and the room was painted a pale blue. She had kept her dressing table, which once belonged to her mother, but that was the only thing left from her childhood. It was a gorgeous room, with an en suite bathroom, but she had barely spent time in it. As she stretched out in bed, she was hit with another bolt of regret. She wished she had visited more, she knew she would feel remorse for not seeing her father – in person rather than on a computer screen – before he died, for the rest of her life. She wished the house hadn't become a stranger to her and she wished she hadn't let her relationship with her siblings drift the way it had. But she also knew that all these thoughts weren't going to do her any good. Self-pity wasn't something that Harriet usually entertained; she wasn't going to start now.

As she slowly sat up, she noticed she was only half undressed. Which meant she had committed the cardinal sin of not taking her make-up off. But then it wasn't every day you buried your last remaining parent, so surely she was allowed this one sinful night? She wondered what time it was in New York. She wondered what the markets were doing, what her trading floor was up to? But then she realised it would be shut, quiet, sleeping right now. As she should be.

She assumed she was suffering from jet lag, as it was only five in the morning, either that or too much alcohol. Harriet liked a drink; her lifestyle allowed for the odd bottle of wine, or a few cocktails at the weekend, but she rarely got drunk. It was one of her many control issues. She had always been charged with being a control freak; she had only a flimsy argument against that accusation.

She reached into her still unpacked suitcase – another unusual thing, normally when she went anywhere the first thing she did was unpack and hang up her clothes – and rummaged for her gym clothes. She pulled them on and made her way downstairs.

The house was quiet as she went to the kitchen, grabbed a bottle of water and then made her way to the basement which her father had converted into a gym and swimming pool. She smiled at the memory of him doing it. It was an ambitious move, turning a dusty basement into a state-of-the-art fitness centre, and they'd all been over the moon at the idea of having a swimming pool. Gosh, she never fully realised quite how spoilt they were. They had had parties there as teenagers; weekends at Meadowbrook Manor were very popular among her friends. Her father liked having the house full, he said it gave the place life, and kept him young.

Andrew also said it was his way of taking good care of himself. He swam every day, and she replayed the pride in his voice when he told her: 'Fifty lengths at least every day, Harry. I'm in tip-top condition.' She felt her heart hurt as she heard his words. Because he was only seventy and for a man who ruled the world as he ruled his world, it was far too young to die.

Feeling angry, suddenly – angry, tired, and fed up – she made her way to the treadmill and started pounding as hard as she could. She wanted to outrun the hangover, she wanted to outrun the grief that was beginning to chase her and she wanted to outrun the feelings that were creeping into her. But she knew she would never really outrun any of it. She put her music on as loudly as she could bear and kept running.

It was nine by the time she had taken a long shower and made it downstairs to the dining room where a full breakfast was laid out waiting for them. Her father had probably studied *Upstairs, Downstairs*, when he first became rich, because breakfast was always laid out, buffet-style, in heated silver dishes on the sideboard in the dining room. According to Gwen, she did it even when it was just him. Harriet felt a pang at the vision of her father sat on his own at the huge dining table, eating a breakfast fit for a king. Not to mention poor Gwen who would have probably been happier serving Coco Pops and toast, but no, there was a full English – fried bread, toast, eggs, even kippers. He was a big fan of kippers.

Gus was sitting at the table, with a newspaper, Pippa was sitting opposite, Mark next to her. Harriet smiled at each of them.

'No sign of Freddie?' she asked, trying to sound breezy as she went to fill her plate. She was glad of the full English, goodness knows her hangover needed it. The treadmill had dulled it a bit but it was still there.

'Probably still in bed,' Gus replied.

'Can I pour you some coffee?' Pippa asked, picking up a silver coffee pot. No sign of a hangover on her face.

'I'll do it,' Mark cut in before Harriet had a chance to reply. 'So . . . does anyone know what the plan is?' Mark asked as he leant across the table to pour Harriet's coffee.

She tried to weigh him up, as she had no idea what he was like. He was older – ten years older than Pippa – but handsome and well dressed. Conservative. Pippa, who had always been quite bohemian growing up, hair flying wildly behind her, barefoot if she could, had definitely changed. She was wearing slacks and a blouse, something the old Pippa would never have owned, and her hair was perfectly done up in a chignon. She sported a full face of make-up and expensive pearls at her neck. But then what did Harriet expect? They had all morphed into adulthood, and she was different now, of course they all were.

'What plan?' Harriet asked, stirring her coffee and hoping it might make her feel better.

'Well, unfortunately I need to get back to Cheltenham, to work . . .' Mark started. He was incredibly attentive to his wife.

'The will's being read today,' Gus said, without looking up from the paper. 'Pip needs to be here for that.'

'Darling, you can go home and I'll get someone to drive me after,' Pippa offered, touching her husband on the arm.

'No, darling, you need my support. I'll stay here. I'll juggle a few things.' He kissed his wife on the cheek.

'But I don't want to put you out?'

'Pippa, I'm staying, that's that. You need me.'

'Oh there you are!' Freddie, looking utterly dishevelled, appeared at the door, interrupting any further debate.

'Fred, are you all right?' Harriet asked.

'I think so, although I need to throw up.'

Harriet wasn't sure who was the most surprised as he did just that, all over the dining room floor.

'I'm going for a walk around the garden if anyone fancies it. Goodness knows, I need some fresh air,' Harriet announced after breakfast was finished. Gwen had not only cleaned up after Freddie but she'd also brushed away any offers of help to clear up after breakfast. Harriet had learnt from an early age that it was best not to argue with Gwen. She was very much in charge of the house, and although that meant clearing up after everyone, she liked it that way. If Harriet so much as tried to move a plate, Gwen seemed to appear from nowhere and snatch it away.

Gwen used to live in a cottage on the estate, which was still hers as far as Harriet was aware, but she had moved into the house after Pippa left home. It always gladdened Harriet to think of her father having Gwen there to take care of him. She wondered what she would do now.

'I'll come,' Pippa said. 'I'm sure Mark will welcome some peace.' She smiled.

'Well I could come—' Mark started.

'Really, no need, you do some work, I want to catch up with the others anyway,' Pippa said.

'I'm in. Shall I try to get Freddie or leave him?' Gus asked.

'No, get him, if he's cleaned himself up.'

As Gus went to see if Freddie was going to join them, Harriet felt her spirits lift a little. They were all together and she was slowly remembering how much she loved her siblings. She wondered if their father was watching them now. Of course she didn't believe in all that life after death stuff, but she liked the idea that he was.

The four of them stood by the back door – Mark had gone off to do some work. Harriet was wearing her gym trainers, the only flat shoes she owned, jeans and a light sweater. Pippa pulled on a pair of wellingtons that she kept at the house, Gus was wearing trainers and Freddie, a pair of ratty Converse.

21

'Shall we go survey the land?' Freddie asked, looking a bit the worse for wear but sounding like someone from *Downton Abbey*.

'Sure, let's do it,' Harriet laughed. 'Or at least the top gardens, Pip said that Dad had done a great job with them lately.'

'He has, they're really beautiful.'

'All we're missing is a gun and a dog,' Gus said, cracking a rare – for him – joke.

Harriet had forgotten how beautiful Meadowbrook Manor was, as they set off. They headed towards the sprawling gardens, out of the back door, which were even more spectacular than she remembered; perfect lawns, lush greenery and the most beautiful flower beds. As she looked to the horizon, the garden, which seemed to stretch for miles, was awash with colour. Meadowbrook Manor spanned acres and acres in total, but the garden was separated by a tall hedge, where her father had secret doors installed so they could get through to the fields, meadows, and woods beyond. As there were public footpaths running across the land in places, he wanted the gardens defined so he didn't find people wandering around them. He was quite welcoming, but he didn't like the idea of people he hadn't invited in his private space.

'Wow the air here is so different from New York, I'd forgotten,' she said, breathing deeply. The warm air, the slight breeze rippling through, was helping her head settle a bit.

'I wish you were nearer,' Pippa said, linking arms with her sister. 'I miss you.' Pippa found affection so easy, Harriet envied that too.

'I'm sorry I'm not better at keeping in touch, just so busy. I should have come home more.' She felt the inadequacy of her words.

'It must be hard being such a success,' Gus said.

'Hey, Gus, I hear your business isn't so shabby,' Harriet replied, light-heartedly. Gus had always suffered from an inferiority complex. It was unfounded, of course. She often thought it must be hard to be the child in between her, always competitive and desperate to achieve, and Freddie who just charmed his way through life. She looked at Gus and, not for the first time, wondered who he actually was, or what he wanted in life. He seemed so, well, just so disappointed.

'It's hardly cutting edge. A successful, yes, but plainly dull insurance company in Bristol. Insurance, I mean who ever thought they wanted to work in insurance?' He laughed, but it sounded hollow.

'I certainly never did,' Freddie unhelpfully replied.

'Everyone needs insurance,' Harriet pointed out.

'Pah. Look at me, I'm divorced, with a job I hate, a daughter who I barely know how to communicate with. It's not what Dad planned for my life that's for sure,' Gus added.

She wanted to tell him that her life wasn't perfect either, far from it in fact. Yes, she was successful, money not an object, but her personal life . . . well that was a mess. But she couldn't find the words.

Gosh, she felt so responsible for them all again. Although she knew she would have to go back to New York she suddenly didn't feel like rushing back. She had taken immediate compassionate leave, but there had been no duration specified. She knew she would need to speak to *him*; her boss and also her lover. The shameful secret she hadn't shared with any of her family, that she was sleeping with Zach, boss and married man. She didn't like to think too much about the wrongs and rights. It was what it was, after all.

They all stood, instead, and admired the rose garden which was filled with beautiful buds, looking as if they were desperate to explode into colour. 'Who does the garden here anyway?' Gus asked suddenly. 'It looks so gorgeous, like those gardens you see at the Chelsea Flower Show.'

'Didn't old Jed die years ago?' Harriet said, bringing herself back to the conversation. Jed had been their gardener and lived in one of the three cottages on the estate, alongside Gwen's and what was now Connor's. He'd been part of Meadowbrook, and insisted on working well into his old age, and when he died, their father was devastated. He loved the old gardener, they all did. Gus, she suddenly remembered, used to trail around after him helping in the garden when he was a kid.

'There's a lady now,' Pippa said. 'She's a fancy garden designer and has a team who work on it, but also the village gets involved.' Pippa gestured to the gorgeous space they were all looking at.

'Right, come on, let's go and walk, that should blow the hangover away before we have to hear the will.' Harriet strode off, feeling purposeful.

'What do you think he's done? I mean, I know there's a lot of money but—' Gus looked uncomfortable, probably because their father used to say that talking about money was common and Gus hated anyone thinking he was greedy.

'Oh, knowing Dad, he's left it all to some home for wayward hamsters,' Freddie laughed. Their father had an animal sanctuary on part of Meadowbrook land, Connor and he had opened it three years ago when Connor first came back. Harriet had heard plenty about it from her father, but she didn't pay too much attention. But it wasn't unlikely that the money would go to it, she laughed, to herself. Freddie pulled out a hip flask and took a slug.

'Freddie, didn't you have enough last night?' Harriet chastised, shaking her head.

'Hair of the dog.'

'Fred, you don't want to be pissed when the will's being read,' Gus said.

'I probably do, especially if he's left everything to the hamsters.' Freddie drained his hip flask. Harriet couldn't help but giggle. Yes, her brother was a bit wild, which made Gus's sensible, slightly dull manner seem even more pronounced, but he was funny with it.

Chalk and cheese, yet thick as thieves. Harriet heard her father's voice. She looked around, of course it was madness, to think he was there, but their dad had always said that about her brothers and she felt warm as she replayed the phrase in her head.

'Right, well perhaps we ought to walk a bit quicker, David will be here soon.' Harriet changed the subject and hustled her siblings on.

'Harriet, I'm so pleased that you are still as bossy as I remember,' Freddie quipped.

'I'm not bossy, Fred, I'm just trying to get you organised.' Harriet tried not to feel offended but she remembered how she used to be called bossy, bossyboots, or 'yes boss' as a child, often preceded by a swear word as they got older. Apparently, she always told them what to do and they were too scared to argue with her.

'Gosh, you used to boss us about something rotten,' Pippa said.

'I'm afraid you did, Harry,' Gus finished.

'Right, well then let's finish this walk and then get your arses back to the house.' A smile curled at Harriet's lips.

'Yes, boss,' Gus replied and he grinned back at her.

Chapter 4

The family solicitor was almost as familiar to Harriet as Gwen. David Castle had been in and out of Meadowbrook for as long as she could remember. He was a few years younger than their father, still practising law, showing no signs of wanting to retire as he wore his customary pinstripe suit and silk tie. He had been at the funeral, of course, where they had greeted him like an uncle, but now he was there in an official capacity and suddenly everything felt serious. It wasn't the money. None of them, as far as she knew, was desperate for money, or the house. Goodness knows, she had already been agonising about what they would do with Meadowbrook now. After all, it was their childhood home, the last place they had to remind them of both parents and it was her father's pride and joy. If they had to sell it, it would be another step in saying goodbye. First was the death, then the funeral and now this. It was all taking their father further and further away from them. She couldn't imagine not having Meadowbrook or another family living here, but then what choice did she have?

They all sat awkwardly waiting for David to speak. Mark had wanted to join them, arguing that Pippa needed his support, but David told him that the strict instructions were that it was only the four of them with him in the room.

'You all know that your father wasn't always orthodox,' David said, as he cleared his throat, tugged at his tie as he stood behind their father's desk. They all nodded. 'And although I told him it was probably a terrible idea, he wanted to make a video recording for you.'

Harriet startled. She wasn't sure how she felt about seeing her father's face on a screen, or hearing his voice again.

'You're bloody kidding?' Freddie asked.

'No,' David continued. 'I'm afraid not. He wouldn't be dissuaded. He said, and I quote, "I want to say goodbye to my children this way and I saw it in a film once." And I also want to warn you that its contents aren't exactly normal either. So, I shall play it for you. Are you ready?'

The four siblings looked at each other. Harriet thought they most definitely weren't ready. But they all stared at the TV screen on the wall of the study as David pressed a button on the remote control.

After a while an ear appeared on screen.

'Can you see me? Well can you?' their father's voice boomed. Harriet jumped. It was as if he was in the room with them.

'Um, only your ear,' Gwen's voice replied.

'Well move the bloody camera, Gwen,' Andrew said and, after a few more swear words, his face appeared.

'Oh my.' Harriet took a sharp intake of breath. She saw his face every week on their Skype calls but seeing him on screen like this, knowing he was buried in the ground, threatened to derail her. For the first time since her father died, she felt tears burning behind her eyes. Pippa was already sobbing; Freddie had his arms around her. Gus was staring at the screen as if he couldn't quite believe what he was seeing and Harriet, who was sat next to Gus, finally felt as if she might be able to cry.

'Right, you all listen carefully now,' Andrew continued in his loud, clear voice. 'I'm sorry that I'm dead. I might be a lot older than I am in this video, but I've a feeling that I'm not. The doctor said my heart wasn't the most stable and I knew that it might give out at any time. I could have maybe had some surgery but I didn't want to do anything which didn't come with a guarantee, and surgery didn't. But living does, because living comes with the guarantee of death. So I chose that.' He paused, turning his head. 'Gwen, are you getting all this?'

'Yes, Andrew, clear as a bell,' Gwen's voice replied. Goodness, it didn't surprise Harriet that Gwen was her father's partner in crime on this.

So, her father shunned surgery, without even discussing it with them. That made her angry but also, it made sense. Her father hated illness, didn't believe it in. As children, they had to be practically hospitalised to get a day off school.

'Right, so I'm dead, and you've buried me now, so all that remains is for you to hear about my last will and testament. And I know, you're not greedy children, but anyway I have money, and I'm dead, so I don't need it and it has to go somewhere.' He took another pause.

'He looks as if he's enjoying this,' Freddie pointed out.

'He certainly likes saying that he's dead a lot,' Harriet concurred.

'It's so strange,' Gus said.

'Daddy could be eccentric,' Pippa pointed out.

He started talking again and they all fell quiet.

'So where was I? Ah yes, my last wishes. Well my dear

friend David will have a copy for each of you, and as I don't know what date it is – I mean, I know what date it is today, but I don't know what date it is when you are watching this, then I cannot say for sure. Gwen, does this make sense?'

'Not really, Andrew,' again Gwen's voice rang out.

'OK, so this isn't exactly my will, I'm not sure how legal a video recording would be, but the thing is that David will read you my final will and testament a year from the day when you are hearing this. To reiterate, this isn't my will, it's kind of a pre-will, and in a year's time you'll hear the final thing.'

'What the hell?' Gus said. The four siblings looked at each other aghast.

'What the hell I hear you ask?' Andrew continued. Harriet shivered, this was beyond bizarre. Seeing, hearing, her father like this, it was both comforting and uncomfortable. 'Well, you see, my dear children, it's like this. I might not have been the best father to you all. I tried, but after your mother died, as your only parent, I feel I was lacking. I tried to give you all you needed, or all I thought you needed, education, money, ambition and strength, but I'm not sure I was able to show you how important happiness was, because after I lost your mum I forgot how to be happy a lot of the time. I missed her, I missed her dreadfully, and when she died a part of me died with her, but I couldn't fall apart, not properly, because I had you four.

'I know I pushed you all to do well, I wanted you to be carbon copies of me, but only because that was all I knew how to do. And I think I made a mistake. I think your mother would have taught you to be who you wanted to be and I fear that I always tried to drive you to be who

I wanted you to be. And at the same time I spoilt you all materially.'

Harriet felt thick with emotion. Yes, her father had been a hard taskmaster but she loved him and it killed her – bad choice of words – that he felt he had failed them. Why hadn't she ever told him that he hadn't failed them? Now it was too late.

'Now I am proud of each of you, I know you didn't always think I was, and I know I didn't say it enough, but I am. My only regret is that I didn't try harder to keep us closer as a family. I let you go too easily.

'Harriet, my darling firstborn, you are such a high-flyer and I couldn't be prouder, but I wish I had tried to get you to visit me more. I would so have loved to see you in person and not just on the computer. Although it's too late for regrets now I know that.' He seemed to look right at her and Harriet felt sick.

'And, Gus,' he continued, 'I didn't support you enough with the divorce. I sometimes think that I only saw you because of Fleur and I adore my only granddaughter but I love my son too and I'm not sure I ever told or showed you that enough.'

Harriet couldn't look at Gus; she couldn't bear to see the hurt on his face.

'And also, Gus,' their father continued, 'I never let you be who you wanted to be. That is my biggest failing. One I wish to rectify now, but more of that later.

'Right, Freddie, well you are the most infuriating of my children, all that party, club stuff, but I wish I had reached out to you and made sure that you were all right and not doing drugs or having sex with women in nightclub toilets all the time.' Harriet glanced at Freddie, she was pretty sure that was exactly what his job entailed. 'Freddie, you

31

might be a party boy, and the only of my children who asked for money on more than one occasion . . .' Now they all looked at Freddie who blushed. 'But I should have tried to get you to settle down, and I feel that I might have failed you in that. If so, I am sorry. You have such potential and if you want to do your parties then that's fine, but you need to grow up I'm afraid, we all do at some point, and perhaps I should have helped you more with that.' Freddie wiped a tear away.

'Finally, my little Pipsqueak, well I saw more of you than the others, but still I worry about you. I don't feel that you are as happy as you deserve to be. I'm not sure if it's Mark – I think it is him – but you didn't tell me and I didn't ask. I think I should have asked more about all of you and I feel if I had been there for you all, then you all would have been closer to each other.' He looked and sounded as if he was choking up. Harriet had never seen her father cry but this was close. 'I love you all, so so very much.' There was another pause where they saw their father pick up a glass of whisky and take a drink.

'This is surreal,' Freddie said. 'I mean, wow, really? Are you sure we can't have a drink?'

'Shush,' Gus told him as their father began to speak again. Harriet felt the familiar voice stirring her emotions. It hurt her, slicing through her. Grief. Finally this was the pain that she wanted to feel, to prove that she was alive and that she loved her father. He was like a god to her. That wasn't in dispute. But now, apart from on the screen where he was slightly left of centre, she would never see him again.

'I will miss each and every one of you, please believe that. And I want to put things right for all of you, so that is why the following might come as a shock to you. My actual will will be read a year from today. David will take care of that. Have I already said that, Gwen?'

'Yes, Andrew, I told you you should have written a script.'

'No, it's all here, I don't need a script.' He tapped his head. 'And until then, I need you to fulfil my last, dying wish. Or dead wish because I am dead of course. Ha!' He paused and stared straight at the camera.

'We are sure he's dead?' Gus asked. 'Because this is madness, and I have the feeling he's going to jump out at any time and say this has all been a ruse to get us home.'

'He's dead, Gus,' Harriet almost whispered.

'And I am dead, so this isn't some kind of sick joke. You know I didn't joke enough when you were young. I was so driven, so busy making money. I should have had more fun, but now is not the time for that. So, you will all be here a year from now to hear what happens to my considerable fortune and the house. But I will tell you this, Gwen is taken care of, as is Connor, and Fleur, but you guys will get the rest of my estate, the money and the house. All equally split of course. I know you always thought I had favourites, but I really didn't.'

'Well now we know that, why do we have to wait a year?' Harriet asked. 'This makes no sense.'

'Why do you have to wait a year in that case?' Andrew continued. 'Well, you see there are conditions to the money. You four will equally divide the bulk of everything; the money, the house, art, et cetera, anything that isn't specifically bequeathed to anyone else. But before you get anything, you have to agree to my conditions. Firstly, you must all live together in Meadowbrook Manor for a year.'

'What?' Freddie yelped, making Harriet jump.

'Yes, I repeat, you will live here, all of you together. It's

33

time you were a family again and this is the only way I can make it happen. And I know you are all going to say that it's impossible because of your jobs and, Pippa, of course you're married to Mark, but actually you can all take a year off. I have looked into it and given it a great deal of thought. Here's how I suggest it will work.

'Harriet, you've been working since you graduated, you never take holidays, you don't seem to have a personal life, or if you do it's not one I would approve of, so for you to take a sabbatical wouldn't be difficult, plenty of people do. You say you have to sort out your father's estate, which is true. But I think the break from the city, from the rat race and New York, will do you good and give you a chance to reconnect with your siblings.'

Harriet sank back into the sofa. Her father was clearly mad and this was impossible, she couldn't even conceive such a ridiculous idea.

'Gus, I know you hate your life. You don't like your job, your wife left you for another man.'

'I'd forgotten that,' Freddie interrupted as David sighed and pressed pause. 'I mean that your wife went off with another man.'

'My squash partner,' Gus said, sadly.

'I didn't know people played squash these days,' Freddie replied, looking confused.

Harriet rolled her eyes. 'David, can we get back to this?' she asked.

David nodded and resumed the video.

'So, I feel as if that is my failing too,' their father scratched his head, 'oh, not your wife leaving you, I'm not going to take responsibility for everything, but the job. You loved painting, do you remember, just like your mother, and you showed talent but I said painting was only for vagabonds who wanted to cut parts of their body off. In retrospect, that was possibly a bit harsh, but I'm not an art expert and I only really know the story of Van Gogh, so I kind of tarnished them all with the same paintbrush. Ha! Anyway, the truth was that your mother loved to paint and we built the summer house as her studio. After she died, I turned it into a den for you and I couldn't bear to be reminded of her in the early days so I dissuaded you from painting.'

'Dissuaded? He banned me from painting.' Harriet squeezed Gus's hand. Gosh, she'd forgotten that Gus had the artistic gene, inherited from their mother, but it had been knocked well and truly out of him. He looked about as much like an artist as any insurance salesman did.

'Of course,' Andrew continued, 'if I knew that would send you to work in insurance I probably wouldn't have stopped you. I mean, insurance! Come on, Gus! You got married young, and wanted to be the man you thought I wanted you to be, and that was my mistake. I want you now to be the man you want to be. So take a year off work, I know your company is in good hands. Take time off and paint for God's sake.' They all jumped as he slammed his hand down on the desk. 'Ow. Sorry, but, Gus, if you go to the attic you'll find all your mother's paints still there. Take them. And I'm sorry. I'm so sorry, son.'

Both her father's eyes and Gus's were full of tears now.

'I don't know if I can bear this?' Pippa said.

'Freddie, oh my boy. You could always charm the birds out of the trees. But you like the finer things in life and you seem to have a misguided way of getting them. This party, or clubbing business, well it's not fulfilling you, I can tell. It's time for you to settle down, grow up and do

35

something which satisfies you, but not just in a hedonistic, superficial way.'

'How well he thinks he knows me,' Freddie quipped, but he looked downcast.

'And finally, my Pippa. You are so like your mother in many ways, not with the art, you were always totally rubbish at that, but in other ways. Not least your looks. And I want you to be happy. I didn't care that you didn't have the ambition of your siblings, I didn't care that you didn't want to work, but I did care that when I gave Mark permission to marry you that I may have made a huge mistake. In the last year I've seen a change in you and I don't know what's caused it. So, anyway, I know if you live here with your siblings for a while you'll have some distance from him at least. I'm not saying leave him, but I am saying if you do as I ask, you'll have options and maybe some space to think.'

'God, Pip, I had no idea your marriage wasn't great,' Harriet said.

'It is great. Dad's wrong, our marriage is good, and I really don't know what he's talking about,' Pippa shot back.

'And if you want to stay with him then that's your decision and I will respect that from my grave. Although if I can figure out how to haunt people he'll definitely be on my list.' Andrew laughed so hard he had a coughing fit.

David Castle pressed pause. He looked slightly uncomfortable. 'Are we all all right up to now?' he asked.

'I'm a little confused.' Harriet took charge as she always did. 'I mean, he really expects us to live here for a year, and only then will the proper will be read? Is that correct?'

'It's bloody insane,' Gus blustered.

'What about Mark?' Pippa added.

'Are you sure I can't have a drink?' Freddie pleaded.

'Right, well, of course, as his solicitor I am privy to the exact terms, and I'll hand them out to each of you when the video is over. But now I'll try to make it clear thus far. Your father indeed expects you all to live in the house together for a year. It's the first condition. It's not the only one.'

'And if we refuse?' Harriet asked. Her life was in New York. She owned her apartment, she had a job, a highly paid, important job. She had a group of friends that she went for cocktails with at least once a week. She had a personal trainer. How could she leave all that? She couldn't. It was impossible.

'Then the estate will be disposed of as per your father's instructions. He was serious about this – if you don't live here, then you don't get a penny.'

'Well how about if one of us agrees or two of us and the others don't?' Freddie asked.

'That won't work. Either all four of you live here or none of you. There are no variables.'

'And what are the other conditions?' Harriet asked. This was ridiculous. She loved Meadowbrook, but she didn't need the money, so she could walk away. But, on the other hand, what about the others? And what about the fact her father wanted them to do this. She'd be defying him, letting her family down. Her head started aching, it was all so confusing.

'You're about to find out.' David pressed play and their father's voice rang out in the room once more.

'I hope you all living here in Meadowbrook Manor for a year will redefine your relationship with each other. As children you were all so close, but well, I know when I sent Harry to boarding school it started to change. I do

37

take responsibility for that but I can't turn the clock back. I am sorry. I want you all to find your way back to being a family and this is the only way I could think of to do that. Now, you guys know about my animals.' David pressed pause again.

Harriet had never seen the sanctuary, but she'd heard plenty about it from her dad. Harriet had to admit she had only shown a very cursory polite interest in it. She had sort of put it down to him going slightly mad with loneliness, if she was honest. Rescuing animals in order to rescue himself. But she never said that.

'I visited Daddy's animals all the time,' Pippa said. Pippa probably encouraged him to get more as well, she was so soft.

'Fleur loved going with Dad to see them too,' Gus added sadly. 'She helped out at the sanctuary quite a lot.'

'Not you, Gus?' Freddie asked.

'No, unfortunately I seem to be allergic to most animals,' he replied.

'But when we were young we had dogs and cats and you were OK,' Freddie pointed out.

'I obviously developed the allergies as an adult.' Gus was determinedly not meeting anyone's eyes.

'More likely that you just didn't want to get your hands dirty,' Freddie quipped.

'Shut up, Fred.' Harriet was reminded of how much the two boys bickered when they were young.

'Can we please get on with it,' David interrupted gently, looking at his watch. 'I know it's a lot to take in but, unfortunately, I have other appointments.' He looked guilty as he pressed play again.

'Right, so probably all of you know how important that sanctuary has become to me.' Andrew shifted in his chair.

'But it's also important to Connor, and the village and – most of all – to the animals we help. Year on year we have grown in size, had so many different animals, and as well as my children, and the house, it really is my pride and joy. So the second condition is that you run the animal sanctuary with Connor, to ensure it stays open, thrives, which also involves raising money for it; an amount that you will find specified in the exact terms.'

'Oh God, no.' Freddie put his head in his hands.

'Oh yes.' It was scary how their father seemed to hear them. Or maybe, Harriet thought, he actually knew them much better than they gave him credit for. 'I expect you to help Connor, I expect you all to get your hands dirty – you've become too soft the lot of you – but more than that, you will also take over my role, which was the finances among other things. We raise money by holding village fêtes, open days and all sorts of events. It not only brings in money but it helps to involve the community of Parker's Hollow and keeps the sanctuary profile raised. If it thrives under your management, that will also ensure you all get to share the bulk of my estate. But, of course, if you don't raise the funds specified, then you forfeit any right to the money or the house.' He took another drink out of his tumbler. 'And it will all go elsewhere.' He sat back looking triumphant.

Harriet didn't know how to describe the emotions that she was feeling. Just what was her father thinking? They had barely been able to keep a goldfish alive between them as children. How on earth were the four of them supposed to run an animal sanctuary? As well as live together at Meadowbrook? It was utter madness.

'Can I just summarise?' Pippa asked. 'Not only do we have to live here for a year, without my husband, but we also have to run an animal sanctuary, raising money to keep it open?'

'Yes, that's about right,' David replied, his face expressionless.

'I supported Dad's rescue centre, I really did, but I didn't expect to have to work for it!' Pippa looked terrified. 'And how on earth am I supposed to explain all this to Mark? I mean it's not as if we need the money.'

When they were younger, it was clear that although the loveliest, Pippa wasn't the most academic of the siblings. Harriet was academically gifted, everyone said from the minute she started school really. Gus, not quite so, but he worked hard and got very good grades. Freddie was also cleverer than he liked to make out, though he was lazy, but Pippa, well, she was terrible at school. She just got by, but because she tried hard she was never in trouble, but you could see the teachers scratching their heads. How could the Singer siblings have a Pippa among them? Of course, when it was discovered she had dyslexia that explained why she found some things so difficult and it did become easier with the right help; Harriet had spent hours trying to help her with homework back before she went away to boarding school. But Pippa was beautiful, she was sweet, she was kind, and she wasn't interested in school. Harriet remembered being jealous when Pippa begged her father not to send her to boarding school and he agreed. But she felt guilty when she confronted Pippa about this and her little sister admitted that she could cope with being near the bottom of the class at home, but only just. She didn't want to go to Harriet's school and be in the shadow of her clever sister.

When Pippa left school, she embarked on a number of courses. Cooking, flower arranging, she took a childcare course, typing, just about everything available, but she told Harriet nothing felt right. And, of course, being the only child still at home, Andrew was happy to let her carry on doing what she wanted. Soon after, Pippa told Harriet she had met someone and was in love. And that someone was Mark and they had a fairytale wedding. So why did her father seem to think he was bad for her? From what Harriet had seen, admittedly in a very short time, he seemed to take care of her, protect her, which was what their father would have wanted. Surely?

'Right, kids, I am sure I have given you more than enough food for thought,' her father's voice interrupted her. She still couldn't get used to seeing him, hearing him, yet knowing he was gone for good. She wanted to reach out and touch the screen, just to be able to one last time, but she knew it was him but not him at the same time. The voice, the confident, loud, slightly booming Somerset lilt that was so familiar, would soon be gone. She almost couldn't bear it. 'But to conclude. If you agree the terms, the final will will be read in a year's time and you'll all be rich. As for other provisions, Gwen gets her cottage, a sum of money, and she has a job for as long as she wants one, and that certainly includes this year. Yes, she is your housekeeper, but she's there to check on you all, make sure you are all right, take care of you all. And Connor, he gets his cottage, some money, and I expect you to support his work. I've set up a trust fund for Fleur. But I can't stress enough, the animal sanctuary must flourish, it's so important to me and I hope it will become important to all of you too. How you divide the labour is up to you.' There was another pause but no one dared speak.

'In conclusion, my children, I love you. I miss you, but I hope that by doing this I will have given you the best

41

gift that a father can give. You might not think so now, but mark my words, the animal sanctuary helped me, maybe even saved me when I was lost, and as you, my children, are all lost in your own ways, I fully believe it will do the same for you. And at the same time you are getting your family back. And trust me, it might be too late for me, but it's not for you. You will see what's important, I truly believe that, and I will never stop loving you.'

There was a pause as their dad stared straight ahead of him. Harriet looked across at her siblings who all had shocked expressions, which hers probably mirrored.

'Was he of sound mind?' Gus asked.

'Clearly not,' Freddie said.

'He was. I think your father has made his intentions clear,' David stated, gently. 'He was unorthodox, you know that, but he was your father and those are his wishes.'

'And if we want to contest this?' Harriet said.

'There would be no point. Your father was sane, he was very certain of this plan, which I hope you will all respect.'

'But if we do, respect it, as you say, we have to all live here together and run an animal sanctuary?' Pippa looked distraught.

'Yes. I know it sounds unusual, but, well, that was what your father wanted. I've got it all typed up here, a document for each of you with the exact terms.'

'Right, I don't care what you say, I bloody well need a drink now,' Freddie stated, getting up and pouring himself a large whisky.

Pippa rubbed her temples as everyone began speaking at once.

'SHUT UP,' she heard her father's voice say from the screen. As it had gone quiet, they forgot the video was still running. They all obeyed once more, perhaps for the last time. 'You can do this, you will do this; I have every faith in you. I didn't do this for my own enjoyment, if that's what you're thinking. But if you can undertake my wishes, then you will make me very proud. More importantly you will make yourselves very proud, and that is what I want more than anything.'

The four of them stared, open-mouthed, at the screen.

'Gwen, did you get all that?' Andrew Singer asked, standing up. He was tall, like Gus and Freddie, his grey hair was neat and he was wearing a V-neck sweater and chinos, his favoured casual wear.

'I did, Andrew,' Gwen replied.

'And how was I? Was I all right?'

'Just as good as any Hollywood actor, Andrew,' Gwen replied before the screen went black.

Chapter 5

'What do we do now?' Gus asked, waving a copy of the document that David had handed over to them before he scarpered. He promised a meeting as soon as they'd had a chance to digest things. But after what they had just experienced, Harriet wasn't sure they would ever digest it. The feeling of unease that her father's video had left her with sat heavily on her stomach, and she couldn't seem to order her thoughts. Lost, she poured and handed out brandies for them all. After all, it was supposed to be good for shock and they were definitely in shock.

'Go and muck out some pigs, I am guessing,' Freddie joked, but he wasn't smiling. 'Do we even have any pigs?' He stared into his glass.

'Daddy did love that sanctuary,' Pippa mused. 'Oh God, Mark is going to be so upset about this.' She chewed her bottom lip, a habit she'd had when she was anxious since childhood.

'But, Pip, what Dad said about him?' Freddie started.

'I don't know what he was talking about,' Pippa replied. 'Mark and I are very happy. I just don't understand where that even came from.'

'God, are we grasping what he's asking? Run a rescue centre for animals, fundraise and live here, all together?

For a whole year!' Why did their father think that they would, or should, give up their lives? It made no sense. Even his explanation didn't add up. And Harriet felt guilty, but she knew there was no way she could do it, no matter what the consequences were. Oh yes, she could take some time out to sort out her father's estate, but if it was more than a week or two, some hungry younger person would be snapping at her heels to take her place at work. And she would never, ever give up her beloved job. Never.

'It's so much, so so much.' Gus's face was ashen.

'Look, we need time to think. Pip, you need to talk to Mark, so I suggest that we all take some time and I'll go and see Gwen and tell her we'll have a family dinner tonight to talk about it.'

'Still the same old bossy, Harry,' Freddie said.

'And thank goodness – someone needs to be,' Harriet bit back before leaving the room.

She found Gwen in the kitchen, pulling a freshly baked cake out of the Aga and then she saw Connor, sitting at the kitchen table nursing a cup of tea. The large kitchen was the only room which didn't have her father's stamp on it. It had, as long as Harriet could remember, been Gwen's domain and she had made it her own. It felt like a proper country kitchen. Huge pine table, the largest Aga they could get; it was always warm and welcoming, filled with the aroma of delicious food. But the main difference was that Gwen had filled the two ancient dressers with her personal knick-knacks as well as the crockery and dinner services that they used. The array of china chickens, pigs and her extensive egg-cup collection had been growing ever since Gwen had moved into the kitchen. There was something so charming about it. Not least that

45

her father found it horrific, but he quickly learnt not to interfere in *her* kitchen. Harriet remembered her chasing him out once with a wooden spatula when he tried to tell her what to do. No one messed with Gwen's kitchen.

'Hello, love,' Gwen said. 'Can I make you a cuppa?'

'No I'm fine, thanks.' Harriet smiled; Gwen was wearing her apron, Harriet could count the number of times on one hand when she had seen the housekeeper without an apron tied around her waist. There was Pippa's wedding, and of course yesterday, at her father's funeral.

Gwen was younger than her father at sixty. She had grey hair, worn in a sensible bob, and a fair few lines scattered on her face made her look her age, but she was fit and healthy. She had the energy of a much younger person. Her loyalty to the family had been one of the few constants in Harriet's life. Harriet remembered coming home from school to freshly baked biscuits or cakes, but Gwen didn't overstep the mark, she never interfered unless they asked her to. Harriet felt a pang of love for the woman who had always been there for them.

'So, obviously you've seen the video,' Gwen said, chewing her lip nervously.

Connor locked eyes with Harriet; God, his eyes were piercing as she was hit by a jolt. He always had those mesmerising eyes which made her feel he could see inside her. She felt like a foolish little girl again. The girl whose childhood consisted of mainly trying to impress him.

She and Connor had grown up together, along with her other siblings. But the two of them would often sneak off from them to go exploring. Connor was fascinated by wildlife and he always had some plan to find animals which usually involved either climbing trees, looking in hedges or jumping into the lake. Harriet usually got roped

46

into carrying his equipment around, nets, ropes, binoculars, cameras. She was his packhorse. But back then Harriet had been happy to trail around in wellies with him. Having so much land around Meadowbrook meant that they had enjoyed an almost feral childhood. Although of course they also had the best of everything, they were encouraged to explore the outdoors, running through fields, paddling in the lake, climbing trees; it was incredible, but a different world to corporate Harriet. Almost as if it had happened to someone else. Although Connor was clearly still living that life. Whereas for her, in New York, jogging in Central Park was as outdoorsy as she got these days.

'Yes, Gwen "Spielberg" White, we certainly did,' she joked, hoping to cover up how unsettled she felt.

'Oh, Mum, was your filming that bad?' Connor asked, lips curled up in amusement.

'It certainly was not. Well, not for my first time,' Gwen replied, giving her son a swat on the head. 'Although I don't know if I've got a future in it, to be honest.' She smiled.

'I don't think the quality of the filming is the debate we'll be having later,' Harriet said. Gwen looked a little embarrassed. 'Gwen, we're going to have dinner together to discuss it, is that all right?'

'Of course, I've got a roast on for you all, I thought you might need fortifying. What time do you want to eat?'

'About seven-thirty? I think tonight we need to chat about what we are going to do.'

'Quite right,' Gwen said. 'You've got decisions to make.'

'We do. Big decisions.' Harriet's eyes narrowed.

'I know it's none of my business,' Connor said. 'But it must seem quite ridiculous at the moment.'

'Yes, and as it involves the animal sanctuary it is your business. But it's surreal. I heard Dad talk about his animals but I didn't really give it too much thought,' she said, pointing an accusing finger at Connor. 'I guess we also need to have a conversation about the sanctuary, I know it's your baby.'

Connor's eyes lit up. 'Yes, it is my baby and Andrew's too. It's something I'd always wanted to do, and well, Andrew had the land, so when he got involved it was wonderful. He loved it, Harry, he really did, but I'm not going to give you the hard sell. It's important, not just to your father's memory, but you'll see that for yourself. When you're ready.' His eyes were full of passion, which only fuelled her guilt.

'Right, I might go for a bath before supper, I've got so much to think about,' Harriet said, leaving the warmth of the kitchen. She needed to clear her head, after the brandy and the pre-will, or whatever it was called, and, fingers crossed, a relaxing bath would help.

Chapter 6

Harriet lay back, closed her eyes and relaxed in the hot bubble bath. She felt her muscles all easing as she let herself luxuriate in the hot water. This was another unusual step for her, taking a bath rather than a super quick shower. In New York her apartment didn't have a bath, she was constantly rushing, she had forgotten how to go slowly, but Meadowbrook seemed to be gently reminding her. And as she thought about her father, and his will, her siblings and the decisions facing them all, she enjoyed the hot water and the feeling of being still.

Only when she was about to turn into a prune did she get out and change for dinner. She had only a limited wardrobe of clothes with her, after all she expected to only be home for a week or so, but she pulled on a pair of black trousers and a cashmere sweater. She was a little anxious for the evening ahead, it was going to be a difficult discussion, and she had a feeling that she would be terribly unpopular when she told them that she couldn't possibly do as their father wanted. Of course she couldn't. Her father was right in so many ways. Her work life was great, her personal one pretty dire, but he didn't understand how much she had invested in New York. She couldn't give that up, it just wasn't possible.

Freddie was mixing drinks when she entered the drawing room. This was her father's favourite room, it was huge, with three custom-made sofas, a smattering of uphol-stered armchairs, a huge open fire, and floor-to-ceiling windows which looked out onto the small lawn that edged the drive. It used to have a grand piano in it. She remem-bered how when they were young the siblings would sit on the piano stool and bash the keys. But it was her mother's, and her father had got rid of it after she died. He couldn't bear to have it in the house and none of them had ever been encouraged to take piano lessons. A bit like with Gus's art, her father had obviously found it too hard.

'Hey,' she said to Freddie. He smiled. He was too thin, she decided. Fred had always been tall, slender, but his cheekbones jutted out just a bit too much now. Perhaps she would ask Gwen to feed him up. She'd love that.

'Vodka Martini?' he asked.

'Bloody hell, Fred, that's brutal,' she said as she took a sip of the glass he handed her. As the alcohol slipped down, she felt calmer, despite the fact that on sip two she would possibly be drunk. 'But you definitely know how to mix your drinks.'

'It's one of my limited skill set. Dad, when I visited, said I made the best Martini and we'd sit and drink two, only two, together before dinner. It was our way of bonding.'

'Did you get home much?' Harriet felt the swords of guilt stabbing her again. All her siblings were here in their own way, for their father.

'Lately yes. I liked to get away from London.' Freddie's face darkened. 'So I spent a bit of time here. You know, I think that's part of the reason for the weird video-will thing. He worried about us, I know he worried about me.'

'Did he need to worry about you?' Harriet asked evenly. He shrugged. 'I miss him,' she said, feeling an urgent need to think about her dad, to talk about him.

'I do too. God, remember growing up? He used to push us, sometimes I felt he was unreasonably hard, other times I felt we, or at least I, needed it. He told me that my job wasn't a job but an extended party. He kept waiting for me to realise that and find something grown-up to do. His favourite thing to do was to be my career counsellor.' Freddie gave a dry laugh.

'Annoying.'

'Yes, but I would give anything to be annoyed by him right now.' Tears shone in Freddie's eyes.

Gus walked in, downcast, which seemed to be his usual state these days. Harriet wished she could hug him, but they didn't have that relationship, or not right now, but when they were younger, they had been so close that they were practically joined at the hip. Especially after losing their mother, when they both felt as if they needed to take care of the younger ones. But when Harriet was sent to school it changed. When she came home in the holidays there was a distance between her and Gus which they tried hard not to notice. A distance with all of them which had never fully recovered.

Gus had married his university girlfriend, Rachel, when she got pregnant with Fleur at twenty-two, a shotgun wedding hastily arranged, so the distance between brother and sister had increased. They worked hard to maintain

51

some kind of relationship, but Harriet didn't get on with Rachel, or actually vice versa. So they drifted more and when Harriet moved to New York, their contact was limited to emails. She sent gifts for Fleur of course, but Harriet had been about as bad a sister and aunt as she had a daughter.

But when had Gus got so dour? He was never quite as laid-back as Freddie – no one bar a recliner chair was – however, he didn't used to be this uptight either.

'I know, new resolution, whatever we decide about Dad's crazy will, I want us to behave like a family again,' Harriet said, feeling a sudden urgency for her family.

'I'll drink to that.' Freddie handed Gus a Martini and replenished his and Harriet's glasses.

'Blimey, Fred, this will have me under the table in no time,' Gus said, taking a sip.

'Good, you need to loosen up,' Freddie replied with a wink.

'Yes, well you might regret saying that when I'm legless,' Gus laughed. Harriet wished she felt as easy with them as they seemed to be with each other.

'Am I late?' Pippa asked as she entered the room.

'Just in time for a drink,' Freddie said, pouring her a Martini and hugging her warmly.

'Fred, did you make a vat of that?' Harriet asked.

'No, just a jug.'

'Has Mark gone?' Gus asked.

'Yes, he has to work tomorrow and, well, we need to make a decision, of course. I felt as if it would be impossible but Mark made me see that it's not necessarily so—'

They were saved by Gwen appearing. 'Dinner's ready, loves,' she said.

'Gwen, you know we can clear up after dinner,' Harriet

said. 'It's been a tough few days and we'd rather you relaxed than waited on us.'

'Are you sure, I don't mind?' Gwen replied.

'Honestly, it's not on. We are big enough to clear up after ourselves, and I know full well you'll be in that kitchen first thing in the morning making another delicious breakfast. Please,' Harriet begged. She knew Gwen felt the need to work, but not every minute of every day. 'Either go and see Connor or watch your soap operas!' They both laughed. Harriet remembered how her dad hated her watching *EastEnders* back when she was young so she would sneak to Gwen's cottage and watch it with her; their secret. Another memory that she had buried. How many more would there be?

The air was thick with anxiety as they went through to the dining room and they took their seats. It felt formal, serious, and Harriet had a thousand thoughts whooshing round her mind. They all faced each other; their father's chair at the end of the table conspicuously empty. Plates of food sat in front of them, along with empty wine glasses. Gwen, despite being told that they didn't need such formality, said she liked doing things 'properly'. As wine was poured, silence descended. They tucked into their food, Harriet was glad to eat, although she felt a little fuzzy from the Martinis. She barely tasted the food.

'OK, I guess it's time for us to discuss what we are all thinking,' Harriet said, taking charge yet again. Yes she was bossy, but she was the oldest and being bossy hadn't done her any harm. She had become the youngest female Vice President in her department at the investment bank. And she headed up a large team, mainly men, earning a salary that most people could only dream of. So, being bossy worked for her, why change it?

'Well Gwen has surpassed herself again with this dinner. She's such a treasure,' Freddie quipped.

'You know what I mean. Dad, his will, or pre-will. Meadowbrook Manor and the animal sanctuary. Am I the only one who's never seen it?'

'Yup. They've built it out past Gwen and Connor's cottages. Paddocks have been cordoned off, there's housing for all the animals as well as a specific cat home and dog home,' Pippa said.

'I'll see Connor and get him to arrange for me to have a guided tour,' Harriet replied, efficiently. Despite the Martinis and the wine she was currently drinking, her brain had gone into work mode. She knew full well she wouldn't be able to do what her father wanted, but she needed to see what her siblings thought before she showed her hand.

'And animal sanctuary aside, what about living here? I mean how random is that?' Freddie quipped.

'Let's go round the table and discuss what each of us thinks about it,' Harriet suggested. 'I mean, is it even possible for us to put our lives on hold for a year?' No, she wanted them all to say. The idea that she might be the only one to cost her siblings so dearly seemed unthinkable.

'OK, boss,' Freddie laughed. He downed some more wine and topped up his glass, spearing a potato with his fork at the same time. 'Well, I am currently living with my girlfriend, the lovely Loretta.'

'Hey, how come we haven't heard of her?' Harriet asked.

'Well I have, actually,' Pippa replied.

'Me too,' Gus added, leaving Harriet feeling an outsider yet again.

'Why wasn't she at the funeral?' Harriet asked a little more aggressively than she intended. What the hell was wrong with her? She felt a burning jealousy that the three of them all had a part in each other's lives, but she was the one who took herself away from them. It was her fault.

'She's overseas, working – she's a model. So she wanted to come but couldn't. She's gone for about a month. Anyway, although I am not sure I can cope living with all of you, I personally think we should honour Dad's wishes.'

'What about Loretta?' Harriet asked, surprised by Freddie's easy compliance.

'What about work?' Pippa asked, echoing her thoughts.

'Surely they can survive without me for a year. Loretta can stay at weekends and I can still be involved with work, remotely. Did the terms say we could do that?'

'I haven't read them yet,' Harriet replied. She had scanned the document, but because of the impossibility of the whole thing, she had yet to properly read it, was there any point? 'OK, so Fred's in. Gus?' Harriet felt her heart sink. Surely Gus would put a stop to this nonsense?

Gus exhaled. He looked as if he carried the world on his shoulders and he also looked exhausted. His face seemed to wear sorrow which Harriet knew couldn't just be down to their father's death. Yes they were all grieving, but with Gus there was definitely more.

'Well, funnily enough, I was thinking of taking some time off work. And Fleur loves it here, so it might help with our relationship. She's twelve, going on twenty, and I feel that I have no clue how to be with my own daughter.'

'Gus, what's going on?' Harriet asked. First Freddie, now Gus?

'Oh, you know, the usual, premature midlife crisis and

all that. And, you know with Dad dying, it's just been a bit tough, but the point is that despite the fact I'm not keen on running the animal sanctuary, I would be open to living here. You see the alternative, not having the house in the family, seems wrong.'

Harriet had thought about that. Yes it would be terrible not to have Meadowbrook in the family. God, almost unthinkable.

'But say we do this, for a year, then what?' she asked.

'Who knows,' Gus replied. 'I guess we cross that bridge when we need to, at the moment we just need to focus on this year.' Harriet glanced around, surely they didn't think this was a good idea? What on earth was going on?

'Mark and I talked, as I started to tell you when we were in the drawing room,' Pippa explained. 'He said it was my decision, although like you, Fred, he said that we should probably honour Dad's last wishes. In fact, he was rather encouraging, quite disproving what Dad said. I know we'll find it tough being apart all week, but he could come here at weekends. That's all right in the terms actually, I checked with David.'

'But you are prepared to live apart from your husband all week?' Harriet didn't keep the incredulity out of her voice.

'I don't agree with what Dad said on the video, so don't think that. We're happy, Mark and I love each other and he proved that by saying that he would let me decide what to do about this whole thing. So I think that our marriage is strong enough for this, for anything, and I really would like to do what Daddy wanted us to.' A lone tear rolled down her pink cheek.

Harriet remembered Pippa's wedding day, the last time they had all been together. She'd spent a week with her family at Meadowbrook. The wedding was held in the village church and the reception was in a huge marquee in the grounds of the Manor. Pippa was young, not quite twenty-five and so excited. She was so radiant, she glowed. And her dress, a beautiful designer gown, had been stunning. It had almost made Harriet cry, almost but not quite. Mark looked handsome, top hat and tails, and their father radiated pride as he gave his youngest daughter away. Harriet was her maid of honour and, at that time, not wanting to be married, had enjoyed her sister's happiness.

'So, Pip, you're a yes?' Harriet couldn't believe it. 'Not more than a few hours ago we were all saying Dad was mad.'

'Well we still think that, but this doesn't seem to be so much of a hardship,' Freddie said. 'In fact, perhaps Dad was right, it's a gift. I mean, we all get to spend time together, re-evaluate everything, and as has already been said, we should do all we can to keep Meadowbrook in the family. So, Harry, that just leaves you . . .'

Harriet sighed, this wasn't exactly how she thought it would go. 'Look, guys, I get that it's all or nothing and I don't want to take it away from you, but I have quite a job, as you know. I'm not sure I can just take a year off, I'm not sure they'll let me. It's complicated.' She hoped she didn't sound too self-important.

'But you will see if you can, will you try?' Gus asked. 'Look, I've never been after Dad's money.' Gus looked down at his nearly empty plate. 'But you know, he wanted us to have it. And, of course, there are our families to think about. Not just Fleur, but your future kids, if you have any. I'm happy to give as much as needed to the animal sanctuary, I don't need a lot to live on, but I don't want to lose all the family memories and that means keeping Meadowbrook. And it also, to me, means honouring Dad's memory and doing what he wanted us to do.'

'It's all we have left of Mum and Dad,' Pippa said, another tear rolling down her cheek. 'I don't want to lose it but, more importantly, like Gus, I want to do what Daddy wanted us to do. Because he might not be here, but he's still our father.' Pippa's voice was full of emotion and something Harriet had to respect; passion. As her three siblings all nodded in agreement, she felt guilty, wretched. She didn't have such a straightforward decision. If she said yes, she would kiss goodbye to her job, oh and her relationship, or whatever it actually was. If she said no, then she would lose her siblings and Meadowbrook. It was a lose-lose.

'I need to check in with work.' Harriet stood up, she needed to get out of here, have some time to think. She had mixed feelings; panic, anxiety. She loved her siblings, she loved her job; she was sleeping with her married boss. They had had an on/off affair for about five years now; something she hadn't planned but more fallen into. She wasn't proud of that, but Zach, successful, powerful, was a difficult man to resist. And as much as she enjoyed being with him, she loved her job even more.

'Gwen's left an apple crumble in the Aga,' she said, collecting herself, refilling her wine glass, as, heart thumping, she left the room.

She made her way upstairs to the first floor. There were five bedrooms here and five on the second floor. The first floor housed the family's bedrooms, the top floor the guest rooms, but, as far as she knew, her father didn't have many guests. As children they used to play upstairs, but then they pretty much ran around everywhere in the enormous house. They were fairly wild at times, various nannies tried to tame them, Gwen too, but they didn't quite manage it.

Harriet opened her computer. She knew the drill; it would be easier to email Zach, who never took his eyes off his mailbox, and get him to call her urgently. She needed reassurance from him that this was a terrible idea and that there was no way she would be able to stay at Meadowbrook for even a month let alone a year.

Zachary Matthews, the man she had walked into the interview room ten years ago with a desperate need to impress. He was tall, with curly brown hair, dark eyes, and a presence so commanding she was drawn to him like a magnet. She was so focused on the job, nothing would stand in her way of the much-wanted move to New York. Her and Zach worked closely together and at some point they ended up in bed together. It hadn't happened overnight, it had taken almost five years before anything happened. A work trip to Washington, too much wine with dinner, and then up to his hotel room. He didn't sugarcoat anything, romance it certainly wasn't, but that was what Harriet wanted, needed, understood. No strings, nothing to detract from her job, no emotions. Harriet didn't even know if she had emotions anymore. They were the same person; driven by making money, excited by the deal, obsessed by work, by succeeding.

She didn't focus too much on the fact that she was sleeping with a married man. And every time her moral compass seemed to right itself and she decided to end things, Zach would smile at her and they'd end up in bed. Was she the only one? She doubted it. But there was something powerful about him. And something safe. Harriet certainly didn't worry about him falling in love with her and she didn't need to worry about falling in love with him. She had let that happen once and it didn't end well.

But now her father had died. Which made her question what the hell she was doing.

She took a deep breath as she opened up her email and, scanning through the spam, she noticed an email from work. It was from the director of HR, with Zach copied in. As her thumping heart slowed to a dull thud, she felt bile rising in her stomach as she read it.

A knock on her bedroom door roused her back to the present.

'Can I come in?' Pippa asked, tentatively, as her head poked around the door.

'Sure,' Harriet replied, quietly.

Pippa made her way over to the king-size bed and sat down. Harriet was still at the dressing table, staring at the screen in front of her. Shock, fear, hatred all fighting to dominate her emotions.

'So, did you call the office?' Pippa asked. Harriet turned her head to look at Pippa. 'Harry? Are you all right?'

'I just checked my emails.' She could barely believe what she'd just read. 'And look.' She picked up her laptop and took it over to the bed, sitting next to her, so Pippa could read the email. Harriet needed her to do so, because she still hoped she imagined it. It was as if she was in a night-mare.

'It says that they're making you redundant?' Pippa said, eyes wide in shock.

'Yes. Paying me off. Restructuring my department.' Harriet shook her head. Zach hadn't even sent a personal message. Her boss, the man she had been sleeping with on a semi-regular basis, had used her father's death as an excuse to get rid of her.

'But I don't understand, they can't do this, I mean you've come home for your father's funeral.'

'I think they must have been planning it, even they couldn't come up with this in twenty-four hours.' She paused to think. 'Actually they could.' Redundancy packages had been put together in a matter of hours. She should know, she had been behind some of them. Her stomach plummeted even more.

'That's terrible and surely not even legal.' Pippa was outraged. 'Surely you could threaten to sue them.'

'I could, but I won't.' Harriet felt her body deflate.

'Why not, Harry? That's not like you. Why won't you at least threaten them?'

'Because, Pip,' Harriet's eyes swam with tears, 'I'm not proud, but I've been sleeping with my my married boss.'

Pippa's mouth gaped open. She shook her head and shut it. 'But, I don't understand, if you've been sleeping with him, why is he getting rid of you now?'

'I don't know.' She really didn't. But she did know that she would never walk onto that trading floor again. Feel that exhilaration of anticipation of the day ahead. Hear the buzz of the phones ringing, computers beeping – her favourite music. How on earth was she supposed to live without that?

'What a bastard. To do it just after you buried your dad. And not even tell you himself. I mean, I can't condone you sleeping with a married man, Harry, that was wrong. Oh goodness, what a mess.' Pippa sounded distraught. Harriet looked at her. She was no longer the kid that Harriet felt so maternal towards.

'Exactly, without my job I'm nothing.' She felt tears threatening her, and she was almost ready to welcome them.

61

'Oh, Harry, I am so sorry.' Pippa hugged her.

'It's my fault. I shouldn't have done it,' Harriet stated, feeling self-loathing.

Pippa didn't argue with her.

Harriet suddenly saw her life clearly. She worked long hours, mostly six days a week, she went to the gym to stay in shape, one of her closest friends was her personal trainer for goodness sake. She had a best friend, Mimi, who knew most things about her and a handful of social friends, all high-flying single career women who she drank cocktails, ate at the latest restaurants and bitched about work and men with – in that order. She had a beautiful but barely furnished apartment – who had time to decorate a place that she barely spent any time in? A wardrobe of fabulous clothes, ditto shoes, and a city life that she was in no way ready to leave behind. She was struck by the realisation that her life was lacking in real relationships, and maybe a bit lonely at times – was this what her father meant?

'Ah. Well, listen, Harriet, I know now's not the time to think about the future, because it's so raw and such a shock, but we'll sort it out. If you don't want to fight them, then take the money, and at least you've got us and Meadowbrook,' Pippa said.

'Oh, Pip, I don't know, I don't even know how I feel. I mean, I had barely processed the fact that Dad's gone and now I've lost my job, all in one fell swoop.' She stopped for a minute and thought back to her father's video. Was he right about her after all? She had worked tirelessly to succeed, to be the daughter that he wanted her to be, had she lost herself along the way? Surely not. She shook her head. He was just rambling because he wanted his children all together – still trying to control them from beyond the grave.

'I guess that means that you can stay here for the year though,' Pippa said, uncertainly. 'Maybe it's fresh starts all round, and maybe Dad knew more than we ever gave him credit for.' Pippa sounded anxious but Harriet wondered if she could read her mind. 'We'll be together at least.' Pippa squeezed her sister. 'And get to run an animal sanctuary,' she laughed. Harriet did not.

'I'm used to running a trading floor, with millions of dollars at stake every day, so how hard can running an animal sanctuary be?' Harriet asked, and then she finally burst into tears.

Chapter 7

Harriet knocked on Connor's door. She felt nervous. Probably due to the fact they hadn't spent any time alone in forever. She pulled her cardigan tightly around her. It was chilly, not quite seven in the morning, the dew was glued to the grass. Harriet wore skinny jeans, a T-shirt and a cashmere cardigan; dressed down but immaculate. On her feet were her trainers. As she waited for the door to open, she thought fleetingly about New York. She'd be in the office by now, phones ringing, people shouting, and now when all she could hear was the odd squark of a bird, she felt as if she had been dislodged from her life.

After the shock last night, which she still keenly felt, her mind had been whirring with thoughts of living at Meadowbrook for the year; wondering if she could do it. Live with her family, run an animal sanctuary, give up the bright lights of the city, live a 'simple' life. And the answer was she didn't know. Already, she missed those bright lights terribly. She didn't care about her father's money, but she did care about what happened to Meadowbrook and, of course, she cared about her brothers and sister. It was all so confusing, she couldn't think in a straight line. She wished her father was here; he would know what to do. Of course, he would tell her to get on with the year at Meadowbrook, and run the animal sanc-tuary, bond with her siblings. Oh, and stay away from unsuitable married men. As she heard his voice in her head, she choked back tears.

Unable to sleep, she had read the terms of the pre-will – as it was now known. It was actually quite straightfor-ward but bloody annoying – her father really had decided to strip each of his children back to basics.

Living together for a year, each of them was allowed a maximum of a week away from the place. They would be given a very slim allowance; their father thought they were all spoilt and too materialistic. The amount wouldn't have kept New York Harriet in cabs, let alone anything else. Although all food and bills at the house were taken care of, they weren't going to be buying any luxuries for a year. And as soon as they agreed to do it, they all had to hand over their bank cards and any credit cards and cash they had on them to David. Cheating was out of the question.

Harriet felt it was like a bad reality TV show, but one which was her life.

The animal sanctuary was another thing. They had to raise £25,000 in the year, which seemed like a ridiculously high amount for four people who had never raised a penny for charity. Oh, Harriet had given money, she sponsored, she put money in charity collections, she'd been to a number of high-profile auctions and spent thousands in an hour, but she hadn't actually shaken a collecting tin herself. And although used to dealing in millions, getting ordinary people to part with money wasn't something she had any experience in. If only she could use her own money she would pay it right now, but of course that was against the rules.

They also had to get their hands dirty with the sanctuary, they were each expected to take on a physical role to help out such as mucking out or walking the dogs. Harriet just couldn't see it. Not any of it. All she could feel was loss on top of loss. Her father was gone, her job was gone, and she was rapidly losing her sense of self. She might be home but she felt like a stranger in a foreign land.

She knocked on Connor's door again. She could see he was in, lights were blazing from inside. The three cottages that sat in a row belonged to Meadowbrook. Gwen and Connor had lived in the largest, but, when he returned home, he had moved into the second and newly renovated cottage which was next door to his mother. And the third was the old gardener, Jed's cottage, which stood empty ever since he had died a few years ago.

Connor was wearing thick socks, jeans and an oversized jumper when he finally answered his front door. He looked surprised to see her but he smiled, warmly, eyes crinkling.

'Hey, Harry, come in.' He stepped aside.

'Sorry to call round so early.'

'It's fine, I'm always up at this time.' Connor gave one of his cheeky grins, and led her into his living room. It was small and messy, with a large sofa dominating, and a wood burner which was unlit. Papers were scattered around, with the odd mug and plate thrown in for the extra lived-in look.

'Goodness what would your mother say?' Harriet couldn't help herself.

'Don't worry, I tidy up before she ever sees it,' Connor laughed.

'Do you happen to have coffee?' she asked, laughing with him.

'Come through.'

The small kitchen was clean and tidy as Connor set about putting the kettle on, taking out a French press and spooning coffee in. She sat down at the breakfast bar.

'I don't remember coming into this cottage before,' she said as she took it all in. The wooden kitchen was modern but rustic, the back door led onto a small patch of lawn, it was sweet, but after Meadowbrook felt tiny. And six foot two Connor filled the cottage like a giant.

'Silvia lived here, remember she used to help Mum with the cleaning sometimes and she also worked in the local pub.'

'Oh, yes of course, I'd forgotten.'

'Harry, I'm not being rude, but you seemed to have left Meadowbrook and everyone behind with barely a backward glance. Myself included.'

Harriet startled. She wasn't ready to hear that. She wasn't sure why she had found it so easy to turn her back on Meadowbrook when she moved to New York. She thought she was running towards her glittering future, after all, most ambitious people did that. In her world it was totally normal. But first her father, then her siblings and now Connor. Was everyone intent on making her feel that she had abandoned them?

She shrugged. 'I followed my career and I didn't look back. Yes, I kept in touch with the family, but I didn't have much time to think about home, and now I'm here I feel . . . well, I feel a little strange,' she explained.

'But you're back now,' Connor said quietly. The way he peered at her again made her feel he could see inside her, see all her thoughts. When they were young she thought that he knew her better than anyone did.

'What happened to you?' She was desperate to change the subject, he was making her feel too uncomfortable; exposed. 'You were in New Zealand when I came back for Pip's wedding, I recall, with your fiancée?' Her father kept her abreast of Connor's movements, in their exchanges. Yet still, Harriet didn't quite understand how their friendship had fractured quite so much. Connor was one of the most important people in her life, and she had let him become a stranger. But why?

'Ah yes, the lovely Elizabeth. Well, we did go to New Zealand, she wanted to emigrate and we were going to get married, but then we started arguing all the time. I missed home, she didn't. Do you remember her?' Connor asked.

'Of course, I met her on a number of occasions,' Harriet replied carefully, trying not to look as embarrassed as she felt.

The first time she met Connor's girlfriend, they were both home from university and she had been so excited to see Connor. He wanted her to meet someone and that someone was Elizabeth.

That holiday changed so much for Harriet. Probably the fact that Connor wasn't there for her anymore, or perhaps the idea that he now belonged to someone else. Elizabeth. Annoying Elizabeth who clung to Connor's side like a limpet. Elizabeth who was going to be a vet just like him; she and Harriet hated each other on sight. They both wanted to be the most important girl in Connor's life, but there was only one spot. And as Elizabeth was having sex with Connor, Harriet was never going to win. Elizabeth, smug, annoying and with the only man Harriet had every truly felt herself with.

No matter how hard she tried, she couldn't spend any

time with Connor without his annoying girlfriend being there. And after that Harriet felt she had lost him, as things changed irrevocably.

Gus had accused her, when she ranted about 'Limpet Liz' with her frizzy hair and annoying laugh, of being jealous, but she refused to accept it. Harriet smiled to herself, now she was an adult, she knew she had been ridiculously jealous.

'Anyway, I'm sorry it didn't work out, but I guess it's good for Meadowbrook,' Harriet said, collecting herself. It was a childhood crush that didn't go away. That was all it was.

'I didn't realise how much I loved this place until I came back. Now I can't imagine leaving. Well, I won't because I'm invested. I'm at a local practice and I have the sanctuary. It keeps me out of trouble.' His eyes twinkled, years melted away. 'But what about you?'

'I've made a monumental mess of my life. But can we leave it at that?' Harriet asked. 'And as I'm here I wondered if you would be able to show me this famous animal sanctuary. I seem to be the only one that hasn't seen it.' She knew she sounded brusque but it was the only way she could keep it together. Ever since tears had visited last night, they kept threatening to return.

'So you're going to do it?' Connor asked, eagerly. 'You're going to stay here just as your dad wanted?'

'It looks like it,' Harriet replied and was utterly surprised as Connor picked her up and spun her around.

'And they said there wasn't room to swing a cat in this kitchen,' he joked as he put her down. She raised her eyebrows but couldn't help giggling like a schoolgirl. 'Honestly, Harry,' he still hadn't taken his arms away, it felt warm, 'I am so pleased. Not just about Andrew's

69

wishes, or Meadowbrook, or even the animals, but about the fact that we're all back together.'

'Just like the good old days,' Harriet mumbled.

'Are you up for looking for toads then?' Connor joked. 'Or perhaps climbing trees to study squirrels?'

'Nope, but I am interested in seeing these animals. Although, I really do need that coffee first.'

The day was warming up as they set off from Connor's cottage, out through his back garden gate and across the fields to the rescue centre.

'There's a couple of buildings,' Connor explained. 'One for the dogs, another for cats, and an office. Of course, the animals who live in the fields also have sheds, or shelters and they are largely taken in at night. We have only two full-time staff here, who are on rota, but we have a few part-timers, and also a number of volunteers from the village, which means that we are quite well staffed. I tend to make sure the animals are all OK myself before I go to bed and, of course, any medical issues come under my jurisdiction. All the paperwork is in the office.' His face became animated when he spoke, it was as if someone had switched his light on.

'It sounds well organised.' Harriet was already wondering where she and her siblings would fit in.

'It is. Although we are feeling Andrew's absence keenly. We're not enormous, by any means, and we've been lucky to get quite a few of our domestic animals rehomed, but there are always more coming in and some of our animals are definitely here to stay. Until recently there was even a cockatiel, Hamlet. He could never get rehomed because he swore like a sailor, so not exactly a family pet.'

70

'How did he come to live here?'

'His owner, an elderly fisherman, died and his daughter who's local brought him over to us. Your dad had a rule: no animal gets turned away. Unfortunately he died, Hamlet that is. Anyway, running this place is costly, there's food, shelter, the paid staff and we also try to raise awareness, there's enough to keep you all busy.'

'If you pay staff, surely £25,000 isn't enough to keep the place running for a year?' Harriet's head was already juggling figures.

'No, but the wages are taken care of in a trust your father set up, and we also have a number of regular donations. I'll talk you through all the paperwork, but yes, the twenty-five grand is what we need on top of what we already have, to make sure we can stay open this year.'

'My God, you know last week I was in New York, screaming at men in suits because we were about to lose millions of dollars when the markets dipped and now I am supposed to raise money for cockatiels with Tourette's. Who on earth thought my life could come to this?' She smiled, sadly.

'Harry, it might be small fry compared to what you are used to but what we do is important,' Connor snapped.

'I'm not denying that, I'm not being rude.' She was suddenly reminded of how she and Connor used to bicker a lot, and they were on the cusp of it now. She was annoyed, after all she was the one who had just had the rug pulled from under her, but again, she knew that she needed to make an effort. 'I'm sorry, it's just a lot to take in.' Harriet shook her head, Connor pursed his lips as he did when he disapproved. God, he was still a judgemental pain in the arse. Some things never changed.

They were still silent as they reached the first field.

'That's Sebastian and Samantha, they're alpacas,' he pointed out. Harriet raised her eyebrows as she looked at the two of them striding around the field, she wasn't sure she'd ever seen an alpaca close up. 'It became fashionable to knit with their wool, so some bright spark decided that they'd do just that. Only they couldn't take care of them, or knit for that matter,' Connor laughed, as if she was forgiven and Harriet couldn't help but grin. She relaxed slightly. 'They are what we call lifers.'

'They're beautiful,' although that wasn't quite the right description. They looked almost regal, she thought. Connor took her over to meet them. They looked at her, slightly suspiciously, but they let Connor pet them, and then, feeling brave, she did the same.

'The donkey is Gerald, he's quite old but very sweet and he's pals with the miniature ponies, Clover and Cookie.' Harriet followed Connor into the next paddock. Gerald ambled over and greeted them with an ear-busting hee-haw.

'Oh my, they are so cute.' Harriet watched the two tiny ponies as they grazed under the watchful eye of Gerald. She'd never seen ponies that small.

'Yes, but again, they were suffering before they came to us, luckily we were able to bring them here. Gerald, well he was abandoned. You'd be amazed at how many animals just get left to fend for themselves. But Gerald seems to parent the ponies, which is quite sweet really.'

'What is wrong with people?' Harriet stormed. She felt impassioned, which took her by surprise.

In another field there were two large pigs and three goats.

'The pigs were micropigs that turned out to be full-size

72

pot-bellied, there was no way the owner could keep them in her bungalow,' Connor explained. 'Betsy and Buddy.'

'They're enormous,' Harriet laughed and, as she looked out at the fields and the animals, she felt herself begin to relax. She remembered her outdoorsy childhood and although the animal sanctuary wasn't here when she was growing up, it was beginning to feel more like home.

'And the goats are Piper, Flo and Romeo.' Connor pointed to the three goats who were happily munching grass. One of them came over to where they stood, looking at them hopefully.

'Hi, Romeo,' Connor said, picking some grass and handing it to him through the fence.

'Where's Juliet?' Harriet quipped.

'That's why he's here, because he lost his Juliet. She died, and they thought he would too, he wouldn't eat, and when they asked me to look at him, I could tell he had a broken heart, so I suggested trying to bring him here to be with Piper and Flo.'

'Oh my goodness, that's so sad.' Harriet didn't like to add that she knew how Romeo felt. Part of her wanted to pine and never eat again. Over a job not a lover in her case though.

'Luckily when he came they all seemed to get on, and he's perked right up.'

'A sort of goat ménage à trois?'

'Let's hope not,' Connor laughed. 'Piper and Flo are sisters.'

Harriet laughed. Whether it was the warm morning breeze, being able to see lush fields and so much open space, she didn't know, but she felt as if she could breathe a bit. Perhaps she could do this. She felt the breeze in her hair and her head cleared a bit, or at least the fog shifted slightly to the left.

'OK, well we have chickens over there.' He pointed to another field which held a very elaborate looking henhouse as well as space for them to run. 'They're all ex-battery hens but they do lay eggs – at times – and we try to rescue as many chickens as possible. They come to us in such a dreadful state but we mostly get them happy and healthy again. Although, and you have to get used to this, we do lose some of our animals.'

'I guess they all have names too?' Harriet asked. She hated to think about the cruelty aspect to the sanctuary, or animals dying. She knew it went on but she didn't want to give herself nightmares. She might be a hard-nosed city woman but she had a heart. It was just a bit of a well-kept secret at the moment.

'All named after Jane Austen characters, one of our staff, Jenni, is a huge fan so we let her name them. And she can tell them apart, but the rest of us get them mixed up.'

'The chickens look kind of the same to me,' Harriet said, looking at them.

'Don't tell Jenni that. There are also some geese, they sort of roam around, they're quite tame, so you can approach them but don't scare them. And in the far field two Highland bulls.' He pointed and she looked across. They were enormous, and quite magnificent with their horned heads and shaggy coats. 'They're best friends. About a year ago I had a call about them and, well, it wasn't easy as they aren't always the friendliest of animals but we managed to get them here. They clearly adore each other, barely leave each other's side, but they can be aggressive to any other animal and some humans, although they're fine if you approach them properly. Still, we keep them on their own, we named them Elton and David.'

'Gay bulls? Are you joking?' Harriet looked at Connor but he had already turned his attention to other animals.

'And if you look at the far side of the field just beyond the ponies, you'll see that in the shelter we have our blind sheep and her guide lamb. Agnes and Abigail.' Harriet looked to where Connor pointed and saw two white dots.

'How come she's blind?'

'She was attacked by a crow when she was pregnant, blinded, but she managed to deliver a healthy baby and the lamb, Abigail, became her "guide lamb". No good to the farmer so he brought them to us. They trot around together quite happily, it's very sweet, but we do take extra special care of them, almost like domestic pets.'

'God, Connor, the stories, they're quite sad.' Harriet wiped fresh tears from her eyes, for someone who never cried she was suddenly finding it a bit too easy. Poor heartbroken Romeo, the neglected gay cows, the blind sheep and her lamb who took care of her, the ex-battery hens, not to mention the domestic animals. It was so, so tragic. No wonder her father had invested so much in this.

Her threatening tears came, suddenly. Connor put his arm around her shoulders. She felt warm, she almost felt safe as her body danced with sobs that wouldn't subside. There was so much heartbreak, not just hers. She wasn't going to feel sorry for herself, not when there were others who had it so much worse. Even if they were animals.

'Let's go and meet the animals properly. But, Harry, they're happy, they're safe, your father was so committed to this place, it was his vision and his dream to have it, mine too, but I couldn't have done it without him. Anyway, before we go any further, I better warn you that this,' he swept his free arm around, 'gets to you.'

'It already has,' Harriet replied and she looked at Connor who was blurred through her tears and she let him hold her as she cried some more.

Chapter 8

Freddie stood on the drive, smoking and shouting into his mobile phone as Harriet jogged up.

'Hey,' she said.

'Where have you been?' he asked after he hung up. He looked dishevelled, his eyes bloodshot, hair a mess, and reeked of smoke. But she wasn't going to bring that up now. He looked as if he needed help, not a lecture.

'I went for a run. Anyway, who were you talking to?' The run was helping to clear the air after the past couple of days.

'Loretta. She's still away, but I was filling her in about the will stuff. Quite rightly, she thinks it's a bit mad, but anyway she said she'd support me.'

'That's nice, isn't it?'

'Yes, although the line was bad, so she may not have done.' Confusions etched his face momentarily. 'Anyway, you'll get to meet her when she's back.'

'I'll look forward to it.' Harriet grinned.

'However, it leaves me with a bit of a problem. I have no clothes here, well only a limited wardrobe and I could go to London to collect some more but, well, they aren't exactly appropriate for the country.' Ah, Harriet understood. They were expected to muck in with the sanctuary, as per her father's instructions, and she had assured Connor they would be starting as soon as they got the chance to discuss it. But, as she looked at her designer trainers, she realised that she didn't have anything suitable to wear either.

'Oh God. I'm in the same boat. I left most of my stuff in New York, not that any of my clothes would be good for feeding chickens or mucking out ponies.'

'We need country clothes,' Freddie laughed. 'But we have a cash-flow problem, remember?'

'Oh, goodness. What the hell are we going to do?' This was where her father's wishes began to hit home. They had a tiny amount to spend, no access to their own money – they'd handed it all over to David yesterday – and as far as Harriet could see, not many suitable clothes to wear.

'What's going on?' Pippa appeared at the front door.

'Freddie and I were worrying about what the hell we are supposed to wear while we're here. Have you got any ideas?'

'Actually yes. But now breakfast is ready.'

Harriet wondered if her father was playing a massive joke on them. Here they were, sat around an expensive dining table, eating a breakfast fit for royalty, provided for them by their lovely housekeeper as if they were lords and ladies. Yet they didn't have money, and they were expected to literally go and get their hands dirty in order to fulfil their father's wishes. She shook her head, it made no sense.

'So, Pip,' Harriet said, pulling her brain back to the matter in hand. 'What are we going to do about clothes?'

'Well, you obviously both dress very expensively,

which is not suitable for the animal sanctuary, I'm guessing.'

'We know that,' Freddie replied.

'Right, so I thought we could go shopping.' Pippa looked pleased with herself.

'But we don't have much money. We each have to live on forty quid a week after all,' Harriet said. How on earth would they do that? Her face cream cost two hundred pounds and it was running low.

'What was Dad thinking? I mean, I know we have food and bills paid,' Freddie echoed.

'And alcohol,' Gus pointed out.

'Oh yes, perhaps it'll be all right after all.' Freddie seemed satisfied again as he tucked into his breakfast.

'I'll take you shopping, but we'll go to charity shops,' Pippa announced with a flourish.

'What?' Harriet felt the colour drain from her face.

'We have to wear other people's clothes. Dead people's clothes?' Freddie said.

'They probably won't be dead people's. Just cast-offs,' Pippa said, cheerfully. 'Gus, do you have old clothes?'

'Yes, I've got my sort of Sunday clothes, jogging bottoms and so forth.' He sounded so formal when he talked about slobbing out, Harriet thought, such a contradiction. 'I just need to go to my flat to pick them up.'

'Pippa, what about you?' Freddie said. 'You could do with some work clothes. I mean, no offence, but you look like you should be hosting a WI meeting.'

'Ah, I have a stash of clothes upstairs,' Pippa said. 'Although, Freddie, for your information this is how I dress and I like it.'

Harriet looked at her sister, she was wearing a silk blouse tucked into her black tailored trousers, her hair was pulled back in a neat ponytail, she wore pearls at her neck, small diamond studs in her ears and her wedding and engagement rings. Pippa used to wear all sorts of crazy jewellery, she would put on multiple necklaces, huge earrings, and nearly every finger had a ring on it. The old Pippa had had her own style, it was slightly crazy, but being beautiful, looking like a pale, blonde doll-like creature, meant she could pull anything off.

'You used to look different,' Harriet pointed out. 'You always looked gorgeously bohemian actually.'

'I know, but I'm not a kid anymore.' She spoke determinedly and Harriet wondered if she would ever stop thinking of Pip as the baby of the family. At the moment she seemed more grown-up than any of them.

'What is your secret stash then?' Gus asked.

'When I moved out, I left a lot of old jeans and stuff here. They're still there, in my wardrobe. Daddy didn't get rid of them. Actually, Harry, some of the jumpers might fit you, the trousers will be too short.'

'And possibly a bit tight.' Harriet was a UK ten but Pippa was an eight. 'Why don't you go and change then?' Harriet grinned. 'After all, you'll look more at home in a charity shop if you do,' Harriet laughed.

They waved Gus off as he went to his flat to get his belongings and then opened the large, four-car garage that her father had built.

'Wow, I'd forgotten about the Bentley,' Harriet said, admiring the vintage car that was her father's pride and joy.

'Isn't she a beauty? Gosh, do you think I'm allowed to drive this?' Freddie asked.

'No. The will said we could use the Range Rover.' As

well as the Bentley and Range Rover, Gwen's Volkswagen Polo was in the garage, along with a couple of bicycles and a buggy which her father used to drive across his land.

Harriet went back inside and located the keys for the Range Rover, kept in the console table in the entrance hall. Pippa emerged from the house transformed into someone who wouldn't be so welcome in the WI. Her hair was loose, hanging below her shoulders, and she was wearing a pair of jeans, a T-shirt and a pair of flip-flops.

'Gosh, I haven't felt this casual in ages,' she said.

'Pip, when did you get so grown-up?' Harriet asked, shaking her head.

'Being Mark's wife, well, I have to look the part. He's very successful, you know,' Pippa said, sounding a little defensive.

'Pip, you wear what you want, I don't care.' Harriet shrugged.

Freddie decided to drive and Harriet sat in the front passenger seat able to enjoy the drive through Parker's Hollow. It had been so long since she had been in the village, she needed to reacquaint with it. She felt herself choke up as they passed the church where they had buried their father and she turned to see Pippa wiping a tear. They drove past other landmarks of her childhood: the village store, which was now part of a chain, the post office which was attached, and the pub, the Parker's Arms. It was a proper village pub, good simple food, the same locals always propping the bar up, she hoped it hadn't changed. And, she thought, she'd have plenty of time to find out.

The village was just as she remembered it; it was

comfortingly familiar. It was so pretty with the village green, the local primary school, and gorgeous houses and quintessential English cottages. There was a small new modern estate on the edge of the village which was the only addition to it as far as she could see.

Harriet glanced across at Freddie who was humming as he drove. She felt her mouth curling up in a smile; it was beginning to feel even more like home.

'So, you're sure no one died in these clothes?' Freddie asked the elderly lady who was trying to serve him.

'Not as far as I know.' She had a broad Bristol accent. 'Now do you want them?' She was losing patience, and Harriet understood. This was the fourth charity shop they had been in, which had been a bit of an eye-opener. Nothing like Prada, she had been astounded by the first shop they entered. It was neat and tidy but all the clothes were squashed together and there didn't seem to be any order. Thankfully, as she and Freddie exchanged horrified glances, Pippa had taken charge. She found all the clothes in Harriet's size and bundled her into the changing room before doing the same to Freddie. Turned out Pippa had worked in a charity shop for a few months before she married Mark. It was one of her many attempts at having a job without having a job, she explained. Anyway, at least it was paying off. She had a knack at finding the right things and now Harriet was the proud owner of four jumpers, a cardigan and a padded jacket which was from Joules, which Pippa exclaimed to be the find of the day. Freddie had a few shirts, T-shirts and trousers. She'd even found a pair of wellington boots. They were hardly Hunters, but they would do.

Now they were in the last shop where Pippa had found Freddie a couple of jackets and a pair of shoes that Harriet was pretty sure someone *had* died in. After Freddie had reluctantly paid for his belongings, they headed back to the car.

'Well that was fun,' Pippa said.

'Yeah, easy enough for you to say, you don't have to wear dead people clothes,' Freddie moaned. He was fixated on it.

'Well, it was an eye-opener that was for sure,' Harriet said. She had spent all of her forty pounds but she had quite a lot for her money. She just hoped she didn't need anything else this week.

'Never mind, I'm sure Gwen will wash everything for me,' Freddie said.

'Not sure that was what Dad had in mind when he was trying to get us to be less spoilt,' Harriet finished as she sat back to enjoy the journey home.

Harriet put her wellington boots by the back door. They were floral and not her first choice, but then neither was the jumper she was wearing – not cashmere in the slightest.

She emailed her closest friend in New York, Mimi, asking her if they could help her with her apartment. She wouldn't sell it yet, that was far too drastic, but she thought if she could get her belongings packed up, some stored and some shipped over, then she could let out the furnished apartment for the year. When she typed about losing her job, she felt herself crumble. She let herself sob as she finished writing and pressed send. New York was so far away, but still, the idea that she wouldn't be going back to the bank didn't feel real. But then neither did the idea that she would never see her father again.

She needed to get in touch with the rest of her friends but she wasn't quite strong enough for that yet. She felt as if she had a mountain to climb, but at least she had started. She emailed Zach again, saying that she accepted redundancy but he was the biggest dick ever not to have the decency to tell her himself. Of course he hadn't replied to either email. So she then contacted HR to formally accept their offer. She could have fought it, hired a hotshot lawyer, but the fight had gone out of her. She wanted to draw a line. Move on. Get this year out of the way so she could then focus on her future.

'Are you all right, Auntie Harriet?' Harriet wiped the tears from her eyes, as she turned and saw her niece standing there.

'Oh sorry, Fleur, just feeling a bit sad,' she replied. She didn't know Fleur that well so she was surprised when her niece flung her arms around her. Fleur was tall, with long dark hair. She looked more like her mother than Gus, but there was definitely Singer features in there. Her eyes, and her expression, Harriet thought.

'About Granddad?' Fleur asked, her voice wobbling as she hugged her aunt back.

'Yes, God yes, we're all going to miss him. Anyway, I think I need some cake, shall we go and see if Gwen has any for us?'

'Yes, let's.' Fleur smiled, she wore braces, and although she carried herself with the awkwardness of a twelve-year-old, already she was turning into a beauty. Gus would have to watch out, there'd be queues of boys to contend with in a year or so.

'How long are you staying?' Harriet asked.

'Just for the weekend. I come most weekends, unless Mum has something planned. Daddy said we could all go and see the animals tomorrow, he said he'd even come although he's allergic.' She smiled. Harriet saw Gus in her smile.

'Great, it's about time we spent some time together as a family and I might as well get used to the idea of working at the animal sanctuary.'

'Blimey, Auntie Harry, I thought you were some kind of city slicker,' Fleur laughed.

'So did I, Fleur. So did I.'

Harriet hadn't often thought about whether she wanted children or not. The situation had never arisen and she hadn't yet felt a ticking biological clock inside her. She assumed she was one of those women who valued being a career woman above being a mum. But she certainly felt maternal towards Fleur. She felt a bit of envy for the fact that Gus might have a fractured life, like hers, but at least he had a daughter to show for it. Had she missed this? She was thirty-seven, she was single. OK, so she could in theory still have a baby, after all didn't women well into their forties have babies these days? But she didn't know the first thing about how she felt about that, or if she even wanted one. She'd probably make a terrible mother, although she did feel quite maternal towards her favourite shoes . . .

'Well, you all look a bit glum,' Gwen said, as they entered the kitchen.

'I miss Granddad, it feels funny being here without him,' Fleur said.

'I agree.' Harriet smiled sadly as they sat at the kitchen table.

'I know, it's not easy to get used to, I wonder if I ever

will. I keep expecting to see him,' Gwen agreed. 'Look at me, I even baked his favourite lemon cake today. Don't suppose you fancy some?' she asked, looking at Fleur.

'Can I have cream with it?' she replied.

'And me,' Harriet added.

She sent a text to the others telling them to meet them in the kitchen as Gwen made a pot of tea. Soon Pippa, Freddie and Gus appeared.

'Fleur,' Pippa said, kissing her head.

'Hi, Auntie Pip.'

'Right, where's this cake?' Freddie asked, sitting down. Gus stood awkwardly by the Aga.

'Come and sit next to me, Dad,' Fleur said, and Gus flushed with pleasure.

'Gwen this is the best cake ever,' Pippa said as they all tucked into tea and cake. Gwen looked pleased.

'But you know we need to talk about how much work you do for us,' Harriet said.

'Look, pet, it's my pleasure. I love looking after you. I miss looking after Andrew, and Connor, well, he doesn't need me so much; this house, well, it's my life. Please don't worry about me doing too much, I really want to at the moment, I need to keep myself busy.'

'Please keep baking for us,' Freddie said.

'It's just that we feel so spoilt, Gwen,' Gus said, agreeing with Harriet.

'Well I'm not objecting,' Freddie said. Pippa rolled her eyes.

'Would you let us help more around here?' Pippa suggested. 'And, actually, as you run the house so brilliantly you should tell us what you need us to do, so we don't interfere.' Harriet felt relieved. Pippa was always the diplomat of the family.

'Of course, you're welcome to help, as long as you don't take my job away from me.'

'We would never, ever do that.' Harriet went to hug her. 'As long as you want it, it's yours.'

'And my living arrangements?' Gwen asked.

'God, that's up to you. Meadowbrook is your home, you've got your rooms here, and the cottage is yours, you decide where you live.' Harriet's voice was full of conviction.

'I want to stay here for now,' Gwen replied.

'I was hoping you'd say that.' Harriet grinned. 'Right well tonight I'll be your assistant for dinner and, Gwen, will you join us?'

'I will. Connor's out, but I'd be delighted to have dinner with you.'

It was beginning to feel as if they might just find their way back to being a family again.

She wondered if her father could see them now and, if he could, what he would have thought. As Harriet ambled around Meadowbrook, taking in the grand rooms, the high ceilings, the art, the flowers that Gwen arranged every week, she would have loved to have known, when he was making his plan, what his real intentions were.

Did he know what a mess Harriet was in? It was as if he knew more about them and their lives than they ever did. Her father had always seemed clever, but she had never thought of him as this perceptive before. Either that or their first view still held; that he really was batshit crazy.

After dinner she had gone into her father's study to look over paperwork, make lists and check her emails. New York, not quite a distant memory yet, prising her fingers off it wasn't proving easy. Mimi was concerned but on board with helping with the apartment; they arranged to Skype the following day. Apart from spam, there was a message from HR with final paperwork, and, finally, a message from Zach's personal account.

Harriet, I feel that in the circumstances it would be better if you didn't contact me again.

She couldn't believe her eyes. What a jerk. He probably thought it was *him* she was upset about, not the job. Egotistical sod. She had almost hurled the computer at the wall but she didn't because Harriet was far too rational. Reading the simple line again, Harriet realised she needed to find her old self. She needed to find the person she was before New York. If she could find her way back to that person, then everything would be all right. But Harriet had buried her so well, like hidden bodies, she wasn't sure where on earth she was.

Unsure how she was supposed to deal with her emotions, she pottered around the house, looking for answers.

Gus and Fleur were on the sofa in the snug. They were watching a film together and it was the most relaxed Harriet had seen Gus, so she quietly left them to it. She didn't want to disturb some much-needed father/daughter bonding.

Pippa was in the kitchen with Mark. He had arrived after dinner, and Pippa had heated up some food for him. Harriet quietly backed away as they sat at the kitchen table, sipping wine and talking about their respective weeks.

She needed to get rid of her nervous energy so she went to get changed and then headed down to the basement to the gym. Running was her only relief at the moment. As she walked past the pool she saw Freddie, fast asleep on one of the sunloungers, an empty bottle of vodka next to him. She shook her head and covered him with a large towel. She would have to tackle him about his drinking, hopefully it was just because he was missing Dad, but honestly, he was far too old to be passing out like a teenager. They were no longer teenagers, not any of them, and Harriet needed to accept that too.

Chapter 9

'Fleur, I swear I wouldn't do this for anyone but you on a Sunday,' Freddie said, as he pulled on a pair of their father's wellies, which fitted him and didn't seem to worry him that their former owner was in fact dead.

'Uncle Fred, you've got to get used to it,' Fleur teased. He was wearing some of his new clothes. He looked even scruffier than Harriet felt.

'Don't call me uncle, it makes me sound old.'

'But you are,' Fleur replied, looking confused. They all laughed. 'Dad, are you going to be all right with your allergies?'

'I've taken a pill, I'm pretty sure I'm going to be fine, but if I start sneezing then I'll step back.' Gus sounded less uptight, almost verging on happy.

'I'm sorry, have I kept you waiting?' Pippa asked.

'We're just about ready to go. No Mark?' Harriet asked. She was struggling to be as open and as comfortable with her siblings as they seemed to be with each other and she could tell, at times, when they looked at her questioningly that they noticed it. She was trying but falling short.

'No, he's going to stay here and catch up with some work but I promised I'd go out for lunch with him. Is that all right?'

'Pippa, you don't need our permission,' Freddie quipped.

'We're only going to the Parker's Arms if you do want to join us.'

'We don't have any money,' Freddie pointed out.

'Oh God, we can't even buy a pub lunch,' Gus said.

'What's this?' Fleur asked.

'Your grandfather thought it was a good idea to give us a tiny allowance for the year we have to stay here,' Freddie explained.

'He probably thought you were all too spoilt.' They all looked at Fleur, unsure how to react to that.

'Can we take the buggy?' Freddie changed the subject

'Honestly, Fred, it's not that far, come on let's all walk,' Gus said, and they set off.

Connor was waiting for them by the sanctuary office. Harriet tried not to notice how nice he looked in his jeans and polo shirt. It was a dull day, warmish but with no sign of sun. Harriet had brought a jacket, because the sky looked as if it might unleash some good Mendip rain later; the others had teased her for that.

'Hey, Connor.' Fleur ran up to greet him, and Harriet could see they were close. Was everyone close apart from her? She felt something akin to jealousy; their relationships with Connor (as well as each other) were all easier than hers, but she had no one to blame but herself. She felt like an outsider in her family, but then why wouldn't she? It was time to build bridges.

'Hey, Fleur. Do you want to come say hello to the dogs first?' Connor suggested.

'How many dogs are there?' Freddie asked.

'Eighteen. Gus, willing to risk it?'

'Please, Dad,' Fleur said.

'Sure, why not.' Gus forced a smile.

'I'd love to meet the dogs too,' Harriet said, trying to sound jolly. 'Who walks them? I'm assuming they need exercise?' she asked, sounding as if she was in the office.

'We have a wonderful volunteer dog-walking group who come up from the village – not the same people every day but they, and whoever is on duty, usually does one long walk. And as you'll see, their quarters have a large outside space, so they do get exercise. Of course, what they all need is loving homes, but we're working on that.'

They followed Connor to the dog centre. As they entered, dogs in large and what seemed like quite luxurious kennels all started barking for attention. There were so many, all breeds and sizes.

'Oh, can we let them out, just for a bit?' Fleur asked.

'Yes, but not Jasper at the end, he's still too nervous around dogs and people. I'll take him with me later,' Connor said.

Fleur took over as she directed everyone to round the dogs up and let them outside, without a stampede. Harriet was impressed by her niece.

'She's so good,' she said.

'Ah, she's my apprentice, is Fleur. Reminds me of her Aunt Harriet.'

Harriet felt herself flush.

'She's a natural with animals. Shame her father isn't,' Connor continued – Gus looked terrified as dogs whizzed past him.

'It's so sad, why do they all live here. I mean it's nice enough, but dogs need a proper home.' Harriet felt her eyes welling again, and she turned to see an Old English sheepdog standing next to her, wagging its tail and looking at her with an expression which simply said, 'love me.'

'Harry, you all right?' Fred asked, looking concerned.

'Why do people think it's OK to treat or abandon animals like this?' she replied, angrily, and she bent down to stroke the eager dog.

'Meet Hilda. She belonged to a family who downsized and said there simply wasn't room for her. She's lovely though.' She barked as if to agree with Connor as he ruffled her fur. Harriet knew she had to pull herself together. How on earth was she going to survive running this place if she wanted to cry every five minutes?

'I've been trying to rehome a dog or two for ages, but Mark isn't keen, he's a bit worried about the mess,' Pippa said. Harriet looked at her sharply, but she had moved on to play ball with a Labrador.

'Why didn't Dad have one? At the house?' Harriet asked.

'When the last of his dogs, Jimmy, died, he did think about getting another one, but then, well, with his health problems he didn't want to take on that commitment. I wish more people thought like him though, Harry. I've rehomed over fifty dogs so far this year and we're a tiny shelter.'

'Right, well the dogs are lovely and I'm so glad they are cared for, but I'm desperate to see the gay bulls.' Freddie lightened the mood.

'They're not gay, are they?' Fleur's eyes were wide.

'No, darling, just very, very good friends,' Gus replied, a smile curling at the corner of his lips.

Hilda had attached herself to Harriet and when she made to leave, she started whining.

'I'll come back and see you,' Harriet promised, fussing

her. She loved the way that the soppy, shaggy Hilda looked so hopeful. That was what she needed but seemed to have misplaced: hope.

Harriet stayed with Gus as the others wandered off to see the other animals and she began to see how much work was involved in the actual day-to-day running of the rescue centre. Evie, one of the vet's assistants at Connor's practice, worked at weekends, and she helped show them the daily routine. The cats had another impressive space, indoor and outdoor, so they could all have a level of freedom. They pretty much all got on with each other, although the saddest story was that one came in just last week, pregnant, and now they had added five kittens to the place. Fleur had shown earlier that she clearly loved them and Harriet wondered if she could have one.

'Rachel won't hear of it. Mike, my old squash partner, is more allergic than me, apparently.' Gus gave a wry smile.

'Oh, Gus, how did it come to this? Look at your daughter, so happy, what if we let her have two kittens at Meadowbrook?'

'What about my allergies?'

'Gus, when we were kids we had all sorts of pets. Anyway, just man up and take some more pills.' Harriet didn't understand Gus at times. Maybe he had developed some kind of animal allergy, but to her it seemed he had developed an allergy to life.

Gus coughed for good measure. 'It can come later in life. But I seem to be OK here for now,' he grudgingly admitted.

'Listen, bro, you said that your relationship with Fleur

is strained since you haven't been living with her, so maybe this would help. And the house is perfect for kittens. I mean, we might have to keep them out of the drawing room to protect the curtains, but we can make a lovely bed up in the kitchen or utility. Gwen loves cats, so go and speak to Connor.'

'I could let her choose them, as well, and name them. OK, Harry, you're right. If Fleur has pets here then it really will feel like home.' He smiled. 'But what's with the "bro"? Since when did you go all ghetto on me?'

'New York, innit.' Harriet laughed.

'Please, never say that again,' Gus chuckled before his brow knotted seriously. 'Harry, are you all right?'

'What do you mean?'

'Look, I know we haven't been close for years but, well, you seem detached at times, but your old self at others. I know there's a lot going on, but if you need to talk . . .' His cheeks coloured.

She wanted to reach out and hug him, tell him that she missed her brother and was so glad they were together again but she couldn't.

'Sorry, Gus, it's just Dad's death, losing my job, this, I'm going to take a while.' She bristled, and Gus nodded sadly.

Evie came running in to the cattery then. She was breathless but mirth swam in her eyes.

'Guys, Freddie's being chased by one of the bulls.'

They all rushed out to see Freddie trying to jump over the fence followed by a cross-looking Elton. His face was puce, Pippa stood nearby laughing, tears running down her cheeks, she was clutching Fleur who was shaking. The alpacas watched on, as did the goats.

'I told you not to get too close,' Connor was shouting.

95

'They don't know you and they don't like anyone they don't know. It's OK, Elton, he's a friend,' he shouted. Elton looked as if he didn't believe Connor, but he stopped and glared rather than charging.

'Are you all right, Fred?' Harriet asked, as Gus helped him down.

'My goodness, that was a bit scary. If he'd got me with those horns . . .' Freddie shuddered.

'But Connor told you not to disturb them like that,' Fleur reiterated. 'They are lovely and gentle if you know what you're doing.'

'Clearly they didn't like Freddie.' Pippa was calming down. 'Although, that is the funniest thing I have seen in a while.' Harriet had almost forgotten Pippa's mischievous side.

'Well, I don't know why. Gay men always love me.' Freddie was indignant.

'Yes, but, Freddie, they are bulls,' Connor pointed out. 'And there's no evidence they are gay.'

'You named them Elton and David,' Gus replied.

Connor shrugged in defeat.

'Do you think Dad did this thing with his will to punish us all?' Freddie doubled over as he tried to catch his breath again. Elton was still eyeballing him.

It was gone lunchtime when they went back up to the house, but Harriet felt as if they were becoming a unit, a pack, if not yet a family. Connor was with them, Fleur had just been told she could pick out two kittens later, and she was overjoyed. Harriet had snuck back to say goodbye to Hilda, who looked so forlorn as she left that Harriet felt awful, and Hilda had whined and looked very sorry for herself. When was the last time someone had been sad to see her go? Well, not in a long, long time, she thought. Maybe her siblings when she went off to boarding school. Connor even said he'd miss her back then. Pippa had cried, and Freddie and Gus had begged her to stay. But since then no one. Oh goodness, Harriet thought, I must stop feeling sorry for myself. She now realised that she and Hilda were probably kindred spirits. Both wallowing in self-pity. She smiled and walked faster to catch up with the others. As they approached the house, Mark was stood on the drive.

'Are we still on for lunch?' he bellowed.

'Sure, the Parker's Arms serves food all day,' Pippa replied calmly.

'Don't you want to change?' he asked.

'I look fine for the village pub,' she replied.

Mark looked as if he was going to argue but clearly changed his mind.

'Fine, darling,' he said, sweetly, opening the passenger door of his car for his wife.

As per Harriet's request, lunch was laid out in the kitchen. It was a feast of quiches, salads, bread, cheese and Gwen ate with them, as did Connor.

'Honestly, Connor, I don't understand why you don't eat up here all the time, the food is too good,' Gus said.

'I used to come up quite a lot, but, you know, you guys have so much stuff to talk about I don't want to intrude.'

'You would never be intruding, Connor,' Freddie said.

'Gwen, Dad says I can have two kittens here, but we need to check with you,' Fleur piped up.

'Goodness, love, I'm not in charge.' Gwen looked secretly pleased. 'But I'd love that. I miss having pets in the house, and we could make them a nice bed by the cooker, they'd like that wouldn't they?'

'Yes, they'd be so cosy. Am I having girls or boys?'

'You can choose, Fleur,' Connor said. He was smiling broadly. Harriet couldn't help but think he had quite a dazzling smile. It made her want to smile.

'If I got two boys I could call them Harry and Zayn.'

'Interesting names for kittens,' Gwen said.

'They used to be in One Direction but they're my favourite singers now,' Fleur informed her.

'Well that's that then. And I'll look after Harry and Zayn when you're not here, you don't need to worry about that.'

'And, Dad, will you also help Gwen look after them?' Fleur chewed her lip as if she was concerned about her father's commitment.

'Of course, I've got my allergy medicine now. And, if you like, this afternoon we can go to the pet shop and you can choose a bed.'

'Yes, because they'll need toys and collars and things,' Fleur said. 'I should make a list.'

'That's fine but, Fleur, don't forget I've only got thirty pounds,' he said, laughing.

'Don't worry, Dad, I've got pocket money.'

'Let's start, shall we?' Harriet said. She was sitting behind her father's desk, a pile of papers in front of her. Pippa was sat next to Freddie on one of the sofas, Gus was on the other one. They had survived their first weekend in Meadowbrook. Gus had driven Fleur home the previous evening and he'd been quite miserable when he came back. Freddie tried to cheer him up by plying him with wine at dinner, but looking at how green he was today, it might not have been his best idea. Mark had also gone back home on Sunday evening, and his departure had affected Pippa in a different way, she was very quiet. She must be missing him, Harriet concluded. She still seemed to be watching everything with a detachment she didn't know how to stop. One minute, like at the sanctuary, she felt as if she was part of the family, the next something pulled her back.

'Yes, boss. Can I clarify are you actually my boss now?' Freddie asked.

Harriet threw a pen at his head – he ducked and it clacked to the floor.

'Don't be silly, but we need to run this house, and the animal sanctuary, raise a lot of money, and it takes organisation, huge organisation. So, I've been through everything more than once. The work would be best done if we divide it up.'

'So what do each of us do?' Gus asked.

'I'm happy to do whatever you want,' Pippa said. 'It's quite exciting as I haven't had a job for years.'

'Did you ever have a job?' Freddie asked.

'I did, I had a few jobs, once I worked in a florist,' Pippa protested.

'For a day,' Gus pointed out.

'Well, I did lots of courses,' Pippa persisted. 'And I worked in that charity shop, remember.'

'But, Pip, what do you do with your days? I mean not now, but when you're at home?' Freddie asked.

'I see Mark off to work, I then take care of our diaries, we get quite a lot of invitations, you know. I usually go shopping, and then I might meet a friend for lunch before going home to clean up and make supper.'

'You sound like a 1950s housewife.' Harriet failed to keep the horror out of her voice.

'Thanks, Harry. I love my life.' Pippa sounded angrier than she normally did.

'Right, sorry, anyway, guys, going off topic a bit. We need to divide up the work that needs to be done to make it easier for us. I mean, Dad pretty much did everything before, so how hard can it be for the four of us?' Harriet said.

'Famous last words,' Freddie said. 'Right, Harry, what are we going to do?'

'Well, there is obviously going to be an element of pragmatism, but here's what I have so far. The house is Gwen's domain and there is no way I am messing with that. There's a cleaning company who come in twice a week, the shopping is delivered, although she does like to buy locally when she can, but she has made it clear that if we want anything, we ask her. I for one am not arguing with Gwen.'

'I am with you on that,' Freddie agreed.

'Right, so next is the garden. We have a garden consultant called Amanda Owen, and she's brilliant. She comes in once a week with her team, but here's the best bit, there is a gardening club who also come once or twice a week and get to work – under her direction – on the top garden.'

'No wonder it looks so beautiful,' Gus said.

'Yes, and Dad likes to open the garden to the village once or twice a year. He doesn't charge but asks for donations for the sanctuary and Gwen makes cream teas for everyone. Last year it raised about a thousand pounds.'

'Wow,' Gus said.

'It's important to the village, and he wants it to continue. So, Gus, I thought as you are the most creative out of us, you could take care of the gardens. You'll work with Amanda, and also the gardening club.'

'Who are the gardening club?' Gus asked.

'People from the village, here, Dad kept notes.' She handed the papers over to Gus. 'They'll be here tomorrow afternoon and I'll meet them with you, but after that it'll be your domain.'

'You know, I might enjoy that. I used to love helping Jed in the gardens and it'll make a change to get to do something outdoors.'

'And you never know there might be hot women in the gardening club,' Freddie suggested. Gus shot him a withering look.

'But also, Gus,' Harriet continued, ignoring Freddie, 'you need to take on a task at the animal sanctuary. I know you're allergic, but I wondered if you could help with the pigs.'

'Really?' Gus looked doubtful.

'Well, I figured as the pigs don't have fur, you're likely to be less allergic to them. I've spoken to Connor, and basically a list of jobs is drawn up every morning. So, we all report to the sanctuary, every day, see what we've been allocated and get it done.'

'Every day?' Freddie looked horrified.

'We only have to do about two hours work there a day – that's manual work by the way – we still have other stuff to do.'

'So, I have the gardens to look after and the pigs?' Gus didn't look exactly thrilled. Harriet nodded.

'So, Harry,' Freddie rubbed his hands together, 'what am I going to do?'

'Well, Freddie, what is your greatest strength?' Harriet asked. OK so, it might not exactly be high finance but she was enjoying herself slightly. She had familiarised herself with how to run Meadowbrook and the animal sanctuary

101

in record time and it was pretty straightforward. But then she thought, her father had charged them with raising money, and she wanted to make sure they at least hit the target. As always, Harriet felt the need to overachieve. For her father.

'Drinking?' Gus replied.

'Being annoying?' Pippa suggested.

'Parties, of course,' Freddie answered, swatting Pippa's arm.

'Exactly, Fred. And given that, I am putting you and Pippa in charge of organising events, starting with this summer's village fête.'

'Eh?' Freddie looked confused.

'Think of it as a party for the village. I've decided that it's going to be in memory of Dad, as well as to raise money for the sanctuary. I want it to be the best event the village has ever seen.' Harriet grinned, Freddie looked pained. 'I thought we could use it to see how much money an event can raise – it'll give us an idea of how effective they are.' Harriet might be all enthusiastic about raising money, but she had no clue. Twenty-five thousand was a drop in the ocean to her, or to the old her, but how did you get that when you had to ask people and you had very little to offer in return?

'It'll be great, Fred, you and I can work together to plan the best event ever. We could get all the English village traditions: tombolas, raffles, coconut shy, that sort of thing. Oh and maypole dancing.' Pippa sounded excited.

'I'm more an expert in pole dancing,' Freddie quipped.

'Oh, Fred, you'll be fine. So it's a different kind of party to the one you normally organise but you can still use your skills. Just get to know your market and then put together an event that they will all love. Oh, and you are going to feed the chickens and collect any eggs. You'll have help but that will be your role.'

'And me?'

'Pippa, you've been put on domestic animals. It's when the team and volunteers are short, so it'll be more ad hoc but there is always something to do for the dogs and cats, feeding, cleaning, walking the dogs.'

'Great.' Pippa beamed. Nothing ever fazed her sister, who looked genuinely delighted.

'And what are you going to do?' Freddie still didn't look exactly thrilled.

'I'm going to run the animal sanctuary. I'm looking after the admin, financing, building maintenance, fund-raising, staffing and also I am going to work on getting the pets rehomed. And I am going to look after the ponies, Gerald the donkey. If you think I'm not going to get my hands dirty, I am actually going to be mucking out the stables every day.'

'Oh for the summer fair we could have a dog show with our dogs as the stars!' Pippa suggested.

'Great idea.' Harriet smiled. 'See we're all getting it. Imagine if Dad could see us now. What would he think.'

'He'd think we were slightly crazy?' Freddie suggested. 'But, you know, I have a very good friend who has a printing company, so maybe I could get him to do the programmes for free.'

'Great, Fred, as we can't spend any money, we all need to think of anything we can to make this year a success,' Harriet finished. 'Now, Freddie, pour us some of the good whisky.' Harriet felt some of her resolve returning. So, she wasn't exactly thrilled about having to muck out stalls on a daily basis, but she was a strong woman, she always had been, and more than that, she was her father's daughter, she was the daughter he always wanted her to be. And she was determined to make him proud once more.

Freddie did as she asked, and handed the glasses out.

'Right, I would like to propose a toast.' She raised her glass. 'To the Singer siblings and a year at Meadowbrook Manor.'

Chapter 10

The Singer siblings all made their way out of the front door to greet the gardener as she got out of a van whose side read, *Graham's Garden Design*.

Harriet strode forward. As when they were children, her leading, them following.

'Hi, I'm Harriet,' she said, holding out her hand. They shook hands and she introduced the others.

'I'm Amanda Owen.' They had spoken on the phone briefly the previous day and Harriet already had a feeling she was going to like her. Amanda had a slight Somerset accent, was tall, slim with wavy hair pulled back from her face. Harriet guessed they were of a similar age. She was wearing blue overalls, and was pretty, in an outdoors kind of way. 'I'm so pleased to meet you, your father spoke about you a lot, so I kind of feel that I know you a bit already.' She smiled, warmly.

'Dad loved his gardens, didn't he,' Gus said, 'and you've done a marvellous job.' Gus looked at his shoes and Harriet's heart went out to him. Gus needed to be in charge of the gardens; not only were they the most creative part of the house, which would suit him, but running them would, she hoped, bring back his confidence. Or at least allow him to find it. She didn't like to think what the pigs would do for him.

'Thank you, but that's largely thanks to my volunteer gang,' Amanda laughed. She looked at her watch. 'They'll be here any minute.'

'What about your paid staff?' Freddie asked.

'They come once a week, you'll barely know they are there, but I have to say the gardening club are the real stars.'

'And about the open gardens, are you all keen on that?' Pippa asked.

'We love it, especially the gardening club. It's a way of showing off what they do, and the village love walking around, having a nose. Of course it means a lot of work before and after but we don't mind.' She grinned and Harriet felt her earnestness. She wondered how they could turn the open gardens into more of a moneymaker than it was currently. At the moment people could just trample through, and were asked for donations . . . Harriet's mind was whirring.

She pulled her thoughts back as a minibus pulled into the drive. They all watched as it snaked its way up to the house. It parked near Amanda's van, and the driver, a woman who looked as if she was Gwen's age, got out, followed by the others.

'Wow, some gang,' Freddie said, wide-eyed, as a number of silver-haired women appeared.

'This, is your gardening club,' Amanda said, and introduced them all. The women lined up and hugged each of the siblings in turn. The driver turned out to be the youngest member of the gardening club and Harriet wondered how these – to be polite – older ladies managed the physical work.

'We're so happy you're looking after the place for your dad,' Margaret, the driver, said. 'He loved his gardens and we do too, so it's a real privilege.' She had a broad Somerset accent and a twinkle in her eyes.

'Thank you,' Pippa said, impulsively giving Margaret a hug. 'You've done such a wonderful job, don't know what we would do without you!'

'Oh it's our pleasure, love, some of us have had hip replacements, or knee replacements, so fit as fiddles we mostly are now,' one of the ladies, who also had a Somerset accent, stated. The ladies all started doing weird stretches as if to demonstrate the fact. As well as Margaret they were introduced to Rose, Edie, Mary, Dawn, Caroline, Meg, Bev and Lorna. Harriet wondered how on earth she would remember everyone's names.

'Look I can even do a star jump,' Edie said, as she tried, and failed, to lift off the ground. 'Well a star shape at least.'

Rose lunged, then had to hold onto the person next to her to get up again.

'See,' Rose shouted, after she was once again upright, 'fit as fiddles.'

'This is going to be fun.' Freddie shook his head.

Amanda proved very efficient after she rounded her chattering ladies up and led them round to the back of the house. They all headed to the shed and retrieved their gardening tools and, still gossiping, set to work. Harriet was impressed as they all seemed to know exactly what they were doing. She wished she and her siblings were as efficient.

'Wow, they're good,' Harriet said to Amanda. 'They do this because they love it? Shouldn't we pay them?'

'Let's just say your father was very generous with gifts,

because they wouldn't hear of being paid. They love having these beautiful gardens to work on, and as most of these ladies live alone, it's a social event for them to look forward to coming here. Also if any of them need anything, they tell me, and me and your dad would sort it. Sue had a burst pipe in the winter and worried about the cost plumbers, so your dad arranged for it to be fixed for her. He took care of them, of anything they needed.'

'Well, absolutely,' Harriet felt a rush of warmth for the ladies, 'anything they need, please do tell us.' Although how on earth they could help with their allowance, she had no idea. Then she remembered, there was a fund, a provision for anyone in the village that needed help. Now that suddenly made sense.

'Can I help? I mean get involved?' Gus asked. 'I'll be taking over Dad's role with the gardens and stuff.' He sounded slightly awkward and didn't quite meet Amanda's eyes.

'Come with me, I'll introduce you properly to everyone. The ladies are great, honestly, they love the gardens, not many people who love gardening get to work on such beautiful grounds, so it's a real treat for them. My team look after the mowing, strimming, hedges and any heavy work, as well as the design of the gardens, but they also help with the flower beds, the vegetables and the fruit cages. We do have to keep them under control though,' Amanda laughed. 'Dawn wanted to do a bit of topiary on one of the hedges; it was supposed to be a chicken but somehow it looked a bit phallic so I had to put a stop to that.'

'Oh I'm almost jealous I can't hang out with these women, they are brilliant,' Freddie snorted.

'Great, Amanda,' Gus, ignoring his younger brother, said, 'lead the way.'

Harriet, Pippa and Freddie watched them go.

'I think this will be good for Gus,' Pippa said.

'Those women will eat him alive,' Freddie joked. 'But it might help bring him out of his shell.'

'They'll love him,' Harriet said.

'Let's hope so, the poor chap is still so uptight,' Freddie added. 'And that Amanda's not bad-looking. In an outdoorsy kind of way.'

'Oh, Freddie,' Pippa said. 'Let's go inside and we can discuss how we'll start organising the events.'

'Well of course we do need to do that but first I have to make some um, urgent phone calls. I'll find you guys later.' He scarpered before they had a chance to reply.

'He's work-shy,' Harriet said. It was apparent even in the last few days that Freddie was happy to pour drinks – either for them or down his throat – but not much else. Harriet could see why their father referred to him as 'the problem child' so often. The trouble was that now she felt it was her problem. 'But tomorrow he has to start helping with the chickens.'

'I'll believe that when I see it. Right so just you and me, where do we start?'

'Have some coffee and start sorting the paperwork,' Harriet said. Thank goodness for Pippa, Harriet thought as she linked arms with her sister.

'Um, sounds like fun. No wonder Freddie scarpered.' Pippa rolled her eyes as they went inside.

Working in her father's office made Harriet feel uncomfortable. It was as if she was an intruder, rummaging through his desk without permission. Of course she had his permission, and what's more, her father was so organised that it was easy to get all the information they needed.

He had a folder for household expenses and suppliers, another held everything they needed to know about the village fete, and the open gardens; he had kept meticulous records of everything. The only thing he hadn't left them was clear instructions on how on earth they were supposed to raise the money for the sanctuary. It still seemed like a huge amount.

'So, if I take the village fete info, I can read through it later and start to get to grips with it,' Pippa suggested.

'Uh-huh,' Harriet replied. 'It's all quite straightforward, but I still think we need to make this year better than ever.'

'I agree, in memory of Dad and because we need to raise that money. Shall I go and make us another cuppa?'

'Oh please.'

Harriet was grateful that Pippa left her alone for a few minutes. She was suddenly hit with a real pang for New York. She missed it, she missed her life, she still missed her job with an ache that felt as if she'd lost a limb. It wasn't Zach, although of course he was wrapped up so much with her work. She couldn't just turn the tap off on her old life. She wanted to but she couldn't. And she felt lonely, yes she had her family, but she missed Mimi and the girls, she missed how they understood her, how they were like her. And sitting in her father's chair the fact that she was alone seemed to illuminate itself. A big neon sign hanging over her.

Oh, she hoped that throwing herself into Meadowbrook would be good enough, but it wasn't. She tried to tell herself it was early days, but she was beginning to think she would always feel this way. She needed to give herself time but Harriet was impatient. She wanted it all to be better, she wanted to be better.

She was wiping angry tears from her cheeks when Pippa walked in with two mugs of tea.

'God, how on earth did you get Gwen to let you make tea in mugs rather than cups?' Harriet tried to disguise her feelings with a laugh. Gwen was a stickler for bone china cups and teapots, she didn't even know they had mugs.

'Gardening club mug stash that I found and raided,' Pippa laughed. 'Gwen was outside serving cakes so I seized my chance. Are you OK?'

'Yes, of course, I'm fine.' Harriet slumped down on one of the sofas and took the drink.

'No, you're not, you're dealing with so much right now, and, Harry, you might not think so, but you're doing well. Anyone else would have thrown themselves down a well or something by now.'

'Do we have a well?' She attempted a laugh.

'No, thankfully, although there's always the lake.'

'Don't tempt me.'

'Hey.' Pippa sat next to her and gave her hand a squeeze. 'We're all on a bit of journey right now, and some of it is really unpleasant, but at least we're together. Do you remember before you left for boarding school and you made us all sit in your room while you lectured us about how to behave when you were away.'

Harriet remembered her eleven-year-old self doing just that. She certainly was bossy, although at the time she felt that she needed to be in charge; thinking about it, nothing had changed.

'Yes, I remember.'

'And you said that no matter where we were, or what we were doing, we would always be the unbreakable Singer siblings.'

'Oh, Pip, when did you learn to be the motivational speaker?'

'I learnt from my older sister.'

Harriet had to hold back her tears yet again.

'How did you enjoy the garden club, Gus?' Gwen asked as they all ate dinner together, Connor included. The gardening ladies ended up in the kitchen, admiring the kittens and eating cake before they left, chattering animatedly. It was clear they were part of Meadowbrook, a real part, and Harriet liked it; the house needed people. She needed people.

'They were a lovely bunch of ladies, and you won't believe it, but Lorna, the lady who takes care of the fruit, used to be an art teacher, so when we got talking about my sketching she said she'd love to look at it and if she could give me some tips she would. Just hope she doesn't tell me I'm rubbish,' Gus laughed.

'Gus Van Gogh,' Freddie said, affectionately.

'I'd be happy just to be OK really,' Gus said. 'I know I'm not going to suddenly became a famous artist but I enjoy it. I'd love to at least make a hobby out of it.'

'If you could do some sketches or paintings of the house or the gardens we could have a stall at the fête,' Pippa suggested.

'Oh my, that would be great.' Gwen clapped her hands with delight. 'People would love that.'

'Well let's make sure that I can paint first, shall we?' But Gus sounded happier than he had in a long while. 'But I enjoyed today. Amanda is hugely talented and committed to the gardens, she loves them, you can tell from just talking to her.'

'She's quite hot too,' Freddie piped up.

112

'Shut up, Fred,' Gus said, cheeks reddening. 'She's passionate about the gardens which is all that matters.'

'Don't you think she's hot, Con?' Freddie asked.

'Um . . .' Connor replied, staring intently at his plate.

'He took her out on a date last year,' Gwen piped up. Everyone stared at Connor. Harriet felt her cheeks heat up; discomfort jumped onto the dining table.

'Not really, well OK, sort of.' Connor looked dismayed. 'Andrew set us up, as usual gave neither of us any choice, and we went to the pub for a drink, where it soon became apparent that we had no chemistry and very little in common, despite the fact we both like the outdoors. So that was that. Cheers, Mum.' Connor's face was ruddier than normal, and Harriet irrationally felt annoyed. But why?

'So the coast is clear for Gus then?' Freddie asked.

'Oh for God's sake, Freddie, shut up,' Gus reiterated.

'Well at least we've started, I mean properly started on the work that Dad wanted us to do,' Harriet said, desperately wanting to change the subject.

'Yes, we're quite organised, aren't we?' Pippa asked.

'We made a good team today, Pip.'

'Is that a dig at me?' Freddie asked, draining his wine glass and refilling it.

'No, because first thing tomorrow you will be collecting eggs,' Harriet pointed out. Freddie scowled.

'I think you all have a lot to contribute and it might take a while to find your feet properly but you're going in the right direction,' Gwen told them. 'And I for one am happy to have you all here, this isn't a house that likes to be empty, that much is sure.'

'And, Harry, if you're at the sanctuary tomorrow morning, we're getting a Shetland pony, and it'd be good for you to see how we manage a new arrival,' Connor said.

'Great.' Harriet smiled. 'What time?'

'About ten?'

'Does this pony have a name?' Pippa asked.

'Brian. I mean who would call a pony Brian?' Connor scratched his head.

'No wonder it needs rescuing,' Freddie said.

Harriet was looking at a very tragic email inbox – all spam apart from two from friends – when Gus walked into their father's study. She wasn't sure whether it was a bad habit, but she had taken to drinking a very large brandy every night before bed – it reminded her of her father. On top of the wine at dinner she was not only eating more than normal but drinking far more too. Not in Freddie's league of course, but still, something she needed to try to keep an eye on.

'Hi, Harry, can I join you for a nightcap?'

Harriet nodded. Gus poured himself a large measure of brandy, and sat down.

'I'm really glad you enjoyed the gardens today and that you're going to start painting,' she said, smiling. It was at least something he was passionate about. Harriet felt that lacking in her life now. Her passions were all in New York. Work, shoes and being slim; possibly in that order. It wasn't a great list, was it?

'Me too. And you?'

'What about me?'

'Connor?' Gus sat down in the chair opposite Harriet. She felt uncomfortable.

'What about Connor?' she asked.

'Well when he said about going on a date, or when

114

Gwen did actually, you looked incredibly uncomfortable. I mean, probably no one else noticed but I could see it written on your face.'

'I was probably just miles away.' She studied the crystal glass intently.

'Harry, do you know that since I can remember Connor had this effect on you.'

'What effect?'

'Oh come on, look I might be a bit of a stuffed shirt, but I'm your brother and we were so close once that I felt we knew each other better than anyone else.'

'We did,' Harriet admitted sadly. 'And I'm sorry we lost that.' She was sorry, but she still didn't know how to get it back.

'Me too, but, Harry, you would never admit how much you cared about him.'

'It was probably a teenage crush,' she said quietly. She was feeling all sorts of alien emotions and they were all unwelcome. Yes, she had idolised Connor when she was growing up, but then they actually grew up. He met Elizabeth, she met ambition. It took them to the opposite ends of the world.

'It was a crush that sent you to New York.' Gus sipped his brandy.

'What do you mean?' She fiddled with her brandy glass, unable to meet Gus's eyes.

'Harry, when Connor got engaged to Elizabeth you got a job in New York. It can't have been a coincidence, surely?'

'That had nothing to do with it.' She was startled. It hadn't been that that sent her to New York. Gus had it wrong, didn't he?

Did Connor's engagement to Liz really send her out of the country? If it did, it wasn't conscious, she certainly wasn't aware of it? She, at the time, had said to everyone, including herself, that she needed a new challenge and a new adventure. Of course it had nothing to do with bloody Connor's engagement.

'Really? Well the timing was suspicious and I remember trying to talk to you about it but you wouldn't and of course I was married and I had Fleur by then, so it wasn't easy for us, but—'

'Gus, Connor had nothing to do with me moving to New York. Can we leave it? I am mourning my life there, my job, Dad, you know.' She hadn't told Gus and Freddie quite as much as she'd told Pippa, just that her job and her relationship had imploded. It was enough.

'Sorry, Harry, but you are always looking out for us, and I just wanted you to know that I am here for you, if you need me, or want to talk, please feel you can. I didn't mean to dredge up the past but, well, we used to tell each other everything. And I'm sure that your feelings for Connor were a crush when you were young, I didn't mean to suggest you still held a candle for him, I just wanted to check.' He seemed to quickly change tack. 'I just want us to be as close as we once were, that's all.' He appeared lost again and Harriet wanted to grab him and tell him it would all be all right, just as she had done as a child. But she couldn't because she didn't know. She didn't know anything.

Chapter 11

'Morning, peeps.' Freddie breezed into the dining room and took what had become his usual place at the dining table; the others were just finishing eating. He was wearing his pyjamas, his hair tousled; he looked adorable, young, handsome and hopeless. Harriet looked up from the newspaper she was reading – the financial pages, she couldn't break that habit quite yet. They had fallen into a predictable morning routine, having only been at Meadowbrook for barely over a month.

'Hey, Fred,' she said, smiling as he poured a coffee.

'Sorry I'm a bit late, I overslept,' Freddie said.

'Did it have anything to do with the chickens?' Gus asked, not looking up from the paper.

'No, I will go and see to them after breakfast,' Freddie replied. 'I just didn't sleep too well last night.'

'Why, what's wrong?' Pippa asked.

'Loretta. She's coming down this weekend. I'm worried about you all meeting her.' He chewed his lip.

'But, Fred, she's your girlfriend, we'll all welcome her,' Gus said, reasonably.

'I know, I just worry, she's quite different to you.'

'In what way?' Harriet asked.

117

'She's not had the same upbringing as us.' He looked so uncomfortable.

'Who cares about that. Anyway, Fred, it'll be fine, we'll all be lovely to her. And I'm looking forward to meeting her, anyone who tamed Freddie . . .' Pippa laughed. Freddie did not.

'OK, I'm sure it'll be fine. Now I better eat some eggs before I actually have to collect them.' There was an edge to his voice that Harriet couldn't identify.

It had been a whirlwind month at Meadowbrook, in many ways it had been the hardest time of her life, yet it had also been incredibly comforting. New York, not yet a distant memory, was slowly, gradually, slipping more into the past. She was allowing herself to grieve her old life, as well as her father.

She still cried to herself at night at times; she felt her father's loss so keenly, normally when she was alone. She missed him more and more and hadn't accepted he was gone. Nor had she quite accepted that her life in New York was over. She still got up in the morning and felt the urge to don a suit and heels, she would feel a pang of loss as she pulled on her jeans and her charity shop clothes. She knew she was a snob, spoilt, but at the same time, she couldn't help but miss her old life.

It was funny how she barely gave Zach a thought though. She still thought he was all sorts of unmentionable names for what he did to her but she didn't miss him. She didn't miss their relationship in the way she missed her job. There was so much about New York she was mourning – the buzz, the smell, the cocktail bars, Mimi, her personal trainer. And most of all work. But Zach, no.

She was getting on with it. That was the best she could

do. Grief was thick within her, for so many things, but Meadowbrook was also creeping under her skin. She was split in two: the Harriet who missed being a high-flying corporate woman in New York and Harriet who loved spending time with her family, being outside, growing to love the animal sanctuary. She was finding her old self, whilst not quite ready to let go of the other one.

Living with her siblings for the first time since childhood was proving interesting. It was, in many ways, as if they were getting to know each other again; they were finding their relationship with each other at the same time as finding their own feet. There were times she would look at them and feel as if she knew them as well as she knew herself, other times they felt like strangers.

Gus, underneath the uncomfortable, formal facade was beginning to show glimpses of his old self. He was blossoming slightly, now he had been involved in the gardens and was also sketching. He would take his pad out into the gardens almost daily and it had given him a new attitude. He seemed to be growing more confident in himself, he had even taken to having daily conversations with the pigs who he seemed to be almost growing fond of, Connor told her. It was Gus's smile that made her feel familiarity, he had a smile which she knew so well and missed greatly. And despite Freddie teasing him that he should be wearing a smock and carrying an easel, Gus was happier than he had been when Harriet first came home. He was also very interested in the gardens, he worked well with Amanda and her team and he was incredibly popular with the gardening club, who he referred to as 'my ladies'. His ladies certainly loved him. It was almost a spectator sport watching them flirt with him.

Harriet and Gus were tentatively beginning to talk more too, catching up on the lost years as well as reminiscing about their childhood. They were slowly trying to find their way back to each other.

Pippa was more of a puzzle. She was a beautiful carefree girl/woman who, when working closely with Harriet to organise everything, was proving efficient and hard-working, despite never having had a real job. She had been speaking to a number of people in the village who were involved in various activities around Meadowbrook and the animal sanctuary, and it was quickly apparent that her skill lay with people. She had a gentle charm that everyone loved and no one could say no to her. Pippa was also the most emotional of the siblings, she cried about their father the most, heaving sobs which Harriet barely knew how to deal with. However, when Mark arrived for the weekend she became slightly altered. A little more reserved. She did seem genuinely delighted to see her husband, but she held back when he was here, just a tiny amount, but enough for Harriet to notice. She wasn't sure if she should worry about it, but she was going to keep an eye on it.

Freddie was the most unchanged. Still charming, funny, rude, selfish and hedonistic. He was the laziest by far. Yes, he turned up to the sanctuary most days, but Harriet had watched him charming whoever was working that day into doing any dirty work. He collected the odd egg, and carried the bucket of chicken feed, but that was pretty much all he did.

And at night, after dinner, where he would outdrink everyone, he would keep going until he was ready to pass out. He got away with a lot, did Freddie, as always, and Harriet wasn't yet sure how to deal with him. She was going to mention it to Gus; perhaps he could speak to him, man to man.

While she was getting to know her siblings again she was getting to know herself. Mainly through the animal sanctuary. She had got to grips with the structure, the costs, the admin, but more than that she had got to know its heart. And the animals were stealing hers.

She loved going to the office, speaking to the staff, visiting the animals. She was often found in the field with the ponies, Gerald and the goats – raking hay and mucking out – which didn't even bother her – making sure they had food, petting them, and she and Connor were slowly becoming reacquainted too. She'd forgotten how well they always got on, despite the odd bicker. He made her laugh; she enjoyed teasing him. She couldn't help but notice how many women were vying for his attention – but he never seemed to notice – and his lack of ego, the exact opposite of most the men she knew in New York.

At the same time, she and Hilda were becoming an unlikely team. The dog gravitated to her whenever she visited and she had been persuaded by Jenni to take her out. Hilda was a boisterous dog who had a lot of energy and she had become her enthusiastic jogging companion. She was the most endearing dog that Harriet had ever met, energetic, soppy and constantly bouncing around. Jenni and Connor said that the exercise with Harriet calmed her a bit, wore her out at least, but when Harriet left her back at the kennels she would always whine and look sad. Harriet was finding it harder and harder to walk away. Often, Pippa and the dog walking volunteers would be walking the calmer dogs and Harriet and Hilda would bound past them, not sure who was trying to keep up with whom.

121

She would have loved to take her home but Harriet had to be realistic. Not only did they have to think about Fleur's kittens – although she suspected Hilda would have loved them – but also what would happen after this year? They had only committed to a year at Meadowbrook and Harriet had no idea where she would go after, what she would do. She couldn't let Hilda be abandoned for the second time, so, sadly, keeping her was out of the question. But leaving her after their daily jog was becoming increasingly hard.

Weekends at the Manor were becoming routine for different reasons. And wonderfully, Fleur was now here most weekends. Sometimes just for one night, but other times for the entire weekend, and that was making Gus blossom even more. Harriet could see their relationship growing easier with each passing weekend. They were still awkward around each other at times, polite even, and Fleur sometimes acted like a typical teenage brat which left Gus scratching his head, but on the whole their relationship was growing, along with the beautiful gardens. Harriet was also getting to know her only niece and she was so grateful that she finally had the chance to do so. Fleur's mother, Rachel, could be difficult and, at times, tried to change arrangements, but Fleur was now older and beginning to stand up to her, which made things much easier for Gus, who never stood up to his horrible – Harriet's opinion – ex-wife.

And Fleur was so in love with Harry and Zayn, the kittens, that she wanted to spend more time at Meadowbrook, she had phoned her mother a number of times to extend her stay, stating the kittens needed her. Fleur was headstrong, which reminded Harriet of the awful Rachel who had bossed Gus about so much that he barely knew who he was anymore, but Fleur also had her father's compassion and a softer side to her than her mother. Thankfully.

Gwen was also in love with the kittens who were naughty, spoilt and had the run of the kitchen, utility and soon would be going out into the gardens. Goodness help them if they ruined Gus's flower beds. But having Fleur there was good for them all and as each of them got to know their niece better, it cemented the family unit. A family which missed its head, their father, but also was beginning to value each other, regardless.

'So what's everyone doing today?' Freddie asked, nibbling a piece of toast and bringing Harriet back to the present.

'Gardening club,' Gus said. He folded the paper and put it on the table. 'Well later anyway, pigs first.'

'Oh Gus and his hareem,' Freddie laughed. Gus smiled.

'Don't knock it. In fact, Fred, can you come help me today, we've got quite a lot to do and it wouldn't hurt for you to get a bit involved. After all, you're meant to be helping to arrange the open gardens, and the gardening club are pivotal to that,' Gus said, and Harriet shot him a grateful look.

'After the chickens, sure.'

'Don't forget or I'll come and find you.' Gus pursed his lips as if to say that he would brook no argument. Harriet was impressed with his assertiveness. Freddie groaned.

'Great, that's decided,' Harriet said quickly before Freddie could argue.

'While you two are busy with the animals and the gardening club, Harriet and I are going into Bath today,' Pippa said.

'What for?' Gus asked.

'We've got a meeting,' Pippa explained. 'An old school friend of mine, Bella, she just moved back to Bath to set up a small PR consultancy. She might be able to help us with publicity for the animals.'

'We're going to pay for PR?' Freddie asked. 'I thought the idea was to make money not spend it.'

'No, we don't have any, Pippa is going to charm her into working with us for free,' Harriet told him. 'Right, well I have to go and get ready, Pip, see you in fifteen minutes.' Harriet stood up and left the dining room.

She went to her bedroom, brushed her hair, checked her make-up and enjoyed dressing more carefully as she selected a dress and heels. She wore jeans, T-shirts, flip-flops, trainers or wellies most of the time now; putting on something more like her old attire made her feel that her corporate self hadn't disappeared completely. She'd shrunk from view, certainly, but Harriet wasn't ready to hang up her power dressing completely.

'Shall we grab some lunch?' Harriet suggested. They'd had a constructive meeting with Bella, who had said she'd come up with a proposal and also promised to give her time for free while she had it. Harriet was relieved, but actually Bella seemed grateful to have something to kick-start her consultancy, even if she wasn't being paid. Bella was Pippa's age, short, elfin dark hair, big brown eyes, and having failed to meet Mr Right in London had decided to move to Bath to try to sort out both her work and personal life. Harriet liked her. She was attractive, wholesome-looking, and at the same time ambitious and organised.

'Sure, I'm so hungry,' Pippa said. Today she was wearing a wide-legged trouser suit, a scarf in her hair, and she looked so beautiful. 'And I have all the money from my allowance.'

'Should be enough to get us a sandwich,' Harriet joshed.

They found a café, got themselves seated and ordered.

'It's quite nice to be just the two of us,' Harriet said. And rare, so rare.

'And to be out of the house. Did you like Bella?' Pippa asked.

'Very much. I think she'll be good, and well done for persuading her to work for free. I'm thinking perhaps we put Fred in charge of liaising with her.'

'You think Freddie's up to it?' Concern worked its way across Pippa's face.

'He's a bit of a mess, isn't he?' Harriet felt deflated. 'I thought giving him more to do might, you know, help him pull himself together.'

'I think losing Dad might have hit him harder than he's admitting. He doesn't talk about his business at all, and well, I'm relieved we are going to meet Loretta to be frank, I'm hoping she'll sort him out. I'm worried he's self-destructing.'

'I know, so if he has to get involved in the PR it might give him a bit more structure.' It made sense to Harriet.

'Um, she's quite persistent is Bella, he won't be able to fob her off that's for sure.'

'Well, fingers crossed this works.'

'And then we need to do something about you.' Pippa reached out and took Harriet's hand.

'But—' she started but was saved by the arrival of their paninis.

Chapter 12

'This is Loretta,' Freddie said, dramatically. They were gathered in the drawing room, having pre-dinner Martinis, by now a Freddie tradition.

'Hi,' Loretta trilled in an accent that could be London or maybe Essex? Harriet wasn't sure.

'How lovely to meet you, we've heard so much about you.' Mouths gaped open as Mark kissed Loretta's cheek. They had heard very little about her, practically nothing.

'I'm Harriet, Loretta, welcome to Meadowbrook,' she said, hoping she didn't sound as stiff as she thought she sounded. Loretta was what could only be described as a knockout.

'I've been dying to see the old 'ouse for ages. It's like real old, yeah?' Loretta said.

'Well yes, hundreds and hundreds of years.' Gus blushed as he gave her cheek a kiss.

'Yeah, fought so. But it's lovely,' she added. 'I mean, when Fred said he lived in a manor I fought it would be all draughts and leaky roofs and tatty.' Loretta laughed.

'Right, well as you can see it's not.' Pippa's cheeks reddened, the way they did when she was annoyed. Harriet put her hand on her arm. They could all be a bit over-protective about Meadowbrook.

'Oh no, it's actually quite lovely, and I can assure you there are no leaks! Has Freddie given you the tour?' Mark cut in quickly. Harriet was grateful that Mark was taking charge. She had no idea why they were all behaving so awkwardly, but then maybe it was because Freddie had never had a serious girlfriend before.

And Loretta was gorgeous. Almost as tall as Freddie, she was slim, with long, thick glossy hair, which reached down her back, looking as if she had stepped out of a shampoo advert, which she may have done given that she was a model. She was wearing a pair of jeans so skinny they looked painted on, heels, and a see-through black top which exposed a very small black bra. She definitely brought glamour to Meadowbrook.

'Wow, I can't believe you're a model,' Fleur said, impressed as any twelve-year-old girl would be.

'Well it ain't all it's cracked up to be, darlin'. Never eating, always posing, I'm looking to give it up, settle down, maybe write a book or somefing.'

'Great,' Harriet said quickly. Loretta didn't quite come across as the literary type. Even Freddie choked on his Martini at this statement.

'Well, delighted to meet you anyway,' Mark said. 'With the Singers all so close, us partners must stick together,' he laughed.

'Perhaps after dinner we can go to the pub, I love a country pub, with those funny local types,' Loretta said.

'That would be lovely, Pippa and I are definitely in,' Mark gushed. 'I mean, if that's all right with you, darling?'

'Of course,' Pippa replied, agreeably.

'Can we go, Dad?' Fleur asked, looking hopeful.

'It might be a bit late, sweetheart, but if you want we can watch a film after dinner, your choice?'

127

That seemed to placate her.

Gwen put her head round the door, to announce dinner was ready, unfortunately she wasn't joining them, as there was bingo in the village hall.

'This is a top house,' Loretta said, again, as she toyed with her food. 'I can see us living here,' she added. Freddie had a coughing fit, and Gus slapped him on the back repeatedly.

'I agree, and I said the same to Pippa. This would be an ideal house for us to raise a family in,' Mark added, beaming.

Harriet was irrationally horrified. How dare they talk about Meadowbrook as if it was theirs? Or that they had any claim on it.

'Well the house will belong to all of us, so unless we all live here together, that's not going to happen,' Harriet snapped, sounding more severe than she intended.

'And that wouldn't work, would it?' Gus added reasonably, calmly shooting his eyes towards Harriet in warning. 'As fond as we are of each other, I'm not sure all of us could do that.'

'Of course not,' Freddie added, quickly.

Harriet knew she had overreacted, but she was still seething.

'Well, of course,' Loretta started. 'I just meant it was a lovely place, and I'd love to live in a house like this.' She sounded confused, but her face didn't show it, although her face didn't move.

'Sorry, I didn't mean to snap,' Harriet had the grace to apologise. 'I think with Dad gone we're all a bit sensitive about Meadowbrook.'

'Which is understandable,' Mark concurred quickly. 'But, Harriet, we don't mean for you to think we want to take the house off you.'

'Thought never crossed my mind.' Harriet smiled. Although it had. She had to stop being so ridiculous.

'Anyway, what with Freddie's business and stuff, it's all up in the air, isn't it?' Loretta said.

All eyes turned to Freddie. He turned the colour of Loretta's nails.

'I haven't told them,' he hissed.

'What haven't you told us?' Harriet asked.

'I need a cigarette.' Freddie jumped up and almost ran outside.

'Should one of us go after him?' Pippa asked.

'I'll go in a minute,' Loretta sighed. 'I'm sorry, I fought he'd told you.'

'Told us what?'

'His business went tits up, a while back. Poor Fred was terrified of telling your dad, so he didn't. He sold his flat to cover the debts and moved in with me. Virtually penniless he is.'

'Ah, that might explain why he didn't sleep last night,' Gus reasoned.

'And why he was so keen to stay here this year, even when it involved chickens.' Harriet and Gus raised their eyebrows at each other. Poor Freddie. When the year was up, he would need his share of the money, unlike them he had nothing else.

'Chickens?' Loretta asked.

'Go after him, Loretta, tell him we're all here for him when he's ready to come in,' Harriet pleaded, her heart going out to Freddie.

It explained a lot. His drinking, his moments of running off to be alone, the slightly hopeless air that he'd worn since their father's funeral. Why hadn't Freddie told them? They would have helped him, she would, although she guessed being the other side of the world she couldn't have done much. But she was here now and she wasn't going anywhere, she was determined that she would do all she could for Freddie and her siblings.

Meadowbrook was a house that needed people, they all said so, but it was strained after Loretta's revelation. Dinner was pretty much abandoned as Freddie, sheepishly explained how they'd been silly with the business, how younger people had come in and taken over the party scene and they'd been too arrogant to move with the times. Instead of selling up, they ran up more debts and finally it caught up with him. Freddie sold practically everything he owned and thankfully Loretta had taken him in. He had no income, no clue what to do next and he was ashamed.

'Freddie, there's nothing to be ashamed about.' Pippa's eyes were full of tears.

'Just, bad luck, old chap,' Mark offered.

'And you've got us,' Gus pointed out.

'And this year you're taken care of,' Harriet said, after all she was pretty much in the same boat – apart from being penniless and having a model partner of course. 'You can have a long think about what you want to do with your life, just like the rest of us.'

'Not Pippa,' Mark said quickly.

'No, Pippa's sorted, but the rest of us, Mark,' Gus said, reasonably. 'Fred, Harry's right, you can take this year to have a long think about what you really want to do with your life.'

'Or you don't have to do nothing. Because surely at the end of this year you're going to be rich, aren't you?' Loretta said. No one spoke as all eyes turned to her.

What the hell? Harriet wanted to scream but, sensing this, Gus moved to her side and hissed for her to stay quiet.

Harriet woke early the following morning, still unsettled about the events of the night before, about Freddie. She found herself at the animal sanctuary where, despite the rain, she went to fetch Hilda. Connor was feeding the dogs when she arrived.

'Morning, how are you?' she asked, cheerfully.

'Well, this little man,' he picked a small terrier called Barney up, 'is going to his new home today.' Connor beamed.

'Ah, Barney, we will miss you,' Harriet said. Barney yapped. Harriet felt emotional. When the animals were rehomed it was a moment of triumph. They were going to carefully vetted families and would be part of a home, rather than here, which although lovely wasn't the same. But it always struck her that so many more were left behind. And when a dog or cat did get rehomed it just seemed like a matter of time before more came in. Harriet hated that aspect. She wanted them all to have loving homes.

'But he's going to a lovely couple who just lost their dog and so they'll really spoil him. Hey, Harry, you look as if you're going to cry. Are you all right?'

'Well, not really, last night was hideous. Freddie's miserable. His girlfriend told us that his business went bust and he's penniless.'

'Oh God, I had no idea, poor Fred,' Connor said, concern etched across his face.

'And now he's acting as if he's a failure, and well, I'm worried he might be depressed. Not that Loretta seems to have noticed.' Harriet didn't mind Loretta at first. But after the comment about the house and then about Freddie being rich, she wasn't so sure.

'What's his girlfriend like?' Connor asked.

'Hot, very hot. But I'm not sure she's a member of Mensa.' Harriet hated to sound like a bitch, especially in front of Connor who never said anything bad against anyone.

'Anything I can do to help, let me know?' He smiled and Harriet tried not to notice the dimple on one side of his lips. An angel's kiss, Gwen always said. She felt herself flush at the thought of kissing his dimple. What the hell was wrong with her?

'What are you doing tonight?' she asked, impulsively.

'No plans, why?'

'Will you take me somewhere, anywhere away from here. I just feel I need to get away for the evening.' She was once again on the edge of tears.

Connor's eyes flecked with concern. 'Hey, how about we go out for dinner? Just the two of us; a change of scene?'

'Thanks, are you sure you don't mind?' Harriet felt embarrassed she was a charity case and Connor, who was so nice, had taken pity on her, but at the same time she needed to get out of the house. She was finding it hard living with the others. She was so used to living alone and making decisions that were hers alone, having to think about the others, the sanctuary, her father, it was a struggle. She loved them dearly, of course, but living and working with them 24/7 was hard for them all, especially as they had so much to come to terms with in their own lives.

'Why would I mind?' He looked at her as if she was

crazy. 'Harry, it'll be great to spend some time with my old pal.' He shook his head.

'Thank you, although less of the old. But if it's more expensive than McDonald's you'll have to pay, my pocket money isn't what it once was,' she laughed.

'Fine, my treat.'

'Right, where's Hilda, I thought we might go for a walk.' She changed the subject before she could feel even more of a charity case.

'Good luck, Hilda hates the rain.'

'Don't be silly, she loves being with me.'

Harriet fetched the lead, clipped it on Hilda, who although looked delighted to see her, took one look outside as they approached the door and sat down. Harriet tried to push and pull her, but Hilda wouldn't move. As she tried coaxing, cajoling and then physically dragging her to the door, all Harriet could hear was Connor laughing.

'Right, Hilda, if you won't come with me then I'll go alone,' she said as a last threat, but the dog merely wagged her tail. Harriet shot Connor the evil eye, dropped Hilda's lead, and walked out. The sound of Connor's laughter and Hilda's bark following her. Instead she went to visit the animals, taking apples to Gerald and the ponies. She saw Fleur, wrapped in a rain jacket and wellingtons, and Gus with the pigs.

'Auntie Harry, I think the pigs know Dad now, they actually come up as soon as they see him and you know how lazy they are.'

'Glad he's made friends,' Harriet said dryly.

'Hey, could do a lot worse. They are very good listeners and don't talk rubbish,' Gus smirked.

'Oh, Dad, you can be so funny,' Fleur stated.

'We're all soaked, so how about we go and get some

hot drinks?' Gus replied, flushed at the compliment his daughter paid him. Fleur started running, leaving Harriet and Gus to take up the rear.

'Harry, are you all right?' Gus asked. 'You seem a bit . . .'

'A bit what, Gus?' Harriet ran her hands through her hair.

'Detached, I guess. Since you've been home, you started to open up a bit more, I even saw glimpses of the old Harry, and I guess that I'm the same, but now it's like you're guarded again.'

'Freddie's news bothered me, and, well, I can't put my finger on it but something felt a bit wrong last night.'

'I know, but, Harry, I was wondering, do you feel a bit lonely? Is that what's bothering you?'

Was it? She was lonely, but then she was used to being alone. She felt suspicious, as if something was up, but maybe that was her too. She had no idea, but if this was grief, then it was playing with her.

'Probably,' she mumbled. It was easier than trying to find the truth. 'Maybe I should start talking to the pigs,' she joshed.

'Don't knock it until you've tried it,' Gus replied, a grin curling at his lips as he reached over and gave her a hug.

Harriet bumped into Pippa as she tried to sneak out the front door. She had dressed up, wearing a black jumpsuit and heels. Not too out there for Parker's Hollow, but she felt a bit like her city self, which was a nice feeling. She explained to Gwen she would be out for dinner, and Gus would be too, he was taking Fleur out to the cinema and then for pizza.

'What are you doing?' She hadn't seen Pippa since breakfast.

'Just going for a bite to eat with Connor, I fancied a change of scene. Anyway, are you all right?' She tried to sound breezy.

'Yes we had a lovely lunch at the pub with Loretta and Freddie. She's sweet, Loretta, and Freddie seems to adore her. She was disappointed not to get to know you better.' Pippa sounded a little accusatory.

'I'm sure there'll be plenty of time for that.' She smiled at Pippa and left before Pippa could object further.

She had intended on walking down to Connor's cottage, which she soon realised wasn't a great idea in her heels, but as she closed the front door she saw him waiting outside in his jeep. He saw her, leapt out and walked round to the passenger side.

'Your chariot awaits.'

Harriet laughed. He looked so handsome in his shirt and jeans, and although she tried not to notice how mesmerising his eyes were, she felt like a youngster on a first date and she wasn't. Either young or on a date; she chastised herself for being so silly, as she climbed into the car.

'Thank you.'

'There's a gastro pub, ten-minute drive and the food is really good, is that OK with you?'

'Anywhere away from here is great. Thank you for this, Connor.'

'Please don't, it's nice to spend some time with you. I mean, we've talked a bit, but I don't know much about your life in New York, or what you gave up to come back here.'

'Um, and I don't really know why you and Elizabeth broke up.'

'Touché. Are we keeping off personal stuff then? I mean

we can, but I don't know how we are supposed to rebuild our friendship if we keep things from each other.' He sounded so sincere, so sensible, she wanted to tell him everything, suddenly.

'I tell you what, if you buy me a decent glass of wine, I'll tell you everything.' Suddenly she wanted him to know, the good, the bad and the ugly.

He sat back, took a sip of his pint and seemed to be thinking before he spoke.

'Wow, some story. I'm not sure I would have guessed it of you, I mean, Harry, you were always so bright, so in control.'

'I bet you never thought I would have an affair?'

'I guess it's a bit of a surprise, I know how moral you are, were, but then they say you can't help who you fall for.'

'I don't think I fell for him exactly. I was so into my job, Zach was the boss, I think I confused the two. I certainly admired the way he worked and I wanted to be like him, that ended up with me being . . .'

'Was it love?' Connor looked right into her soul, she felt as if she was naked.

'No, it wasn't love.' She remembered the only time she ever thought she was in love and that felt nothing like it was with Zach. But she couldn't talk about that. She could barely think about it. She didn't really even know Zach and vice versa. Zach never asked about her home, he never showed an interest in her family, he didn't know how she spent her childhood. He didn't know the Harriet who would tuck her skirt into her knickers, climb trees, catch frogs, swim in the lake even in winter. No one knew her like the man sitting opposite her. 'Connor, order me

136

more wine, please,' she said, quickly. 'And then tell me about you.'

He went to the bar and came back with a bottle and two glasses.

'OK so I'll tell you about Elizabeth. You know the background, we met at uni and I thought she was perfect. She was confident, beautiful, we were both going to be vets, we both adored animals, and we both had that youthful ideological need to make a difference, to save the world. Basically, we both wanted the same things. To live in the country, to own our practice, to have a house full of pets,' he laughed dourly. 'I mean we were perfect for each other.'

'When you were together she was quite territorial if I remember rightly.' Harriet bristled.

'Funnily enough, only around you. She felt threatened by you, I guess because I told her all about you, our childhood, our friendship.'

'She was threatened by me?' She felt shocked. After what Gus said, the implications, Harriet knew she had felt jealous of Elizabeth for whatever reason – and she still didn't think it was anything like as simple as Gus thought – but why would Elizabeth have felt threatened by her? Connor only ever saw her as a toad catcher after all.

'Because of our history together and apparently I talked about you a lot. I had to reassure her quite often – I mean, as if we were anything but friends, what an idea!'

'Thanks, Connor.' Harriet couldn't believe how hurt she felt, as her cheeks reddened.

'Oh you know what I mean. You wanted the glamorous city life, I wanted the country. In fact, what you and I wanted was opposite ends of the spectrum. Anyway, after uni Elizabeth and I started working together, we lived together, and we got engaged. I think around the time you moved to New York.'

'Um.' Harriet tried not to acknowledge that, after the seed Gus had sown and she was still smarting about the fact Connor said they were such opposites. Although, of course, he was right. 'So what happened next, you didn't get married?'

'No, we were planning the wedding, not that either of us wanted a big fancy do, but then a job came up in New Zealand for both of us. We left just before Pippa's wedding actually. It was a great opportunity, and Elizabeth was particularly keen. The posting was meant to be a year, but one became two and, well, then I wasn't as happy there as she was. We kept rowing. I wanted to come home, it might sound pathetic to a jet-setter like you but I was homesick. I worried about Mum, I mean I know she had your father and Meadowbrook, but I'm the only family she has, and I missed her. Liz called me a mummy's boy and it got so bad that we could barely stand the sight of each other.'

'I think the way you look out for your mum is special,' Harriet said, resting her hand gently on his arm. Connor had been the man of the house since he was a young boy. When his father died, it was a huge loss, just like Harriet's mum. They had bonded over that as children, both having lost a parent far too young, the only difference was that Connor was an only child. Gwen was a strong woman, and she applied for a job at Meadowbrook, because it had a cottage with it, and it would offer security for her son. And Harriet knew her father would have hired Gwen even if she couldn't cook. The minute he found out she had been widowed and left with a young son, the job was hers.

Connor continued, 'Neither of us ended it when we

should have though, I'm not sure why, I was clinging onto the fact that I believed I loved her, she was clinging onto to the same, I guess, or maybe it was habit, but she met someone else, and then she told me she wanted to be with him.'

'Oh goodness, how did that feel?'

'That was the worst thing, it felt like a relief. I flew home, guilt-free, and well, I learnt a lesson.'

'Which is?'

'I shouldn't have let the relationship get to where it was, I should have left it sooner. But, you know, we live and learn.'

'We certainly do. And now here we both are.'

'I never thought we'd both be living back at Meadowbrook, you know. It's crazy. How are you finding it?' Connor asked. His voice was so gentle that Harriet just wanted to tell him every thought she had. But of course she wouldn't.

'I really don't know yet, honestly, losing Dad, the job . . . everything that's happened, there is still so much to process that I can't be sure how I feel.'

'I'm here for you, Harry, I want you to know that.' Connor reached over and gave her hand a squeeze. 'You were my best friend growing up and I want to us to still have that.'

She concentrated on her wine because she didn't trust herself to speak.

'Can we have a nightcap at yours?' Harriet asked, feeling reckless as Connor approached Meadowbrook. She felt drunker than she was – although she had polished off the majority of the wine – because Connor was sober, and she didn't want the evening to end. Spending time with him was reminding her of why she adored him so much when they were younger. The way his eyes crinkled when he smiled, the warmth that radiated from him. His terrible jokes. He was the polar opposite of Zach and she couldn't help a thought snaking into her head that perhaps that had something to do with why she had been drawn to Zach in the first place.

'Sure, I could do with a drink.' He let them both into the cottage, flicked on a light.

'It's tidier than last time I was here,' Harriet observed.

'Mum, she came and cleaned. I know, I know, Liz was right, I am a terrible mummy's boy.'

'Don't forget I know Gwen, she wouldn't have it any other way.'

'I said I was going to get a cleaner once and I thought she might actually kill me!' Connor laughed and poured them a generous measure of whisky.

'You know I never drank whisky or brandy in New York, since being home I feel like I'm swimming in the stuff.' Harriet swished the liquid round the glass.

'It's Meadowbrook isn't it? I think the first time we got drunk it was your dad's brandy.'

'Oh yes and stupidly I took his good stuff, he was furious and, well, I never made that mistake again.'

'You were so sick, I have never seen anyone turn that shade of green.'

They were teenagers, and she had sneaked a bottle to the summer house. She couldn't remember what triggered it, but Connor and she had shared a few drinks, before he became all sensible and tried to stop her. She remembered they were both in big trouble, although it was all her fault.

'Oh my goodness, remember I insisted on going

swimming in the lake, and you tried to stop me because I was drunk.'

'I actually had to jump in the lake and drag you out, H, and that wasn't fun, believe me.'

'I did try to say it wasn't your fault.' No one but Connor called her H, her stomach felt as if it was on fire, from the drink or the memories.

'You did, but I still got into big trouble. Mum grounded me for a month if I remember rightly.' Connor laughed. 'I didn't mind, we had such fun in those days.'

'We can again.' Harriet felt alive, inspired and crazy. She had been such an adventurous, impulsive person once. What had happened to her? The most impulsive thing she did in New York was to buy coffee from a different coffee shop once in a while.

'What are you thinking? You've got that look in your eyes?' Connor narrowed his eyes.

'The lake. Come on, grab towels.'

'H, you are crazy!' He had a twinkle in his eye.

'The rain earlier will have warmed the water, come on.'

'I am not saving you again, not even if you drown,' Connor said. But he was already running upstairs.

'Last one in's a loser,' Harriet called as they headed out the back. Just how they were in childhood.

Harriet felt the wind in her hair as she ran barefoot across the grass. She felt free and wild, the way she had growing up at Meadowbrook. Although it was dark, she knew the way to the lake, as if she had never been away. But sensible Connor was following with a torch, which illuminated her path along with the large moon.

Harriet reached the lake first and recklessly shrugged off her jumpsuit. She let it fall to the ground; she had shed her inhibitions just as easily. The idea of Connor seeing her in her bra and knickers didn't occur to her; they'd spent most of their childhood running around half naked after all. She looked at him, he'd put the torch down, and had pulled off his shirt and jeans. He had a strong body, she couldn't help but notice how hot it was; not too muscly, but not an ounce of fat on him. Oh God, she felt exposed as it hit her that they were no longer children. She was glad it was dark as she felt herself turning beetroot and she looked away. Taking a deep breath, she stood right on the edge of the lake and jumped in.

The cold of the water immediately sobered her, but as she immersed herself, it felt so comforting. This was home. This was her life, and she had turned her back on it for the city, but why? Why would anyone turn their back on this?

As she swam on her back, she realised that nothing made her feel as alive as this did. Not making millions of dollars, not shouting at a room full of men, not having sex with Zach. This was the best feeling ever; she had really come home.

'I can't believe you made me do this.' Connor swam up to her. She could feel his presence so near to her.

'I can't believe we're doing it either,' she giggled. She had never wanted to be close to anyone the way she did now. But she didn't want to make that mistake, she didn't want to confuse things any more than they were in her head. She diffused the moment – which she acknowledged would only be her moment – by splashing him.

'I'll get you for that,' Connor shouted and, as he chased her, she swam as fast as she could through the lake, remembering just who she was.

She was dripping as she wrapped one of Connor's towels around her, and freezing. Her teeth chattered.

'Right, crazy lady, let's get you home.'

'Connor, I can find my way back to the house, you go home otherwise you'll get hypothermia.'

'Let me walk you to the back gate at least,' he said. She shrugged and followed him.

She could almost feel him watching her as she passed through the gate through to the back garden. She wanted so much to have him with her that she felt scared. There was a massive history of feelings there. She didn't even know how to process them, or how to acknowledge them. She didn't know if she could think about it, it scared her too much, as she opened the back door and crept in. Connor was her first love but they'd never been lovers. And she wasn't sure what sort of love that was. A crush or something more? But nothing had ever happened between them. Not even a kiss. Connor had said that evening how they were totally wrong for each other, so why was she feeling like this? What if her father dying and losing her job was making her yearn for something she thought she had buried years and years ago? What if it wasn't real? But what if it was?

Bloody Connor, it always came back to him. Bloody, bloody Connor.

She pulled the towel tighter around her as she walked through the hall towards the staircase. It was dark as she scrambled to find the light switch. She startled as she put the light on and saw Mark lurking outside her father's study, his hand on the door handle.

'What are you doing?' she exclaimed.

'Sorry, Harriet, I was just going to help myself to some of your father's brandy,' Mark answered quickly, like a rabbit caught in the headlights.

'There's brandy in the drawing room,' she said, feeling confused.

'I know but the one in the study is the nicest and I, well, I hoped you wouldn't mind.' He again looked awkward as he shuffled from foot to foot. Harriet did mind. She didn't know why but she did.

'Of course not. Right, well goodnight,' she said. He smiled at her and went upstairs without bothering with the brandy. If he thought it was odd that she was wrapped in a towel dripping water over the floor, he didn't say.

Chapter 13

July beckoned and the summer fête loomed and Meadowbrook took up more of Harriet's time. The summer fete was scheduled for the August bank holiday weekend and Harriet was delighted that Pippa and Freddie had thrown themselves into it, even Freddie was actually enthusiastic, although some of his ideas – wine tasting, beer pong, a pole dancing competition – had to be vetoed. She felt almost redundant when it came to that and the gardens, although the animal sanctuary was keeping her busy. They hadn't had any major fundraising projects; the summer fete was the first, so afterwards she was hoping to have an idea about how to raise the rest of her father's target. Although this was a tiny amount in comparison to the money that Harriet usually played with, it was also proving slightly perplexing as to how to actually raise it. She had no charity experience apart from some sponsored swim she was forced to do at school.

The sanctuary was expensive to run, so the money allocated to it was getting eaten up quickly. Animals seemed to be coming in all the time, and they had a policy of never turning any away. They had a few regular donors, the dog walking volunteers stood outside the local supermarket once a month to raise money, but it was nowhere near enough. Harriet needed to come up with ideas. And fast.

Working with Connor was also keeping her occupied, or distracted, she didn't know which. She was finding being so close to him agonising and wonderful at the same time. Since the swim in the lake she knew she couldn't discount her feelings for him, feelings she'd quite probably had since she was aware of her own sexuality. Feelings that she had buried successfully for years. She needed to bury them again. She was so good at hiding how she felt, so surely she'd be able to do it, right?

'Fred, are you ready?' Harriet called, knocking as loudly as she could on his bedroom door. She heard a few swear words and then he emerged, wearing jeans and a T-shirt. He looked thin still, and pale, but she was hoping that having a purpose might make him pull himself together a bit, as she tried not to notice his bloodshot eyes. He refused to talk about his business still, just saying that it was gone and that was the end of it and he also seemed reluctant to talk about Loretta. Harriet was increasingly worried that if they didn't do something he might slip down into depression or alcoholism. Or both. Gus said she was overreacting, he just needed time, and Pippa backed him up, but Harriet didn't agree. She was going to keep a close eye on her youngest brother.

'Ready, boss,' he said with a grin.

'I'm not your boss, Fred,' she replied, swatting him on the arm. 'And we're late,' she added. They were due to join Bella and a photographer for a photoshoot at the sanctuary.

'Oh good, let's take the buggy then.' Freddie bounced. Although the sanctuary was only a short walk from the house, Freddie had taken to driving the buggy everywhere. He liked to survey 'his land', he said, which stretched for acres. No wonder Loretta had already adopted the lady of the manor role; Freddie had driven her around the whole weekend – although she gave the animals a wide berth. She didn't even go and help when Freddie was being pecked at by the chickens, which was his fault as he'd been too busy showing off and he'd forgotten their feed.

What was returning to Harriet's consciousness was the dynamic they had shared as children. Harriet was the oldest, yes, she also tried to be maternal, but that sometimes led to being judgemental, she was also hotheaded, and would jump in first and think – or repent – later. Gus was the level-headed peacemaker of the family. His gentle and creative way of looking at things meant he would look at any situation from all angles before passing judgement. That was coming back, too. He was once again becoming the calming influence he'd always been. Harriet had almost forgotten that. Freddie always liked to get his own way and was so funny and charming he usually did; Pippa and Freddie were similar in many ways. Although Pippa was the most unselfish of them, but also she had a habit of digging her heels in when something was important to her – she was more complex and contradictory than she appeared.

Harriet had often tried to tell them what to do when they were children, there would be a huge row, and then Gus would broker peace in an effort not to bother their father. Well, hello, that seemed to be the situation now as well. Not that they could bother their father anymore, she thought with a huge pang.

'Freddie do you have to drive so erratically?' Harriet

147

screamed. Luckily the buggy didn't go very fast, but the way Freddie drove was reminiscent of a dodgy fairground ride.

'Yes, Harry, I do,' he replied.

Harriet clutched the handle for dear life as they made their way across the fields and down to the sanctuary. As they drew nearer, she saw the photographer, barking orders to his assistant and Bella watching them.

'Oh thank goodness you're here,' Bella said, rushing up to them as they climbed out of the buggy.

'Are we late? What's wrong?' Harriet asked.

'No, you're not late, but – oh.' Bella noticed Freddie for the first time.

'Sorry, this is Freddie, Bella, you two are going to be working together on the PR.'

Freddie removed his sunglasses. 'Frederick Singer at your service. Charmed to meet you.' Freddie bowed dramatically, taking a surprised Bella's hand and kissing it.

Harriet rolled her eyes; she noticed a slight flush on Bella's cheeks, although Freddie had that effect on most people.

'Lovely to meet you too,' Bella replied. She looked the part, Harriet thought, jeans, Hunter wellies, a Barbour jacket. Dressed for the country, for an animal sanctuary, quite unlike when they met at her office in Bath.

'So what's the problem?' Harriet asked.

'It's Connor, he's being difficult. I hadn't pegged him as a diva but . . .' Bella looked unsure.

'Connor, difficult? I find that hard to believe,' Harriet replied, frowning.

'Harry will sort him out,' Freddie offered.

'He's in the office,' Bella said, 'and we don't have much

time.' Harriet left the two of them and went to find him. Connor was trying to wedge himself behind a filing cabinet.

'What on earth are you doing?' she asked.

'Trying and failing to hide. I thought you said she was professional.'

'She is, and she's also free, which is why we hired her. But that's irrelevant, what is going on?'

'She keeps trying to get me to take my top off.' Connor looked so distraught, Harriet couldn't help but laugh.

'Why on earth would she do that?' Harriet wasn't sure she blamed her. After all he did have a very nice chest . . .

'She says sex sells and I tried to point out that this was an animal sanctuary and I'm a vet, not a sex symbol.' Harriet wanted to tell him that he was a sex symbol actually, but she never would.

'Wouldn't you take your top off if it meant lots more animals getting rehomed?' she asked.

'No, I wouldn't. I'm not exactly a muscleman and it gives off the wrong image. We are an animal rescue and rehoming centre, not a knocking shop.' Connor sounded so outraged that Harriet hoped her amusement wasn't too apparent.

'Good point. OK, if I tell them you are definitely keeping your top on, will you do me a favour?'

'Anything, if I get to keep my shirt on.'

'Cooperate with everything else, and then this will be as painless as possible.'

'OK, deal.'

'Good, let's get this hot vet photo shoot over and done with.'

'Your father would never have made me do this,' was his parting shot.

They made their way outside where Bella and Freddie seemed deep in conversation.

'Everything all right?' Bella asked, nervously.

'Yes, sorry, I stormed off but—'

'Connor's shirt is staying on, Bella, that's non-negotiable,' Harriet explained. 'This is a serious subject after all.'

'Of course, sorry if I upset you, Connor, I just got a bit enthusiastic.' Her eyes shone as she looked at him. Harriet smarted; was she flirting?

'I offered to take my shirt off, but apparently that's not going to help,' Freddie added.

'Can we get started? I have to do some house calls later.' Connor was still tetchy. Harriet couldn't help but be pleased he wasn't flirting with Bella.

Their star human was definitely not a natural in front of the camera, but luckily many of the animals were. Gerald especially enjoyed the limelight and Seb and Sam, the alpacas, managed to look almost flirtatious, despite trying to eat the camera at one point. Hilda took an adorable photo, although she kept rushing to Harriet when she was supposed to be still, so it took a while to get the right shot.

'Hilda, sit,' Harriet commanded in her sternest voice, but Hilda just wagged her tail and looked at her with those big eyes before running round in circles.

'It's OK, I'm used to shooting animals,' the photographer, who thus far hadn't spoken, said.

'Oh my God, you kill animals!' Freddie was horrified.

'No, Freddie, he means, photographing them,' Bella explained.

Bella was going to send out a press pack to local papers, radio stations, and even TV, to try to rustle up some coverage for the sanctuary. Harriet managed to slip back into professional mode as Freddie, she and Bella chatted over details of the campaign. Connor, as soon as he was allowed, scarpered without a backward glance.

'Freddie, why don't you give Bella a tour of the estate on the buggy?' Harriet suggested as they wrapped up.

'Would love to and I can tell you all about our big summer extravaganza,' Freddie said.

'Great.' Bella beamed. She really was nice.

'Right, your chariot awaits.' Freddie ushered Bella onto the buggy and then took off; Bella's squeals could be heard for quite some time.

'So, I should thank you properly for persuading them not to turn me into a sex object,' Connor said when Harriet found him in the office.

'You can buy me lunch,' she said. 'Oh, I forgot you said you had house calls.'

'Ah, yes they seem to have been cancelled.' His lie was evident. Clearly he just wanted to hurry the photo shoot up. 'Pub?' he asked. A bark rang out and they saw Hilda sitting looking hopefully at them.

'Come on then, Hilda, you can come to lunch too.'

Harriet was surprised to find Gus in the pub, a pint in front of him.

'Hey,' she was a little disappointed that it wouldn't be a cosy lunch for two (plus Hilda), but it was possibly for the best.

'Caught red-handed,' Gus laughed, awkwardly.

'You are allowed a drink, you're a grown-up,' Connor teased. 'Speaking of which, glass of wine? I'll grab some menus.' Harriet nodded.

'Can we join you or did you want some alone time?' Harriet asked.

'Harry, I have so much alone time, that it's ridiculous.'

'Maybe it's time you started dating again? I hear there's this new thing called online dating.'

'Oh god, can you imagine me doing that? My profile will read, sad, divorcee, one kid, dead-end job, pretty crap wardrobe, but might inherit a share in a big manor house and some money, which negates all that.'

'Fleur's right, you are actually quite funny,' Harriet said.

'What have I missed?' Connor returned and set the drinks down.

'Gus, doing his Tinder profile.'

'Hell, Gus, don't do it. I hate all that online stuff. Swiping left or right for an actual person, it's dehumanising.' Harriet was surprised by the passion in his voice.

'I had no intention of it. I'm far to stuffy and old-fashioned. The last date I went on was pretty disastrous and, well, I am concentrating on Fleur, the gardens, the pigs and my painting right now.'

'You know, Amanda is quite lovely and I believe she's a single parent too,' Connor said, reading Harriet's thoughts. She smiled as she thought about Gus and Amanda; perhaps she could be Meadowbrook's own personal matchmaker.

'And your cast-off?' Gus raised an eyebrow.

'No, don't be silly, we got on fine but we both lacked the spark.'

'Amanda's passionate about her work which I like but, well, why would she be interested in me?' Gus looked genuinely baffled.

'Why wouldn't she?' Harriet said fiercely. 'After all, as you said, you might have a dead-end job and be a sad divorcee, but you are going to inherit a share in the house and gardens,' she teased.

'Well there you go, she'd be a fool to turn me down

and we'd save a fortune on garden fees if she was obliged to do them for free,' Gus laughed.

'See I told you, you were funny.'

'Honestly though,' Connor said, interrupting her Cupid thoughts, 'what do you think will happen when you do inherit the house?'

'We can't think about that,' Harriet said. She bristled. She wasn't ready to think about what would happen after this year, yet. Perhaps not ever. Would she stay in the UK, go back to New York? Would she want to work in the city again or was she going to take a totally different path? It was all too terrifying to think about, not least the fact that she didn't have the first clue what she actually wanted to do with her life since losing her job. How could you get to thirty-seven and not know anything? Well, she guessed losing your father, being made redundant and single might have something to do with it.

Connor stared her down, Harriet felt sick. She had no idea what was happening to her, what these feelings were that were pulsing through her, but she couldn't begin to process them. She was far from ready. She might never be ready.

'Let's order,' she said, quickly.

As Hilda barked, she reached down to stroke her. If only everything in life was as straightforward as animals were, then things would be so much easier.

Chapter 14

Freddie rushed through the front door, out of breath, red-faced and panting as he slammed it shut, knocking into Harriet as she was about to step outside.

'Help,' he shouted, as he grabbed her to maintain his balance. He then slumped against the closed door, once safely inside.

'What the hell?' she asked. He looked as if he was going to combust. He had clearly been running, his clothes were dishevelled, his eyes bloodshot and he wreaked of stale alcohol.

'There, out there.' He squeezed the words out.

Pippa and Gus appeared from upstairs to see what the commotion was.

'What's wrong?' Pippa asked.

'There's something out there?' Harriet asked.

'The village, out there.' Freddie bent over double, trying to regain some composure.

'Freddie, slowly, tell us what's wrong. Has someone been chasing you?'

'They are. The villagers. We had a bit of a disagreement and they've formed a lynch mob . . . After me!' Freddie spluttered.

'What do you mean? Fred, you were supposed to go

and meet the committee to finalise the fête details,' Pippa said.

'Yes.' He nodded as his breathing started to ease, slightly. 'Yes. I. Did.'

'Um, Pip, why weren't you there?' Gus asked. Harriet was thinking the same.

'I had a headache,' she said, quietly. 'I gave him my notes and thought Fred could handle it.'

Harriet swivelled to face her, Pippa looked terrible; face pale, eyes red-ringed as if she'd been crying.

Harriet sighed. For the last few weeks everything had been going swimmingly at Meadowbrook. With just under a month left until the fête, she felt that Pippa and Freddie had everything in hand. Bella had been a great help with publicity, Freddie and she worked together well – working being the operative word – and along with Pippa's people skills they were all set for the best summer fête in the history of Meadowbrook summer fêtes. Or so she thought.

'OK, so Freddie what did you do to the villagers?' Harriet folded her arms.

'I just made some suggestions,' Freddie said, innocently. 'But that doesn't mean they should have chased me out of the hall. The only thing missing was pitchforks – however, that morris-dancing vicar was waving a big stick at me.'

'Oh boy,' Gus said, lips curling.

'But, Fred, we went through what needed doing,' Pippa said, sounding distraught. 'You were just meant to finalise everything. Agree the finer details!'

'I know, I know, Pip, but I'm not a robot, I just had some ideas—' They were interrupted by banging on the front door. It did sound like a mob. Parker's Hollow was a lovely village, friendly, welcoming, but also fiercely protective. Harriet knew that if anyone criticised the village they would be put in stocks, which knowing Parker's Hollow they still had somewhere; the majority of the villagers being older and having had family in Parker's Hollow for generations. Young families were beginning to move in, but high house prices, and the fact that once people moved there they rarely left, meant that the older generation were definitely in charge. A bit like the gardening club.

'Hide,' Freddie shouted, and before anyone could do anything he fled towards the kitchen.

'Right, time for the grown-ups to handle this,' Harriet said and, turning to Gus and Pippa, she opened the door.

There was a small but very angry group of villagers pressed up against the front door, they almost fell inside when she opened it. They were all members of the Meadowbrook fête committee, a group her father had put together to help him with the annual summer fête. They were headed by John, the leader of the morris dancers and also the local vicar, he was flanked by Hilary, his wife who was helping to organise the Meadowbrook bake-off, Edie and Margaret and Rose from the gardening club, Samuel who supervised the placing of the stalls, and a few others, some Harriet didn't know yet. They were all a bit red-faced, having pursued Freddie from the village hall to the house. And they weren't spring chickens, although John the vicar with all his dancing was possibly fitter than even Harriet.

'What's going on?' Harriet asked. 'Are you all all right?' She was worried that some of them might keel over.

'That Freddie, he's bang out of order,' John said. He was

wearing his morris dancer white costume, and had cymbals strapped to his knees. He was still waving the stick around, quite aggressively for a vicar. Before Harriet could speak, they all started talking at once

'OK,' Pippa said, everyone fell silent as they looked at her. 'Why don't you all come in, you look like you might need to sit down, and then we can talk about it calmly.'

They didn't need asking twice. Harriet stepped back, everyone rushed in, and Pippa ushered them into the drawing room.

'Please, make yourselves comfortable. Shall I get some water?' Gus asked.

'Please, Gus, bring a big jug and some glasses,' Harriet said. Gus nodded and left.

'Edie, you shouldn't have walked here, you said your hip was playing up,' Pippa said, sounding concerned as Edie slumped onto the sofa.

'Well, I didn't think about it, to be honest. That brother of yours was so out of order, so we all just rushed up here. I'm a bit tired, mind,' Edie said.

John sat down next to her, his knee cymbals crashed together. Everyone jumped.

'Maybe I better stand,' he said, heaving himself up.

When everyone was settled and had glasses of water, faces began to return to normal colours.

Pippa stood in front of the fireplace facing them, Harriet and Gus stood next to her.

'Right, so one at a time, tell me what happened. John?' Pippa asked.

'He said that us morris dancers had to modernise our routine. He was talking about us doing our dances to Rihanna and learning to twerk. I didn't even know what twerking was before he showed me. And it's certainly not suitable for a family event. It's obscene!'

'Yes, well I can see how that might upset you,' Pippa concurred, a smile curling at her lips. Harriet could almost hear Freddie suggesting that, as she suppressed a smile.

'We beat sticks together, have bells on our knees and I have the cymbals.' He bashed them together to demonstrate. Poor Samuel jumped again. 'I ask you, twerking! We are an almost award-winning morris dancing troupe! We entered a competition and came sixth out of twelve. That's not to be sniffed at.'

'No, John it isn't,' Pippa replied.

'Not to mention God. What would He think if we all went round shaking our bottoms?'

Harriet struggled to contain her mirth.

'And 'e said I was too old to look after the stalls. I mean too old, I've done it for years!' Samuel exclaimed. 'I was good enough to supervise when your dad was alive.'

'And you are now.' Pippa smiled. 'Samuel, ignore Freddie, you are valued and we need you for this fête.'

'He said that the Meadowbrook bake-off had to be cakes, and they all had to be in the shape of famous people, but I had planned to do my best quiche,' Hilary piped up. The vicar and his wife were very well matched, Harriet thought. Apart from the fact she didn't have any instruments strapped to her, they looked fairly alike. Tall, angular, both with grey hair and glasses. But they were good people, central to the village community and John had conducted their father's funeral after all. 'My quiches are famous, everyone loves them and I thought we were allowed to bake what we wanted.'

Pippa opened her mouth to respond but was cut off before she had the chance by Rose.

'Not to mention he said my tombola wasn't good enough. He said we weren't allowed any talc or Spam, or Old Spice gift sets as prizes, and well I have to tell you that I have collected all of them so far, and I donated the Spam myself, it always goes down a treat. He told me that I should have champagne, and caviar and something called Dippy candles.'

'Diptyque,' Harriet said, quickly regretting it when Rose glared at her.

'No one's ever complained about my tombola before.' Rose looked close to tears. 'I've been running it for years and it's always a big hit.'

'Right, well let's address each point,' Pippa said. Harriet was trying and failing not to find it amusing. She could just imagine her loose cannon of a brother trying to turn the Meadowbrook summer fête into a Chelsea event.

'Oh and he wants us to get girls in bikinis to sell the raffle tickets,' Edie said. 'And I can't possibly wear a bikini at my age, neither can Mary or Doris,' she pointed at the two women Harriet hadn't yet met, 'although I was a bit keen to have a go at the twerking.' Out of the corner of her eye, Harriet noticed Gus's eyes twinkling.

'And he also said my coconut shy would make more money if a girl wore a coconut bra and hula skirt. I don't even know where I'd get one of those,' a man Harriet didn't recognise said. 'I'm Gerry by the way,' he said, coming over to them and shaking their hands. 'I'm fairly new to the village, only lived here for ten years, but I ran the coconut shy for your father for the last five years, I did.' Gerry looked about sixty, so fairly young among the other villagers, and was well dressed and well spoken. Harriet fleetingly wondered if he'd met Gwen. She shook her head, she must stop trying to matchmake everyone.

She knew she was only doing it so she didn't focus on herself, but all the same, she wasn't sure Gwen would welcome it.

'OK, well I am so sorry, all of you, that my brother, Freddie, upset you. Firstly, he has no right to tell you what to do. Yes, we are organising the fête, but only with you being fully involved. It's a community event, a village event, and it's important to us, as I've said before, that Parker's Hollow is all on board with everything,' Pippa said.

Harriet grinned, she sounded impressive, confident and in control. The group began to look a little less disgruntled and a little less likely to collapse.

'John, you do what you do best, you are, as you say, nearly one of the best morris dancing troupes in the country, so we trust you. No, of course you don't need Rihanna or twerking.' Pippa grinned. 'I remember the fêtes from when I was a child, before they were even held here at Meadowbrook, and I always loved them, the tradition is so important. You all keep that tradition alive and that is what we will continue to do.'

'So we just carry on as we were?' Rose asked.

'Yes. Same with all of you. No one will tell you what to do from now on. If you want to discuss anything, then I am here, but we aren't making any major changes, and please, can we just pretend today never happened. After all it's only a month until the event and we really do need to try to pull together. I'm here to support you, so anything you need, please come to me,' Pippa said, sincerely.

'What about Freddie?' Hilary asked.

'Right, well he has been suffering terribly from missing Dad,' Pippa explained. Harriet thought she was right, a combination of a failed business, losing Dad, drinking too

160

much and Loretta was the cause of him being an out-of-control nightmare. 'He's very sad, full of grief, but don't worry we'll talk to him.'

'Oh, poor Freddie, it's like Hamlet all over again,' Edie said. 'I said to you didn't I, he's so pale and always looks like he's seen a ghost. Oh my!' Edie looked quite excited. 'Maybe he saw a ghost of your father and it made him mad with grief. I said, Rose, didn't I? That poor boy looks like he's haunted.'

'You did, Edie, you did,' Rose concurred.

'Ladies, there's no such thing as ghosts,' John the vicar pointed out. 'And anyway, if he is feeling like Hamlet then we need to support him, because he might challenge me to a duel next.'

'Well I'm pretty sure that won't happen,' Gus pointed out. 'He is full of grief, but I'm not sure we can compare him to Hamlet.'

Harriet didn't know whether to laugh or cry.

'That's settled it.' John bashed his knees together again, making the ladies jump. 'We'll all rally to make this the best fête ever, and support Freddie in his hour of need.'

The villagers nodded vigorously in agreement. It was more than an hour of need, Harriet thought.

'Right, well that's all fabulous,' Pippa said. 'Now, would anyone like a lift back, Gus can take some of you.'

'Oh yes please,' Edie said. 'That twerking's played havoc with my hip.'

Gus was dispatched with some of the ladies, all who seemed to be vying to sit next to him in the front passenger seat, the others, pacified, all set off back to the village – John's cymbals were still clanging as he walked down the drive.

161

'Why aren't there any younger people on the fête committee?' Harriet asked. 'I know the village is dominated by the silver-hair brigade but I thought some of the younger members of the village might get involved.'

'We do have quite a few participating though, don't worry. Especially the bake-off, it's become fashionable with a group of yummy mummies who are all taking part. But you know most of these guys have known us all our lives, and they are the heart of the village. We need to take care of them, like we would have wanted for our father.'

Harriet put her arm around Pippa.

'You are definitely the good sister.'

'Shall we go and find Freddie and see what possessed him to try to get the morris dancers to twerk.'

'I guess it's wrong but I would so have paid to see that,' Harriet laughed.

Freddie was at the kitchen table, his head in his hands. Gwen was sitting opposite him, looking concerned.

'Right, explain yourself,' Harriet said, sharply. 'Half the village were after your blood. The village fête could have been a disaster.'

Freddie looked upset.

'I may have had a few drinks before the meeting.'

Harriet studied her youngest brother. They were all aware, since moving back to Meadowbrook, how much Freddie was drinking but normally only in the evening. Yes, she had caught him passed out by the swimming pool that one time, but he was Freddie. The partying, fun one of the family. And although she thought, privately, that he drank too much, she had put it down to his business falling apart and losing Dad. After all she had been through, she wanted to drink herself into a stupor most nights, so she could hardly blame him. But he clearly was using drink as a crutch and something would need to be done about it if he continued this way.

'Why? Why would you do that?' Pippa asked, she still sounded annoyed, in the sweetest way.

'Things are getting a bit on top of me, to be totally honest. Moving here, losing Dad, feeling lost, and then Loretta . . . She wants me to settle down a bit and when she says that it freaks me out.'

'But why?'

'I don't know, I can't explain it, I just feel out of my depth. But, I promise I'll drink less, and I'll apologise to the fête committee. I'll do everything properly but don't try to make me make sense of it because I can't.' Freddie put his head in his hands and his body shuddered; he was crying. Harriet couldn't remember the last time she'd seen him upset, even at the funeral he'd been cracking jokes.

'Oh, Fred, I'm sorry.' She sat next to him and put her arms around him.

'I miss Dad. He always knew what to do and I never listened to him, but if he was here now, I would.'

Tears filled Gwen's eyes, they streamed down Pippa's cheeks, Harriet felt emotions choking her. It was all such a mess still. And they were all grieving, sometimes she forgot they were in the grip of grief, but then there were the ugly reminders.

'It'll be OK,' Harriet said, and she fervently hoped it would be.

Gus walked in, then stopped as the saw them all.

'Old ladies delivered home,' he said, carefully.

'Thanks, Gus,' Pippa stuttered. Gus's eyes trailed to each of his siblings, finally resting on Harriet.

'I wish the old man was here,' Gus said, as his voice choked up.

'Me too,' Harriet added.

'Me three,' Freddie said.

'And me four,' Pippa finished.

Chapter 15

Harriet had just climbed off the treadmill when her phone beeped. She looked – it was a text from Connor asking if she could help him at the sanctuary as soon as possible. It was only seven in the morning, but Connor was at the place most days at the crack of dawn. She not only admired his passion but she was beginning to share it too; it had definitely gotten to her. She quickly typed back that she was on her way, she didn't stop to change, or even to look at how sweaty she was. As she jogged over, she sent Pippa a quick message saying she wouldn't be at breakfast and then, picking up the pace, she went to find Connor.

He was in with the ponies.

'Is everything all right?' she asked, before even greeting him.

'It's Brian, he's hobbling, and crying out, so I need to check his hooves, but no one else is here yet. I hope you don't mind me asking you.'

'Don't be silly, of course I don't.' Harriet was fond of all the ponies but she and Brian had a sort of affinity. He was the new boy in the paddock, and she felt a little bit like the new girl at Meadowbrook. Brian had been welcomed by Gerald, Cookie and Clover, the goats were indifferent, but he was still unsure of his place in the paddock and she knew that feeling. 'What can I do?'

'If you could hold him and keep him still, comfort him, then I can check out his hooves.'

'Hey, Bri, it's OK, it's me.' Harriet put her arms around his neck, and stroked him, whispering into his ear. He was still making a bit of a racket but started to calm. She watched as Connor gently checked his hooves and found what was causing discomfort.

'Somehow he's got an old bit of nail stuck. Harry, I'm going to have to pull it out but he won't like it.'

'Hey, baby, keep calm and Connor will fix you,' Harriet cooed nervously. She felt a little foolish talking to the pony this way, as if he was a baby, but she didn't know what else to do.

Connor opened his vet bag, took something out and started to yank at Brian's hoof. Brian cried out so loudly that Harriet nearly lost her grip. She tightened it, hushing him, stroking and whispering into his ear.

'Nearly there,' Connor said. He was getting a bit sweaty as he worked, trying to be gentle. Finally he released the leg. 'Done!' he shouted triumphantly.

Brian, surprised at his leg being freed, broke free of Harriet, headbutting her so she fell over.

'Bloody hell.' Harriet lay splayed in the paddock, Brian looming over her to see if she was all right, alongside Connor. 'Brian, don't act like you care now, you pushed me.' She felt a little red at the undignified way she was sprawled on the grass.

'Here, take my hand.' Connor reached out and pulled her up. Brian trotted off as if nothing had happened.

'Stop laughing,' Harriet snapped.

'Sorry, but it was quite funny. Thank you for helping,

you'd make a pretty good assistant. Can I get you coffee, or breakfast to make it up to you?'

'Yes, because I've missed your mum's yummy breakfast actually.' Her pride was bruised, as well as her bottom.

'Can't promise anything so grand, but I probably have toast, and the bread might not even be mouldy.'

'Great. What an offer.'

Fortified by toast and marmalade – she loved how old-fashioned Connor was in so many ways – they set back out to the sanctuary. He wasn't due at the practice until later so he said to make up for this morning he would help her muck out the stables.

'Who knew that city girl Harriet Singer would enjoy getting her hands dirty,' Connor teased as she started raking up old hay. She threw it at him.

'Shut up, Connor, this is temporary remember,' she said as he brushed the hay off.

'Ah, not converted you yet then?'

'I have to admit, I don't mind it as much as I first thought, but I still think I'm probably more of a desk sort of person. Hey, shall we go and check on the rest of the animals.'

'Lead the way, m'lady.' Connor pinched her bottom and Harriet flushed. 'Sorry, I couldn't help it!' he laughed. She shook her head and walked off, trying to hide her blushes.

'Hey, Fred,' she shouted, waving as he was feeding the chickens, something that she was getting used to seeing.

'Jenni's had to go to sort out something, so I'm doing this alone today,' he said, as the chickens clucked happily around him.

'You look almost at home with them.' Connor grinned.

'Oh I am, honestly, although Elizabeth Bennet and

Emma seem to have a bit of a rivalry for my attention.' Two of the chickens looked up at that point.

'Nothing surprises me here, nothing,' Harriet said. 'Right, see you later, Freddie, we're off to check on the others.'

They just entered the field where the pig pen was when Harriet stopped. Betsy and Buddy had been joined by two more pigs, Napoleon and Cleopatra – two more fully grown micropigs. But as Connor strode forward, Harriet grabbed his arm and pulled him back slightly.

'What?' he said.

'I think Gus is talking to them.' Gus was stood leaning on the side of the pen; while the pigs ate, he did seem to be chatting away.

'Shall we eavesdrop?' Connor asked.

'Oh God we really shouldn't,' Harriet said, before dragging him behind a tree where, of course, they listened to what Gus had to say. Harriet clamped her hand over her mouth to stop herself from laughing. Poor Gus. He was such a sweetheart, but honestly, he was talking to the pigs as if they were human.

'So, I'm trying not to worry about the future of Meadowbrook and live in the present, something I've never been very good at,' he was saying. 'Always planning ahead me, even as a young boy, Harry will tell you that.'

Connor looked at Harriet, who shook her head.

'Anyway now, with the loss of Dad, the painting and the gardens, I feel as if I can breathe again and so I am trying to be more impulsive. Which brings me to Amanda—'

'Come on,' Harriet hissed and dragged Connor away through the other entrance to the field so Gus didn't see them.

'Hey,' Connor said when they were out of earshot. 'Why did you drag us off, I wanted to hear what he had to say about Amanda.'

'But it was too private. If Gus wants to talk to either of us, he knows where we are. But it's not fair to spy on him.'

'I know, you're right. Do you remember when we spied on him when we were teenagers, when he brought Rachel home for the first time?'

'Oh God, yes, we hid didn't we because we wanted to find out what she was saying about us.'

'Yes, but only because she didn't like us,' Connor pointed out.

'Me, Connor, she didn't like me. Told Gus I was far too sure of myself.'

'Well, you were quite.' Connor grinned.

'Maybe then but not anymore,' Harriet finished. 'Anyway, poor Gus, if he likes talking to the pigs we shouldn't ruin that for him.'

'No, we shouldn't. Besides, it's well known that they are very good listeners,' Connor said.

'That's what Gus said. Oh, look there's Pippa.' She waved over to her sister.

'Oh hi,' Pippa said, running up to them. 'Guess what, I've just taken the dogs out with the dog walking volunteers and one of them, Pat, said that he's managed to find homes for three of the dogs, they're coming in later to do the paperwork.'

'How did he do that?' Harriet asked.

'He's been telling everyone and anyone who'll listen at the local golf club and it's paid off.'

'Who needs PR when you've got Pat?' Connor said. 'Right, ladies, I need to get off to work, but, Harry, why don't you meet the people who want to rehome, with Jenni of course, see how the process works?'

'Sure,' Harriet agreed, although she suddenly had a thought which made her heart drop; she hoped it wasn't Hilda they would be taking.

Chapter 16

'Oh God, it's going to rain,' Pippa lamented as she discarded the piece of toast she had been playing with.

'Pip, it'll be fine,' Harriet replied, trying to comfort her sister. The summer fête meant a lot to all of them and all their nerves were a little shredded. However, as usual, Harriet felt that she had to be the one to keep it together. She looked out of the window and her confidence dipped slightly. The dove grey sky looked a little threatening.

'Besides, we've set up a lot of marquees,' Freddie stated calmly. 'We'll just shove as much as we can undercover if we need to.' Freddie and Pippa actually made a complementary team; he was laid-back, she was slightly neurotic; a perfect mix to organise a summer fête, it seemed. They had also become closer than ever, which was doing Freddie no end of good. He had drunk a lot less and been busier than Harriet had ever seen him. She hadn't wanted to make too much of a big deal about his drinking, Gus had warned her against it, but they had all cut down. Not having wine every night, or brandies or cocktail hour, and Freddie had joined them. He even said waking up without hangovers was a revelation. But then he was busy and happy, which probably helped keep him away from alcohol a bit more.

'And anyway, we all have the Meadowbrook spirit, we won't let a bit of rain ruin the village's best annual event,' Gus announced. 'The gardens have never looked better. We're expecting a record number of visitors.'

'And I've spent hours training Hilda,' Fleur piped up. Harriet smiled. The dog show was going to be quite an event. Not in the same league as Crufts, more 'Crusts', as Freddie had named it. But what their rescue dogs lacked in pedigree and talent they made up for in enthusiasm and personality. Everyone involved in the sanctuary plus the volunteers from the dog walking group were taking part, the aim being to rehome some of the poor loves. Connor had reluctantly agreed to host the show and Fleur had begged to be allowed to partner with Hilda.

It had given Harriet an opportunity to spend more time with Fleur, and Gus, as he always came out to watch Fleur trying, and mainly failing, to get Hilda to do what she was told. It had been a good, no, a necessary bonding time for them all. Gus was beginning to learn that what Fleur needed from him wasn't money, but love and time. It wasn't that Gus didn't want to spend time with her, it was that he didn't know how. Harriet thought that his ex-wife, Rachel, had sapped so much of Gus's confidence that he didn't know how to be himself, and the way she controlled his relationship with their daughter had ensured that Gus was always insecure around Fleur. But Fleur, twelve, very mature in many ways, and about to turn thirteen, was developing a mind of her own and the great thing was that her love of animals, and of Meadowbrook, meant she was demanding to spend more time with them and therefore her father. Her mother didn't stand a chance.

Harriet had tried gently to encourage their relationship, and Gus's confidence with Fleur was growing by the day.

'Right, well today is for Dad,' Harriet raised her coffee cup in a toast, 'and therefore we need to do our best.'

'I remember last year's fête,' Pippa said, tears welling. Harriet knew it would be an emotional day, she just didn't quite know how she would deal with it yet. 'Dad opened it with such great flourish.'

'Oh yes, I remember Granddad's speech about how special Parker's Hollow was, how much the sanctuary meant to him and how being part of the village community was imperative for Meadowbrook.' Fleur smiled, sadly.

'Gosh, Fleur, you remembered that practically word for word,' Gus said.

Again, Harriet felt a pang that she hadn't been there for her father's final event.

'Even I came down,' Freddie said. The final nail in the guilt coffin.

'Yes, but, Fred, you got drunk in the sherry tent,' Gus pointed out.

'I did, because it was very nice sherry.'

'Tut.' Mark didn't look up from the newspaper.

'What was that, Mark?' Harriet asked. Mark had been in a foul mood since arriving the previous evening. Harriet wasn't sure if it was because Pippa had been so preoccupied with last-minute fête arrangements that she'd barely paid him any attention or maybe he'd had a bad week at work. But this was a side to Mark, a moody side, that she hadn't yet encountered. She thought perhaps this was what her father was talking about when he had said, in his pre-will video, that he wasn't sure Mark was right for his

173

youngest daughter. Harriet had brushed it off when Pippa reassured her that their father had got the wrong end of the stick, for Pippa's sake, but now she was beginning to wonder.

'Sorry what?' Mark said.

'You tutted loudly,' Freddie said.

'Oh, it must have been something I was reading.' Mark smiled, grimly.

'So, Mark, what are you going to do today to help out?' Harriet asked. She knew she was poking the bear but she thought maybe she would begin to find out exactly who the man married to her sister was.

'I've told Pippa I'll support her in whatever she needs. In fact I shall be by her side all day.'

'Thanks, Mark, I do appreciate it,' Pippa said, leaning over to kiss her husband.

Harriet focused on her coffee. Her sister seemed to adore her husband, and kept telling them all she was happy, so why was Harriet questioning it?

'So, Granddad always opened the fête, who's doing it this year?' Fleur broke the silence.

'Well, if you need me to, I'd be happy,' Mark said. Harriet choked on her coffee.

'No, thanks all the same, Mark. I mean no one in Parker's Hollow knows who you are,' Freddie said.

'I'm sure that's not true,' Pippa shot back.

The fête flyers had billed a 'surprise celebrity guest' attending, but no one knew who it was, or even if there was one. Not even Pippa. Freddie had said he was sorting it and the only person he would tell was Bella, as the fête's official PR. To say that this was a worry was an understatement. Parker's Hollow were all speculating who the celebrity would be. The gardening club were hoping for

174

Christopher Biggins or Charlie Dimmock, other speculation was the cook from *Downtown Abbey*, Mary Berry who would judge the Meadowbrook bake-off, or the judge no one could quite remember from *Strictly*. Harriet was more than a tiny bit worried they were going to be bitterly disappointed.

'Well, despite the doubters, we have actually secured a very special guest,' Freddie announced.

'And he hasn't even told me who it is. Frankly though as Bella's involved I kind of trust her,' Pippa added.

'Thanks, Pip, you don't trust me. Right, well I guess I can tell you now, the special guest opening the fête will be . . . drum roll please . . . Hector Barber,' Freddie announced. There was a brief silence.

'Who?' Pippa asked.

'No idea,' Gus added.

'I've never heard of him.' Harriet felt concerned.

'Oh my God,' Fleur said, almost knocking her orange juice over. 'You mean Hector from *Single's Holiday*?'

'What's *Single's Holiday*?' Harriet asked.

'Only the best TV show *ever*,' Fleur said.

'You watch it? You're allowed to watch it?' Gus blustered, like an outraged parent. 'You don't watch it with me and I can't believe your mum would let you. You shouldn't be watching that, not at your age.'

Fleur coloured. 'But Dad—'

'I haven't seen it, it's got a terrible write up in the *Radio Times*,' Gus continued to bluster.

'I can't believe you read the *Radio Times*, Gus. Actually on second thoughts I can,' Freddie added unhelpfully.

'What is it?' Harriet repeated.

'It's an incredibly popular reality TV show where single people go on, couple up, shag and pretend to fall in love so they can come out and make money on Instagram,' Freddie explained.

'Mum doesn't let me watch it,' Fleur admitted. 'But everyone at school does, so I watch it on the computer in my room.'

'Fleur, I forbid you to watch that rubbish,' Gus stormed.

'Gus, remember peer pressure, let's not forget how hard that was,' Harriet said, reasonably. Gus understood more than most. Being a bit sensitive didn't help him at boarding school and he had to change, to toughen up, to fit in.

'Of course. But I don't like the idea of my twelve-year-old daughter watching people having sex,' he said.

'I'm nearly thirteen, Dad,' Fleur piped up.

'It's disgusting,' Mark added, unhelpfully.

'Oh, do you watch it then?' Freddie asked. Pippa hit him on the arm.

'OK, Fleur, we'll talk about it later. But, Freddie, no offence, if only you and Fleur know who this Hector bloke is, no one from Parker's Hollow will,' Gus pointed out.

'He's right,' Harriet added. 'He's no Christopher Biggins.'

'But, you know he's doing it for free and Bella and I thought if we tell everyone he's a celebrity off the telly they'll all be happy. That's how it always worked in the clubs. We always had these reality TV stars doing personal appearances and people, for some reason, lapped it up.'

'Because they were on drugs?' Gus suggested, helpfully. 'I'm pretty sure that most of the people at the village fête won't have had anything stronger than cider, and even the strongest cider might not be enough.'

'I can't believe I'm going to meet actual Hector,' Fleur

said, starry-eyed. 'Dad, I know you don't approve and I promise I keep my eyes closed when they're actually doing it, you know the sex stuff, but can I get a photo with him? The girls at school will be well jell if I put it on Insta.'

'Not sure what "well jell" or "insta" means, but yes, you can have a photo with him, but only if I am there at all times and also if you promise not to date boys until you're at least twenty-five,' Gus said with a wry smile.

'So, did he win this show then?' Harriet asked. She didn't watch TV since being back at Meadowbrook, but maybe she should give it a go. It sounded appalling but compelling.

'Oh no, he was voted out by the other people in the show in week three for sleeping with three of the girls and none of them knew about the others at first. But his banter was really good, so he's secretly quite popular,' Fleur explained. 'And he's well fit.'

'And despite the fact they were living in the same villa he managed to get away with it for a week. He's now known as the bad boy of the nation,' Freddie added. 'Oh and he pranced around in these tight jeans for the three weeks he was on TV, so that helped his popularity.'

'And he's opening our village fête?' Pippa's voice was filled with disbelief. 'Fred, you do know that most of the village are probably the same age as Hector's grandparents. They'll never know who he is and if they did they'd never approve.'

'Yes I know, but as I said, he's free, and you know how important it was for this fête to make money.' Freddie put a good case forward. 'His agent, a good friend of mine, is trying to show that he's a nice guy, so when I said I could get him photographed with some nice old ladies, some cakes and maybe a donkey, they leapt at the chance,

177

not to mention that he will talk about how he supports the animal sanctuary in interviews,' Freddie explained. 'Bella reckons she can get quite a lot of press out of it.'

'Well, I guess that's all good.' Harriet was slightly unsure still.

'But *Parker's Hollow Gazette* is coming and I'm not sure if that's the kind of publicity this Hector is after. What was Bella thinking?' Pippa asked.

'Maybe she thinks he's well fit too,' Gus finished. Harriet couldn't help but think this was a disaster waiting to happen.

After breakfast, when they made their way to the fête site, one of the fields near the animal sanctuary, it was already a hive of activity. Stalls were being put up, the show ring was set up in the centre and it was already looking like a fête. Some of the animals in the adjoining fields ambled nearer to see what was going on; others, Elton and David, kept well away.

Thankfully, the sun was beginning to warm slightly. Yes, Pippa was right, the sky was still grey and rain threatened – but then this was the August bank holiday and Gus had said there hadn't been a rain-free bank holiday that he could remember. But no matter what, they would all make sure it was a success, for their dad.

'Dad, keep the rain way, please,' Harriet said silently, staring at a cloud. If Andrew Singer was up there, she was pretty sure he could control the weather.

'Hey, you OK?' Connor appeared at her shoulder and gave her a hug. Yet again she tried to ignore the physical feelings that he was invoking in her. She had no way of dealing with them, apart from quashing them, and she hoped, prayed, that she was hiding them well.

'Yes. I feel slightly redundant actually, today is Pippa and Freddie's they've worked so hard, so I think I should possibly take a step back.'

'Well, apart from hosting the dog show, I don't have much to do, so maybe we can act as if we're village fête goers.'

'As long as you don't win the Old Spice on the tombola,' Harriet quipped.

'I've got to go and feed some animals, you know, actual work, and then I'll see you back here. It's a date.'

She shook her head, it really wasn't. Harriet wasn't a teenager anymore, despite her feelings being a throwback to her youth. She knew full well what unrequited love looked like and felt like. Connor still treated her as the annoying girl he was far too fond of to say no to.

Whatever his feelings, or hers, it added up to the same thing – telling Connor, telling anyone, how she felt would end up with her being humiliated yet again. And Harriet was going to concentrate on a positive future. If there was love in it, then it would be with someone she hadn't yet met. So it was time for her to move forward. She was worried that the situation with Zach and her job, the loss of her father, was what was making her so desperate to cling to the past. But now it was time to let go.

The fête committee were all here, excited and happy. John was in his morris-dancing regalia, Harriet suspected he liked to wear it a bit too much. The bake-off tent was bustling with activity. Gwen was helping to supervise and, as she felt it wouldn't be right for her to enter the competition she was going to be one of the judges, along with Freddie because he really liked baked goods – which apparently qualified him – and of course the reality TV star who no one would have heard of. A sudden well of emotion opened up inside her: pride at what they had done, love for the unorthodox nature of the fête and the village and hope for the future. She looked at the sky and the sun miraculously appeared.

'Thank you, Dad,' she said, knowing, as an invisible warm blanket enveloped her, that he was here with them today.

Chapter 17

'Ladies and gentlemen and everyone else,' Hector Barber laughed. He certainly was 'fit' as Fleur had said. A besotted Fleur was standing next to Harriet as close as they could get to the stage which had been set up for the opening and prize-giving. It wasn't a big stage, the O2 had nothing to worry about, and Hector, who was actually incredibly posh, seemed to fill it. Freddie and Hector's agent huddled in the background and the whole of Parker's Hollow crowded round, as if at a pop concert.

'Who is he?' Edie hissed from her place near the front.

'He's off the telly,' someone else replied and that seemed to satisfy her.

'I am delighted to be here today, in—' He turned to look at his agent who mouthed something. 'Parker's Swallow, what a charming village you have. Yay!' He cheered and some of the older ladies looked a bit flustered. Harriet could see why. He was tall, over six foot, with dark hair, muscles which did not just happen on their own, and he was wearing a pair of incredibly skinny, skinny jeans and a T-shirt which left nothing to the imagination. His green eyes twinkled and although he was definitely too young for Harriet, and for most of the women here in fact, she could see the attraction.

'Really, who is he?' Connor, who had, as promised, shown up as her escort for the fête, asked.

'Reality TV person.' She whispered an explanation of the show in his ear.

Connor looked confused.

'You mean he's famous because he had sex on TV?' he said far too loudly. Everyone turned to look at Connor. Hector coloured.

'Well, you know there was more to it than that,' Hector blustered. 'I didn't just do . . . well what you said. I do have other talents you know.'

'Did you sing? Will you give us a song?' a voice shouted.

'Well, no I don't sing.' His face was almost the colour of Gwen's home-made strawberry jam.

'Ah, did you dance? Are you going to dance for us?' another voice boomed out from the crowd.

Hector looked at his agent and Freddie, he was clearly not used to dealing with anyone but adoring girls.

'He was very funny,' Fleur piped up. 'I mean, you were really good at making people laugh.'

'Oh good, I love a comedian, like that Tommy Cooper, he was my favourite. Tell us a joke.'

Harriet almost felt sorry for Hector, as did Freddie who quickly rushed to join him at the mic.

'Hector will tell jokes later, if you're all very lucky. In the meantime we need him to open the fête so we can start the festivities.'

'Thank you.' Relief hugged his words. 'I am so delighted to be here, in your lovely village. I am also touched to be an ambassador for the wonderful animal sanctuary at Meadowbook.' He turned again to his agent for approval.

'Meadow*brook*,' his agent said.

'Of course.' Hector grinned. 'I knew that.'

'He's an ambassador now? I didn't agree that,' Connor hissed in Harriet's ear but she shushed him.

'So, without further delay or singing, dancing or jokes, it gives me immense pleasure to announce the great Meadowbrook Summer Fête open.'

The crowd cheered and suddenly everyone was a Hector Barber fan.

'What a lovely young man,' Edie said. 'I'm going to make sure I get a photo later. Not every day you meet someone off the telly, and even if he did have sex, it's not to be sniffed at.' She walked off happily. Connor, Harriet, Fleur and Gus all gaped after her, speechless.

'I was always better at the coconut shy than you were,' Harriet teased as Connor missed again.

'I just let you win, that's all,' he replied, good-naturedly.

'Were we competitive as children?' Harriet asked.

'You were, you couldn't bear to lose anything, I was more laid-back, hence the fact I let you win.' He aimed a ball and hit a coconut as if to illustrate the point.

'God, I was a nightmare,' Harriet said.

'Was?'

'Thanks, Connor.'

'Look, Harry, I always adored you no matter that you were bossy, competitive and always right.'

'Thank you.' She tried to choose her words carefully, she was terrified that she was going to say the wrong thing and ruin the friendship they were building. 'I am still bossy, according to the others, and competitive, and if I was allowed to access my redundancy money, I'd probably spend it all trying to win a coconut right now, but I am certainly not always right. Sometimes I wonder if I ever am.'

'Now that doesn't sound like the Harriet Singer I used to know.'

'She's gone. Not completely, but a bit. Anyway, shush, I have to do this.' She took aim at the coconut, and threw. The coconut wobbled and then fell down. 'First time, eat my dust,' she taunted.

'No, not completely gone at all,' Connor laughed.

'Sit, Hilda,' Fleur was saying as Harriet silently cheered them on. She was rooting both for her niece and Hilda right now, as Fleur was trying to lead Hilda round the agility course that Connor had set up. It was simple, but most of the dogs were more interested in wagging their tails than doing as they were told. Fleur had a pocketful of Hilda's favourite treats, yet she was still refusing to cooperate.

'That dog reminds me of you,' Gus said.

'Thanks, Gus.' Harriet narrowed her eyes. A shaggy, disobedient sheepdog wasn't the most flattering thing she could be compared to.

'She's as stubborn as you,' Freddie added.

'She's a star,' Pippa said. Mark was standing by her side, as promised.

Just then Hilda looked right at Harriet and broke free from Fleur, bounding over.

'Hilda, you're meant to be winning a rosette,' Harriet chastised as she petted her. 'Sorry, Fleur.'

'You know she wasn't this bad in rehearsal.' Fleur rolled her eyes but then she gave Hilda a treat regardless.

'Right, well put your hands together for Fleur and Hilda,' Connor said, before going on to introduce the next contestant. Everyone clapped politely, although Hilda hadn't done anything at all.

'Hello.' Hector approached with his agent, Greg, who slapped Freddie on the back.

'How's it going?' Freddie asked.

'Fantastic,' Greg replied. 'We've taken some photos with a couple of old dears, and in the cake tent, on the coconut shy, and also having a go on the tombola.'

'Did you win anything?' Freddie asked.

'Yes, a tin of Spam,' Hector replied, looking slightly bemused.

'Um, can I take a photo with you?' Fleur asked, blushing furiously.

'Sure thing, love.'

'She's twelve,' Gus said.

'Yes but, dear brother, twelve is legal to have a photograph taken,' Freddie teased.

'Just keep your hands where I can see them,' Gus said.

Fleur insisted on taking the photos herself on her phone – it had to be a selfie apparently – and then Hilda got in on the act. Facebook, or sorry, Insta, would be busy tonight, Harriet thought, glancing fondly at her niece. Oh to be that age again. If only she could go back, she would definitely not have messed her life up so spectacularly. Embarrassed at the force of her thoughts, she turned her attention to the dogs again.

Hector was being approached by Gus's gardening club ladies now.

'Hector, we'd like a photo with all of us,' Margaret said. 'But do you think you can take your T-shirt off? It's just we googly'd you to see who you were and you have got quite a nice chest.'

At least Hector was obliging, Harriet thought as he

whipped his T-shirt off and, surrounded by ten swooning old ladies, Freddie took a number of photos as Hector posed patiently, charming the women as he did so.

'Gosh,' Hector said, once they'd gone. 'I thought the girls at the PAs I do at the clubs were bad but these ladies act as if they'd eat me alive.'

'Oh they most certainly would,' Harriet replied with a laugh.

'Now you could eat me alive any day.' Hector suddenly snatched Pippa's hand and held onto it.

Pippa blushed, Mark looked incredibly uncomfortable.

'That's my wife,' he stated.

'Sorry, old chap, I thought she was your daughter,' Hector replied, non-plussed.

Mark suddenly looked murderous, as Pippa quickly dragged him away, which was lucky as the rest of them couldn't hide their sniggers.

'She's probably a bit old for you,' Fleur said, sounding a little jealous. 'She's my aunt and she's almost thirty.'

'Nah, not too old at all, I'm twenty-five and I like the older ladies.'

They crammed into the tent for the results of the Meadowbrook bake-off. Gwen had taken her job as judge seriously; Harriet couldn't say the same for Freddie and Hector, who just seemed to eat a lot. Hector seemed to be relishing his role as the celebrity guest, as he picked up the microphone.

'Ladies and gentlemen, I have the great honour of announcing the first ever winner of the Meadowbrook Bake-Off—' He broke off and turned to his agent. 'Do you think we could get in touch with the real *Bake-Off* people? I didn't realise how much I liked baked goods.'

'I'll pop it on the list. If we do a photo, and hashtag *#hectorbarberforbakeoff,* you never know,' Greg replied.

'Can we get on with it?' Gwen asked, good-naturedly.

'Of course, so without further ado. In third place is,' he squinted at the paper in front of him, 'Mrs Wells with her show-stopping gingerbread recreation of Meadowbrook Manor.' He began clapping and the packed tent cheered. It actually looked like a normal gingerbread house and nothing like Meadowbrook, but Freddie, as he handed over the certificate, praised her creative thinking. 'In second place, with the tastiest chocolate cake I have ever tasted, is Simon someone.'

Simon, a man who Harriet had never met, stepped forward.

'It's Simon Torque,' he said, shaking hands with Hector and taking his certificate.

'Couldn't read the bloody writing,' Hector complained. 'Anyway, the big prize. Well, it is my honour to announce the winner of the Meadowbrook Bake-Off is Hilary, the vicar's wife.'

As the tent erupted in cheers, Harriet blinked in disbelief. It wasn't the most professional, but as Hilary ran to grab the trophy that Freddie had managed to get for free, she didn't seem to care.

After a lengthy speech where she thanked her husband, most of the village, her grandmother for teaching her how to make quiche, and shed a few tears, it was finally over. However, when Freddie tried to get the trophy back off her to get it engraved, there was a bit of a tussle.

The raffle was drawn – also by Hector – who pulled John the vicar's ticket out first and after a ten-minute argument about how he couldn't possibly accept it, he finally took the hamper with aplomb, before donating it to the local community group.

As Harriet and Connor watched the morris dancers closing the fête with an enthusiastic stick-thumping, knee-shaking performance, she felt a bit sad it was over. It had been a perfect day, even the mishaps had added to the charm and she knew her father would be proud.

Later, when she had taken Hilda back to the dog home, she felt her usual pang at leaving her, but at the same time she needed to go home. She was exhausted, it had been a very, very long day. But a fabulous day and one her father would have enjoyed greatly. She wished, with all her heart, that he had been here. As she walked back to Meadowbrook, a single white feather appeared in her path and she wondered, not for the first time if he was here after all.

'I propose a toast,' Harriet said that evening. They were all in the drawing room, along with Gwen and Connor. They'd eaten leftovers from the fête, quiche, sausage rolls, all manner of cakes and scones, and as the fête had been such hard work for Gwen, she hadn't even tried to argue. Harriet had put some of her father's vintage champagne in the fridge, so they could toast their success in style.

The fête had been amazing. Everyone agreed it was a wonderful day and that Andrew Singer would have been so proud of his children. Harriet, being the self-appointed financial director, hadn't yet had time to count all the money, but the high attendance meant that they expected to have made a tidy sum for the animals, and Hector had given them a generous donation – a thousand pounds. He'd been promoting a manly fake tan, which paid ridiculously well. Connor kept muttering that he was in the wrong job, but he accepted the cheque and the publicity photos that came with it, almost in good grace. Connor couldn't quite let go of his disbelief that a man who had sex with three women on television was able to earn money off the back of it. His reaction had just endeared him to Harriet even more, irritatingly she found his naivety about the modern world very attractive.

'So,' Harriet continued, champagne saucer held high, 'I think the toast should be firstly to Freddie and Pippa. You guys pulled off such an impressive and wonderful Meadowbrook fête. Honestly we are all so bloody proud of you, and I know Dad would be too.' Emotion stuck in her throat for a moment. 'Here's to Freddie and Pippa and the best Meadowbrook summer fête so far.'

'To Pippa and Freddie,' they all echoed.

'And how lucky were we that the rain stayed away?' Connor added. 'Maybe we should toast that.'

'I expect your father had a hand in that,' Gwen said, quietly. 'He always seemed to be able to control everything, why not the weather?' She grinned. As Harriet had thought the same earlier, she squeezed Gwen's hand.

'We were lucky that Hector went down so well, pardon the pun,' Gus said. Fleur giggled.

'Have you posted all those photos on Facebook?' Harriet asked.

'*Instagram*, Auntie Harry. Facebook is for old people,' Fleur replied.

''Course it is,' Freddie agreed. 'Talking of old people, where's Mark?'

'Fred, shut up,' Pippa replied. 'He went back to Cheltenham, he wasn't feeling well, and he didn't want to put a dampener on our evening.'

'That was nice of him,' Harriet said carefully. Her feelings for Mark were becoming more mixed. At times he was charming but, lately, the mask seemed to be slipping and she wasn't sure who exactly her sister's husband was.

'You've got to admit he was a bit weird today, at the fête, one minute acting as if he was the Lord of the Manor, and the next face like thunder,' Freddie pointed out, echoing Harriet's thoughts.

'He wasn't feeling well, but he was trying his best to support me. Honestly, Freddie, I wish you'd make more of an effort with him,' Pippa said, crossly.

'Well I thought that Hector was a nice young man,' Gwen said, diffusing things. 'I mean, a bit orange if I'm honest, but apparently that's all the rage, so he told me, and those jeans were so tight you'd have trouble getting a shoehorn down them, but all in all I liked him.'

Harriet had no words.

'Well, I think we need to thank the village fête committee,' Pippa said, the threatened row with Freddie thankfully aborted.

'Why don't we invite them all to dinner here?' Freddie suggested. 'We can get the good wine out, have a nice meal.'

'Which I expect you want Gwen to cook,' Harriet pointed out, still worried about the workload. 'And can we afford it? I mean, I know we have access to enough wine to last us for a hundred years – well not at Freddie's rate, but you know what I mean, and also the food is taken care of, but I'm not sure our allowances stretch to entertaining.'

'I know, I mean I thought that I wouldn't need money, not living here and being fed and watered, or wined, but actually the pittance we get doesn't go anywhere, does it?' Gus said. Harriet agreed with him. They were still spoilt, lucky and indulged, but when it came to buying anything, they really had to stop and think for the first time in ages. Last week she had been to the pharmacy and her whole allowance had gone on essential toiletries and she was no longer able to use her usual brands. Oh she knew she was still luckier than so many people, but it was making her think about how frivolous she was with money before, which may have been her father's point.

'I would love that,' Gwen said, going back to the proposed dinner party. 'This village is so important to Meadowbrook and the sanctuary, not to mention your father, and it's been a while since I've done a big dinner. And I think we can do it without spending any of your allowances.' She smiled.

'Will everyone fit at the table?' Connor asked. 'There's quite a lot of people.'

'Ah, you don't recall Dad's magic table?' Gus asked.

'It expands to seat twenty. Dad had it made when he first bought the house, he said Mummy loved having dinner parties. We never used it after she died,' Harriet explained, quietly.

'Then it'll be good to use it now. You invite everyone and just tell me what you want me to cook.' Gwen glowed at the idea.

'I just hope Vicar John doesn't turn up in his morris-dancing outfit,' Freddie said.

They all thought he probably would, cymbals and all.

Chapter 18

'Pip, can I talk to you?' Harriet said, grabbing her sister after breakfast. It was Friday, the day of the dinner for the village fête committee to say thank you for all their hard work.

It was almost a month since the fête, they were nearing the end of September, but it was the first date that everyone was available. As Freddie said, for a bunch of old people the fête committee had very busy social lives. Not like the Singers, who barely had any social life at all. The occasional trip to the Parker's Arms was the social event of Harriet's life. She and her siblings tried to go once a week, which was pretty much all they could afford. Steve and Issy, the landlord and landlady, had almost become friends now, and Harriet loved the community spirit she felt when she walked in there. In New York going out was so anonymous. Beautiful people wanting to be seen, or her and Zach trying hard not to be seen. Nothing as friendly, warm or comfortable as going to the village pub. It might not be as glamorous, but to Harriet it was so much more real than her old life had been. She was beginning to feel more real too. Not necessarily happier though. That still eluded her. And now Harriet had a problem.

'Sure, what it is?' Pippa smiled, in her good-natured

way, as Harriet practically dragged her into their father's study.

'You know how I don't have any money.'

'Well none of us do really do we? I mean, you'd think Dad's allowance would be plenty living here, but I had to give my money to Mark this week.'

'Why?' Harriet asked, sidetracked from her own disaster briefly.

'He needed petrol and he lost his bank card so had no access to cash.'

'Right.' It made no sense to her, but she had bigger fish to fry. She had decided she wanted to look her best for this dinner. No, she needed to. 'Pip, I've got grey hair.'

'OK. Well, yes I can see your roots are a bit . . .' Pippa grimaced.

'I normally have my hair coloured every six weeks, it's been months and now I'm going properly grey.' She sounded hysterical. 'Not only that but my hair is a mess.' How could she not have noticed this before? Had she let her looks slide that much? Yes, she clearly had.

'Well, it's not that bad.'

'Pippa, what am I going to do? I have twenty pounds to my name and I'm pretty sure that no hairdresser will do anything for that sort of money.'

'No, they probably won't. I see what you mean.' Pippa suddenly beamed. 'I know, I'll do it.'

'You'll do my hair? Was one of your many courses a hairdressing one?'

'No, don't be silly, but we can get one of those home dye kits, everyone uses them, and I can give you a trim. After all, I cut Mark's hair.'

'Oh God, how the mighty have fallen.'

* * *

'Bloody hell this thing is heavy,' Connor huffed, as he and Gus, supervised by Freddie and Gwen, heaved the extra leaves to insert into the table.

'We did it.' Gus gave Connor a triumphant high-five as they slotted the last piece in. They then slumped down on chairs.

'No time for that,' Gwen said. 'We need to get this table set.'

'I'll help with that,' Harriet said, 'the boys look as if they need water, or a paramedic or something.'

'I'm fine,' Freddie said.

'That's because you didn't do anything.'

There were going to be nineteen people altogether for dinner, including the Singers, Mark, Loretta, Connor, Gwen, Amanda and Bella. The only absent family member was Fleur who had her best friend's birthday sleepover to go to and no one, not even Harry and Zayn, could compete with that. Although if they'd done as Edie requested and managed to get Hector to come that may have done the trick.

Gwen had reluctantly agreed to letting Harriet and Pippa help her with the dinner party. And that was only because Harriet pointed out she was joining the dinner and it would be too much to serve and clear up as well as dine with them on her own. Gwen really didn't like to accept help – getting her to agree took Harriet's most persuasive negotiating skills and left her exhausted.

For the dinner Harriet had again taken a step back, letting Pippa and Freddie take charge. She was trying to be less controlling, a tiny bit more laid-back even. When she spoke to Mimi in New York now, she didn't even feel the urgency to jump on a plane as she had done in the early days. Yes she missed her, and her other friends, and the job, or the way the job made her feel, but she was also beginning to embrace life here. It was as if she was two different people and she wasn't sure which one was the forever Harriet, or if either of them were.

And, of course, she had the challenge of the sanctuary to deal with. It might not be quite the knife-edge job she was used to, but now they were a few months into their year already and she was aware that they had a lot to do to fulfil their father's terms. The fête had raised just short of five-thousand pounds, which was an amazing achievement, although that included Hector's money and the subsequent donations that his publicity generated. However, along with regular collecting tins and other fundraising bits and pieces they still had a long way to go. Harriet was beginning to panic, because it seemed like such a long haul. She was planning on spending the weekend reviewing fundraising ideas; clearly they needed to up their game.

She dressed carefully for dinner. It was nice to make the effort, which was so rare these days. Pippa and the hair dye they bought from the chemist hadn't done a bad job. She actually wondered why she felt she needed to spend so much as it didn't look that different from when she spent hundreds of dollars.

There was a knock on her bedroom door.

'Come in,' she shouted.

The door opened slowly and Gus poked his head round.

'Oh you look nice,' he said.

'Thanks, I was going for something a bit more than nice,' Harriet retorted. She was wearing a designer black dress, long, fitted at the top, flowing at the bottom. She had put on a pair of her favourite heels and clipped her hair back on one side with a diamanté hair slide, and she felt glamorous. Yes, it might have been a bit too dressy for a dinner party at home, but she didn't know when the hell else she would get to wear it. Not to feed the ponies, that was for sure.

'It's a beautiful dress.' Gus smiled. 'But you're my sister, so nice is probably the best I can offer you. But do I look all right?'

Harriet studied her brother. He was wearing a tailored suit but no tie, which suited him, he looked smart but not as if he was going to the office, and more trendy than an insurance salesman. He was less uptight than usual. As she studied his face, she realised he looked young too, handsome. Better than she had seen him in a long while, actually.

'Very nice, but why are you worried about what you're wearing?' She thought, having almost overheard his conversation with the pigs, that it was for Amanda's sake but she didn't want to let on.

'I'm not,' he replied quickly. 'But you know, this dinner, I know the ladies coming from the gardening club are making an effort, they've been telling me about getting their best dresses out all week, so I didn't want to let them down.' Even though his confidence seemed to be growing by the day, the insecurity was still there at times.

'You look great,' Harriet said and gave him a reassuring hug. 'And your ladies love you, so I really don't think you need to worry.'

Freddie was mixing drinks in the drawing room when Harriet and Gus walked in together. Loretta was sitting on the sofa, trying to look demure, but in a dress so tight Harriet was sure she could count her ribs, she was failing. She gave her a kiss on the cheek. After she got over her comments on the house, Harriet quite liked Loretta, although they didn't spend that much time together. Her stories of the fashion industry fascinated her. She was still a little bit confused as to her and Freddie's relationship, but only because they seemed so different, but that might just be Harriet being a snob. After all Loretta was so good-looking, what man wouldn't want to date her?

Pippa was wearing a smart but very middle-aged shift dress with kitten heels, pearls at her neck and her hair swept up and off her face. She looked lovely as she always did, if not a little old-fashioned and different to the style she adopted during the week. Weekend Pippa dressed very differently, and Harriet found it puzzling. Mark had opted for a suit with a tie and since the summer fête had gone back to being his usual charming self. Harriet thought maybe he was just ill and she vowed to give him the benefit of the doubt. After all, neither Pippa nor Freddie gave her any reason to think they weren't happy in their relationships, so who was she to judge?

'Right, try these.' Freddie handed out drinks, some kind of vodka-based cocktail.

Harriet took a sip. 'Bloody hell,' she said. They were good but strong.

'Listen, Fred, put some more mixer in or the oldies from the village won't even make dinner, actually not sure even I will,' Gus instructed and went to help Freddie dilute the cocktails to a safer level.

'How are you, Loretta?' Mark asked.

'Yeah, pretty good actually. Nice to see you again, Mark, you all right?' Loretta shrieked.

'Yes, I'm very well thank you.' Harriet liked the fact they made such an odd pairing. Mark, charming, traditional and a little uptight, and Loretta, gorgeous, sexy and uninhibited. Mark always blushed when he spoke to her, but Loretta didn't notice as she flashed her long legs at him.

When Connor escorted Gwen into the room, Harriet could almost hear her own sharp intake of breath. He was wearing smart trousers and a shirt, and he looked incredible. She couldn't help herself weaken, as she let him kiss her cheek.

Everyone greeted each other and then, with Freddie's safer cocktails in their hands, they waited for the rest of their guests.

Bella and Amanda arrived at the same time. Bella looked pretty in a floral dress, wholesome with her short hair held off her face with an Alice band – she had an old-fashioned look about her. Amanda had also definitely scrubbed up well. Her long red hair hung down her back, she was wearing a trouser suit and she had make-up on. Harriet had always thought she was attractive, but tonight she looked stunning. She could see why Gus had fallen for her, even though he hadn't told her as such.

Introductions were made, Harriet noticed Gus flush with pleasure when he gave Amanda a kiss on the cheek. Shortly after, the village fête committee arrived en masse, led by John, who wasn't wearing his morris-dancing outfit, but a normal grey suit. Harriet felt irrationally disappointed.

They were all welcomed into the drawing room, cocktails were distributed, and as the older guests sat down, they all started chatting excitedly.

Samuel was sat next to Loretta and he seemed quite

smitten with her as he proudly told her how many stalls he had erected in his time.

'Oh well unfortunately I couldn't come to the thingy,' Loretta said. 'I had to do a weekend cleanse for a modelling job.'

'What's a weekend cleanse?' Hilary asked. She was wearing a suit which was similar to her husband's, although with a skirt rather than trousers.

'You don't eat, but drink juice and have colonic irrigation,' Loretta explained.

'What's colonic irrigation?' John asked.

'They stick something up your bum and—'

'Right, well that's all lovely but perhaps we should go through for dinner,' Pippa said quickly. Freddie was almost doubled over with laughter and Connor was staring very intently at the curtains.

As Loretta stood up to take Freddie's outstretched arm, she managed to give a bit of a flash of her crotch, and no, she wasn't wearing knickers. Harriet rushed to Samuel's side, he looked as if he was going to collapse.

'I've never seen one like that,' he said to Harriet, shaking his head. 'Not in all my years.'

The table looked spectacular, if she did say so herself. Although Gwen deserved most of the credit. The two silver candelabras were lit, the cutlery glinted and gleamed. Vases bursting with short-stemmed roses were dotted along the table, giving off a heady aroma. Heavy crystal glasses were laid out, for both red and white wine and water.

'Wow,' Margaret said as she saw the table. 'This is beautiful.'

'You did this for us?' Dawn asked.

'I've never seen a dinner table this beautiful,' Gerry added.

Gwen beamed.

'We did it for you all.' Harriet smiled, feeling warm towards their guests.

'We did,' Pippa said, bursting with pride. 'So, let's all sit down and enjoy a lovely dinner.'

Freddie and Pippa had put out name places and Harriet wished she hadn't trusted them with it. Or at least she could have come in and changed them round. She was wedged between Samuel, who still hadn't recovered from Loretta's flashing, and Gerry, who had Gwen on his other side. And the first thing Samuel told her was that she was sitting next to his bad ear so she'd have to shout. She was further annoyed that Connor was at the other end of the table to her, wedged in between Bella and Loretta who was already making him laugh.

'Right,' Freddie said, standing up. He had taken the position at the head of the table, Pippa was at the other end to him, as tonight's hosts that seemed appropriate. 'We are here because of the success of the summer fête and that is down to everyone in this room. Well, not quite everyone, Mark, you did nothing, Loretta was too busy starving herself to come, but everyone else played a crucial part.' He paused and laughed.

'What Freddie is supposed to be saying is that we'd like to welcome you here tonight to say a big thank you for your help and support with the fête, for making it the success it was; Mark did help, he supported me and Loretta supported you, so anyway, we are looking forward to building on it in years to come,' Pippa finished. Everyone clapped and the starters arrived.

'Shall I say grace?' John asked. And before anyone could reply he did just that.

'Amen,' the table echoed before they started eating. Harriet couldn't remember the last time she'd said grace – school, of course.

'So, we thought tonight would be a good time to talk to you about our next idea,' Pippa said. 'We want to do something at Christmas and we'd like you all to be involved.'

'First I've heard of it,' Gus said. Harriet was in the same boat.

'The idea is to create a winter wonderland here, possibly over a weekend. Connor, we thought we could get the ponies to act as reindeer to pull a small sleigh, we'd get fake snow and the villagers could all come, have a mince pie, mulled wine and carols.'

'Is it a bit ambitious, do you think?' Gerry asked. 'I mean, fake snow . . . where do we even get that?'

'If we kept it small, in one of the paddocks near the sanctuary, we could do it. We thought that perhaps a simpler event, but one which would be lovely for children and adults alike,' Freddie explained.

'Could we set up a stable nativity scene, you know with real people?' John sounded excited. 'And the other animals could join in with that.'

'I could play the Virgin Mary,' Hilary offered. Freddie choked on his wine.

'And I'll be a wise man,' Gerry said. 'I was always a shepherd at school.'

'Well, we've got a donkey.' Connor grinned.

'Great idea, and we can also have a grotto with Santa. Mark, you fancy being Santa?' Freddie asked. Mark spluttered. Harriet wasn't sure why Freddie had decided to

201

tease Mark so much tonight – maybe because he had flirted with Loretta.

'As we said, it's in the very initial stages, but we thought we could raise some much-needed money and have a lovely community event at the same time. What do you think?'

Harriet listened as everyone chipped in ideas and said what a great event it would be; normally Meadowbrook didn't have a big Christmas event, although their father invited most of the village up for a party when he put up the Christmas tree. And Amanda said she and her team could create a Christmas display with holly, ivy and Christmas trees, which Gus enthusiastically said he would help with. Bella said she already could see the PR opportunities, wondered about celebrities, as everyone around the table got swept up with the excitement of the idea.

'You're having Santa, he's the biggest celebrity, the only one you need at Christmas,' Margaret pointed out.

'Well, apart from Jesus of course,' John said, quickly.

'There you go, we've got Jesus and Santa, what more do we need?' Freddie said.

'It'd be nice if you could get Christopher Biggins too though,' Edie finished.

By the time the starters were cleared away, the Meadowbrook winter wonderland was looking like a reality. Harriet thought it was a great idea and was proud of how Freddie and Pippa were throwing themselves into it. Loretta said she would dress up as a sexy Mrs Claus and Samuel yet again looked as if he would have a heart attack.

'I was thinking, Connor, we could do a photo calendar to sell around the time of the event,' Bella suggested, clapping her hands excitedly.

'I'm not dressing up or taking my shirt off,' Connor added quickly.

'Connor, you might be a good-looking bloke but I think she meant a calendar of the animals,' Gus said, good-naturedly. Connor blushed. Bella put her hand on his arm.

'I was, but if you want to be in it, then . . .'

'No, no, the animals would be great.' Connor's cheeks reddened.

'I'll get it set up.' Bella smiled at him.

Harriet narrowed her eyes; was she flirting with him again?

'What about cost? We don't have any money,' Harriet said.

'I'll get a sponsor. It won't cost a penny and if we can sell loads of copies . . .' Bella might look sweet, but she was also determined.

'Hilda would make a great December, if we could get her in a Santa hat. What do you think, Harry?' Connor said.

'She'll probably refuse to wear it, but it's worth a go,' Harriet mumbled.

She tried to quell the feelings of jealousy shooting through her. She sipped her wine and tried to concentrate on Samuel. He was a dear man, even if she had to shout into his ear. Luckily before she was almost hoarse, John began talking about the morris-dancing competitions he'd been to, and the correct way to use the sticks and hand-kerchiefs. It was quite an education.

'Edie,' Pippa said. 'Can I ask you about your hip?'

The table went silent and, for a moment, Edie looked upset.

'Hey,' Gus asked, putting his hand on her arm. 'What's all this?'

'Oh nothing much, I need a replacement, but what with waiting lists as they are, it's taking a while. I mean I've been on the list ages now and my mobility is getting worse. But I don't like to make a fuss.'

Harriet glanced at Gus and Pippa.

'What about if we arrange it for you?' Harriet said. She knew it was what her father would have done, and David had said that money was available to help those who were involved in Meadowbrook. Apart from his own children, it seemed. Edie had been helping with the gardens for years now, and she was a big part of the Meadowbrook community, so she was pretty sure they should help her.

'How? Can you jump waiting lists?' Margaret asked. 'Only, if she could have it done, it'd be a new lease of life for her. She's worried, really worried, that she might have to give up the gardens.'

'Margaret, don't tell them that,' Edie chastised.

'But it's true isn't it, love,' Rose said, looking concerned.

Edie was flushed as all eyes were on her.

'I had my knee done last year and it made such a difference,' Dawn said. 'At the fête I was almost running around selling raffle tickets, like a spring chicken I was.'

'And my Brian had his done and, well, let's just say it reignited sparks which I thought were long gone,' Mary said, which was too much information for anyone but especially poor Samuel. Harriet thought if he lasted the night it would be a miracle.

'Well, Edie, you are one of our most valuable gardening club members so I need you to have it done,' Gus pushed gently.

'Are you saying you are going to pay for her to go privately?' Mark asked, loudly. Everyone looked embarrassed. Harriet glared at him in the hope that it would shut him up.

'Shut up, Mark,' Freddie hissed.

'No, I couldn't let you,' Edie said. 'I wouldn't dream of it.'

'And who will pay for it? I mean whose money will be paying for it,' Mark continued. Charming Mark had once again been replaced, it seemed.

'Certainly not yours,' Freddie snapped.

'I'm not a charity case,' Edie said, lip trembling. 'Never have been, never will be.'

'That's ridiculous,' Harriet started. 'You work on our gardens for nothing, if anyone is a charity case it's us. If you let us do this it only benefits us after all.'

Gus looked at her gratefully.

'How so?' Edie asked, suspicion etched on her face.

'Well you're my star gardener, isn't she, Amanda?' Gus asked.

'Certainly, Edie, I mean you're all great, but, Edie, no one knows roses like you do. I learn from you, so what would we do if you can't help us because of your hip?' Amanda backed Gus up. 'The rose garden is pretty much all down to you and it was one of our star attractions at the open day. Everyone said so.'

'Well, if you put it like that.'

'It's non-negotiable,' Pippa said as she looked directly at Edie.

'For God's sake,' Mark muttered under his breath.

Harriet sat alone in her father's study nursing a brandy. The door was shut and the lights were off; she didn't want anyone to join her, so she was almost hiding as she sat on the sofa, blending into the dark colours. She was feeling conflicted. It had been such a lovely evening in many ways, but then when it had been time to leave, the fact that Harriet was alone hit her hard, almost winded her. She was beginning to resent how much time self-pity seemed to be taking up, but she couldn't help how she felt.

Connor had walked Bella to her car and then she heard him say that he'd love for her to drop him home, she felt a stab of jealousy, especially when Bella said it would give them the chance to discuss the calendar.

Amanda took a taxi home, she'd had quite a lot to drink, but Gus insisted on calling and waiting with her for it.

Gwen had gone to bed, Mark and Pippa had headed off together, and Freddie and Loretta had talked about a nightcap before heading up.

Despite not missing gutless Zach, as she now thought of him, she missed the physical intimacy. She missed having someone kiss her, take her hand, take her to bed—

She almost jumped as the door opened, interrupting her thoughts, and two shadowy figures emerged. She stayed, camouflaged on the sofa, as they both stood with their backs to her. She almost didn't dare breathe.

'Look, we better not linger here in case we're seen but, Loretta, this family is intent on giving all the bloody money away,' Mark said.

'Yes, but it's their dad's money,' Loretta pointed out.

'No, it's ours. I mean, it will be theirs, after this year. You see, I'm not sure how much Freddie told you about this pre-will business, but at the moment our partners are pretty much penniless. But they won't be. Soon they'll be rich, but not if they give all the bloody money away. Which is why I asked you to meet me.'

Harriet couldn't believe her ears.

'I see, you mean the animals, old ladies' hips, whatever.

You fink, there'll be nothing left for us,' Loretta replied. 'You know I fought you were being a bit dramatic when you said we needed to take action, but maybe you're right. I mean, what if Freddie never has any money? What would I do then?'

'Exactly, Loretta. The bloody Singers are too intent on being do-gooders to even think rationally. Look, I think we need to join forces. I've been giving all this a great deal of thought; the house is a problem. It will always belong to the four of them, so the best thing we can do is to get them to sell it. Then we can split the money four ways. Along with the rest of Andrew's money, we'll all be sitting pretty.'

'But how do we do it, they seem to quite like this 'ouse?'

'I don't know, but if we put our heads together we'll come up with something, surely? I mean, the ideal would be if Harriet buggered off back to New York for a start. She's far too in control of the family. She's our main stumbling block.'

Harriet had to stuff her hand in her mouth to stop herself from shouting out. Thank God she was a stumbling block. But where had this come from?

'But not now? I mean, you don't want her to go now?'

'No, of course not.' Impatience was creeping into his otherwise charming, and very quiet, voice. 'No, darling girl,' the charm was back, 'we need to get this year out of the way, so they get the money, but we can plant the seeds for selling the house at the same time. I'll work on Pippa, you do the same with Freddie, and we'll meet up regularly for updates. Basically, we need to make sure that Harriet doesn't make them do anything stupid with the money.'

'OK, Mark, after all, I've been bankrolling Freddie for long enough, it's about time he took care of me. So yes, what you're saying makes sense. And I thought that Harry was a bit cold if you want to know the truth. She's all right, but she doesn't exactly try that hard to be friendly.'

'You are so right, she seems to treat us both like we're outsiders. Before I go tomorrow I'll give you my mobile number you can text me if you need to.' Mark sounded almost excited. 'Right, we better go now, but Team Get-Rid-of-Meadowbrook it is.'

'All right, Mark, I'm right behind you. After all, Freddie and me are going to get married and have kids, so we need all the money we can get.'

'Same for Pippa and me. I'm not letting anyone stop us from getting our hands on that inheritance.'

As they left her alone again, Harriet didn't know what to think. So yes she had had her doubts about Mark before, and she was pretty sure that Loretta was just being swept along with him, but she didn't think he was that desperate to get his hands on Pippa's money. And she had been nothing but nice to him, hadn't she? And all along he'd been trying to trick them all.

Chapter 19

'Gus, would you take a turn with me around the gardens,' Harriet asked, sounding like someone from a Jane Austen novel.

'What?' Gus shot a sideways glance at his sister. She shrugged. 'Sure, but it's cold, so we'll need coats.'

'OK, Dad,' Harriet teased.

'Why aren't we invited?' Freddie asked.

'I want to talk to Gus about something, and no it has nothing to do with you two,' she lied. In fact it had everything to do with those two.

It was October, the nights were drawing in, the mornings were dark and Harriet was bracing herself for her first Meadowbrook winter in years. Of course New York was cold, freezing even, and snow far more frequent than in the UK, but it was different back home. The chimneys had been swept – which again made Harriet feel as if she was in a different century. The chimney sweep was actually Samuel's son, he was sixty, and looked like a younger version of his father. The fires were ready to go, they had enough logs from the estate to last forever, although they offered them to the villagers who still had open fires and Gus was going to be delivering them with Freddie in tow. See, Dad, she said, even Freddie was throwing himself into village life now. They were such a part of Parker's Hollow at times even Harriet felt as if she'd never been away. And they were living the way their father wanted them to. Harriet didn't think about luxury items, despite living in luxury. She spent hours in second-hand clothes at the animal sanctuary. She worked on figures, she thought strategies, but instead of doing so in a swanky office, she did it in her father's study wearing thick woollen socks with her feet up on one of the sofas.

But Harriet was still swinging on her emotional pendulum. One minute she was fully ensconced in Meadowbrook, as if she'd never been away. Her and Connor's friendship was growing with the work they did together at the sanctuary, she felt closer than ever to her siblings and she was throwing herself into her ambitious fundraising plans which were keeping her busy. But then, at the same time, she was feeling like a kid who had never grown up. She knew it was time for her to think about her future but those thoughts kept making her want to run away from them. So she did. She hadn't heard anything else from Mark and Loretta about their plans, but Loretta hadn't been at Meadowbrook that much because of work, and Freddie had even visited her in London last weekend.

Harriet had decided that she would keep quiet about what she overheard until there was something concrete, but now, as that hadn't happened, she decided to ask for Gus's advice. Hence the suggested walk around the garden.

She pulled her coat on, wrapped a scarf around her neck and slipped her feet into wellingtons. It was amazing how this was becoming second nature to her the way power dressing used to be. They were one month short of being halfway through the year and although she couldn't believe how fast it had gone in many ways, in others she felt as if she had been here forever and New York was another life.

'Ah there you are,' she said, as Gus joined her. He was also wrapped up against the cold. 'Come on, let's go.'

They started walking along the back path and up towards the vegetable garden which was growing in size. The flower garden was looking very different now, it was all being prepared for winter, the rainbow colour was fading away, but it still looked neat and green, luscious and healthy.

'So, I think I know what you want to talk to me about,' Gus said with a wry smile.

'You do?' She linked his arm, brow wrinkled.

'And I appreciate you taking me away from the others,' he continued.

'Well I had to.' Harriet was a little confused.

'You didn't, I mean you could have said it in front of them, but I appreciate that you didn't. I mean, I will tell them soon but it's good to discuss it with you first.'

'What would you like to tell me?' Harriet said carefully.

'Oh, Harry, I am so happy.' Yup, Gus had no idea. Harriet sighed, this was obviously not going to be the conversation she thought she was going to have.

'I'm so pleased.' Her mind was ticking over.

'I mean, when I asked her out, well I never thought she'd say yes.' Ah, the penny dropped.

'So you finally asked Amanda out?'

'Isn't that what you wanted to talk about? I mean, I know it's taken a while, but for so long I have felt so disjointed from everything. After my divorce I lost myself, or maybe I lost it when I was married, but I didn't feel I could be close to anyone. Dad, well he noticed but when he tried to talk to me about it, I closed up.' His words were gushing out, tempered with excitement. 'But I felt distant, estranged from everyone in my life, you, Pip, Freddie, Dad, and especially Fleur. I didn't know how to be Fleur's dad so I just bought her presents, and hoped she wouldn't need anything else. For the longest time I felt like a shrunken version of myself, I guess.'

'I understand,' Harriet said, her heart going out to him. 'I've been feeling a bit like that since New York. When you're hurt, it's sometimes easier to retreat.' There was a degree of this still.

'Exactly. But, you know, being here, with you all, and the gardens and painting again for the first time since childhood, I began to feel myself coming back. Bonding with Fleur and with you all, well, it really has helped me, healed me, does that sound cheesy?'

'Totally cheesy but also quite lovely.' Harriet wiped a tear from her eye. She loved Gus so much, and his happiness, well, that was enough for her. For now anyway.

'So, I've been spending time with Amanda as you know and she's lovely. So down-to-earth, normal, but also attractive and funny. Nothing like Rachel! So it took a while, but I asked her out. I felt like a teenage boy who'd never been on a date ever, but I did it, she said yes and, well, we've been out a few times.'

'Ah the mysterious trips.' She couldn't believe she hadn't noticed, but Gus had been going out more, mumbling about painting. And of course she didn't question him.

'It's not been easy, dating on my allowance. God, it really is like being a teenager. But we've had a picnic, and I took her to the cinema, we both enjoy walking so that's good and cheap!' His voice was rich with happiness; a different Gus to the one she first encountered when she came home. This was the Gus that he should be.

212

'Oh God, what was Dad thinking putting us on this budget. I can't even afford my usual brand of face cream let alone Botox. If I end this year looking like a wrinkled old hag, I shall not be happy.'

'Ha. I think Dad wanted us to be dependent on each other and Meadowbrook. I think he thought if we all had access to money, we'd be out having fun, not doing what he wanted us to do at all.'

'He really wanted us to reconnect as a family, didn't he?' Suddenly sadness crept back in.

'He did, and this was his slightly ridiculously bonkers way of doing it.' She reached out and squeezed his hand. As Gus squeezed hers back she felt the warmth and the closeness of their childhood in that moment.

'Anyway, back to you and Amanda.' She needed to keep her emotions in check.

'Yes, I didn't want to involve anyone else in our relationship, not until it was a relationship, but last night we talked and we've decided to give it a proper go.'

'Yes!' Harriet hugged him. 'Have you told Fleur?'

'I'm going to tell her tonight when I pick her up from her mum's. I think she'll be pleased, and I've invited Amanda to have dinner with us tomorrow night, and her daughter if that's all right, as long as Fleur is happy with it.'

'Wow, I'm sure that Fleur will be happy for you.'

'What if she's not? What if she doesn't like it. Not only have we only just bonded, but she's never known me to be with anyone but her mum, so I really don't want to upset her.' Suddenly the confident happy Gus fled and the insecure one stood in his boots. Harriet hugged him again.

'She wants you to be happy. Trust me, tell her as soon as you pick her up. And if for any reason she does object, tell her you'll let her watch *Single's Holiday*.'

'Not in a million years.' They both laughed. Harriet shelved the conversation she actually intended. Gus didn't need his happiness being rained on right now. No, she didn't have it in her to burst that bubble. She was back to being the only one who knew that Loretta and Mark were planning anything and the only good thing was that they would both be at the house this weekend so she could keep a close eye on them.

'Right, well let's go back, I've got animals to take care of.'

'You enjoy the work at the sanctuary, don't you?' Gus asked.

'More than I will ever admit,' she laughed.

She was hoping to see Connor as she slipped Hilda back into her kennel and went to the office, but he wasn't around. Since the fête quite a number of dogs and cats had been rehomed but more had arrived. They had received donations from the families that took the animals, but then when they had to process the new arrivals, the money wasn't coming in fast enough. And if they didn't up their game and raise more money . . . Well she couldn't think about what would happen then.

It seemed for each animal they found a home for, two more would arrive. Harriet didn't understand it, how people treated their animals, and it made her sad, angry and also determined. And poor Hilda was still there; Connor said she was too big for most houses and too boisterous for most people. Every time he talked about families coming to see her, Harriet had mixed feelings. She loved Hilda so much but she knew she couldn't take her, not when her life was in such limbo. If she did go back to New York – and she had to face it at this point in time she wasn't sure what would happen – then Hilda couldn't possibly go with her. It was no life for a lovely, friendly dog who needed company to live with someone who worked fourteen-hour days.

'Hey, Harriet.' Jenni walked into the office. She was wearing a thick jumper and wellies, and had obviously been seeing to some of the animals.

'Hi, Jenni, is everything all right?'

'Yes, fine, all running efficiently as always.' She smiled. 'We have two families coming in this afternoon who want a cat, the radio interview that Connor did locally has led to a flood of donations and some more enquiries from people interested in rehoming, I've put it all down there for you to see.' Connor hated doing any publicity but he grudgingly admitted it worked for them.

'That's so good about the donations. But the sanctuary runs efficiently because of you guys mostly,' Harriet said.

'Actually, don't tell Connor I said this, but it's running so much better since you started. I mean, the systems you put in place make everything so much easier but, well, that's between you and me.'

'Mum's the word. By the way, where is Connor?' Harriet tried to sound nonchalant.

'Oh he's with Bella, they're looking through the final calendar today.'

'Really? No one told me.'

'Those two have been quite secretive about it, wouldn't be surprised if she wants to show him more than the calendar, if you get my drift.' Jenni winked.

Harriet pursed her lips; she did get her drift, but she certainly didn't want to.

By the time she headed back to the house Harriet had taken Hilda for her second walk, worked in the office, fretted for hours and as she reached home, to finish her day off nicely, she bumped into Mark on the doorstep.

'Harriet,' he said, looking awkward. He must have noticed how she had been a lot less friendly to him lately, ever since she overheard him in the study. She tried to act normally, but now she knew he had some kind of agenda, she didn't trust him and she didn't like him. Not that she knew what to do about that.

'Mark. Is Loretta here yet?' she asked, raising an eyebrow.

'No idea, how would I know?' he replied.

'Oh, it's just you two seemed awfully pally last time you were both here.' She grinned, enjoying Mark's discomfort.

'Oh there you are.' Pippa came out of the house. 'I thought I heard you arrive.'

'Darling,' Mark said, dramatically. 'I've missed you.' He kissed his wife as if to illustrate the point.

Harriet left them to it before she said something she'd regret. She went to her father's study, something she often did to feel close to him, but just as she'd settled at his desk, Pippa bounded in and closed the door. She was wearing her cross look.

'What?' Harriet asked.

'Why were you rude to Mark?' Pippa demanded.

'I wasn't,' Harriet replied, innocently. She kept forgetting that Pippa was no longer the sweet baby of the family. She had grown up and, although still a sweetheart, she had a tough side, more like Harriet than either of them realised.

'But he said you were.' She looked a little doubtful. Harriet was glad, until she had something concrete she didn't want to worry Pippa and, also, Mark might just think he was acting in her sister's best interests. Although she doubted it.

'I'm sorry he thought that. I'm happy to apologise.'

'Oh.' Pippa was wrong-footed. 'Well thank you, Harry, he can be a bit sensitive, you see.'

'Pip, you know in Dad's pre-will, why did he think Mark made you unhappy?' Harriet had tried to broach this subject with her before but she'd always got the brush-off.

Pippa slumped into the chair opposite.

'Daddy was wrong.' Her mouth was set determinedly.

'Dad was never wrong.' Harriet was glad of having his nearly last words to back her up. 'I mean, he was right about how messed up my life was, right?'

'Look, I might have been a bit down once or twice, but it wasn't Mark's fault. There's always more going on behind closed doors, it's just that Dad didn't realise that.'

'And are you going to tell me?' Harriet wanted to know what was upsetting her sister.

'OK, so no one else knows but we've been trying for a baby.'

'Ah.' So that made sense.

'I desperately want one, but it's been two years now and nothing. I went to the doctor and he ran tests and I'm fine but Mark, well . . . he won't go. He says that it just takes time.'

'Ah.' Harriet saw it more clearly; poor Pippa and it couldn't be easy for Mark either. 'But you need to insist he gets tested, so then if there is a problem you guys can find a way round it.'

'He's promised to think about it. With Dad's death I told him I wasn't going to wait forever. I think Mark is worried that he can't father a child and then I'll blame him or something, and part of me hopes that it will just happen but it hasn't, has it? And he knows that.'

'I'm here if you ever want to talk, Pip. I really am, and if you need anything.' She was a bit taken aback, because now that complicated everything, didn't it. Was that why he was so concerned with selling the house and securing Pippa's inheritance? But then, Mark was successful so they didn't need the money . . . Was it because he was scared that Pippa would leave him? Just what was it?

'Thank you. Harry, I am glad we're all back together. I know you thought this idea of Dad's was crazy but it feels as if we are becoming a family again, doesn't it?'

'Yes, baby sister, it does.' And it did – a family with problems, happiness, issues and dastardly partners, it seemed, but a family all the same.

Chapter 20

Harriet felt proud of her siblings as she listened to Freddie speak. They were in the dining room for the grand unveiling of the final plans for the winter wonderland and although both Freddie and Pippa were acting as if they were organising something on a par with the Hyde Park event, it was impossible not to get caught up with the buzz that could be felt in the room.

The village fête committee had become the winter wonderland committee and they were all brimming with enthusiasm. Because morris dancing wasn't right in the winter, John the vicar was in charge of the nativity scene and one of the shelters in Gerald and the ponies' field was being commandeered for Mary and Joseph's stable. All the animals who were comfortable with each other were going to be involved, so the ponies, Gerald, the blind sheep and her lamb guide and the three goats were all being roped in. The ponies were going to masquerade as reindeer, the rest would be in the nativity scene, although, as Connor tried to point out, they couldn't be guaranteed to stay still. Agnes the sheep probably would though, and her lamb never left her side so they would be fine, but Gerald and the goats would possibly wander off. The pigs, who had another two members to their community – it seemed micropigs that grew to be full-sized pigs were quite common – were being excused, as were the alpacas, and Elton and David on the grounds they would possibly kill someone, or in the pigs' case, eat them. Harriet listened patiently as Connor explained which animals they could use and tried not to think of him as being ever so slightly mad.

They were holding open auditions the following day to find a Santa and all the Singer siblings were going along. Although it was Pippa and Freddie's show, Harriet and Gus wouldn't miss that for the world.

Winter had properly enveloped Meadowbrook, and with less than two months to go until Christmas, it was also getting incredibly busy. The animals needed more care in the winter, some dealt with the cold better than others. But many of the outdoor animals spent most of their time in their sheds and stables. Harriet worked mainly with the full-time animals, as she called them, the ones who would never be rehomed, and not only were she and the alpacas now on good terms, but she also had managed to be accepted, albeit grudgingly, by Elton and David. Of course Hilda was still her best pal here at Meadowbrook, and Harriet found that increasingly she dreaded her getting rehomed, which was selfish of her.

It was funny how they had all now become so involved in the animal sanctuary that it was part of their normal routines. Freddie would skip off from breakfast to feed the chickens who he now claimed he was fond of. He also took photos of various animals for social media, which he and Pippa worked on together. They usually concentrated on the ones who needed rehoming, and Harriet had to guiltily admit she took Hilda for her walk whenever she saw them approach with cameras.

They had hired an extra member of staff full-time, a young lad called Damian, who had left school with few GCSEs and had no idea what to do, but loved animals. Connor had taken him as a sort of apprentice, so he was cheap. And although at seventeen he was too old for her, Fleur had developed a bit of a crush. The good thing was that she wanted to spend even more time at Meadowbrook, the downside was that Gus looked as if he was going to kill the poor lad, although he'd done nothing to encourage Fleur.

Harriet was more concerned with the money they needed to raise, the figure was still vast and she was reminded of this every day. They were nearing the ten thousand pound mark, but it was no way nearly enough at this stage in the year. After the winter wonderland, fundraising would be her priority; if she had to go and roam the streets, knocking on doors herself, then she would do it.

She turned her attention back to Freddie who was still talking. As well as the winter wonderland plans, Bella was also going to show the final proofs for the Meadowbrook Animal Sanctuary calendar this evening. Gwen had jumped at the chance to do some baking so they were going to have a buffet and cakes rather than a sit-down meal.

She snuck a glance at Connor who was standing just a bit too close to Bella for her liking. When Harriet had asked if anything was going on between them, he told her they were friends, just working together closely on the calendar, but she didn't quite believe him, and she was being eaten up with jealousy along with everything else.

'So, in conclusion,' Freddie said with a great flourish, 'this is going to be such an amazing community event that we hope will be the first of many winter wonderlands in years to come.' Everyone applauded.

'Oh it will, I'm sure of that,' Rose said. 'I've already got my Angel Gabriel costume ready.' Harriet tried not to laugh. Rose was the angel, John and his wife Hilary were going to be Mary and Joseph, the rest of the committee were either shepherds or wise men, which meant the average age of the nativity was about sixty-five. Thank goodness Edie was getting her new hip and wasn't going to be able to participate, she wanted to be the baby Jesus and Samuel had even offered to make a full-size manger for her out of a coffin he had lying around – no one dared ask why he had it lying around.

Instead, they were making a small manger and using a doll, which was a relief, because when Margaret started suggesting they go and see the village's new mums about borrowing an actual baby, Harriet almost had kittens.

'Right, well now I would like to show you our Meadowbrook animal calendar, which we are going to sell at the winter wonderland and also if any of you want to take some to sell, then that would also be great, well necessary really,' Bella explained. She pulled a sheet off the easel.

'This is the mock-up, which is why it's so big, but it'll be A4-size when it's printed.' Harriet looked and saw a photo of Elton and David, horns entwined on the cover. It read 'Meadowbrook Calendar' and then the name of a sponsor, which was a soft drinks company based in Somerset who were also one of Bella's clients. They had paid for the calendar to be made so they got their name plastered on every page. Harriet had to admit, as Bella turned the pages, the woman had done a great job. And Connor, of course. If it hadn't been for him, the animals wouldn't have looked so good or as natural in front of the camera. Hilda was December and she had a Santa hat on and looked so incredibly adorable that Harriet felt a tear rolling down her cheek. Connor saw and came over and hugged her, which she was grateful for.

They all burst into applause when the calendar presentation was over and agreed that it would be a huge seller in the village. Translation – they would make everyone buy a copy.

Once the house had been cleared and Gwen established that no one wanted dinner because they'd been eating all afternoon, Harriet decided to hit the gym, because once again she found herself alone. Gus had taken Fleur to Amanda's house. The two girls, Hayley, Amanda's daughter and Fleur were getting on really well and Gus and Amanda definitely seemed serious about each other. Both divorced, both with one child and both still fairly young, so well suited. Mark had taken Pippa out to dinner, Freddie was off somewhere, she wasn't sure about Loretta, and Connor had left at the same time as the others saying he needed to go and check on the animals.

Running gear on, Harriet made her way down to the gym. She was amazed to see a phone sitting on one of the tables by the pool as she passed, then she noticed Loretta was in the sauna. She spent a lot of time in the sauna, trying to sweat off any calorie that may have accidentally passed her lips, she told Harriet. After hearing her with Mark, Harriet was struggling with her relationship with Loretta, up until then she had liked her, even if she didn't quite 'get' her relationship with her reckless brother, but she was quite entertaining and didn't mind taking the mickey out of herself. But now she felt angry and suspicious. Did she just want Freddie for the money he would have one day?

Feeling furtive, she seized her opportunity and picked the phone up. She couldn't believe her luck when she saw it was unlocked. Glancing around, she opened the text messages and bingo! Loretta wasn't smart or deceptive enough to delete her messages and so Harriet, one eye on the sauna door, scrolled until she found some from Mark. There were quite a few; she read as quickly as she could. Feeling totally enlightened, well a bit, Harriet returned the phone to the position she'd found it in and carried on to the treadmill. She wished she'd brought her phone with her so she could photograph the messages as evidence, but she was a bit of a novice at this spying business.

As she ran, she sank into deep thought about what she'd read. Money was clearly the motivation and Mark was the brains behind the operation. His messages reiterated to Loretta that the family, left to their own devices, would probably let Harriet decide the fate of the house and the money. And he was sure that Harriet would use it to control them all forever – she really didn't think she had given him any reason to think this, although of course she accepted she was a bit bossy and had sort of taken the role of head of the family. But when and if their father's money went to them, her siblings would do what they wanted with it, Harriet had no interest in trying to control them. Meadowbrook, similarly, would be a decision they would all make. Why was Mark trying to make her the bad guy? Or was it because he wanted control of Pippa's share, so by making out Harriet was a threat he could not only get Loretta on board but, down the line, maybe Pippa too? Well it seemed it was working, as Loretta had said in her messages that she loved Freddie but she didn't want the poor version for too much longer, so she would do what was needed to make sure that he didn't fritter anything away.

The grand plan, thus far though, seemed to revolve around splitting the family up, making the siblings fall out somehow, especially with her. She was a little unimpressed; reading the texts, the plans weren't exactly military grade, but then Mark and Loretta weren't either. In Loretta's last text she said she needed to get Freddie to marry her, and Mark said he had some ideas that he would share with her when he saw her. Harriet realised that now she needed reinforcements and the only person she could turn to was Connor.

The hot water cascaded onto her, and Harriet felt her nerves rising up. She wasn't sure why, but she felt anxious about going to see Connor. Which was ridiculous, he was her friend, someone she saw practically every day and their friendship had been rebuilt. There was no friction between them, apart from her unresolved, bubbling feelings, of which he knew nothing. She gave herself a pep talk – she was a big girl, it was time to act like it.

She dressed carefully in skinny jeans, an oversized charity shop jumper and her boots. She blow-dried her hair and added just a touch of make-up to hide the lines that seemed to burst onto her face with increasing regularity. If she was in New York she would be having regular Botox but here, well, it wasn't something she thought about – not that she could afford it. Had she forgotten how to take care of herself? In New York, she was always groomed and one Saturday a month the whole day would practically be taken up with it all, although the cost of that day was about six weeks' allowance. God, she never thought about spending money before, but now that was a jolting thought. But then, in New York, natural was a dirty word.

She walked briskly to Connor's cottage, playing in her head what she would say. She would tell him about the night in the study, how Mark and Loretta joined forces and then she would tell him about the text messages. She hoped that he would know what to do.

Lights blazed in the cottage, and she knocked at the door. She waited a few minutes – for a small cottage, Connor seemed to take a time to open the door, but finally he was there, facing her. She ignored her little flutters and smiled, this was important, more important than her silly feelings after all.

'Harry?' He looked confused.

'Sorry to drop in unannounced but—'

'Who is it, Con?' a voice said. A voice she immediately recognised as Bella. Her face ignited; she felt her cheeks burning.

'It's Harriet,' he called back, still looking a little uncomfortable. Within seconds, Bella was at the door.

Shit, Harriet thought, what now? She wished the doorstep would open up and swallow her whole.

'Hey,' Bella said. Harriet noticed how comfortable she seemed as she put her hand on Connor's arm. Why had no one told her they were together. Why hadn't he? Friends, my arse, she thought as she noticed that Connor couldn't meet her gaze.

'Hi, I'm so sorry I interrupted your evening,' she started, with no idea where to go from here. 'I had no idea . . .'

Connor looked embarrassed, she noticed, but Bella seemed oblivious.

'I told Connor we should have told you all that we've been seeing each other, but he thought we ought to keep it professional. I knew you wouldn't mind though?'

'Er, no?' Harriet replied. She glanced at Connor who was studying his socks.

'I mean it's been a month now so it is time we came clean.' Bella beamed like the cat who got the cream. The bloody PR who got the Connor.

Harriet tried and failed to process the words. A month! Her insides burned with something akin to humiliation again. She had vowed after Zach she wouldn't be humiliated again, but look, here she was standing on Connor's doorstep feeling like a lovesick teenager. And that wasn't even the reason she was here.

'Well, that's great, and as I said, sorry for interrupting your evening. I just wanted to—' What the hell could she say? 'I wanted to check on Hilda, she seemed out of sorts earlier.' The tips of her ears felt a bit hot, she hoped the lie wasn't too obvious . . . Of course it was bloody obvious.

'Oh she's fine, H. I put them all to bed an hour ago and she was wagging her tail happily.'

'Hilda's such a lovely dog, it's a shame we can't adopt her,' Bella said.

We? They'd been seeing each other a month and they were a we. And besides, over her dead body would they get her dog. She scowled.

'Are you all right?' Connor asked, noticing.

'Yes of course, just worried about Hilda,' Harriet snapped. 'Right, I'll be off then, enjoy your evening.' Harriet kissed Bella on the cheek – in her head she slapped her – and totally ignoring Connor she left.

The big heaving sobs took her by surprise, but as she walked home her body convulsed. She had kept telling herself that nothing would ever happen with Connor, but now it was clearer than ever. Despite her pep talks, deep down she obviously still hoped he would suddenly realise it was her he wanted all along. But no, it was Bella. And who could blame him? Bella with her Audrey Hepburn hair, her tea dresses and Alice bands, whose pink cheeks were so naturally wholesome, and her prettiness, her sweetness, was there for all to see. She had the whole package. Lovely young lady who any man would be lucky to date. Not anything like her.

If Connor wanted a woman like Bella, it was apparent that he would never want someone like her. Ball-breaker Harriet, with her razor-sharp tongue and a hairstyle to match. Who could reduce grown men to tears in under ten words or sometimes with just a look. Who was ambitious and intelligent and no shrinking violet. She was so far from Connor's type, that was brilliantly clear to her now. Time to move on, and it was definitely time for Harriet to move forward. She had been stuck in the Meadowbrook mud for quite long enough.

Chapter 21

'If you could state your name, age and why you are here,' Freddie asked, doing his best Simon Cowell impression.

'You know my name,' Samuel said, scratching his head.

'Well yes, but I'm trying to be professional.'

'Oh, right you are. I'm Samuel and I'm here to audition for the role of Santa.'

'Your hearing's pretty good,' Harriet said, they were behind a desk and he was a fair few feet away from them.

'Oh yes, I've got a new hearing aid, got it off the telly.' He sounded very pleased with himself.

'Can we please get on with it,' Freddie stormed.

'I think the high-waisted trousers have gone to his head,' Gus chortled.

'Samuel, do you like children?' Pippa asked, the only sensible one among them.

'No, can't stand the little blighters.'

'NEXT,' Freddie shouted.

'Freddie, can I just say, that we are looking for someone to dress up in a red suit and hand out presents, not the next big thing,' Harriet said. They had seen six potential Santas so far. In Freddie's eyes they were either too old, too young, not fat enough, or in the case of Samuel not keen on children.

'That last guy, Julian, he looked shifty.'

'Freddie, he was an accountant,' Gus said, exasperated.

'Exactly.' They all shook their heads.

Gerry walked in.

'Hi, I'd like to apply for the job.'

'Aren't you too busy with the winter wonderland?' Pippa asked. 'I thought you were one of the wise men.'

'Well I was,' Gerry said. 'But then I got to thinking, anyone can be a wise man, especially as John said all we had to do was stand there looking wise.'

'Well, after today, I'm not sure anyone could do that actually,' Freddie said.

'Go on, Gerry,' Harriet sighed.

'Well, I thought that maybe someone else could be a wise man and I could be Santa.' He wrung his hands nervously.

'OK, but you're a bit thin,' Freddie said. 'And do you like children?'

'I really do. And not in a bad way. And I was thinking, what if we made the grotto look a bit like Santa's house? I mean I could do that, I could put up a shed easily and we could decorate it, and make it look like the kiddies are coming into Santa's front room. I'd do it all for free, you know, to raise money for the sanctuary.'

'I'm liking this.' Freddie leant in closer.

'And I thought we could get Gwen to be Mrs Santa, and she could help me hand out the presents.' Harriet was sure she could see him blushing.

'Why Gwen?' she asked.

'Just thought she would make the perfect Mrs Claus really.' Gerry studied his feet.

'I agree,' Freddie said. 'But I'm not sure you really could pull off Santa.'

'Give me ten minutes.' Gerry left, then came back with a bag and nipped into the loo. When he emerged he was wearing a Santa outfit, complete with cushion stomach, beard, glasses and was carrying a sack.

'Wow,' Harriet said. 'He's not bad.'

'Not bad, I think he looks fantastic,' Pippa said.

'I agree,' Gus added.

'OK. You're hired, but on the condition that you get the grotto done and you have to persuade Gwen to be Mrs Claus,' Freddie said.

'Thank you, thank you, I cannot tell you how much this means to me. It's everything.'

'Hang on, Gerry, where did you get the costume from?' Harriet narrowed her eyes.

'Ah, well I just happened to have it lying around. You know.' He shrugged. No one knew quite what to say.

'Can you believe this is our first Christmas without him?' Pippa's voice choked with emotion as they sat at home later. Harriet, blinking back tears, merely shook her head.

Harriet had quickly realised that when you lose someone you love everything immediately became a notable first. For example, her first birthday without him, which largely went uncelebrated so soon was it after her father's funeral, the first summer fête, and now the first Christmas was looming. Her father had been gone for nearly seven months. They were more than halfway through their year at Meadowbrook and with every passing month, the further away he felt. She missed him every day, it had become part of her, a part she welcomed because it kept

231

him with her, but she also despised because it broke her heart anew when she woke most mornings. The contradictions of grief.

She knew her siblings were feeling their father's absence keenly as well as they prepared for the Meadowbrook Christmas event. Andrew Singer loved Christmas. For the first few years after their mum died, she vaguely recalled a slow-down in festivities but then as they had got older, at some point, he had rallied again. Christmas retook its rightful place as the highlight of the year at Meadowbrook. They had the biggest tree, which always took a few men to haul into place, piles of presents that, when they were still kids, their father's long-suffering PA would spend hours in Hamleys collecting, and a big party every year. He had done this up until last Christmas and Harriet had been the only Singer not there for both the cocktail party and Christmas Day. They had Skyped her, all of them, and after she'd hung up she had cried, real, fat tears, because she felt then as if she was estranged from her family and her old home.

She shook her head. Memories haunted her, at the time she felt justified in her life, now she felt anything but.

Her father tentatively asked her to come home every year since she moved to New York – and now she would give anything to reverse her decision and say yes. Instead she always told him that work made it impossible, which was true, but only because she was so married to her job. Last Christmas she had worked Christmas Eve, then on the day itself she had gone to Mimi's apartment where six single New Yorkers had drunk cocktails and eaten sushi in front of a fake designer Christmas tree. She had gone into the office the day after Boxing Day and that was Christmas over. She told her father that she couldn't get a flight back in time, which she couldn't for just two days, but she should have tried harder.

However, Christmas this year was going to be different; she was determined to make up for lost time. She would never fully forgive herself for the time she had missed spending with her dad, but she would try to make it up to her siblings who were still very much here.

Harriet had taken charge of decorations and the tree which, as per tradition, was delivered from a local forest. It was huge and dominated the grand hall. It had taken them nearly all day to dress it, but as they rediscovered the decorations collected throughout their childhood it had been a bonding moment for them all. Emotional, moving and cathartic. Luckily it was also included in the household expenses. If the siblings had had to fund a tree themselves, it would have been little bigger than a twig.

They worked together as a team: Harriet, of course taking charge, Pippa doing exactly what she was told, Gus quietly moving decorations to make it more artistic and Freddie teasing everyone. Fleur joined in, the excitement of youth still apparent as she gabbled about what she was hoping to get for Christmas.

'Fleur, you know I told you about Granddad's will? I literally have very little money, in fact I am pretty sure your allowance is bigger than mine,' Gus said grimly. Harriet knew he was worried about Christmas, about how he was going to spoil his daughter the way he usually did.

'I know, Dad, but you don't need to spend money on me, what I'd really like from you is a painting of Zayn and Harry.'

'The kittens not the popstars, right?' Freddie asked.

'Of course the kittens.'

Gus reached out and hugged his daughter. 'I might not have got much right in my life but I got you right.'

'Yeah but Mum takes the credit for it,' Fleur teased.

Gwen appeared with mulled wine. She'd been feeding them all day, and bringing drinks as well. This was an event for her too.

'Dad would approve,' Harriet said as she stood back to admire their handiwork. The four siblings stood in a row, Fleur slightly in front of them and Gwen to the side, beaming.

'He really would.' Fleur gave her aunt a hug.

'I just wish he was here,' she replied, furiously wiping tears from her eyes.

Freddie had decided that the Meadowbrook tree light switch-on would rival the Oxford Street event and that they would hold their father's traditional cocktail party for the occasion; live music – carols from the church choir – guests, and of course a celebrity to switch the lights on. And all for free. Gwen had managed the catering, she had done her fair share but Hilary had made a number of quiches and someone else mince pies, so they were well taken care of. And luckily her father's alcohol supply had not been totally diminished. Whether it would last the year was another issue. Even though Freddie had cut down drastically on his drinking, with the support of his siblings of course, they still managed to get through a fair bit.

Rising to the occasion, Freddie, had taken total charge of everything other than the food. Harriet watched with amusement as he walked around with a clipboard, making notes and barking orders at Pippa, who was sweetly humouring him. He was in his element, not thinking about drinking but actually throwing himself into making it work. Pippa had organised a Christmas-themed raffle, and although they weren't charging their guests, they had pots for donations all round.

The winter wonderland committee, plus the gardening club and those who were involved with the animal sanctuary were attending, along with the family, Mark and Loretta. Over fifty guests, including Hector who was fast-becoming the Meadowbrook resident celebrity, roped in to do the switch-on. His reputation was being turned around. Despite still displaying no discernible talent, he was always on morning TV, in gossip magazines and there were rumours that he was going to be on the next series of a celebrity jungle show that Harriet hadn't seen. According to Greg, pictures of him singing with the church choir might help him secure the show, as long as he could pull off looking angelic convincingly. Amanda and Hayley were joining them along with Bella who was now very much a part of Connor's life. It hurt Harriet, but she managed to keep out of their way as much as possible and did her best not to think about them. Harriet was good at shutting her feelings down, but she wasn't quite good enough anymore.

Harriet put on a red cocktail dress and it looked striking with her pale skin, even if she was the only one to say so. Although she had put on a few pounds since eating Gwen's food, it suited her, and she felt a little softer, less angular, although still slim. She secured a simple pendant around her neck, which looked long and slender. She'd bought the Valentino dress last year. Gosh, she had baulked at the price tag, it was scarily expensive, but so beautiful and it flattered her more than any other dress ever. As did the saleswoman, who kept telling her how stunning she was.

And Harriet had felt stunning. She'd bought it for a big charity event – goodness how different from the events they had here at Meadowbrook. It was an event to be seen at, her bank had purchased two tables, she was on one with clients, Zach and his wife on the other. It was the only time she had met Zach's wife actually. And she knew that she wore the dress as a statement – she didn't want to be overshadowed by anyone. And not only that, but they had drunk so much champagne – vintage, of course – that in the auction she had paid a ridiculous amount of money for a weekend on Long Island. One which she still hadn't gone on. It made her feel a little sick actually, the obscene amounts of money they spent in the name of doing something good but actually just indulging them-selves. She couldn't even remember the cause. God, for the first time since being home she felt ashamed about her lifestyle, as well as ashamed about Zach.

And she was also guilty about Connor. She knew that on some screwed-up Harriet level, she was hoping that he would notice her tonight. Would see how stunning she looked in her designer dress and feel *something*. She knew she probably needed years of therapy, but she wanted to believe he would look at her and suddenly the room would fade away. The penny would drop that he was in love with her and he would finally find the courage to tell her. She pinned a lot of unrealistic expectation on that red dress. But then, for what it cost, it should have delivered her a whole happily ever after.

There was a knock on her bedroom door.

'Hello,' she bellowed, Pippa walked in. 'Hey, Pip, are you wearing the same dress as you did to the dinner party?' she asked as Pippa appeared in a black shift dress.

'No, that was a different dress,' Pippa replied. She went

to sit on Harriet's bed. 'You look gorgeous,' she enthused to Harriet. 'That colour really suits you.'

'What's wrong?' Harriet asked, sensing something in her sister.

'Nothing, I just wanted to get away from Mark for a few minutes. I know, I know, he's only been here a short time, but he's in a terrible mood and I don't know what's wrong with him.'

'Have you asked him?'

'Of course and he just mumbled something about being tired and having to carry so much of the load without me at home. Then he went silent.'

Harriet hugged her sister, she loved her so much, if only she could expose Mark for what he was, not that she knew exactly. And with that and the fact that he was holding Pippa off about the fertility tests, she didn't have a good feeling about him, about them. She was beginning to think that her dad was right.

'Oh, I need to get myself in a better mood, poor Mark's probably just working too hard and I should cut him some slack. I mean, look at it, it's all around us at Meadowbrook this Christmas. Gus and Amanda, Connor and Bella and I even heard Gerry say he was going to ask Gwen if she'd like to have her tea with him as soon as he could pluck up the courage,' Pippa giggled, her bad mood evaporated. 'Hopefully not when they are dressed as Santa and Mrs Claus though.'

Harriet was still smarting from the mention of Connor and Bella. 'Gwen?'

'Yes, they've grown quite close over the plans for the winter wonderland. He's the same age as her, why can't they find happiness?'

'I would like nothing more, but you know how Gwen

was, she vowed she never would look at another man, like Daddy did after Mum.'

'Things change when you're facing being alone. She misses Dad, they were almost in relationship if you think about it,' Pippa pointed out. Harriet baulked, appalled at the suggestion. 'Tut, Harry, I don't mean a sexual one, but having her here stopped him from being totally lonely and vice versa. Now if Connor marries Bella—'

'You think it's that serious?' Harriet wondered if she had managed to keep the horror out of her voice.

'She's smitten. She keeps asking me if I know how he feels about her. She's so neurotic about him, it's cute.'

'And do you?'

'Do I what?'

'Know how he feels about her?'

'No, Connor doesn't say anything to me, you know what he's like. Has he said anything to you?'

'No,' Harriet admitted, not that she'd given him the chance.

'Well anyway, let's hope next year we see Meadowbrook weddings. Freddie and I could organise them!' Pippa looked so alive, so full of happiness for others, which was characteristic of her. But Harriet was determined: one of those weddings would take place over her dead body.

Her feet were killing her, but as her Jimmy Choos were telling her, they needed to be worn, and they did look perfect with her red dress. She had practically run in heels on a daily basis in New York, but since being home she was always in flats, so her feet had forgotten how to cope. She sat down on the stairs, to give her feet a break and studied the party.

The Christmas tree looked magnificent, her father

would approve, Hector, had made rather a meal of turning on the lights – the old ladies lapped him up. Edie, still recovering from her hip operation, had still managed to pursue him with an impressive amount of vigour, despite a walking stick.

Now the party was in full swing. Carols had been sung, mulled wine and Freddie's Christmas cocktails were being drunk, chatter filled the air, as the guests spilled into the drawing room and dining room as well as the grand hallway. Mark was holding court as if he was the lord of the manor, Freddie was charming everyone, Pippa was playing her hostess role perfectly and Gus and Amanda were almost inseparable. Fleur and Hayley had slunk off to Fleur's room to watch Netflix and Harriet had promised not to tell, although she was tempted to go with them. Gwen was laughing at something Gerry was saying and Harriet wondered if there could be happiness for her again, she sincerely hoped so; no one deserved it more than Gwen. And finally, Connor and Bella. It wasn't the first time she had seen them as a couple but it sucked more and more each time. The longer they were together, the happier they appeared, the worse it felt. Having to greet them, be nice, when she wanted to tear Bella's perfectly neat dark hair out and kick him where it hurt, almost killed her. Just look at them, the perfect couple! Bella was gazing adoringly at Connor who had his hand on the small of her back, in a way which made Harriet burn with jealousy as she choked back tears.

'What's up?' Hector sat down next to her. He was wearing a ridiculous Aran jumper and a pair of smart trousers which made him look about fifty from the neck down.

'I was just thinking how happy everyone looked.'

'Yeah, it's that sort of party, isn't it? A happiness party.'

'My invite must have gone astray,' she stated.

'I'm having a marvellous time, although if I get groped one more time by one of your old ladies, I'm going to sue for sexual harassment.' Hector was deadpan, Harriet glared at him in surprise but he burst out laughing. Harriet giggled.

'They've got no money,' she pointed out.

'Ah, then I'll just have to avoid them.' He looked at her, his blue eyes were quite hypnotising. 'By the way, Harriet, you look bloody sexy tonight. I don't suppose you know anywhere to hide, you know, your bedroom perhaps?' He raised an eyebrow suggestively.

Harriet threw her head back and laughed. 'You are far too young for me,' she said. 'Although that doesn't seem to be deterring Edie.' She pointed to where Edie was approaching them.

'They're going to do my favourite song, "Rockin' Around the Christmas Tree", Hector, so will you dance with me?' Edie asked as she reached the stairs.

'Are you sure you should be dancing, with your hip?' Harriet said. Hector looked terrified.

'Well he can hold me and we can just sway,' Edie suggested.

'Off you go, Hector.' Harriet pushed him up. It had almost cheered her up, but then as she saw Bella kissing Connor under the mistletoe she knew she had to escape.

She grabbed a bottle of Prosecco from the side and made her way to the back door, where without looking back she slipped her stockinged feet into wellingtons and took off for the summer house. She opened the door which they still never locked and made her way inside. It smelt of paints, Gus had been painting more than ever since he'd been dating Amanda, just as their mum used to. Her throat choked with emotion and her eyes filled with tears. Here, among all these people, among her family, she felt so lonely. She never cared about being in a relationship in New York. Probably because she was still harbouring feelings for Connor. They might have been buried so deep that she didn't even know they were there, but that didn't mean they weren't. It was crazy. She was so devoted to her job because she didn't have to worry about emotions and now, at home, it was all emotions and she didn't know how to deal with them.

Just as she took a swig from the bottle, the door opened.

Panicked, and without thinking she dived over the back of the sofa so she was hidden. Harriet's first thought as she heard footsteps approach was she hoped it wasn't Connor and Bella.

'I thought we would never get away.' Mark's voice rang out in the dark.

'I know, those randy old men kept trying to look up my skirt. Even the vicar,' Loretta replied.

'Who can blame them, you look ravishing, my dear,' he said.

'Fanks, Mark, you're well nice.'

'Yes, well, that's why we need to get our partners to sell Meadowbrook. Because I'm desperately trying to do the right thing, because I *am* nice.'

'OK?' Loretta sounded as confused as Harriet felt.

'You know Pippa is so sweet and innocent in so many ways, now she seems convinced that they will run Meadowbrook as an entertainment venue, all of the Singers working together, like the Waltons or something.'

'And that would be bad?'

241

Harriet had no idea if that was what Pippa was thinking, she hadn't mentioned it at all.

'Of course, it would be a disaster. I mean apart from lack of experience, it's a very risky business, they would have not only to pay for the upkeep of Meadowbrook but also set up an expensive business which would probably take all their inheritance and then they'd probably lose it all.'

'But Freddie's run a business before,' Loretta argued. Not the best argument, admittedly.

'Which folded. Do you see what I'm saying?'

'Ah, yes, I do see. After this year they still won't have no money and then they'll lose the lot.'

'Yes, exactly. So I am trying to protect Pippa's inheritance from that disaster.'

'And I need to do the same with Fred. I mean my work isn't what it was, what with me being nearly thirty.'

Harriet had to stop herself from choking. Loretta was way past thirty.

'And, I want to get married and have kids and stuff. Oh and I've always fancied a yacht. Will we be able to buy one?' she continued. Harriet shook her head.

'Yes, if you do as I suggest, you will.'

'Right, so what's the plan?'

'I've been thinking and as I said before our main problem is Harriet. We need to isolate her from the others, because without her they won't be able to do anything. So my first idea was to let some of the animals out of the sanctuary one night, and then make out that it was Harriet. We'll leave an item of hers there to incriminate her.' Mark chortled.

Harriet bristled.

'But how do we do that? And how are we expected to

let the animals out?' Loretta sounded horrified. 'And don't forget, the animal sanctuary needs to survive in order for them to get the money.' Goodness, Harriet thought, she had been paying some attention.

'We'll pay someone to do it. I have someone in mind already, don't worry I've thought it all through. This person will let the animals out and then someone will find Harriet's scarf or something. And, of course, it won't be enough to shut the sanctuary down, but you and I can step in like heroes and help clear up afterwards! Gosh, it'll be perfect. Harriet will get the blame and everyone will turn against her. And they'll start listening to us more. Then we convince them that Harriet has lost the plot, and ta-da, she has no influence over the house or the money any more.'

Harriet couldn't believe it. What had she done to become his enemy?

'But that's not going to be enough, is it?' Loretta said, and Harriet agreed, it sounded like the thinnest plan she had ever heard.

'We're also going to sabotage the winter wonderland. What I thought, and I think it's quite genius if I do say so myself,' he laughed. 'We could kidnap the baby Jesus, and leave a ransom, then we plant the doll on Harriet, and when we, being very good citizens of the village, lead them to her, the village sees her for what she is and turns against her. It will divide the siblings, make Harriet unpopular all round and hopefully as soon as the year is out she'll scarper back to New York.' He laughed. Dastardly bastard, he really had it in for her. 'I'll say to Pippa that I'm worried about Harriet as she seems so miserable and strange and I'll convince her that Harriet's having some kind of breakdown and you can do the same to Freddie.'

'Oh, Mark, you're well clever. So, I tell Fred that I'm worried about 'Arriet because she seems to be getting more unhinged, so it will seem like she would do the fings you said.'

'Oh, Loretta, we're on the same page. Yes, we'll both bring up concerns for Harriet's mental health first. I always thought she was a bit of a weirdo anyway.' Harriet had to stop herself from getting up and throttling him.

'Oh, Marky, I can't wait, and then they'll sell the 'ouse because none of them will want to live at Meadowbrook or with each other.'

'Exactly, Loretta. And we'll be not only rich but also rid of the bloody annoying siblings and life can get back to normal. Only a better normal.'

'Right, babes, we better get back, Fred'll be missing me.'

'I wish I could say the same for Pippa,' Mark sighed. 'She's too busy for me these days. But soon, it'll be just the two of us again and she won't have any need for Meadowbrook or her bloody awful siblings. Or you for that matter,' Mark muttered, just loud enough for Harriet to hear.

'What?' Loretta asked, already by the door.

'Nothing, let's go.'

Harriet drained the bottle. She didn't feel nearly drunk enough to forget about what she had just heard and what it meant for both her and Meadowbrook. Oh, of course she could foil their silly plan, although she had to admit she needed to get Connor involved now, but why did they have it in for her?

Chapter 22

'So, you're telling me that sometime between now and the winter wonderland weekend, the animals are going to be let out?' Connor said. 'That's less than a week.'

'Yes, I'm aware of that,' Harriet replied, sounding tetchy. She thought Connor would be outraged when she told him of Mark and Loretta's plotting, instead he looked, well, almost amused. 'And so I thought we should hire security. But of course we can't afford it.'

'Right, so you think it's that serious?'

'I do, I've overhead Mark and Loretta plotting, they want us to sell Meadowbrook, so they'll have the money from the house as well as the inheritance, well their partners will, and by default they think they'll get their hands on said money, they want us all to fall out so that there's no question of Pippa not running back to Mark and letting him have everything. They also want to make out I am mad. I wanted to hire a private detective to look into Mark, but I couldn't afford that either.'

'Sorry, Harry, this is crazy. You wanted to hire a detective?' Connor shuffled from foot to foot. He scratched his head and glared at Harriet with something akin to disbelief.

'Yes.'

'What would Pippa say?'

'Hopefully, when we've exposed Mark for what he is, thank you.'

'Harry, you know it's dangerous meddling in people's relationships.'

'Whatever.' God Connor was a sanctimonious idiot sometimes. 'But you know this involves all of us, so I'm not just going to stand by and let Mark disrupt the sanctuary, the village and my family. And I thought you would be concerned about the welfare of your animals. I thought you might care a bit that they were going to try to discredit me!' she shouted.

'OK, OK, fair enough.' Connor held his hands up in mock surrender. 'Let's start again. So, the plan to let the animals out, tell me about that.'

'He said he was going to pay someone, he said he had someone in mind. So I thought, as we can't pay for security, we need to get John the vicar and his morris dancers involved.' Harriet tried not to think how ridiculous that sounded.

'You are going to get the morris-dancing guys to be security?'

'They've got sticks,' Harriet smarted.

'They also have bells, which would warn off any would-be perpetrator,' Connor said. Then he burst out laughing.

'You are not taking me seriously.' She almost stamped her foot in frustration. 'Do you have any better ideas?' Harriet folded her arms. 'Connor, it's not funny.' He was almost doubled over laughing.

'It is a bit. I mean, kidnapping the baby Jesus, which is in fact a doll, and pinning it on you, I mean, genius. John would be so angry, he'd never speak to you again.'

'They are going to tell everyone that I'm unhinged. Me! I'm the most sensible member of my family.'

'Well apart from Gus—'

'Shut up.' Harriet thumped Connor on the arm, something she did a lot when they were younger. He rubbed his arm. 'Anyway, now I know everything, I am going to put a stop to it. And before you ask, no I'm not going to tell Freddie and Pippa yet, not until I have concrete evidence.'

'Right, so we're in cahoots on this, just me and you?'

'Yup.'

'Fine, if you need to talk about it, then talk to me and I agree to whatever you want regarding security. But how did you find out?'

'I happened to be in the summer house, you know the night of the cocktail party, when they both snuck in.'

'What were you doing in the summer house?' he asked.

'I needed some space, you know I was a bit drunk and I often go to the summer house to be alone.'

'And while you were there,' Connor asked, 'Mark and Loretta came in to talk about their plan?'

'Yes.'

'Right, well I guess we better go and see John then.'

He might not be taking her seriously but she was glad that she had Connor onboard now – it made her feel slightly less alone.

'John, we have a bit of an odd request,' Harriet said as they found John in the pulpit practising his sermon.

'What can I do for you, Harriet?'

'Well, we need the skills of your morris dancers actually,' she said.

'Ah.' He smiled, suddenly.

'Although not to dance,' Connor added quickly.

'Well that's all we do really.' His brows furrowed.

'John, as I said this is a bit odd, but, you see, the animals and the nativity scene might be in a spot of bother.' Harriet explained about the threatened sabotage without naming Mark or Loretta, but instead saying they had an anonymous tip-off. Connor had his hand over his mouth, clearly trying not to laugh. 'You see,' she said as she finished. 'We can't take any chances, not with the animals or the baby Jesus.'

'No, no, of course not. Right, well it's four nights until our big day, so how about I draw up a rota of my men to be in place overnight until then.'

'Oh, John, would you? I mean, I'm not sure we're dealing with master criminals but—'

'We will have our sticks with us, and our bells and anything else we could use.'

'Your handkerchiefs,' Connor suggested. Harriet scowled at him.

'Yes, in case we need to apprehend the villains, we can use them to tie them up, good thinking, Connor.'

Harriet rolled her eyes. She hoped she wasn't going to regret this.

'If you need anything, call me or Connor, but, John, we are going to try to keep this from the others, I don't want them to worry.'

''Course not, Harriet, we will be very discreet. It's in the morris dancers' code, you know.' Of course she didn't. She didn't even know they had a code.

Two nights later, the phone woke Harriet, she reached out, grabbed it and put it to her ear.

'Hello.' She blinked her eyes open and yawned.

'It's Connor. You were right, John just called me, can you come to the sanctuary office?'

'I'm on my way.'

Harriet managed to drag herself out of bed, she pulled a cardigan over her pyjamas and, pushing her hair out of her eyes, she quietly made her way downstairs. She put her wellies on, grabbed Gus's coat, picked up a torch and, glancing at the time – 2 a.m. – she made her way to the office. It was freezing and she almost skidded on the icy ground as she rushed, taking the short cut down to the office.

She walked in, and in front of her was Connor, also in his pjs, John, Steve and Burt from the morris dancing squad and Damian, Connor's apprentice, whose wrists were bound with a yellow handkerchief.

'Oh dear,' Harriet said. So this was who Mark had paid, a clueless kid. 'What's going on?'

'This young man was apprehended trying to let the donkey, the ponies and the goats out of their shed. When asked what he was doing, he said he was checking on them, but obviously our job was to apprehend him, and notify you,' John explained, sounding incredibly formal.

'Our bells alerted him, but as he tried to run off, Steve here tripped him up,' Burt explained.

'You guys are amazing,' Harriet said, impulsively hugging them. They were a bit taken aback but they let her.

'What the hell were you really doing, Damian?' Connor asked. He sounded calm but he looked furious and his eyes flashed angrily.

'Nothing, I was just—'

'Don't bother lying, we know. What we want to know

is how much Mark paid you,' Harriet took charge. She almost felt sorry for Damian, barely seventeen he was out of his depth, but she guessed he was cheap.

'How do you . . .?' Damian's eyes swung between Harriet and Connor. He looked petrified.

'It doesn't matter, but I know that Mark put you up to this. Were you also supposed to kidnap the baby Jesus?' Harriet almost wanted to laugh at her words.

'Yes, but I've been watching, they never leave it in the manger overnight. They guard it like it's a real baby rather than a doll.' Damian shook his head.

'Well he is the Messiah,' John said. 'And a lot of work went into all of this. I bet you didn't think of that, did you?'

'No.' The poor kid looked shamefaced. Harriet just felt relieved that nothing had happened to the animals.

'Damian, I gave you a chance because your parents said how much you wanted to work with animals. I don't understand why you would mess it up, risk it, for what? A few quid.'

'A hundred,' Damian replied. 'I'm sorry, but he said there would be more money if I did this job and I'm saving up for a car.'

'A hundred quid, that's ridiculous. You do know we could have you arrested, for breaking and entering. You could have a criminal record, all for a hundred pounds.' Harriet saw him cower at her words. 'And those lovely animals could have been badly hurt when you opened the gates to the field as you were trying to do.'

'Please, please don't have me arrested.'

'We won't,' Connor said. 'But I hope it was worth losing your job over.'

'What will I tell my parents?' He looked terrified.

'The truth, because otherwise I'm going to tell them,' Connor offered. 'First rule of being an adult is that you have to take responsibility for your own actions.'

'Sorry,' Damian mumbled again.

'I'll walk you home, if you make me a hot chocolate,' Connor said. John, Burt and Steve had frogmarched Damian out and were taking him back to his house.

'Isn't Bella waiting for you at the cottage?' Harriet asked, caustically.

'No.'

Silently they made their way to the house.

'So, what do we do about Mark and Loretta?' Connor asked as they nursed their hot chocolate, which she'd added a generous slug of whisky to.

'We need a plan. At the moment, if we go to Pippa and Freddie, I think Mark and Loretta will manage to wheedle their way out of it, well Mark will at least, and I'm worried that they'll turn against me. I've only just rebuilt my relationships with my siblings, I don't want to lose that.'

'No, but it's unlikely Mark will give up.'

'I need to find out what is going on with Mark.'

'But you can't hire a detective.'

'No.' Harriet had a sudden brainwave. 'But I have an IT guy in New York who used to work with my team and I can email him. I'll offer him a luxury weekend in Long Island in exchange for getting me some info.'

'Bloody hell, Harry, remind me to never cross you. But how are you going to afford that?'

'Oh I bought it in a charity auction ages ago, didn't know what I was going to do with it, so now . . .'

'Perfect.'

'Well let's see what he comes back with, but I just know there's something going on.'

'And if you do find out more, will you tell Pippa and Freddie then?' His voice was so gentle that Harriet had to resist throwing herself into his arms.

'I don't know, Connor, I feel so out of my depth.' *And with you*, she silently added.

'H, your methods might be slightly unorthodox but, look, you got this sorted. And to be honest, I think the morris dancers were quite enthusiastic as security guards, I'm thinking of making it a permanent thing!'

'Nice of you to say.'

'H, you're so capable, no wonder you're this successful investment banker, God I always knew you were destined for big things, you left the rest of us behind, and I don't mean that in a bad way. You really are amazing, you know.'

'I'm also jobless right now.'

'Hey, come on, stop feeling sorry for yourself. You stopped Mark and Loretta, and I know you'll make sure they don't let anything happen to Meadowbrook, I have every faith in you.'

'I wish I had your confidence, because I just don't know how to tell the others.'

'All right, how about we get Christmas out of the way, and then you and I will put our heads together.'

'Thanks, Con.' They clinked hot chocolate mugs and Harriet tried not to feel as if her heart was about to stop. At least she had someone on her side now in this, unfortunately though, it was the someone she wanted by her side for good and she was struggling to stop her feelings from betraying her when he was so close that she just wanted to be in his arms. She took another sip of her drink and had a little chat with herself. As she watched him, from beneath her eyelashes, she realised she needed to put those feelings aside, for now, for the future, and concentrate on getting rid of Mark and Loretta. After all, he was never going to be hers and the sooner she accepted that, the better.

Chapter 23

'Seriously, Hector, you'll be telling me you're moving into Meadowbrook next,' Harriet teased as Hector, today wearing some seriously strange country garb of tweed jacket, trousers, hat and green Hunter wellies, officially opened the winter wonderland.

'Well, I may be mistaken, but I believe I was so drunk at the Christmas party that I may have agreed to marry Edie.' They both laughed. He was becoming a bit of a Meadowbrook fixture, but as he was drawing quite a crowd and also generating a lot of publicity, she was happy to have him. And he was amusing, especially with his outfits.

The winter wonderland was packed. And as everyone had to pay a five-pound entrance fee, Harriet felt confident that that, along with Santa's grotto and some other stalls, would make quite a bit of money. She seriously hoped so. John was offering for people to take selfies with the baby Jesus for a pound a go, which she wasn't sure was strictly ethical, but who was she to argue?

Gus had hand-painted some lovely Meadowbrook Christmas scenes, which he and Fleur were selling, Gwen was busy being Mrs Claus, but Margaret and Edie – who said she was fit as a fiddle again – had the cake stall. The refreshment tent was run by the rest of the morris dancers, who were tucking into the mulled wine already, but were also paying for it, so she couldn't object. All in all it was looking to be another successful event, with the whole community involved. The ponies were standing around by the sleigh that Gerry had made, cordoned off in a pen, that he had also made, in front of Santa's grotto, which of course Gerry had made. He had spent weeks getting it all perfect and it really was, although they knew now that it was all to impress Gwen.

Connor was happy that the event was going off without a hitch. All that remained was for them to keep an eye on Mark and Loretta, she didn't think there would be any trouble, but she wanted to check. Mark looked pretty unhappy though, as he had done increasingly lately, whilst Loretta was the same as always; dressed inappropriately for a family event that was for sure, as she caused quite a stir among the men of the village and elicited scowls from their wives.

Harriet, with Connor as her partner in crime, had told the family at dinner the other evening that Damian had been fired for breaking into the animal sanctuary – Mark's face had been a picture. Loretta's smile froze as Gus spoke.

'What the hell was he doing?' he'd asked.

Harriet had replied, as innocently as she could, 'I think he wanted to see if there was any money in the office. He said he was checking the animals, but he obviously wasn't. But never mind, he's been fired and we have stepped up security at the sanctuary and also at the winter wonder-land. No one will get past us now.' Harriet made sure she looked directly at Mark, smiling sweetly at the bastard. He seemed to think she was a threat and, by God, now she actually was.

Harriet saw a local news crew arrive now, setting up to film the nativity scene. Well, as Bella billed it as the only real live nativity scene in the area, how could they resist? And despite the fact that Joseph and Mary were well past child-bearing ages and one of the shepherds – Samuel – kept falling asleep on the hay, it was quite a sight.

'It's great isn't it, Harry?' Freddie said, putting his arm around his sister. Mark and Loretta stood awkwardly next to them.

'You and Pip have done a fantastic job yet again. You know, you two make such a good team, you should go into business together.'

'Do you think so? Really?'

'Meaowbrook Events. Has quite the ring to it, doesn't it?'

'Oh my, Harry, it really does.'

Harriet stifled a giggle as Mark's jaw dropped to the ground and Loretta even had the grace to blush.

'Oh God, guys can you come here,' Pippa suddenly shouted. They all rushed to the nativity scene where everyone seemed to have gathered.

'Whats wrong?' Freddie asked, breathlessly.

'Gerald bit the sound guy,' the local news presenter, Sally Miles, explained.

'I could sue,' the guy said.

'You really couldn't, we don't have any money,' Freddie said, good-naturedly.

'What did you do to make him bite you?' Connor demanded.

'I tried to put the mic near him so he would do a donkey sound, but instead he headbutted the mic away and bit me.'

'Bella, sort these guys out, will you?' Connor said

crossly. 'Gerald doesn't know you and he doesn't need to make a "donkey noise" for you.'

'I'll sort it, Con,' Bella said calmly. But then Gerald took the hat off the sound guy's head with his mouth and started eating it.

'Oh boy, he really doesn't like you,' Freddie said.

'Not many of us do,' Sally said, laughing.

Harriet was exhausted. The field was emptying and everyone was congratulating them on the event on the way out. The kids all clutching their Santa gifts – the grotto had been a huge success, Gwen and Gerry made a great team. Gus had sold out of his paintings, the calendars had also sold out, ditto the cakes and, well, the mulled wine didn't last the day. John was delighted he had made a hundred pounds for them with his 'baby Jesus' photo opportunity.

'Right, I vote we go back, open some of Dad's good wine and all collapse in the drawing room,' Harriet suggested.

'God, yes, I am exhausted,' Pippa said.

'I thought we could spend the night in Cheltenham for once,' Mark said

'Really?' Pippa looked at him. 'You didn't say before, anyway I'm too tired.'

'Pippa, since being here you've only spent about two nights at our actual home.'

'Yes, and you know why. Dad's will. Anyway, Mark, another night, but not tonight, as I said, I just want to collapse with my family.' Her voice was strong and Harriet felt proud of her.

Mark started to speak but seemed to change his mind. Harriet had figured it out a bit more, the stronger and more independent Pippa became, the harder Mark found it to deal with. Every weekend now he was trying to get her alone, he had even suggested Christmas at their house, just the two of them, but Pippa said that as it was her first without Dad she needed to be at Meadowbrook. And Harriet got the impression that Mark wasn't used to not getting his own way, which explained why he was so worried about the money, well to some extent. She was still waiting to hear from her guy in New York, to see if he had discovered anything about her brother-in-law. She was sure there was more to it. Her instincts when it came to work were always spot on and she had a strong feeling they were in Mark's case too.

Chapter 24

Harriet took Gwen's arm as they walked across the fields to the church for midnight Mass. There was something so magical about Christmas Eve; she'd always loved it at Meadowbrook. It was cold, and frost filled the air as they strolled along; Harriet could see her own breath, hanging like a cloud in front of her. She snuggled into Gwen taking comfort from her.

Midnight Mass was a Singer tradition, for as long as she could remember. As kids, they had moaned a bit, but their father said that staying up late meant they wouldn't have so long to wait for Santa. They bought into that logic, of course.

They weren't a big churchgoing family. Their father went fairy regularly with Gwen after they all left home, but Harriet thought, with a pang, that it was more for something to do. Harriet knew stepping into the church tonight would be hard for them all, it was the first time they had done so since their father's funeral. She had a pocket full of tissues at the ready.

'Harriet, love,' Gwen said quietly.

'Yes?'

'I wondered if tomorrow, after church, I mean when I go to church not you, would it be all right to invite Gerry up to the house for lunch?'

Harriet was taken aback by the request, not because she minded but because Gwen never invited anyone to the house.

'You don't need to ask me,' Harriet said, breathing in the icy air.

'Well, I thought, I'd check. I know we're not having a big Christmas lunch tomorrow, but still it's a family day and Gerry is on his own. His daughter is having him on Boxing Day, but I didn't think that anyone should be on their own on Christmas.'

'Of course they shouldn't. And you're family, so any guest of yours is welcome.'

They were having their Christmas Day on Boxing Day because Fleur wasn't joining them until then. She always spent Christmas Day with her mother and although she said she wanted to be at Meadowbrook, Gus had gently suggested just delaying their Christmas by a day. He was willing to stand up to Rachel now but he also didn't want to cause trouble. And Harriet had reasoned, it didn't matter that they were having Christmas a day late; they were grown-ups after all.

Harriet had helped Gwen plan the big Boxing Day Christmas feast. Traditional, of course, smoked salmon and Buck's Fizz for breakfast, turkey with all the trimmings for lunch, then leftovers for supper. Amanda and Hayley would be joining them – they were also coming to midnight Mass tonight, along with Loretta and Mark. Thankfully Bella was visiting her family in Kent; Harriet wasn't sure she could cope with watching her and Connor fawn over each other over the Christmas table without stuffing the turkey up one of their arses.

On actual Christmas Day they had decided to just have a quiet day and Gwen was banned from cooking, or even making a cup of tea. They were going to see to the animals in the morning – when Gwen went to church – have sandwiches for lunch, and the plan was to watch Christmas TV in the afternoon – there were some things they needed to do, including the Queen's Speech, because that was another of their father's traditions and funnily enough without him, his traditions felt more important.

Harriet wasn't that excited about Christmas, although she had enjoyed the preparations. Last-minute shopping in Bath with Pippa, who again had led her to the charity shops to find gifts for everyone. And actually, Harriet had taken quite a lot of joy in finding bargains. She got an old cookbook for Gwen, retro food which she knew she would like, a hip flask for Freddie – she didn't like to think too much about it being second-hand – she found a book on the Impressionist painters for Gus, and a hideous Christmas tie for Connor, as a joke. Pippa had seen a pair of very hippy-ish earrings that she liked, dangling feathers, and so Harriet had got them for her. They couldn't find anything to suit Fleur, so they pooled their resources and got her a voucher for River Island. It was Christmas for under a hundred pounds in fact, and despite her looking longingly at the goods in all the expensive shops that she coveted and would have normally bought without so much as a glance at the price tag, she felt a little bit pleased with herself.

'So,' Gwen said, reeling her thoughts back to Gerry as they reached the church. 'It's really all right?'

'Of course, although it seems that all my family is paired off apart from me and Fleur and she probably has a secret boyfriend.'

'I'd hardly say we're paired off, Gerry and me. He's a nice man though and I am aware that now your dad isn't

261

around, I need to fill my time. I mean, if you lot go from Meadowbrook, which you are perfectly in your right to do, then I have to find other interests.'

'Well, if Gerry is an interest . . .' Harriet teased.

'Oh, Harry, you are awful. Anyway, there is someone out there for you, you know.' And just as Gwen said that a feather appeared from nowhere and it settled on Connor's head as he stood at the church door waiting for them.

Bloody hell, Harriet thought, shaking her head. 'Come on, let's go in.'

They all sat in the same pew as each other, Gus was next to Amanda but Harriet was on the other side of him and he gave her hand a squeeze. She could feel her father's presence, tears welled up and she knew that this Christmas Eve, she was missing him more than ever. And as she let the tears fall, Gwen handed her a tissue and put her arm around her, she felt she would give anything, anything, to have him there with her just one last time.

Her father, so strong, so certain. She wanted him to tell her what he meant when he said she needed to take a step back from work and sort out a personal life. She wanted him to explain that when she had done as he asked, it was as if her personal life had disintegrated totally. OK, so it wasn't great in New York, no she didn't have love, but she didn't mind that, but now, in Meadowbrook, she wanted love but couldn't have it. She accepted that now she didn't have her job, she was changing, or changing back to the old Harriet a bit, but it was coming with insecurities, uncertainty, worry that she couldn't do for the animal sanctuary what she needed to do, longing over Connor and then her family . . . She thought of the email sitting waiting on her computer for when she got back. How was her father so sure he was doing the right thing, when it felt, at this moment if it was anything but.

Harriet lay in bed. She was tired, yet she knew sleep wasn't going to come easily, she was too unsettled, the tears had lasted for most of the service, leaving her with a throbbing head. It didn't help that she couldn't stop staring at her laptop screen. She read the message from Nick for the hundredth time, the message telling her all she needed to know about Mark, and as a sick feeling settled into the pit of her stomach she really had no idea what the hell she was going to do. Although, of course, tomorrow was Christmas Day, so she wouldn't be doing anything just yet.

'The animals don't know it's Christmas, so all hands to the pump,' Connor ordered as the Singers lined up in front of him. Mark had even been persuaded into a pair of wellies to help walk the dogs, although he looked thunderous. Harriet, thinking of the email, of the information she had about him, wanted to shove him into the mud, but she couldn't. Not without anyone noticing anyway.

They had all got up at the crack of dawn, not, as when they were children, because it was Christmas, but because of the animal sanctuary. The full-time staff had all been given the day off, so it was down to them to run it for the day. And as they were having their proper Christmas tomorrow, no one objected. Apart from Loretta, who refused to wear wellingtons and said she would come down later. They all knew she wouldn't.

But despite a near sleepless night, Harriet had managed to find some Christmas spirit. She had taken the leftover

263

Santa hats from the winter wonderland and insisted they each wear them – yes, Mark included. They had got treats for all the animals, apart from the ones who only liked grass, and she had already taken Hilda a new collar. It had cost her more than most of the presents she bought for her family, but as Hilda wagged her tail, looking resplendent in the diamanté pink, she knew it had been worth it.

'Hello, ladies, and a very Happy Christmas to you,' Freddie trilled at the chickens. Harriet was helping him feed them. They all looked at Freddie, slightly suspiciously, Harriet thought as their heads wobbled a bit. 'See, they love me,' Freddie said.

'Just as every lady does,' Harriet giggled. 'So, are you excited about spending Christmas with Loretta?'

'I was, but she's been a bit weird. When I told her I could literally only spend pocket money on her present this year, she said she had been expecting something special. Then she asked if I had any of mum's old jewellery, like her engagement ring. When I told her that that had gone to Pippa, she went ballistic, I don't understand it.' Freddie scratched his head as the chickens scratched at the ground.

'Oh, Fred, I think it's clear she wants you to propose.'

'Propose what?'

Harriet shook her head and sighed. What was wrong with him. 'Marriage, you idiot. She wants you to ask her to marry you. Hence the chat about the ring.'

'Oh bugger, I forgot that she mentioned that before.'

'Well she hasn't told me herself, but it would make sense.' She better not admit to reading her text messages. 'Bur, Freddie, you've been living with her, so it's natural she wants to marry you.'

'Good Lord. I love Loretta, but when the business went tits up, I literally had no idea about my future, then Dad handed me this gift and, well, I'm still muddling through this year. What am I going to do?' His voice was panic-stricken.

'You don't have to do anything, Fred.' Harriet was slightly relieved that Freddie wasn't leaping to propose, it gave her more time to sort the mess out. 'No one can force you to propose or marry someone and it's a huge decision. Just tell her you need to get this year out of the way and then you can look to the future.'

'For someone so bossy you do talk sense sometimes.' He gave her an affectionate hug. 'Come on, Elizabeth Bennet is looking decidedly put out that I haven't paid her any attention today.'

'How can you tell that a chicken looks put out?' Harriet was slightly bemused.

'That could only be said by someone who knows nothing about hens.'

Harriet found Connor with the ponies and Gerald. The goats were munching grass on the other side of the paddock. She handed out carrots and stroked Brian who was the most affectionate of the ponies.

'Gus is singing carols to the pigs,' Connor said.

'Oh goodness.' Harriet looked over to where Gus was raking up, and he was clearly singing, she caught a faint 'Jingle bells' coming from across the field. 'He's so happy, isn't he?'

'He's in love, Harry,' Connor said. The way he looked at her, again as if he was seeing into her head, made her want to run away and run into his arms in equal measure.

'I know and I'm so glad he's got Amanda, she's lovely.

Which can't be said for my other siblings partners. I didn't want to tell you at Christmas, but I found out about Mark.'

'Is it bad?' His brow furrowed.

'It's really not good,' Harriet replied honestly.

'I tell you what, how about we sneak off into the summer house later and you can fill me in. We won't ruin Christmas for anyone, but it would probably do you good to be able to share.'

'What about Bella?' Harriet hoped she didn't sound as snarky as she felt.

'She's staying at her parents'. But talking of her, I must go and call her now. Can you take over here?' He handed her a bucket and walked off. She watched him go, feeling as if her heart was going to stop beating. He looked so good as he strode across the field. How could love make you feel so good, like Gus, or so terrible, as in her case? It really wasn't fair. As if sensing she was about to cry, yet again, Brian came and nuzzled her. If only people were like animals, Harriet thought not for the first time, the world would be a better place.

By the time they all met back at the office, all work was done. The animals were happy: the dogs walked, the cats fed, the chickens charmed by Freddie and the pigs sung to. Pippa came in, face flushed, followed by an angry-looking Mark.

'What's wrong?' Gus asked.

'Those bloody dogs,' Mark started. Harriet saw his back was covered in mud.

'Oh poor Mark isn't used to walking so many, the leads got tangled and, well, it was an awful mess, and he was pulled over.' Pippa's face was full of concern but her voice full of mirth.

'Not only that, but they dragged me. *Dragged* me through the mud before Pippa could stop them.'

'Oh dear,' Freddie said. 'You do look like you've been dragged through a hedge backwards,' he added.

'Not funny,' Mark said. 'I could have been seriously hurt.'

'But you're fine, come on, let's all go up to the house, it is Christmas Day after all,' Connor said reasonably.

'And I'll run you a hot bath,' Pippa said. 'You'll be cleaned up in no time, darling.'

'Couldn't have happened to a better person,' Harriet muttered.

'What was that, Harry?' Gus asked.

She blushed. 'Nothing, Gus, nothing.'

Harriet ran her fingers through her hair, dabbed a little of her cut-price lip gloss on and spritzed some of her favourite perfume, which was rapidly emptying. She had some time to collect herself before she was meeting Connor for a debrief in the summer house.

After Mark had calmed down Christmas Day had passed harmoniously. They had yet to exchange gifts, promising Fleur they would wait until she was with them, but they had a lovely lunch, Gerry had proved entertaining and clearly besotted with Gwen, and when Freddie organised a game of charades they had all joined in, even Mark gave it a good go. Loretta seemed to have cheered up as well and it had been a pretty good day all in. Gus had gone off to see Amanda for the evening and the others were all exhausted, so it had been easy for her to make her excuses.

The summer house, although filled with traces of Gus and his paintings, still reminded her of her mum. She wished she remembered more about her, she wondered if she was with their dad now. She hoped so. He had loved her so completely that she hoped they could be together. She felt the fat tears falling before she even realised, and when Connor opened the door, he caught her furiously wiping them away.

'Were you thinking of Andrew?' he asked, shuffling awkwardly.

'Yes, and Mum actually. I know how much they loved each other, I was thinking I hope they're together.'

'Oh, H, under that tough exterior you really are a romantic,' Connor teased. He always used to tease her when she was upset in order to diffuse the situation.

'Don't tell anyone,' she teased back.

'Your secret is safe with me. Right,' he said, sitting down, 'tell me about Mark.'

'It's really simple. He's broke.'

'What?'

'Yes, Connor, the successful businessman is on the verge of losing everything. The house is mortgaged to the hilt, his business has hit the buffers, a combination of bad decisions on behalf of clients and the financial climate. The problem seems to be, the more trouble he encountered, the more he panicked and the result is that he's lost a lot of money and clients. He's hanging on by a thread. So my thinking is that Pippa's inheritance, including her share of Meadowbrook, is all that stands between him and financial ruin.'

'Hence his desperation, with the stupid plan.'

'Yup, and for some reason he thinks I have too much influence over the family.'

'It's not influence exactly, H, is it, but you've always been their big sister, they do look to you.'

'And I am incredibly bossy, you can say it, Con, I do know.'

'Well, it came with the territory. When your mum died, you tried to mother your siblings, and well, perhaps you became more of a parent than a sister.'

Harriet nodded, he was right. But now they were all grown up and they needed a sister, but did she know how to do that? Was that another reason for her going to New York all those years ago? Because she didn't feel needed at home anymore when they all flew the nest? Oh God, it was so complicated.

'But what am I going to do with this information?' Harriet asked.

'Well, I don't know. I mean, you could tell Pippa, but would she believe you?'

'I have it in black and white. I mean, I know it's not strictly orthodox, but in this case I think it's for the right reasons.'

'Yes, although I can't quite believe how dodgy it all sounds.' Connor raised his eyebrow, he was so bloody sensible, Harriet thought.

'When you're employing someone on a million-dollar salary, you kind of need to know everything about them,' Harriet shot back.

'Yes, well, I pay minimal wage, so not sure I'll need his services,' Connor replied, sounding tetchy. Why did they always bicker?

'Can we not argue about the morals of this? After all, Mark is possibly going to take Pippa's money and lose that too.'

'Yes, sorry, that is a good point. Harriet, I understand we need to stop him, but let's tread carefully. I mean, he could talk his way out of this, or he could blame outside forces and say he was trying to protect her, and if Pippa believes him, then you are going to look like the bad guy for poking around.'

'OK, I'll think about it, but you know, having you as an ally, well, I need you right now.' She tried not to meet his eyes, because she felt that hers would betray just how much she needed him.

'Hey, I'm always here for you, H, my best mate.' He gave her a jokey punch on the arm. Not quite what she was hoping for.

'But Connor—' she started, unsure where she was going to go with this, but she was in agony with her feelings for him.

'What?' he asked. She did meet his eyes and she searched them for answers.

A phone rang, interrupting them.

Connor pulled it out of his jeans pocket. 'Sorry, it's Bella. Are we OK here?'

'Sure.' Harriet had to drag the words out of her. 'You go, I'll see you tomorrow.'

She hoped her voice didn't betray how she felt, but Connor didn't seem to notice. She saw him smile as he answered the phone and he looked happy.

And then there was one, she thought as she curled up on the summer house sofa.

Chapter 25

Harriet looked around the empty cottage, shivered and wondered what the hell she had been thinking. OK, so she needed space from everyone; Connor, her siblings, Mark and Loretta, and some space from her thoughts. She knew she couldn't just switch them off, but she also knew that being with the person who was breaking her heart wasn't helping her to deal with anything. She couldn't think about the sanctuary and what needed to be done there without thinking about her feelings for Connor; she couldn't think about her siblings without thinking about Mark and the state he was in. They had such a short time left at Meadowbrook, and she needed to focus on that, but at the moment she couldn't focus on anything much.

She realised she was in trouble when, in trying to figure out ways to deal with the Mark and Loretta situation – most especially Mark – her thoughts kept going back to Connor, and his deep eyes, his warm arms, his kindness, and his gorgeousness. Which wasn't helpful at all. She needed to deal with her feelings for him, and she couldn't do that at Meadowbrook.

Harriet told her family she was going to spend a few days in London over New Year with friends. A lie that she clearly hadn't thought through, because she had lost touch with all her friends from her London days. She had happily left them behind when she skipped off to New York and although they had stayed in contact at first, it hadn't lasted. In fact she wasn't in contact with any friends from the UK. Another tragic realisation about her life. And, of course, the old Harriet would have just booked into a hotel, but she had a total of five pounds to her name, not even enough for a youth hostel.

Gus looked so happy for her that she felt ashamed about her lie. Instead, she had pretended to go – even so far as getting Gus to drive her to the train station – before she somehow managed to figure out how to get a bus home, heavily disguised in a big hat that belonged to her father, and now she was in Meadowbrook's empty cottage – the one that used to belong to Jed the gardener, practically next door to Connor's.

Stupidly it had seemed a good idea at the time. Well, in fairness it was her only idea. But it was anything but a good idea. It was cold, and she couldn't put any lights on in case she was seen, so she was practically hiding in one of the rooms furthest way, with a lit candle and picnic food which didn't requite heating, plates or cutlery. And now she was stuck here for two whole days and nights. Well, at least she would probably be able to think, as she had nothing else to do – unless she froze to death before the days were up of course.

Boxing Day had been lovely; their Meadowbrook Christmas. They had all exchanged gifts, which were cheap, fun and, in Gus's case, free, as he painted for them all. When he gave Harriet a picture he'd done of Hilda, she had choked back tears.

Mark had been on his best behaviour, as had Loretta,

and she hadn't caught them together, or even exchanging a glance and she had watched them like a hawk. The day was all about Fleur really though, and she brought excitement to the house as they opened presents, ate delicious food and went for a long walk, and then back for a quiet evening in. There had been a slight issue when Fleur, who had been given a glass of champagne by Freddie, let the kittens, who were getting quite big now, out of the kitchen and they tried to climb the Christmas tree, but only a minor disaster. Connor had managed to coax them down with only a few baubles as casualties.

Connor. It always came back to him. He was her sticking point. She realised as she replayed their teenage years together, she had fallen in love with him along the way. However, back then, deep down she believed they would be together at some point and she was almost biding her time. She got her degree, a job on a graduate trainee scheme at an investment bank and she waited. But then that fateful day when Connor had announced that he and Elizabeth were getting married, she felt her world collapse. Her response had been to throw herself even more into work and when there was talk of a job opening in New York office she jumped at the chance. She buried her feelings for him as deeply as she could, but they weren't ever going to go. Coming back to Meadowbrook had shown her that. They could be buried, she could get away from them, but they had never been fully eliminated. And now she needed to deal with them.

At home, Freddie was probably mixing cocktails for their New Year's Eve. Bella was going to be there; each of the siblings would have a partner with them. Fleur had a teenage party to go to, so it would be all the adults and their partners, including Gwen and Gerry. The party had been the trigger that made Harriet want to run away, hide away. When Pippa announced they were organising a small get-together for New Year, she quickly came up with the friends in London line. She didn't want to be, no actually couldn't be, there with them, the single sister, the spinster. She tried hard to keep the bitterness out of her head, but her thoughts were beginning to drown in it.

She needed to focus on her life now, and then the future. As her father always used to say, if she let herself be happy, then the future would reveal itself to her, or something like that. But being happy, the only thing she could think of, the only thing she wanted, was Connor. If she had him then she could see herself living at Meadowbrook. She'd happily live anywhere. Without him, she just wanted to run away again.

The idea of the future was bringing her out in hives. Or perhaps the cottage was so neglected it had mites or something.

Being alone was proving therapeutic in some ways and destructive in others – her life had become a constant contradiction. She couldn't leave the house, barely risked leaving the room, and she would only flush the loo if absolutely necessary. Clearly she had finally lost the plot. She needed answers, she knew that, but she had only questions. Harriet, the grown-up, oldest Singer, ex-successful banker, emotionally hampered woman, had no clue what to do next.

And like Hilda she was just running round and round in circles.

She passed into the new year – yay – on her own, with

a bottle of champagne she'd nicked from the house and a packet of crisps.

Her phone woke her. She opened her eyes, and saw daylight streaming through the windows. She was sleeping in a sleeping bag she had managed to sneak into the cottage, on a bed which had clearly seen better days. She didn't like to think that it might have been where Jed, the old gardener, had died. She did wonder briefly why the cottage had been left empty all this time – typical Harriet always looking at the practical – because with some work it would be lovely.

She looked at the screen, it was gone ten, this was the latest she had slept in ages. Her laptop was on the edge of the bed still, she had been typing, deleting and retyping notes late into the night. The bottle of champagne lay empty on the floor. Pippa's name was flashing insistently on her phone's display, so she pressed answer.

'Hey,' she said, sleepily.

'Sorry, did I wake you?'

'Yes, Pip, you did.'

'Happy New Year! You must have had a great party, because you never sleep this late.'

'It's only ten.' She rubbed sleep from her eyes.

'Oh yes, well anyway, I was too excited and I wanted to tell you.'

'Tell me what.' Harriet hoped she didn't sound as irritated as she felt.

'Well, the party was great, although we missed you.'

'Pip?'

'Oh yes, so two things happened. Mark and I talked and he said it was time for him, for us, to get serious about having a baby.'

Harriet groaned inwardly.

'Right?'

'So, we are going to see a fertility specialist as soon as the bank holidays are over, isn't that great.'

'Great.' Harriet felt her heart sink. If Pippa had Mark's child, she would never be free of him.

'And Freddie and Loretta got engaged.'

Oh shit. She couldn't believe it. They called her bossy, but the minute she left the house, Mark and Loretta had clearly taken advantage of her absence.

'You're kidding?'

'No, she came downstairs today with a ring that they got in a cracker – you know, until Freddie can afford something better than plastic. Freddie looked a bit shell-shocked, but you know what he's like.'

'So they're actually getting married?'

'As soon as possible, according to Loretta. And she said she'd love to get married at Meadowbrook.'

'Right,' Harriet said carefully. 'And any other news, Gus not eloped with Amanda or Connor impregnated Bella?'

'No, don't be silly, although they do all seem happy. Oh and Gerry is taking Gwen out for a proper dinner later. He asked Connor's permission, it was so sweet.'

'Well I'm happy for her.' Harriet really was. She wished she could say the same for the others. Apart from Gus, of course.

'Oh, how was your party?'

'Wild.' Harriet looked at the empty, littered, floral carpeted room. 'Which is why I'm probably not reacting the way you expected, but I'm so hungover. Pip, I'll call you later, I need to have breakfast.'

'Love you, Harry.'

'Love you too.'

Again, why the hell hadn't she thought this through, she couldn't even have a cup of coffee and she couldn't go home for another twenty-four hours.

She revisited her to-do list and, feeling determined and more than a little bit annoyed, she deleted what she'd written last night and retyped:

Expose Mark and Loretta
Tell Connor how I feel

Those two things were all she needed to do for now, but despite the fact she was tired from being up half the night, and perhaps a bit hungover from drinking a bottle of champagne on her own, she felt, on the first day of the new year, a sense of clarity at last. Because wherever her future lay she knew that if she could do those two things then the rest of it would fall into place. She knew it in her heart.

Chapter 26

'Oh I'm so glad you're back, did you have the best time?' Pippa gushed.

'Pip, I was gone for two days, you're acting as if you haven't seen me in months.' She didn't let on just how relieved she was to be in civilisation again. She had had to sneak out of the cottage, making sure no one saw her, to take a bus to the station, which meant waiting for an hour in the rain, her big hat pulled over her face in case she saw anyone she knew, and then let Gus pick her up from said station as if she'd just got off a train from London. She had learnt that subterfuge wasn't her strong point.

'Sorry, it's just I am so used to having you around now.' Pippa flung her arms around her. She looked so happy, it was heartbreaking.

'So, what is happening here?'

'Ah yes, well, Loretta wants to move in. Freddie looks a bit terrified about it, and he's drinking more again. I mean, not just in the evening. We were talking about doing an Easter event – I know, Christmas is just finished but we thought combining an Easter egg hunt for the kids, perhaps doing an *Alice in Wonderland* theme, remember how much I loved that book as a child, with the open gardens, and it also will be shortly before the year is up,' Pippa gushed, words spurting from her lips almost faster than Harriet could catch them.

'Pippa,' her sister was so hyper, anyone would think she was the one who'd been drinking, 'what does that have to do with Freddie's drinking?'

'Oh yes, so we thought we'd have a meeting, Gus, me and Fred, and we thought you'd be impressed that we were doing stuff not relying on you so much, but Fred turned up and he was reeking of alcohol and it was only lunchtime.'

'OK, maybe he's freaking out about Loretta.'

'Well, you see, he kind of broke down a bit at the meeting, and he says he doesn't remember proposing, doesn't remember getting the ring in the cracker, and now he thinks he's going mad. And he was almost paralytic on New Year's Eve when he did propose, anyone will tell you that.'

'Did you see the proposal?' Harriet asked.

'No, he did it when they were alone in bed.'

'But how, if he was paralytic as you say?' She couldn't be the only one who was suspicious about this, surely.

'Well, apparently he did, and that's that.' Pippa shrugged her shoulders.

'Ah.' Harriet wondered if the engagement had been concocted between Mark and Loretta. What if they cooked it up and because Freddie often lost his memory when he'd been drinking and they were pulling a fast one. But surely even Freddie would know that he would never forget proposing? It was all beyond shady.

'But he says that he can't tell Loretta that he forgot because she'll think he doesn't care and it might be easier to marry her than have her think that.'

'Please tell me you're joking?' Harriet widened her eyes. Pippa shook her head.

'Mark and I have an appointment at a clinic in Harley Street.' Pippa glowed with happiness.

'Gosh, isn't that expensive?' Harriet decided to tread carefully.

'Mark says it's worth it. You know, he works hard and I'd rather have this than all the fancy holidays we used to have. I told you before, Mark was reluctant to get checked out but now he's all for it, and he said if he was going to, then we may as well go straight for the best. And we're both so happy, our sex life has improved no end.'

Harriet held her hand up. 'Please spare me the details.'

'OK, sorry, but, Harry, I want a baby so much, and this time next year we might have another member of the family.'

Pippa looked so radiant that Harriet wanted to cry for her. It was almost too much to bear. She was going to single-handedly burst that bubble, but she had to, didn't she? She was doing it for their own good, after all.

Once she'd unpacked she went to the sanctuary, picked up a very excited Hilda and then popped into the office on her way to walk her. Connor was there, at the desk.

'Ah you're back?' He grinned. Her heart did a little dance at the sight of him.

'Yes, I am. Do you have time for a quick walk with Hilda? I want to run something by you.'

He stood up and her heart skipped a beat. If anything, a few days away from him had made him even more attractive. But that would have to wait, Mark and Loretta first, as per her list.

'So how was your New Year's? Did it make you realise how much you missed the city life?'

'No, actually. I didn't.' She bristled. Of course she didn't, because she was nowhere near a bloody city.

'Well that's good. All's fine here. Quiet without you,' he teased.

'Ha, bloody, ha. Listen, I'm sure you know, but there have been a couple of worrying developments. Firstly, Pippa told me her and Mark are going to see a fertility expert in Harley Street.'

'Yes, Mark kind of announced that on New Year's Eve with a bit of a flourish. He's definitely changed tack, and you should have seen him with Pippa, he was being so nice, attentive, he was all over her.'

'If Pip gets pregnant, then he'll always control her.'

'I agree.' Connor turned to Harriet. 'We need to stop him.'

'Right, and Loretta. She says Freddie proposed and gave her a ring, but he doesn't remember. And, well, if he doesn't remember proposing, then he didn't.'

'But he was very drunk.'

'Yes, but still, he doesn't do things like propose when he's drunk, he just passes out. And don't forget, he's been drinking much less lately.'

'You're right, even at Christmas he didn't get really drunk, did he?' Connor scratched his head. 'So what are you going to do?'

'I'm going to tell them what I know. About the plotting, about Damian, and the fact that Mark is broke.'

'Ouch, it's going to hurt, but you don't have any choice, do you?'

'Nope. I'm going to do it over dinner tonight, while neither Mark nor Loretta are here. I was hoping that you and your mum would be there.'

'We will. I was going to see Bella, but I think this is more important.'

'So you think I'm doing the right thing?' She was desperate for reassurance.

'I have no idea, but I also don't see what choice you have.' He looked so sincere as he spoke to her, she felt comforted.

'Connor, your support means everything.' Harriet welled up. Connor hugged her.

'You've always got it.'

As Harriet walked Hilda back to the dogs' home, and then made her way up to the house, she wondered if she did always have his support. Because, after what she was soon going to confess to him, she wasn't sure that she would have it ever again.

Nerves jangled as Harriet sat at the dinner table. Gwen served chicken with roast vegetables and sweet potato mash, which was one of Harriet's favourite meals. However, she knew she wouldn't enjoy a single mouthful. Her eyes kept shooting to Connor, who was trying to appear reassuring. She took a sip of her wine, looked around at everyone, and decided to get it over with.

'I need to talk to you all,' Harriet said. 'Connor knows some of what I'm about to say, but well, this isn't easy.'

'What's wrong?' Pippa's voice was coated with concern.

'OK, there's no easy way to say this.' Harriet took a breath, Connor nodded his head slightly. Gus's eyes widened. 'I didn't want to tell you this, in fact I kept it quiet until now but, well, it seems with your latest announcements that I'd never forgive myself if I didn't speak up.'

'Bloody hell, Harry, can you just spit it out, you're making no sense,' Freddie said.

'OK, right, well here goes.' She told them everything.

She told them about overhearing Mark and Loretta, the text messages, foiling Damian and Mark being broke. Her voice shook and she felt awful. She almost didn't dare look at Pippa or Freddie as she spoke, concentrating on Connor for strength. When she finished, she sat back in her chair. The room was so silent that she could hear her own breathing. She took another drink of wine.

'Let me get this straight, you are saying that Mark and Loretta are in cahoots to get their hands on Dad's money,' Freddie laughed. He actually laughed.

'Yes, Connor?' Harriet thought she could do with an ally.

'Harry told me because we knew they were going to try to do something with the animals at the sanctuary, we stepped up security and we caught Damian, who basically admitted he'd been paid by Mark to let the animals out and also to ruin the winter wonderland, pinning the blame on Harriet.' Connor spoke calmly, his voice steady as if to reassure Harriet that she wasn't alone.

'That proves nothing,' Pippa started. Her tone wasn't exactly friendly. She sat back in her chair, arms folded. Harriet rolled her eyes.

'Right, I agree,' Freddie concurred. 'It's preposterous.'

'But, well, how would Harriet have known if she didn't overhear them?' Gwen said, quietly. 'And why would Damian say it was Mark if it wasn't?'

'And I hate to stick the boot in, but Harry doesn't lie,' Gus backed his sister up.

'I'm not saying she does lie,' Pippa said carefully. 'But she is clearly mistaken. Mark said you had been acting up a bit with him lately.'

'Actually, Harry, Loretta said the same. She's very concerned about you,' Freddie added.

'I'm fine,' Harriet stormed.

'You've always had it in for Mark.' Pippa threw the accusation like a ball, right at Harriet.

'Where did you get that from?' Harriet tried to keep calm, but this wasn't panning out as she hoped. 'And anyway, I wouldn't make all this up just because I didn't like someone.' She was trying to keep her cool but it was far from easy.

'Mark told me how awful you are to him when I'm not around and I thought he was exaggerating but now it seems he wasn't.' Pippa's voice was riddled with sadness.

'Loretta said the same!' Freddie exclaimed. 'And your accusations are quite ridiculous,' Freddie added. 'Why would Loretta say I proposed, if I didn't.'

'You have no memory of it,' Harriet pointed out.

'Harriet, perhaps you're unwell.' Freddie was red-faced.

'What about the money thing, Pip?'

'That is something I need to speak to my husband about, but I am sure there is a perfectly good explanation. I really think it's taken its toll on you, you know, losing your job, losing Dad. Harry, it's understandable that you're very unhappy, but that doesn't mean you should sabotage our happiness,' Pippa added.

Harriet felt her blood boil.

'Harriet wouldn't make it up,' Gus reiterated.

'She isn't,' Connor concurred.

'Really? She's just convinced you both because she is so controlling, but it's clear she's the only one causing trouble here,' Freddie said. Harriet felt confused, why on earth where they reacting like this? She expected them to be upset, maybe question her, but to dismiss her altogether? 'I love you, Harry, but you always tried to control us when we were kids and now, coming back here, it's

284

like you wanted to just take up where you'd left off. But we're not kids anymore.'

'Oh no you don't, don't put this on me. I am unhappy yes, but I am not mad and nor would I ever try to sabotage your happiness, but for God's sake your partners only care about Dad's money and, Pippa, when Mark gets his hands on it, it'll all go to paying off his debts, then what? You might have a baby to think of and what if you're left with nothing.'

'Mark is a successful businessman, he may have hit hard times but he'll be a success again.'

'Pip, read the email,' Harriet begged. 'Come upstairs and read it now.'

'No, no I won't. I am not going to let you poison me against my husband.'

'Oh for God's sake, surely you can't be that stupid,' Harriet shouted, knowing she had gone too far but unable to stop herself.

'We're going to have a baby,' she screamed back. Harriet had never heard Pippa sound so angry. Even Freddie looked taken aback.

'You're not pregnant, Pip, you're just going to see a doctor.'

'Please, calm down,' Gus begged.

'No I won't calm down. How dare you lie just to get rid of Mark. What is it, Harry? You want to get your hands on this house so you're doing all you can to make sure no one, no one who cares about mine or Freddie's best interests, is around. You're the one who's lost her job, so maybe you are the one who wants to get her hands on the money and the house. I guess you think you can wrap Gus around your little finger.' Pippa's accusation was worse than being slapped. 'And Connor, but you can't do the same with us.'

'Hey—' Gus started.

'I don't want that at all,' Harriet stormed. She couldn't remember ever feeling this angry. 'I love you both, and I was trying to do the right thing to stop you both being hurt. If you want to accuse me of lying, then that's fine. But don't, don't even think about trying to have a relationship with me. Ever again.'

Pippa and Freddie both stood up and left the room.

Harriet put her head in her hands.

'That didn't go the way I thought it would,' she said.

'Harry, I'm sorry but . . .' Gus said, sounding grim.

'They'll calm down, honestly just give them some space,' Connor said.

'You think? I don't think they will, and if they do, I'm not going to bloody calm down. How dare they accuse me of lying, of being manipulative, of wanting Dad's money and of being mad?'

'But, love, they just had a shock, and it's not simple is it, relationships never are. I think deep down they both know they are wrong but Pippa believes marriage is for life, and now with the much-longed for baby situation being in the spotlight, she's bound to be confused. And Freddie, well, he thinks that he needs Loretta. I know he comes across as the most confident man but he isn't, and she makes him feel better about himself in many ways. You know, having a gorgeous woman on his arm, it sort of reinforces him. I think he's scared that having lost his business and his dad if he loses her, he'll have nothing,' Gwen said, gently coming over to Harriet and putting her arms around her. She made sense, of course she did, but Harriet was too angry to think rationally.

'But after what I just told them—' Harriet couldn't believe it. How was she made to feel like the bad guy?

'I know, but it's a shock, as I said, love, give them some time,' Gwen pleaded. Harriet let herself feel the warmth of Gwen's hug, she needed it so badly because she felt so close to falling apart. She believed she was only doing what her father wanted her to do, but look where that was getting her?

'And, Harriet, in the meantime don't do anything crazy, don't leave here,' Gus begged. 'Don't run off and ruin everything just because of the way they reacted.'

'You know the old Harriet would be on a plane right now to New York, but no, Gus, I won't. No matter what happens, Meadowbrook means too much to us all for me to risk it. Even if I have to spend the next four months avoiding those two, I will stick it out. For you and Fleur more than anything,' she explained. Although how she was going to live here after this, she had no idea.

She thought of her dad's will, and how she managed to mess everything up. And now she was still supposed to tell Connor how she felt, but she wasn't sure if she could bring herself to. She couldn't cope with losing anyone else in her life, even if she didn't have him in the way she wanted, she wasn't going to let him leave her too.

Chapter 27

The end of the week was knocking on the door and Mark would be here again, along with Loretta. Harriet had successfully managed to avoid her siblings, Mark and Loretta, for almost three weeks. She had spent a lot of time on her own, a lot. Gwen despaired when Harriet insisted on eating breakfast and dinner in the kitchen, but she wasn't going to play happy families when they were anything but.

Freddie and Pippa had not only been happy to avoid her but they had joined forces, were thick as thieves, and Gus was stuck in the middle, trying to keep the peace, but thankfully he had Amanda to turn to when things got too much, as they normally did.

During the week, Harriet spent her days at the animal sanctuary. There was a kind of peace spending time with the animals. It also made her feel closer to Connor, although she wasn't any closer to the second thing on her to-do list. Nor were they close to hitting the target for the sanctuary, which had now been added to her list. It had become a matter of pride for her, which was all she had left. She would not fail to raise the money, she wouldn't fail at something else in her life.

The mess at Meadowbrook had to be sorted out first,

she felt that keenly, but she had no idea how. The atmosphere was heavy with accusations, and pain. Gus, although civil, hadn't fully been forgiven by Pippa and Freddie; he said they were treating him as a polite stranger. Freddie and Pippa had united, and didn't seem to move without each other.

How she would deal with the weekend, she still hadn't figured out. She'd been trying to come up with a solution and failed and felt as if her father was further away from her than ever. God, she could just imagine how, if he was there, he'd bang their heads together and tell them to sort it out. Although, now Harriet thought about it, he clearly didn't trust Mark, which was why he had spoken up in his pre-will.

So she ran with Hilda, she helped with all the animals, she even got closer to Elton and David who seemed to accept her in their field now with almost friendliness. She confided her fears to them, to the pigs – Gus was right, they were good listeners – to Hilda and yes, maybe she had gone mad. Although the alpacas seemed particularly uninterested in her issues, all the animals needed her in a way her siblings clearly did not. Sleep was erratic, and her heart ached for all that she'd lost but she didn't feel any closer to getting it back. She didn't feel as if she'd ever get it back.

On Thursday evening, she was hiding in her father's study, desperately asking him for answers, when there was a knock on the door. It opened and Freddie, Gus and Pippa walked in. The way they looked at her made her feel a little like they were staging an intervention.

'Harry,' Freddie started, standing awkwardly in front of the desk, 'we, Pippa and I, are sorry at how we handled things.'

'Right,' she replied. Pippa sat on the chair opposite her.

'I've spoken to Mark and he's explained everything,' Pippa started. 'Yes, he did speak with Loretta but only because they were worried about us. They felt that Meadowbrook changed us and they thought that if we sold the house then we'd be ourselves again.' She said it as if this was the most reasonable explanation ever.

'Right.' Harriet didn't quite know how to respond.

'Loretta totally confirmed what Mark said,' Freddie said. 'Basically, you must have misunderstood them. They weren't out to ruin things, they were just trying to help.' He looked determined. 'I am going to marry her, and Pippa and Mark are going to try to have a baby, you need to accept it.'

'Fine.' Harriet held her hands up. She had lost her fight and she didn't have anything left. That wasn't to do with them, it was to do with her.

'Mark is desperate to apologise to you when he sees you this weekend. I know about his money problems, it was the recession, you see, but he is bouncing back right now and he doesn't want my money at all.'

How could they be so stupid? She shook her head, silently.

'Harry, we have to find a way past this,' Gus said. 'I know this is little to do with me, but I love us being close again and we don't want that to fall apart.'

'So I just have to accept things?' Harriet asked. She might as well. Her head was already mushed up and she didn't know if she cared about any of it anymore.

'Look, when Daddy died, I know you felt guilty about not being here,' Pippa said carefully. 'And grief messes with people. I should have seen how unhappy you were.'

'Exactly, we were our usual selfish selves and we forgot to check on you. I know it must be hard seeing us all so happy, and I know that you want us to be happy, but we do think you rather put your unhappiness onto us,' Freddie added.

Harriet threw her head back and laughed. Freddie eyed her with suspicion and Pippa took a step back. Christ, if they thought she was mad, then she might as well be. What they were accusing her of was ridiculous, but she had no intention of arguing with them. She didn't even have the energy for that.

'That's what you think I was doing?' Harriet asked. They both nodded. Gus shook his head but shuffled from foot to foot, uncomfortably. 'OK, well you are adults, you've told me that, and I should respect both of your decisions. You won't hear another word from me on the subject.' They wouldn't. She had failed. She'd failed her father, her siblings and herself. It was over, she felt that. Yes, she would stay at Meadowbrook as long as she had to but not a minute longer. She just now needed to figure out what, where and how, and she'd be off.

'Right, well let's have a brandy and put it behind us,' Freddie said, decisively.

Harriet shrugged. 'Fine,' she reiterated.

As the siblings toasted their broken reunion, she plastered a smile on her face and tasted failure in every sip she took.

After an awkward dinner where Harriet refused to say a word, Connor asked her to go for a walk with him.

'But it's freezing,' she said.

'You never felt the cold before,' he said. 'You used to run around all winter in barely a coat.'

'Well I do now,' she replied. 'But OK.' She reluctantly followed him.

'You really aren't in a good way, are you?' he said at length as they trotted out. She shook her head. 'You've done wonders with the animals, Harry,' he said as they walked out towards the summer house. 'I wanted to speak to you, to check you were all right and also to ask you what you think about the future of the sanctuary.'

'Well, I am worried about the money side of it, we still have a way to go reaching the target, and not long in which to do it,' she said, honestly, feeling hollowness opening up inside her with every step.

'You know I'm sure you'll do it. I mean, you're used to making millions and millions.'

'Not quite the same thing,' she said. With the whole Mark and Loretta business and also her feelings for Connor, Harriet hadn't been as together about raising the money for the sanctuary as she normally would be. She calculated that they had about four months left to make up the shortfall which was considerable and the old Harriet would have had a million plans up her sleeve to do it. What had happened to her? Was this what love did to a person? No wonder she'd avoided it thus far. She would never have kept her job if she behaved like this.

They reached the summer house and, without a word, Connor opened the door and they went in. Gus had now filled it with easels holding paintings, which took her breath away. It was as if happiness jumped out from the canvases she could see; he'd been painting a lot. Landscapes, the gardens, Meadowbrook and there was one of the four of them, which brought tears to her eyes. They looked so happy, so together, they looked like a family. He must have painted it from a photo of them at the summer fête. She started crying.

'Oh, Harry, I am so sorry,' Connor said as he saw her looking at it.

'Look at us, we've tried so hard to be a family, but we're never going to be the Singer siblings again.'

'But you were happy, up until the whole Mark and Loretta debacle, you were,' Connor pushed.

'No, I wasn't. I was missing something, I've been missing something for years. I was so busy being successful, living a life in New York that is a million miles away from all this.' She swept her arm around. 'But now I can't do it, I'm empty, Connor, I've been empty for years. I just didn't realise it until coming here.'

'And what can we do about it?' He stood by the window, the night glistened, illuminating his face.

'What can you do,' she said quietly. The realisation that she had nothing more to lose hit her full on.

'What do you mean?'

'Oh, Connor, I never thought I could say this, but I have to.' It was her last chance, she knew that. Her last chance to salvage any hope of a future at Meadowbrook.

'Harriet, you're not making any sense.' He seemed bemused as he stared questioningly at her.

She gathered any strength she had left.

'Whatever happens in the future, I need to be honest, with you and myself.' She felt the tears sliding onto her cheeks but she knew she couldn't stop now. 'I love you, Connor.' Saying the words gave her a huge sense of relief, along with a terror that gripped her bones.

'What?' He tipped his head.

'It's always been you. When you got engaged to Elizabeth, I ran away to New York because it hurt too much. I've loved you for as long as I can remember and I still do.' She felt her father's arm on her shoulder as she spoke, willing her on, giving her strength. Pushing her to do this, no matter how much it was going to hurt her. How hard it was going to be. Harriet was brave again. Stupid maybe, but brave.

'Why now?' he said, quietly. He turned away from her and looked out of the window.

'I've been trying to find a way to tell you, without ruining things, but now everything's so messed up, so what's left to lose?' She realised that humiliation wasn't the worst thing, the worst was not ever saying how she felt.

'But Bella . . .'

'You're in love with Bella?'

'Yes, no, I don't know. Oh Christ, Harriet, why did you have to tell me now?'

'I'm sorry.' She wasn't sorry. He refused to meet her eyes.

'Look, Harry, I've always been so fond of you – no, sorry, more than fond of you, and yes, when we were younger I had this crazy idea that we were meant to be together.' She felt a tug of hope, immediately followed by dread of what was to come. 'But we are such different people. I love the country and I love Meadowbrook. You're a city girl, you date men who earn salaries I could never even dream of, or even want. You're sophisticated, you're smart and beautiful and intelligent, and I adore you, but there's no way we would ever work out. I don't even know half the shoe designers you talk about, or the fancy cocktails you mention, our lives are too different, we're too different. You'd be bored here, you're already thinking about the next thing; being here, it won't be enough of a challenge for you. I can't even think about living in a city, this is enough for me, but it isn't for you.'

'What will happen to the animal sanctuary?' She felt the nails being hammered into her coffin, one by one.

'I was hoping you would set up such a great model that someone could easily run it in the future, I didn't expect you to want to do that.'

'I don't know if I do,' she replied, honestly. She couldn't see herself doing it, not without being with Connor anyway. But then if she was with Connor, everything else would fall into place, wouldn't it?

'That's what I thought. So us, we'd never work out, would we? I'm nothing like the men you normally go for.' He crossed his arms.

'If you say so, Connor.' She'd given it her best shot; she wasn't going to beg.

'Harry, don't be mad at me, you've dropped a bomb. I've been seeing Bella for months and you haven't said a word. I don't mess people around, I don't hurt people, so for you to say this now . . .'

'Sorry, I guess I'll add it to the list of the things I've screwed up this year.' She turned from him. She suddenly had all the answers: she needed to leave Meadowbrook as soon as the year was through and stop looking back. It was over.

'Please, Harry, let's talk about this.'

'Connor. There. Is. Nothing. To. Talk. About.' Holding her head up as far as she could, she walked out. She heard him calling her but she refused to look back as she made her way to the house. Not home, it didn't feel like home anymore, whatever happened at the end of this mad year that her father had somehow thought was a good idea, she would definitely be saying goodbye to Meadowbrook forever.

*   *   *

Harriet didn't know if she believed in fate, well she briefly flirted with it after her father's death, but she had always felt that people made their own fate. With Connor's words ringing in her ears, she finally knew how it felt for her heart to be shattered. This was something that she knew would always be part of her. Devastation, and as much as her father said she needed to feel this, she couldn't quite comprehend it. Her heart had been pillaged, ravaged, left with nothing.

But fate had a funny way of showing up when you'd dismissed it, she thought, as she sat cross-legged, like a teenager, on her bed, with her laptop in front of her, trying to stem the bloody annoying tears that had become her constant companion. Blurry-eyed, she was surprised to see an email from Bradley Fisher, her old work colleague in New York. She opened it.

Harriet, please can you call me when you have a second, I assume you still have the number. Brad.

That was all, but in the bank they always used the fewest words possible, always in too much of a hurry to waste precious seconds with any pleasantries – *how are you?* was not necessary. Emails were to the point of the point.

Harriet smiled as she thought of the long chatty emails she now sent about the animal sanctuary, trying to raise money or awareness, and how she used as many words as possible to invoke interest. Well, goodness, her two worlds were so different, she didn't even know where to begin comparing the incomparable.

She pulled out her phone and dialled. She was intrigued, glad almost of the distraction, as she dried her tears. The five-hour time difference in New York meant she knew she'd find Brad at his desk.

'Brad Fisher.'

'It's Harriet,' she said, surprised at the familiarity of his voice despite her months away.

'Oh, Harry, thank fuck you rang.' The urgency in his voice was also reassuringly recognisable, along with the swearing, which was a prerequisite of the trading floor. Brad was her equivalent at the bank, a VP with a team of unruly traders to control. They got on well, had a mutual respect, as well as a healthy dose of competition. She was also friends with his wife, Macy, who was a high-flying lawyer. They were the definition of power couple.

'What's wrong?'

'Well, nothing's actually fucking wrong. But where to start— What the hell are you doing?'

'Who me?'

'No, an idiot broker who's screaming in my ear. Right, back to you. So, guess what, Harry? Zach's gone.'

'What do you mean, gone?' She could hear the trading-floor noise in the background and she felt a slight tug, as if she wanted to run to it.

'Fired. Marched out of the office like a thief.'

'What did he do?' Harriet felt both interested and also a little cold. Did karma actually exist? If it did, she was going to start making another list, with Mark and Loretta on the top of it.

'Remember that little intern, Fiona, well he did her basically. And yes, Harry, we all knew you were shagging him, but no one cared because you had a career already and were good at your job, but he had been seeing her before you even left. Apparently, according to the stupid girl, he promised her a fast track to the trading floor, in

297

return for – well, let's say he had quite a few Bill Clinton moments, and most of them in the office. Anyway, they got rumbled, he got fired, she threatened to sue for sexual harassment, but her internship came to an end and she knew she was lucky to get away with a reference. Apparently it was all on CCTV, not that we've been able to find the footage – and I've got my best men on the job.'

'Wait, Brad, what?'

'Sorry, Harry, but don't tell me being in the English countryside's turned you into a fucking prissy.'

'Actually it has rather, but never mind. So what's the upshot, have you got Zach's job?'

'Yes, and I've promoted Melvin to my old job.'

'Ah, good choice.' Harriet couldn't help but think if she'd still been there they might have offered her Zach's job. Although probably not if everyone knew she was sleeping with him. She suddenly got a sense of clarity about why he'd been so keen to get rid of her. 'What about my old job?'

'Well we couldn't fill it because you'd been made redundant and so Zach was trying to figure a way around it, he really was a first-class tosser, but basically I want you to come back.'

'What? To my old job?'

'Yes, and yes you'd have to work for me, but you know we always did work well together. You were one of the best traders in New York, let alone this bank, so what do you say?'

'Christ, I don't know, Brad. Whatever I decide, I have to stay at Meadowbrook until the end of May, it's a condition of my father's will.'

'Yeah I don't even want to know why, but that's cool. Look we've been covering here without you, but the balance sheet isn't what it was. I want you back, working with me and making this the most profitable trading floor in New York. Again. If I have to wait for you, I will, but please think about it, Harry. We fucking need you.'

Harriet felt the thrill of the challenge coursing through her veins. Remembering the buzz of making money, of closing the deal. So since being here she hadn't missed it as much as she thought she would, but that didn't mean that she didn't love it, did it? Besides, Meadowbrook had been taken from her and here she was being offered her old life back on a plate. Maybe her father had got it wrong after all. Maybe she needed to be here to find out that she didn't belong. She wasn't like her siblings, she definitely wasn't going to have a happy ever after with Connor. And the animals, as much as she loved them, well, anyone could do that job. She wasn't needed, or wanted here, but New York . . .

Suddenly she believed in fate.

Chapter 28

'Right guys,' Harriet said. She had called a meeting with her siblings, and Connor, in the sanctuary office. She had renewed energy since the job offer which could take her back to New York, but she also wanted to make sure that if she went, she went out with a bang. She no longer felt the overwhelming despair and defeat that had characterised the last couple of weeks. She had brushed off any attempts for Connor to talk to her beyond the usual pleasantries, ditto Pippa and Freddie, and she was going to be polite, civil even, but personal relationships were no longer a priority. She had switched fully into work mode, where she felt safe, and although her father had been wrong about them rebuilding the family this year, she didn't want him to be wrong when it came to the animal sanctuary. Therefore she was going to put all her efforts into raising the money to ensure that when she left, the animal sanctuary was in safe hands. Meadowbrook and the money, well that was another issue.

It was the end of February, and Harriet had spent minimal time with both Mark and Loretta who had put on a show of being gracious, apologetic that they *may* have given her the wrong impression, while at the same time treating her as if she was deranged. Harriet, having decided not to care anymore, just shrugged it off and blocked them out. If Pippa and Freddie were going to be so stupid, then she wasn't going to stand in their way. Let them lose everything, let them learn the hard way. She didn't want to be heartless, but they'd made it clear how they felt about her, she was out.

Gus tried to get through to her but she'd closed herself off from him a little too. She wrapped a cloak around herself to keep all feelings out while she thought about how she just had to survive a few more months before she could leave them all behind. She knew she would miss the way she had felt at Meadowbrook before all the drama but, at the same time, that had gone, she would never get it back again, time to close off the past.

She managed to avoid Connor, although the glaring reality was that it felt as if he was avoiding her. He stopped dining at the house, and when she was at the animal sanctuary he seemed to be elsewhere. She pulled that cloak a little bit tighter.

The only person she felt bad about was Gwen. Dear Gwen who kept urging her to keep trying to get through to her siblings, who was so desperate to keep the family together, but Harriet had to explain that it was too late. She hated hurting Gwen who she loved so much, but she couldn't, she absolutely couldn't do it anymore. She hadn't told anyone about the job offer, but she was pretty certain that she was going to take it. The idea of slipping back into her old life – the heels, the salons, her friends, her personal trainer and the job – didn't exactly have her jumping for joy, but it didn't feel like such a bad idea either.

The house was ruptured, she felt it in every room that

had been carefully decorated, every glass that had been drunk out of, plate eaten off – their split, their collapsed relationship permeated everything at Meadowbrook. No amount of effort on Pippa and Freddie's part could fix it, and Gus's entreaties couldn't paper over the cracks. Even Fleur had noticed it, and although Harriet felt worse for her than for anyone, there was nothing she could do. It had gone too far, the damage was too severe, the house, the relationships within the house, were nothing more than rubble to her now.

'So what's the meeting about?' Gus asked.

Pippa and Freddie faced her, looking sheepish, and Connor was refusing to meet her eyes. Hilda snored contentedly at her feet. The rest of the sanctuary staff were off dealing with the animals.

'We're in trouble,' Harriet stated. She always felt it best to start a little dramatically; it worked – she now had everyone's attention. Even Connor's. 'In the terms of Dad's pre-will, or whatever we want to call it, he said we needed to raise twenty-five thousand pounds for the sanctuary this year. This had to be done in any way possible but we weren't allowed to give any of our money, mainly because we weren't allowed any. For example, and I've checked this with David, Pippa couldn't give any of her money but if say Mark wanted to donate, then he could, as long as we were sure it wasn't anything to do with Pippa.'

'Mark hasn't got any money,' Pippa said.

'Well, yes, I know that, it was an example. I could have used Loretta.' Harriet knew she sounded harsh, unsympathetic, but then that was how she was feeling. 'But I didn't. My point is that the money had to be raised by us, not from us, and well, at the moment, with only three months to go until our deadline, it's not looking good.'

'Oh gosh.' Gus looked genuinely stricken as he always did when things were going wrong. 'What on earth happens if we don't raise the money?'

'That I was hoping Connor could tell us.' Harriet raised an eyebrow at him.

'OK, so here's the thing, we need that money to pay for next year.'

'But surely twenty-five thousand isn't enough to keep the sanctuary open for a year?' Freddie said, sensibly, Harriet thought.

'No, not entirely, but we have other sources. But you see, without that twenty-five thousand the sanctuary could be in trouble.'

'But that makes no sense,' Pippa said, she sounded suspicious. 'Because if we fail, all of Dad's estate goes to the sanctuary. And if we succeed, then we'll all make sure it stays open, surely?'

Harriet was impressed, she hadn't thought of that.

'Yes, well.' Connor reddened. 'I don't know all the legalities, but with probate and all the process that wills have to go through, it could take some time. I think that was why your father was charging you with raising that money. Because otherwise it is going to be hard, maybe even impossible, to keep the sanctuary open next year.'

'I was hoping that you wouldn't say that,' Harriet stated. 'But then, we have to do it to fulfil the terms, regardless of the fate of the sanctuary, which of course I care about, before you say anything. I just don't believe that Dad would have let anything happen to it no matter what we did.'

'Look,' Connor said. 'I agree, H, but you know your father said there was no way that you guys would fail. He had every confidence in you.'

'Enough to put the future of this place in jeopardy?' Harriet was incredulous. Connor nodded.

'But if we want to fulfil the terms of Dad's will . . .' Gus started.

'Oh say it, Gus, if we want the money and the house, we have only three months to raise just under ten thousand pounds.'

They all stared at her.

'We all said we'd make Dad proud this year,' Pippa said. 'We have to do it.'

'Then let's do it. Harry, what did you have in mind?' Freddie asked, just as Jenni ran screaming into the office.

'What is it?' Connor said, jumping up.

'It's Elton, bring your bag.' Jenni, looking wild, grabbed him and they ran out. Harriet, Gus, Pippa and Freddie followed him.

'What happened, Jenni?' Connor shouted as they ran to the field.

'David was making a racket.' Jenni could hardly get the words out through her breath. 'So I went to see, and he's just on the ground.'

As they ran into the field, she saw the colour drain from Connor's face. Even Harriet startled at the noise coming from David. She'd never heard a noise like it, it was loud as a siren, but a wailing which was so filled with pain. Elton was lying on his side. Connor rushed to him. Harriet was rooted to the spot with her siblings at her feet.

'He's dead, isn't he?' Harriet said. Connor nodded, his eyes full of tears as he tried to examine him. David wailed even harder and Jenni tried to comfort him, but he was distraught. Harriet had never seen a dead bull before and she'd never seen a grieving one but she understood how David felt.

'Oh no, poor Elton, poor David.' Pippa was the first to cry, Harriet held her as her body rocked with sobs. She rubbed her back as she used to do when they were children and she stroked her hair to calm her. Gus put his hand on her shoulder, his eyes full of tears, and Freddie was wiping tears from his eyes.

Connor, stood up, mud-splattered, shaking his head. He looked at Harriet, and she handed Pippa over to Gus and Freddie before she went to him.

'I can't believe it,' he said, voice choked with emotion.

'I am so, so sorry,' Harriet replied, wrapping her arms around him as he leant down and sobbed into her neck.

It took hours before Elton was removed. He was a big bull, and they needed a small crane and tractor and a trailer to get him out of the field, while David tried his hardest to go with him, almost taking down the fence. In the end Connor had to sedate him.

'What's going to happen to David?' Freddie asked quietly.

'We don't think he'll cope without Elton, those two belonged together,' Connor said, shaking his head.

'They really did,' Pippa concurred.

'They were the most functional couple at Meadowbrook after all,' Freddie tried to joke.

'It says something when the most functional couple here were gay cows,' Gus pointed out.

'Bulls,' Freddie corrected and they smiled.

Everyone could see that the love that Elton and David had for each other was something else. And if that sounded crazy then Harriet didn't care, because that was the magic of Meadowbrook.

Harriet decided to support Connor the only way she

could. She took care of the organisation. Connor wanted Elton buried at Meadowbrook, so Harriet spoke to John the vicar who promised her two gravediggers – they were only part-time, what with cremations being popular, but they were coming up the following day. She also spoke to the others who worked at the sanctuary to see if there was anything to be done about David, but they all agreed that grief, in animals as with people, didn't have an easy fix.

As they all sat down to dinner, the atmosphere in the dining room was heavy, but in a different way to how it had been lately. Thankfully Bella wasn't there, but Mark's attempts at cheering them up didn't work and Loretta's latest wedding ideas were met with even less enthusiasm than usual. Gwen was watching her son closely; Amanda seemed concerned as her eyes darted to each of the siblings; Connor barely ate; Harriet felt so full of pain she didn't know what to do. It was the first animal loss – death – since they'd been at Meadowbrook and Elton was such a part of the animal sanctuary that it wouldn't be the same without him. Just like her father. Meadowbrook wasn't the same without him either, yet it would have to learn to live without them both.

'Can I make a toast,' Harriet said, realising that the dinner felt more like a disaster by the minute. Everyone mumbled their agreement as she raised a glass. 'I want to raise a glass for Dad and for Elton. Both missed, both very loved. In fact both who experienced the purest of loves, the most enduring love that most of us can only dream of.' Harriet fashioned a glance at Connor who was staring at his plate, although his glass was raised. Mark grinned smugly as he took hold of Pippa's hand, and

Loretta blinked, as if she had no idea what Harriet was talking about. Freddie glanced at her and then quickly looked away. Gwen smiled encouragingly and Gus looked at Amanda bashfully. 'So,' she continued. 'My toast is for both man and bull, who should teach us what love is and if we listen to their lesson, then none of us will settle ever again. I would rather be on my own for the rest of my life than have a relationship that doesn't measure up to theirs. So, to love.'

Everyone awkwardly toasted as if they didn't know whether Harriet's toast was a dig or not – it was. Not at Gus though, Gus and Amanda she believed in.

'To love,' Gus echoed.

'And I know we've had a tricky time lately, but today, well, I felt it bringing us all together again.' Harriet was emotional she knew, but it was true, they had bonded over grief, again, and she realised that no matter how angry she was with Freddie and Pippa, they were her family, along with Gus, Gwen and Connor, all she had left. Even when she went back to New York, they would still be her family.

'Harriet,' Pippa said. 'Thank you. Thank you for not being angry and for taking care of me today.'

'I'll always love you, Pip, and I'll always be here for you.' She meant it, even if she wouldn't literally be here. 'And that goes to all of you.'

'Thank you.' Amanda tried to smile.

'Thank you,' Gus repeated, awkwardly. 'And we would like to share our plans with you.' He looked at Amanda who nodded, reassuringly. 'We've talked about moving in together, after the year. Into Amanda's house. Fleur has given her blessing.'

'I think you and Amanda living together is great. You'll

really be happy, I can tell. But what about work?' Harriet asked.

'Yes, now you will think I've lost the plot, but I'm going to retrain as a gardener. I've looked into courses and that's what I want to do.'

'Bloody hell, you're giving up insurance and going to dig things!' Freddie exclaimed.

'Yes, Fred, that's exactly what I'm going to do. I love gardening, really do, and I also love painting, so I am going to do both. Painting will be a hobby, of course, but quite an important one.'

'Well I think that's wonderful,' Gwen said. 'Your father felt he'd suppressed your creative side, Gus, but now you've found it again and it isn't too late. It would be just what he would have wanted.'

'It's never too late, I think I've learnt that,' Gus said.

'But it will be if we don't raise this money,' Harriet pointed out. She felt a stirring of something as she suddenly had a brainwave.

'What's that?' Mark asked. Harriet took a moment to take in his greedy eyes.

'By the terms of Dad's will we only get the money if we raise a certain amount for the sanctuary. And we are quite a way short.'

The colour draining from Mark's face told them all that he wasn't expecting that.

'What, you mean you won't get no money?' Loretta wore her horror blatantly.

'Not a penny.' Harriet was enjoying this, she even let Loretta's double negatives go.

'And, well, raising that much money, in what, three months, isn't going to be easy, it might even be impossible,' Connor added.

'If only we had a plan,' Harriet said, scratching her head for good measure.

'Well, surely you'll will think of something?' Mark said, not bothering to disguise the panic in his voice.

'Well, Mark, you're normally full of good ideas, if you have any, I'd be delighted to listen to them,' Harriet told him. Mark fell silent but she could almost see his brain whirring.

'Gwen?' Harriet said sweetly. After all, she did have a plan, which by the look of Mark and Loretta was already working. And it was almost genius, if she did say so herself.

'Yes, love.'

'Let me help you clear up, the rest of you go through to the drawing room, after the tragic day we've had you all probably need a brandy.'

She grinned at Gwen as she followed her out to the kitchen.

Chapter 29

Gwen opened the built-in cupboard where the large TV was hidden. It was a rarely watched television, except when they were all together, like at Christmas. Harriet felt irrationally nervous, but it had worked. The plan she concocted the night after Elton died had come to fruition. She confided in Gwen, banking on the fact that if Mark thought the money was out of reach he would concoct a meeting with Loretta. He had done, that very same night. Harriet loved predictable people.

'I was hoping it wouldn't come to this,' Gwen started, pointing the remote control at them. 'But it has. Your father would be very disappointed. He wanted this year at Meadowbrook to bring you all together, to see you behaving like a family again, but it's torn you all apart. And I think that it's only fair now to sort out the reason for that.'

'But—' Mark said.

'No, you don't get to talk.' Gwen waved the remote threateningly at him. 'You've been very unfair on Harriet.'

'But I—' Pippa started, but Gwen silenced her, holding up a hand.

'Well, luckily for all of you she didn't just leave you all to get on with it,' Gwen said. Harriet was quite enjoying the Gwen show; she'd never sounded quite so forceful. 'I did it for you all, especially poor Harriet, but more importantly I did it for your father. He loved you so much and he loved Meadowbrook and if he could see you now, which he probably can, he'd be heartbroken. The idea that Pippa and Freddie would let these two destroy the home he put his heart into doesn't bear thinking about.'

'Now hang on,' Mark started.

'We don't want to destroy nothing,' Loretta protested.

'He's my husband,' Pippa interjected.

Freddie stared, open-mouthed, at Gwen.

'Really, well we'll see. But you all have to take responsibility for what you are about to see. And think of your poor dad and how much he loved you all, and Meadowbrook.'

Gwen pressed play and went to stand next to Connor.

The video was a bit jerky but soon two bodies appeared on screen, after a while the heads appeared.

'So, Mark, what are we going to do?' a voice shrieked, Loretta's face became clearer, although they could already identify her voice. Pippa gasped as Mark's face came into picture.

'STOP THIS NOW,' Mark shouted and lunged for the remote control, Connor batted him away.

The video continued.

'Right, well whatever happens, we need to make sure they get that money,' Mark said.

'Can't you donate it?' Loretta asked.

'I wish I bloody could. Only I don't have that sort of cash lying around. Do you?'

'Nah, I mean, my mortgage is quite big, my income's

gone right down and it costs a fair bit to look this good. I was relying on Freddie to take care of me.'

Harriet giggled, then she realised that Loretta was being serious.

'And now, look at them all, playing happy families. Unwittingly we had them where we wanted them, Harriet was an outcast, but now they seem intent on being pally with the bloody woman, again.'

'If there's no money, then what are we going to do?'

'OK, don't panic, you need to make sure Freddie and you set the date – I can't believe you made him think he'd proposed, so you won't find it that hard. I'll find a way to come up with the shortfall for the sanctuary and then get Pippa pregnant. But we need to come up with another plan to get rid of Harriet.'

'You don't mean bump her off, do you?' Loretta asked. Pippa gasped.

'No, as tempting as that sounds we're not bloody gangsters, Loretta. No, we just need to turn the others against her.'

'How?'

'Leave that with me, and when I get Pippa pregnant and you marry Freddie, we'll have control of fifty per cent of the Singer siblings. Gus is a pushover, and Harriet will be in Coventry. Even though it wasn't exactly our plan at first, I think we can get safely back on track now,' Mark finished.

'She's moving to Coventry?' Loretta asked and Harriet burst out laughing as Gwen stopped the tape.

Freddie gaped, Pippa started to turn a startling shade of red. Gus shuffled awkwardly and Connor went to his mother's side. Mark looked as if his mind was whirring a million miles an hour, and Loretta started crying. Harriet hoped her fake eyelashes would fall off.

'How on earth did you—' Mark started.

'Harriet and I came up with a plan and I followed you. One thing about you, Mark, is you never notice me, you think of me as staff, it was easy enough to keep track of you. And, Loretta, you always left your phone lying around, unlocked. I knew you were going to the summer house, so I took Andrew's video camera and hid behind the curtain.'

'Look, I am sorry that you had to find out this way, but I have been trying to tell you, Pip, surely you're not going to let him talk his way out of this, are you?' Harriet said, still finding it all more amusing than she should.

'No, I'm not. Mark, you're a bastard, I wish I'd listened to Harriet in the first place. How dare you try to turn me against her? I was so under your spell.'

'But darling, I did it for—'

'Shut up, shut your lying mouth.' She slapped him across his face, even Harriet felt startled by the force of the blow. 'Now listen to me, Mark, you are a fraud, I know that, I know Harriet wasn't lying, but I couldn't admit that I'd made the biggest mistake of my life marrying you. You made me so unhappy lately but I still blamed myself and I almost lost my family over you. Now here's what's going to happen, you are going to leave this house, and I'm going to divorce you. I have grounds, so you won't contest it. You can keep the Cheltenham house, or what's left of it after all your debt, but you get nothing more from me and if you even so much as try, this video goes public.'

'But, Pippa, you can't do that to me.' Desperation oozed out of his mouth, you could almost feel it coming out of his skin. 'I love you, I need you.'

'No, you don't and more importantly I don't need you.

Yes, you need my dad's money, but you know what? You are not getting a penny. Just try.'

Suddenly Mark's eyes darkened.

'You'll regret this, you stupid little bitch, I will see to it that you regret it.' He rounded on her threateningly.

Gus took a step forward and lunged for Mark, punching him square on the jaw. Mark fell back into Loretta who shrieked.

'I'm sorry I didn't stand up more strongly before, Harry, Pip and Fred, but I'm not letting anyone hurt my family again,' Gus said, rubbing his fist.

'Oh, Gus, that was incredible,' Amanda said, throwing her arms around him.

'Fred?' Loretta looked at him, Bambi-eyed.

'You know, Loretta, I probably could have forgiven you for wanting me to be rich, but I can't forgive you for what you and that idiot were prepared to do to my family, and I certainly can't forgive you for letting me think I was going mad when you said I'd proposed. How could you lie like that to me?' He looked incredibly hurt, Harriet saw.

'Well if you weren't such a drunk then you'd never have fallen for it,' Mark pointed out.

'You're right.' Freddie slumped down. 'But I didn't drink much that night.'

'No, Fred, you'd been drinking a lot less lately,' Harriet said.

'Oh for God's sake. I slipped one of my sleeping pills into your drink, knew you'd never remember a thing. I could have told you that we were married and you'd have believed me.'

'Get out of here,' Freddie shouted. Harriet went to his side. He had worked so hard in controlling his drinking

314

and done so well, she knew how much that must have hurt him.

Connor and Gus became all macho as they marched both Loretta and Mark off and away from Meadowbrook.

'I'm sorry I had to do that,' Gwen said, as they all sat round nursing whisky for the shock.

'I'm glad you did,' Pippa said. 'I'm just sorry that we didn't believe you, Harry, will you forgive me?'

'Pip, I'll always forgive you but it hurt, you know, the way you treated me. Accusing me of being a lonely, bitter old spinster, who tried to ruin your marriage was incredibly unfair.' Harriet was relieved but she still wasn't over it.

'I didn't exactly say that . . .' Pippa protested.

'But we didn't treat you right, did we?' Freddie said. He'd been pretty quiet since the incident.

'No, you didn't.'

'But we will from now on. We'll make it up to you,' Freddie said. 'I am going to throw myself into events here at Meadowbrook and I'll clean up my act and, when I meet someone, if I meet someone, I'll be myself,' he said. 'Not shallow, or silly, but someone with some self-worth.'

'Me too,' Pippa said. 'I think I'll need a lot of strength to get through this, I've been with Mark for so long, and under his control for all that time, I need to find my way back again.'

Harriet looked at her siblings, at Gwen, at Connor, it was time. She knew what she was going to do and now seemed like a good time to tell them.

'Look, I'll forgive you both, of course I will, and I'm so glad you are both going to face the future. But you know, you were right in some ways; I am too bossy, too interfering, and I need to take a step back, a step away. I've been offered my old job back in New York, and as soon as this year is over I'm going to take it.' Harriet stood up. 'I love you, perhaps too much, but anyway, that's what I am going to do. I've made my mind up.'

'But—' Connor said.

'Harry, no—' Pippa shouted.

'Please, just hold on a minute—' Gus started.

'Oh God, look what we've done,' Freddie finished.

With that she left the room and it wasn't until she made her way upstairs and into her bedroom that she held the door frame, bent over double and let the tears fall.

Chapter 30

'I've sold two hundred tickets for the event,' Freddie announced proudly. They were meeting to discuss the upcoming Easter egg hunt. As per usual, Freddie and Pippa had organised the event, as they'd discussed before, an *Alice in Wonderland* theme. Pippa, a perfect Alice, was dressing up as her, and of course Freddie was the Mad Hatter. Gerry, who liked dressing up a little too much, Harriet thought, was the white rabbit and Harriet had reluctantly agreed to be the Queen of Hearts. Having forgotten the story, Harriet first thought she'd been totally miscast, until she read up that she happily handed out death sentences. Gus had got out of dressing up because they were opening the gardens again, this time also ticketed.

Costumes had been made by the Easter egg hunt committee, formally known as the winter wonderland committee, formally the summer fête committee. Same people, but they insisted on changing the name every event. John and his morris-dancing troupe were also going to be performing, but only because they insisted.

Bella had got all the eggs donated and Freddie who had been in charge of selling tickets had done a brilliant job. They had already raised a considerable amount, but Harriet knew that after this event, the last of the year, she would know exactly what was left to be done. She wouldn't let the animal sanctuary get into trouble, she couldn't bear anything bad to happen to it, or the animals. She still found it hard that her father was willing to gamble it, but then she remembered how much faith he had in them, and how he pushed them to succeed in everything, so it did make sense.

'Harry, please, will you reconsider?' Pippa asked, as she had done every day since Harriet announced she was returning to New York. Mark had stayed away, but in the days that followed, he called Pippa constantly, and Pippa had finally opened up about the reality of her marriage to him. Harriet, although still angry, felt her heart breaking again as she listened to the details, the clothes he insisted she wear, the isolation from all her friends, the tight budget he kept on her – no wonder she was the only one happy with their father's allowance. It wasn't physical abuse but it was a systematic eroding of Pippa's personality. She offered any practical advice she could, as her residual anger dissipated. Harriet got Pippa a new phone, so Mark didn't know how to reach her, she went with her to see a lawyer, one recommended by David, who said, given the situation, Mark wouldn't have a leg to stand on. Bizarrely, although they had no money, David said a contingency fund was available for Pippa's legal fees. It seemed their father had expected this all along.

The divorce would soon be underway and the solicitor was already playing hardball with Mark. When he was uncooperative, he was threatened with court, with being fully exposed, and Mark couldn't bear to have his reputation – if he had one – publicity slated so he had no choice but to tow the line.

'No, sorry. My mind is made up. I need to get on with my own life and I can't do that here. I'm booking a ticket for the minute that the will business is over. I'll let you guys decide what you want to do with Meadowbrook, I don't care about what you do with the house, I don't need any money from it. End of discussion.'

'Harry, this isn't like you,' Gus said. 'What's going on?' They were sitting around the breakfast table as they had for the last few months, but what a ride it'd been. One which Harriet was looking forward to coming to an end.

'Nothing. This was just a year, Gus, and when it's over, which is soon, I have a life, a job to go back to. My apartment in New York will be waiting for me.' She knew she sounded cold. She felt cold. Yes, she would do anything for them, but she would do it from the safety of New York. There was no way she could protect herself here, but of course she wasn't going to tell them that.

'Harry, we screwed up, I know that,' Freddie said. 'But we are all just finding ourselves now, we don't want to lose you.'

'You'll never lose me, but I have to do this. It's not all about you, you know, Fred. Right, now, let's get this Easter Eggstravaganza under way.'

'Oh God, Harry, I might miss you but not your terrible jokes,' Freddie said.

'Why are Agnes and her lamb wandering around where the hunt is taking place?' Harriet asked as they reached the field. She was wearing a ridiculous red wig which itched her head, bright blue eyeshadow, a red dress covered in hearts, and white stockings. She looked ridiculous; Helena Bonham Carter had nothing to worry about.

'It was my idea, Auntie Harry. Lambs are to do with Easter.'

'Usually for lunch,' Freddie pointed out.

'Shut up, Uncle Freddie. Anyway, it just adds to the occasion. Now, what time is kick-off.'

Fleur had thrown herself into the event, helping Gwen make hundreds of jam tarts – heart-shaped of course, as well as helping out with the organisation.

Harriet was trying to be gracious about it, yes they were set to make about three thousand pounds, which was a great amount, but still not enough, and time was ticking. Ha, she thought that was yet another reference to *Alice in Wonderland*.

Bella and Connor approached, which was all she needed when she looked so awful. Bella looked lovely, wearing normal clothes, pretty make-up and her hair glossy.

'Oh, Harriet, you look great,' Bella cooed.

'I really don't.'

'You look bloody funny actually,' Connor said.

'Connor, don't be mean, she's doing this for the animals.'

'Yes, I don't see you in bloody costume,' she pointed an accusatory finger at him.

'I'm supervising,' he said, still laughing.

She sat up against a tree trunk, idly stroking Agnes while her lamb grazed nearby. Being nice to children was so exhausting and Harriet had never really had to interact with them so much before. But she had had so many photos taken, even signed autographs – as the Queen of Hearts of course – and her face ached from smiling. They had one more hunt to go today and she was looking forward to getting home, getting the costume off and having a bath and an enormous glass of wine.

320

'Hey.' Connor sat down next to her.

'Hi.' Although Harriet's heart still flipped when she saw him, she was hoping that soon, when she'd gone, she would finally get over him. Having to see him every day was proving so difficult, hurtful, and even worse when Bella was around.

'I wanted to talk,' Connor said.

'So talk.' Harriet knew she sounded a bit tetchy, but she wasn't feeling very warm towards him, especially not dressed like this – no, she would soon scream 'off with his head' if she wasn't careful.

'Look, I know you've been avoiding me since that night. And I've tried to talk to you about it so many times but either someone else turns up, or I can't find the words . . .'

'Right,' she sighed.

'I just, well, Harry, having you back in my life has been great and the fact that you're going back to New York is so awful, we want you here, we need you.'

'What for?'

'You're part of the family, Meadowbrook needs you, the sanctuary needs you. I don't want you to run back to New York because of me.'

'Bit egotistical, isn't it? It's not just you, this year has been a huge upheaval for me. Trying to learn to run the sanctuary, losing Dad, losing my job, not to mention the whole business with Freddie and Pippa. I said I would try my best to get the money before the year is up, I'll do all in my power, but really, staying is not an option.'

'Harry, are you sure? Your siblings, well, I think they need you?'

'What about you, Connor?' She glared at him, as Agnes ambled away slightly.

'I'm your friend, H, you know that, I love you.'

'It's not enough,' Harriet said. 'I can't do this, Connor, I can't be around you like this, and please, please, don't you think the way I'm dressed is humiliating enough, I don't need you to humiliate me further.'

'But—'

'Go and find Bella, Connor.'

Harriet stood up and with all the dignity that she could muster with a stocking that had fallen around her ankle and a slightly tilted wig, she stalked off.

Chapter 31

Harriet felt marginally better. The Easter egg hunt was so successful – she had even got over her terrible costume – the open gardens a big hit, and having counted the money, this month they had added another four thousand pounds to the annual total. Ten cats and seven dogs had been rehomed this month as well, which was a record for the sanctuary. She worried about Hilda now she was leaving. Oh goodness, she really didn't know what she would do about her. She was thinking of asking Pip, who said she always wanted a dog, to take her but something stopped her from doing so, just yet.

She picked up the phone and called Bella. Not that she wanted to but she was desperate. There was no answer which was annoying, so she left a voicemail. She looked at her list. She had five companies to try to hit up for the remaining money, Harriet's idea was to go back to her roots; to go corporate. She was going to approach – attack – local companies, offering them sponsorship deals for the sanctuary in return for money. Some could sponsor actual animals and have that plastered over social media, they could also have their names associated with the events which were growing in popularity. She assumed Pippa and Freddie would continue to organise them, not that they had decided that. The Meadowbrook gardens were already attracting people from much further afield and they'd had enquiries about having coach trips come down in the summer. So she was going to present it as an investment, sell the hell out of it and raise the money before the end of the year. Failure was not an option, but having to do without Bella was irritating. Anyway, Harriet picked up the phone. She just had to raise that money.

Freddie walked into the office just as she finished with her list. It had gone OK. Not wonderful, but she had used her best sales skill and secured another couple of thousand pounds. They were close now, so close.

'Freddie, have you heard from Bella?'

'Ah, yes, I was going to talk to you about that. Pippa, well, she said that Bella is no longer working with Meadowbrook.'

'What? Why?'

'Well I think you'll have to ask our favourite vet. But we have lost a bloody good PR thanks to him.'

'They've split up?' Harriet's heart sped up.

Freddie sat down in the chair opposite. 'I think so, but she wouldn't really say, according to Pip.'

'Where is Pip?'

'Dog walking.'

'Right, well you'll have to do. We are close, very close, we need four thousand pounds to take us just over target, which sounds like nothing, but to be honest I'm not exactly sure where we'll get it. I have another few companies coming back to me later so I'm hopeful, but I don't want to leave anything to chance. Ideas?'

'Call Hector.'

'What, he'll give us the money?'

'Probably not, but he's just been confirmed as going in that celebrity show where they have to learn to do all sorts of modern dance. It's quite a big show, so he's about to embark on a big media round of interviews . . .'

'Great thinking.' Harriet picked up the phone.

Freddie stayed put so she put the phone on speaker.

'Hector, it's Harriet.'

'And Freddie.'

'Hi, guys, are you well?' Harriet was fonder of Hector than she ever thought she would be. He was actually quite a sweetheart.

'Very and congratulations on the dance thing. I might even watch this one.'

'You're too good to me, Harry.'

'I know. And I am about to ask you a massive favour so perhaps I should have buttered you up a bit more.'

'Harriet, you know I would do anything for you.'

'Well good to know, because we need money.'

'OK, how much?'

'No, Hector, I am not asking you to give it to us, although you can if you like, but I thought perhaps now you're doing all this media for the TV show you could ask for donations or something.'

'Yes, you know, you could link our *JustGiving* page to your social media and stuff,' Freddie added.

'OK, but why would people just give money?' Hector asked.

'Because they like you?' Harriet suggested.

'Well, yes, there is that but, you know, I think perhaps if you want to raise serious money we need to offer something.'

'How about we auction something off?' Harriet said, thinking of her overpriced charity purchases.

'Oh yes, let's auction off a date with you,' Freddie said, springing out of his chair.

'Great idea.' Harriet felt enthused. 'People will bid to go out for dinner with you.'

'But I could end up having to go out with anyone!' Hector sounded a little scared.

'Yes, but they might be nice.'

'Or gay, you're very popular with gay men,' Freddie unhelpfully pointed out.

'Oh God, what am I getting into? Can I agree on the condition that Edie doesn't win me,' Hector said.

'She's got no money, which would be no good to us. Right, Hector get your social media people on it right now so we can then share and retweet, and let's get that money.'

'How much do you actually think people will pay to go out with me?'

'I'm hoping a few thousand at least,' Harriet said. God, that might just bring them up to the target. What would someone pay for a date with Hector though? She had no idea, after all she didn't fancy it, but hopefully, fingers crossed, someone would.

'Gosh, not sure I'm worth that much, but you know I'm on Radio One this week, so I can push it then, and I'm in the gossip magazines, so I can mention it . . . You know, Harriet, this might just work.'

'Bloody hope so, Hector, and thank you, you might have just saved the animal sanctuary.'

'Really? Greg would love it if he could put that on my CV.'

Harriet chuckled as she hung up.

'This might just work, you know.' She had a good feeling.

'I'll go and get our social media all ready,' Freddie said, leaving her to it.

Her phone rang then. She looked at the screen, it was Connor.

'Why's Bella quit? What the hell is going on?' she snapped.

'Oh hello to you too, H,' Connor replied.

'So?' she demanded. She wasn't in the mood for small talk. 'Did you guys have an argument? I mean, I know we didn't pay her but she was good at her job and I for one could have done with her help right now.'

'Look, I'll explain everything, but first of all there's something I need to tell you.'

'What?'

'It's Hilda, she's been adopted.'

'No, but how—' Harriet couldn't believe how much hearing the news physically hurt her. She felt as if someone had just punched her in the stomach. Was everything and everyone she cared about being taken away from her? She knew she was leaving Hilda for New York, but she hadn't allowed herself to think about that, and now she realised why. She adored the bloody dog.

'I know, I know, it's very sudden, and I wanted you to be the first to know. Listen, I'm taking her for a last walk, meet me by the lake.'

Harriet's heart was already broken but now it was shattering into thousands of pieces. 'I don't think I can,' Harriet breathed.

Surely there were no tears left; rock bottom just found a new low.

'But, H, you need to say goodbye. You need to, if you

327

don't then you'll never forgive yourself.' Connor's voice was gentle.

'Like with Dad?'

She hung up and let the tears flow. As soon as the hiccupy sobs subsided she knew she had to go. Rushing to the back door, she pulled on her wellies, and a coat – how funny to think in a few months she would be back in her high heels and suits, she thought, as she made her way as quickly as she could.

Her heart skipped a beat when she saw Connor, looking so handsome standing by the lake with her beautiful Hilda by his side. She wasn't sure she could bear it as tears filled her eyes once more and she wrapped her coat around her, tightly. The sky was grey and threatening, matching her mood. She slowed as she approached them, terrified about how she would manage to say goodbye to Hilda, and a loud sob involuntarily escaped from her lips. She realised how much Hilda meant to her, how much of a companion she had been. Their daily jogs, walks, how she had sat at Harriet's feet in the office at the sanctuary, how she had stopped her from feeling alone.

Hilda jumped up, tail wagging as soon as she reached her. Harriet fell to the wet ground, letting Hilda climb all over her as she fussed her, before she looked at Connor, eyes blurred.

'She's been adopted?' she said, her voice choked. She wanted nothing more for Hilda than a loving home, but the selfish part of her almost couldn't bear it. As if the last piece of her heart was being snatched away.

'Yes,' Connor said simply.

'Who?' Her words cracked in the middle. 'I mean I hope they're nice.'

'I hope so too. It's me, H.'

Harriet felt her heart skip, she looked at him. 'What? I don't understand.'

'I decided the other day. When the Queen of Hearts talked to me.' Connor sat on the grass next to Harriet. Hilda was sat on her legs, rendering her immobile as her heart thumped. 'I saw her, all dressed up, in a ridiculous wig and awful make-up, cuddling a blind sheep and it hit me, but I couldn't find the words.'

'What?' she stuttered.

'After you stormed off, I realised, or I admitted, that I had loved you all my life. That I was so scared that you didn't want the same things as me, that I couldn't even think about being with you. Liz wanted the same as me, I thought you and I would never be able to want the same things.' He laughed, nervously.

'You would have hated London.' She understood how right he was.

'Yes, I would, and you would never have wanted to move to Yorkshire with me while I started work.'

'No, I don't suppose I would.' Harriet accepted that although they loved each other, they had wanted such different things back then. But now? 'And that led to you deciding to adopt Hilda?' She felt as if fireworks had been set off in her stomach.

'I love Hilda, and I love you.'

'Why did you tell me you didn't feel the same as me when we talked?' Her eyes widened with confusion. He looked at her and she almost drowned in his eyes; she could barely breathe.

'Because I was scared, terrified. I pushed my feelings for you so far back that I didn't think they were still there. But they were and I didn't know how to tell you.

You were so sophisticated, I wasn't, and then there was Bella.'

'But I lay my heart out for you and you, well, you rejected me!'

'I know, it seemed like the best option at the time. I was scared, H, and confused.'

'But now?' Harriet couldn't comprehend that he did have feelings for her, because if he did, he had hidden them so well. She looked up and saw a bird flying overhead, Hilda barked, the trees swayed in the breeze, her heart was swaying too, unsure what was happening to it right now.

'I really didn't think you would give your old life up, and then when you said you were going back to New York I thought maybe I was right. Then I got to thinking, perhaps you didn't actually want to go back to New York, and I had to give this a chance, I couldn't regret not telling you how I felt for the rest of my life.'

'Oh God, you're a bloody idiot.' Harriet shook her head.

'I know. But you have to understand, I was terrified of my feelings for you, I still am.'

'But I love you. And I will never want anything else.' She knew with even more certainty that it was the truth. 'I don't need New York, not if I've got you.'

'I feel the same. No more nonsense, Harriet. I'm taking Hilda to live with me and, well, you have a bit of an open invitation on that front. After the year at the big house of course.'

'What about Bella?'

'We split up. I knew that my feelings for her weren't strong enough when I realised how much I wanted you.' Hilda went to sit on Connor's lap, her tail wagging in his face.

She saw the Connor she'd always known. He was so gorgeous, clever, so good, yet scared, and she knew how he felt, because she was scared too. But this was her one chance at true happiness, and she wasn't going to let it go again.

'You know your cottage isn't big enough for you and Hilda, let alone me,' Harriet tried to joke. A million thoughts were whizzing in her brain. 'I mean, if you meant what you said about us being together.' A warmth spread through her cheeks.

'There's time for us to work out logistics, Harriet Singer, can't you just enjoy the moment for once?'

'You know how hard I find that!' Harriet couldn't believe the feelings she was experiencing. As if her heart was putting itself back together as they spoke, happiness swelled inside her. It was so much to process but it felt so right that, for once, she wasn't second-guessing anything, especially not her feelings. Nothing had felt this right, and she had never been so certain.

'So, what do you say? Could you stay here with me?' he asked, as Hilda stood up and walked in a circle, barking at nothing as she did so.

'I don't know, after all, Con, we haven't so much as kissed yet,' she teased.

He grabbed her waist, pulling her into him, and kissed her. As she sank into him, she felt sensations she never knew existed. She pulled him as tightly into her as she could, and when they finally, reluctantly, parted, she knew everything.

'Wow, that's only taken me over half my life to do.'

'It was worth the wait. And to answer your question, yes I can stay with you and Hilda, and yes, we can figure out logistics later and I can see myself working with the animals, and maybe one day I'll do something else too, but now I just want to be with you.'

'And what about New York?' he asked, eyebrow raised.

'What about it?'

A single white feather landed in her lap.

Epilogue

'Any questions?' David asked. The four Singer siblings shook their heads. They were in their father's study, David behind the desk, the siblings spread out on the sofa, much as they had been when they first saw their father's video. A year ago. Harriet could hardly believe that it really had been that long. 'Right, well I'll be off, but before I go I wanted to say how proud I am of you. This mad will of your father's, well, even I tried to talk him out of it, but you've done it, you even raised the money for the sanctuary. You've all done amazingly well and your father would be overjoyed with each of you.' They all nodded. David hugged Harriet and Pippa, shook Gus and Freddie's hands, then left.

'Wow,' Gus said.

'I can't believe it,' Pippa said.

'I can. I mean all that bloody fuss with Mark and Loretta and we can't sell the house anyway,' Freddie laughed.

'And all that pressure to raise the money, well that was just him testing us,' Gus said.

'You really thought Dad wouldn't try to control our lives from beyond the grave?' Harriet grinned.

The will had finally been read, a year to the day since they buried their father. There was no video message this time, no theatrics at all in fact, but the will terms were incredibly clear. The money that wasn't bequeathed elsewhere – to Gwen and Connor, Fleur, and the animal sanctuary – was split equally between the four of them. And it was a large enough sum to keep them all in comfort, even after death duties and so on.

Their father had never lived a ridiculously extravagant life but he'd lived the one he wanted. And now he was asking them to do the same. They were charged with looking after the house, the gardens and the sanctuary as they had been a year ago and also of being mindful of the village they lived in and helping anyone who needed it.

They were allowed to do what they wanted with the house as long as they didn't sell it. He made it clear he hoped the family would stay close, but he wasn't going to tie them literally any more. Luckily, he didn't need to. Harriet had already committed to the animal sanctuary, Gus to his gardening course, Freddie and Pippa hadn't yet said what they were going to do but they both said they wanted to stay at Meadowbrook.

The sanctuary was safe. Her father had a contingency fund if for any reason they didn't raise the money but he hadn't told anyone that, not even Connor. And of course they had raised the money. It might have been the eleventh hour but they did it. Harriet's local business idea brought in an extra five thousand pounds in the end, and Hector actually got ten thousand for a date with him – poor Edie was outbid by about nine thousand nine hundred and ninety-five pounds. It was a famous ex glamour model who frankly had been desperate to stay in the limelight and Hector was terrified, but it was worth it, and Harriet promised she would try to persuade Pippa to take him out to lunch to thank him if he survived the date. He still had a crush on Pippa and although Harriet couldn't exactly see them together, stranger things had happened. Especially at Meadowbrook.

Meadowbrook. They inherited the house equally and it had to stay in the family as long as the family existed. It was theirs now and then it would pass to Fleur and any other grandchildren, and so on. If the family came to the end of the line, then it would go to charity. Their father had thought of everything.

'I can't believe he left you the Bentley, Harry,' Freddie complained but with a smile. 'I so wanted that car.'

'Don't even think about it,' Harriet said. 'I am the oldest after all.' It was the only thing their father had stipulated. All the rest of his belongings they would divide up among themselves in whatever way they wanted. But she got the fabulous car. She almost felt she was being rewarded for what she had gone through this year, and she couldn't wait to take it for a spin.

'Well, there is one thing I would like to know,' Gus said. 'What are we going to do with the house?' He stood up and moved to the desk, perching on the edge so he was facing all his siblings.

'I'm moving in with Connor and, if you agree, we wanted to knock the end two cottages together.' Gwen was going to swap cottages, so Harriet, Connor and Hilda would not only have the bigger house but they could also knock into the next, still empty cottage – the one Harriet had hidden in – to make a decent size, four-bedroom cottage. They would be on hand for the animal sanctuary and Harriet couldn't wait to start living properly with Connor, forging their future, which looked so incredibly rosy she almost couldn't believe it was real. They'd barely been apart since the time at the lake, but somehow it felt as if it was getting better and better every day. Harriet wasn't suddenly romantic and whimsical but she was annoyingly in love. She was behaving the way that, if it had been a year ago, she would have found incredibly irritating.

The funniest thing was now they had money, Harriet had no desire to go throwing it around like she used to. She was going to give her redundancy money to the sanctuary – it meant she could work on expansion plans – and as for the inheritance, she had decided to give herself an annual amount to live on. She was going to treat herself to a nice haircut in Bath, goodness knew that was overdue, but as for the ridiculously expensive beauty products, personal trainers and clothes, well they belonged to the old Harriet and she didn't need them anymore. Although she was having all her shoes shipped back from New York now she had decided to sell her apartment.

Harriet didn't know she could feel this happy. She was sure she had once, probably before she ever left Meadowbrook but she couldn't remember. Turning down the job in New York had been easy, and now she was going to fly back to sell her apartment, sort out her last belongings and say goodbye properly to her friends. She was closing that chapter of the book for good, although she resolved she would still keep those she cared about in her life, she had learnt that lesson. She asked Connor if he wanted to go with her but he didn't want to leave Hilda – lest she think she'd been abandoned again, and he was right. Although she thought the real reason was that he'd find New York quite terrifying. Maybe one day she would get him there.

'Of course,' Gus said. 'I think that's a great idea. And,

as I've said, I'm moving in with Amanda, so I'll only be down in the village.'

'So, Pip and I,' Freddie started, 'we need to stay at the big house for now but we have been talking.'

'Really? You do surprise me,' Harriet teased. Pippa and Freddie were still thick as thieves, they were both a bit bruised from their broken relationships, but the great thing was that instead of Freddie going off the rails, Pippa had kept him sane, pretty sober, and they were both mending. They had each other, and Harriet, having been able to fully forgive both of them, could see that they were going to be just fine.

'So what have you been thinking?' Gus asked. Her new laid-back brother was quite a revelation. They were all new people. Reborn. As was their relationship with each other.

'Well,' Pippa said. She looked more beautiful than ever. Her hair gleamed, she'd given up her politician's wife look for a more modern wardrobe which made her look a decade younger. She said she felt free and she certainly wore it well. 'We thought, and the details need to be worked on, this is just a very rough idea, but we thought that we could maybe turn Meadowbrook into a boutique hotel and event venue.'

'Right, wow?' Harriet was intrigued. She hadn't thought for a moment about what they would do with the house and she was a little taken aback. A hotel? Well it was an interesting idea.

'But with a difference as well. We thought that we could offer holidays, or breaks, including gardening, or working with the animals, or maybe painting with Gus. Sort of healing holidays for those who need it,' Pippa said.

'You are kidding, you're going to bill them as "healing

holidays"?' Harriet gasped. 'We'll attract all kinds of crazies.'

'They'll fit in well then,' Gus quipped. 'I mean, we might just attract people like us.'

'We're not going to bill it like that. It'll be a luxury hotel, small, like I said, boutique, and it'll attract people who need a break in the beautiful Somerset countryside, but we will offer a bit extra so we can stand out,' Pippa explained. 'We'll need to really come up with a great marketing strategy but we think we can make it work.'

'We figured that Pip and I could move into two of the attic rooms, and we could let out eight bedrooms at a time, either for couples or single guests. We have the pool and the gym, we were going to ask Gwen if she wanted to stay on here and help out, but if she decides to retire—'

'That'll never happen,' Harriet said.

'Right, well that's what we were hoping,' Freddie finished. 'She could be in charge of the food, and we'll see if we can open a bar, somewhere, I was thinking the drawing room, offering the best in cocktails.'

'So, you have thought about it a lot then?' Harriet smiled.

'But we need your help, both of you, especially your business brain, Harry. Because if we do this, we'll need a full business plan, and we'll have to figure out how to run a hotel.'

'It'll be nice to be involved in another project, I've enjoyed working with you this year,' Gus said. 'And I'm guessing I'll still be needed to run the gardens.'

'Of course, they're going to be part of the attraction,' Pippa said. 'And we will keep going with the Meadowbrook events of course.'

'So, it'll be a break with the added extra that you can

garden, paint, or work with animals?' Harriet clarified. Her brain began to whirl – if they did this, along with the animal sanctuary, she could see that perhaps she would be occupied, challenged enough. She knew that being with Connor was the most important thing but she still needed to work, it was part of her.

'It's kind of going to be like Meadowbrook: the hotel that mends broken hearts,' Pippa said.

'Please tell me you're not going to call it that?' Gus said.

'It's a bit of a tall order,' Harriet pointed out, she was partly amused and party excited at the prospect. 'We might get sued if people's hearts don't actually mend.'

'Well, that might not be the exact name, but you get the gist.' Pippa held her hands out, exasperated. Out from under Mark's shadow, Pippa was finding her assertive side again. 'After all, in its own way Meadowbrook mended all of our broken hearts.'

'It did but it broke them too though,' Harriet said. 'Pip, Fred, it's got the bones of being a very good idea, you know. Although we do need to put more thought into it. And do research, I mean none of us knows much about the hotel business, do we?'

'Exactly, bossy. And now can I pour us all some of Dad's good brandy?' Freddie asked.

'Yes, I think we need a drink, but shall we get Gwen and Connor to join us,' Harriet asked. She knew they were both in the kitchen, waiting for news, and she wanted them here, after all they were both such a part of the family.

'I'll go,' Gus offered.

Gwen and Connor entered the office as Freddie was pouring and handing out drinks.

'So,' Gwen said, 'I'm guessing you know everything now.'

'Did you know all along that we couldn't sell the house?' Pippa asked, eyes narrowed at Gwen as she gave her an affectionate hug.

'I was sworn to secrecy. But I also knew there was a lot of money and I couldn't have lived with myself if Mark and Loretta had got their hands on it.'

'Did you know?' Harriet turned to Connor.

''Course not, Mum didn't breathe a word.' He put his arm around her and she felt the familiar tingling of warmth that she was getting so used to. It was funny how alien having someone around full time was, but how normal it felt too.

'I'm not sure I can get used to seeing you two together,' Freddie said.

'It is weird,' Pippa added.

'I knew they'd end up together,' Gus finished. 'I remember when we were young, she mooned after him all the time . . .'

'Did not.' Harriet gave Gus a playful swipe.

'You do know your girlfriend is rich now.' Freddie pointed his glass at Connor.

'Fred!' Pippa chastised.

'I don't care about that,' Connor said, flushing slightly.

'Oh, mate, he's only teasing, we all know that you care less about money than anyone we know,' Gus laughed. 'If you had your way you'd give it to the animals, anyway.'

'Although perhaps Harry can use some money to buy a new Elton,' Freddie suggested.

'We can't replace Elton.' Pippa was wide-eyed.

'No, but we are looking to get David some company, I think if he had a friend, it would make it easier. He is still missing him so much,' Connor explained. 'Poor thing is really, really in mourning.'

'And, it made it easier on all of us, didn't it?' Pippa said. 'I mean we wouldn't have coped with losing Dad without each other.'

'When I think how close we came to losing that though,' Harriet said. Both Freddie and Pippa looked shamefaced. 'I'm not blaming you, not anymore anyway,' she teased.

'Yes, Harry, it might be time to let them forget it now,' Gwen said, assertively. Harriet grinned at her. This woman knew her too well.

'A toast,' Gus said.

'To surviving the year at Meadowbrook?' Harriet suggested.

'To coming out of bad relationships?' Pippa suggested.

'To some of us finding love?' Gus beamed.

'To us all being together again, a proper family,' Freddie said.

'To Dad, who might have known what he was doing after all,' Harriet admitted.

As Connor kissed her, she said a silent thank you to her father. It turned out he did know exactly what he was doing, but then, he always did.

Acknowledgements

It was such fun to write this, so I want to thank everyone who helped me along the way. To my lovely agents at Diane Banks Associates and to all at Avon, especially Victoria for a great editing process and to Helen who listened to me over a lovely lunch when the idea for this book was born.

Thanks to my mum for all her help with childcare and ironing when I was busy writing away, and also to Helen and Becky and all the Langmead family; knowing my son has such great people in his life is invaluable.

A huge thanks go to Jenny and her sister Claire for letting me visit her lovely animals.

Inspiration as always comes from Jo and Keith, especially with the animals in this book. I am always grateful to have both of you in my life.

Thanks as always to my friends for maintaining my – sort of – sanity and ditto my family. But a special big thanks goes my son, Xavier, who I simply love with all my heart.

I hope that you enjoy reading this book as much as I did writing it.

If you enjoyed *A Year at Meadowbrook Manor*, then you'll love this stunning new series from Phillipa Ashley.

Escape to the Little Cornish Isles this spring.

Loved your year at Meadowbrook Manor?
Now it's time for a new adventure . . .

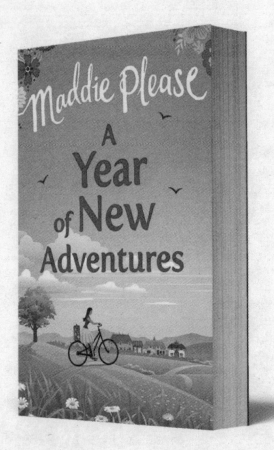

Join Billie Summers as she gives her life a
much-needed makeover.